PRAISE FOR \

"This first-hand account, by a leading Formalist, of a society in turmoil owes much to Sterne—utterly unsentimental, detached, fragmentary, paradoxical, the memoirs tell of experiences at the front, in Persia and in St. Petersburg, philosophical asides jostling with vivid recollections, literary reference with political comment."

—*Times Literary Supplement*

"A rambling, digressive stylist, Shklovsky throws off brilliant aperçus on every page. . . . Like an architect's blueprint, it lays bare the joists and studs that hold up the house of fiction."

—Michael Dirda, *Washington Post*

"Shklovksy's *A Sentimental Journey* is both a major historical document and an important literary experiment."

—*Clio*

"The recollections of almost anyone who lived through the Russian Revolution have historical interest, and the memoirs of a major literary figure like Viktor Shklovsky are a priceless document."

—*Virginia Quarterly Review*

"*A Sentimental Journey* is one of the most gripping memoirs of the Soviet period."

—*Russian Review*

"One would be hard pressed to decide whether the book is more notable for what it says or for how it says it. . . . Viktor Shklovsky's *A Sentimental Journey* is highly recommended."

—*Library Journal*

OTHER BOOKS BY VIKTOR SHKLOVSKY IN ENGLISH TRANSLATION

A Sentimental Journey: Memoirs, 1917–1922

Viktor Shklovsky

Translation and Literary Introduction
by Richard Sheldon

Historical Introduction
by Sidney Monas

Dalkey Archive Press
Champaign/Dublin/London

First published in Russian by Helikon Publishing House, 1923
First published in English by Cornell University Press, 1970

Translated from the Russian and edited by Richard Sheldon
English edition copyright 1970, 1984 by Cornell University Press

Literary Introduction copyright © 1970, 1984 by Richard Sheldon
Historical Introduction © 1970 by Sidney Monas

First Dalkey Archive edition, 2004
Second Printing, 2012

Library of Congress Cataloging-in-Publication Data available
ISBN: 1-56478-354-5

Partially funded by grants from the National Endowment for the Arts, a federal
agency, and the Illinois Arts Council, a state agency.

www.dalkeyarchive.com

Printed on permanent/durable acid-free paper and bound in the
United States of America

Acknowledgments

THIS work is an unabridged translation of the first Russian edition of *Sentimental'noe puteshestvie* (A Sentimental Journey), which Viktor Shklovsky published in 1923 while living as an exile in Berlin.

A Sentimental Journey was republished twice after Shklovsky returned to the Soviet Union: in Leningrad, 1924, and in Moscow, 1929. Part One, "Revolution and the Front," was omitted from the 1924 edition, and Part Two, "Writing Desk," was severely cut in the predictable places. The 1929 edition contains both parts, with deletions in Part One and still more drastic deletions in Part Two.

A Sentimental Journey has recently been translated into French (1963), German (1964), and Italian (1966). The French translation contains approximately two thirds of the original text, most of the abridgment occurring in Part Two. The German translation, while basically intact, lacks several pages of the original, as well as many individual sentences and paragraphs. The Italian translation is complete and equipped with notes of particular excellence.

In preparing the English translation, I have frequently consulted my colleagues Walter Arndt, Peter Jarotski, and Basil Milovsoroff, who gave generously of their time and knowledge. Antonia Glasse read the translation against the original and made many valuable suggestions for its improvement. Patricia Blake and Max Hayward read Part One of the manuscript at an early stage and gave much-appreciated editorial advice and encouragement.

I want to remember with special gratitude Vera Dunham and Deming Brown, who imparted to me their appreciation of the

Soviet period; Dimitri von Mohrenschildt, who during his last and my first year at Dartmouth extended to a new colleague all the resources at his command; and my wife, whose support in all phases of this operation was constant and total.

Excerpts from Part One of this translation first appeared in the July 1967 and January 1968 issues of *The Russian Review*, and are reprinted with the permission of that journal.

The portrait of Shklovsky is used by permission of the artist, Yury Annenkov. It was recently reprinted in his remarkable book of memoirs, *Dnevnik moikh vstrech: Tsikl tragedii* [Diary of My Encounters: A Cycle of Tragedies] (New York: Inter-Language Literary Associates, 1966).

RICHARD SHELDON

Hanover, New Hampshire
May 1969

EDITOR'S NOTE, 1984

The word "Aissor" is used throughout this translation to designate the nationality more commonly known as Assyrian.

Contents

Shklovsky is not only a writer, but a special figure of a writer. In this sense, his position and role are exceptional. In another time, he would have been a Petersburg free-thinker, a Decembrist, and, with Pushkin, would have wandered through the south and fought duels. As a man of our time, he lives, of course, in Moscow and writes about his life although, like Dante, he has hardly reached its middle. In another time, he would have been called a "master of ideas"; in our stern, stingy time, he is called, if you please, a "master of the phrase"—to such an extent has his manner entered not only into literature, but into the letter, into everyday life, into conversation, into student papers.

Few undertake to praise Shklovsky in print, because all who write . . . must first of all emancipate themselves from him. They rail against him as against the injustice of fate. He has offended many—some because he was able to revive Sterne without knowing the English language and German scholarship, others because he wrote remarkable works on prose theory and then proved no less remarkable as a practitioner. . . . Shklovsky in his time threatened the old generation of Russian intellectuals with Opoyaz—just as one hundred years ago, the future Russian "classics" threatened the academicians and Shishkovites with their "Arzamas."

BORIS EIKHENBAUM
in My Chronicle, 1929

Making Armored Cars and Novels:
A Literary Introduction

*D*URING the years 1910–1930, Russia experienced an unprecedented surge of creative energy that produced experimental masterpieces in painting, poetry, prose, theater, and cinema. This movement, inspired by contemporary tendencies in western European art, arose as a reaction against the stultified doctrines and techniques of the Russian symbolists. The new generation rejected the musicality and the metaphysics of symbolist poetry, but they retained the interest in form fostered especially by Andrei Bely. Although they wanted an art rough in texture, coarse and down to earth, they believed that art could not and should not mirror the real world. Accordingly, they used formal techniques involving substantial distortion. They preferred to dismember an object and rearrange its components in unusual ways that would jolt the public and compel a strong, even hostile, response. They cultivated the grotesque; they used staccato transitions, spatial and temporal displacement, montage, hyperbole, antithesis, and paradox.

The movement's preoccupation with the "intensive detail" led Viktor Shklovsky to describe the period as "baroque."[1] Emphasis on the part at the expense of the whole characterizes the paintings of Larionov, Goncharova, Tatlin, Malevich, Rozanova, and Filonov; it also marks the theater of Meyerhold, the cinema of Eisenstein, and the poetry of the futurists, as well as the works of those whom they influenced, such as Pasternak, Tsvetaeva, Mandelstam, and Zabolotsky. "Reification of the component part" describes Russian formalism, with its roots in futurism and its concern for the device; and it describes the highly reticulated "ornamental" prose,

[1] *Poiski optimizma* [The Search for Optimism] (Moscow, 1931), p. 115.

a major tendency of the early twenties. Zamyatin, Pilnyak, and Vsevolod Ivanov all wrote in this manner, and Shklovsky produced a prime example of ornamental prose in *A Sentimental Journey.* Its form and content, perfectly matched, embody the vital concerns of this "neobaroque" period in Russian culture.

The quest for radically new, perceptible forms dominated the period. Above all, it motivated Viktor Shklovsky, who began his career as a futurist and who, throughout the twenties (and also at the famous Writers' Congress of 1934), continually demanded innovation in his literary criticism and demonstrated it in his artistic prose. Born in St. Petersburg in 1893, Shklovsky was attending secondary school when the strident paintings, poems, manifestoes, operas, and plays of the futurists first appeared. Strongly attracted by the poetry of Velimir Khlebnikov and Vladimir Mayakovsky, he neglected his studies to attend their readings and the public debates that accompanied them.

During the years immediately preceding World War I, the prominent artists of Petersburg frequented an avant-garde cabaret known as The Stray Dog. It was there, in December 1913, while a freshman at the University of Petersburg, that Shklovsky read a paper entitled "The Place of Futurism in the History of Language." In his talk he maintained that futurist poetry emancipated words from their traditional significance and restored them to perceptibility by calling attention to their sounds. The function of art in general, he concluded, should be to force such new perceptions of the word and the world.

Recalling that evening, Benedikt Livshits declared the debut of this "pink-cheeked youngster in frock coat and high collar" to be a turning point in the development of the futurist movement. Shklovsky's association with the department of philology at the University of Petersburg made him a formidable new ally for the futurists. Only Khlebnikov had some training in linguistics and his pronouncements tended to be too incidental and lyrical.[2] Shklovsky's report demonstrated convincingly that the futurists were not just a coterie of bohemians, but a major new force in the history of Russian poetry.

Now recognized as an important theoretician of futurism, Shklov-

---

[2] Livshits, *Polutoraglazii strelets* [The One-and-a-Half-Eyed Archer] (Leningrad, 1933), pp. 200–201.

sky began to participate in the group's platform appearances. In 1914 he published his paper under the title *Resurrection of the Word*.[3] Shortly after its appearance, he took a copy to his teacher, Jan Baudouin de Courtenay. The famous linguist introduced Shklovsky to his most gifted students, Lev Yakubinsky and E. D. Polivanov. Although the master objected to Shklovsky's apotheosis of sound in poetry, his students responded enthusiastically.[4] They felt that the sound patterns of poetry offered a fertile new field for linguistic analysis. Under Shklovsky's leadership, these students of Baudouin de Courtenay joined forces with the futurists in 1914. This new alliance was called Opoyaz—*Obshchestvo izucheniia poeticheskogo iazyka* (Society for the Study of Poetic Language); it eventually evolved into the full-fledged critical movement known as Russian formalism. *Resurrection of the Word* is usually considered the first document of that movement.

When Russia entered World War I in the summer of 1914, Shklovsky enlisted in the army. He was trained in vehicle operation and maintenance and dispatched to Galicia and the Ukraine. In 1916 he was reassigned to Petersburg, now Petrograd, as an instructor in a school for armored-car personnel.

In Petrograd, Shklovsky resumed his ties with Opoyaz and met the newest members of the group, Osip and Lilya Brik, friends of Mayakovsky. During 1916, the members met every week to hear and discuss reports on verse language and the function of art. Brik and Shklovsky published one anthology of these reports in 1916 and another in 1917.[5] These literary activities were interrupted by the February revolution, which flung Shklovsky into the tumult recorded in *A Sentimental Journey*.

In this book a decade of world war, revolution, and civil war, now comfortably abstracted and analyzed by historians, re-emerges in fresh and harrowing detail, as related by one of the most brilliant and provocative figures of the era. *A Sentimental Journey* is not only a superb specimen of ornamental prose; it is also a major historical document that has been unaccountably ignored by historians of the revolutionary period. Part One records Shklovsky's impres-

[3] *Voskreshenie slova* (Petersburg, 1914).

[4] Viktor B. Shklovskii, *Zhili-byli* [Once upon a Time] (Moscow, 1964), pp. 95–96.

[5] *Sborniki po teorii poeticheskogo iazyka* [Studies on the Theory of Poetic Language], vol. 1 (Petrograd, 1916), vol. 2 (Petrograd, 1917).

sions of the events that he witnessed in 1917: the February revolution, the Kerensky offensive, the Kornilov revolt, and the occupation
of Persia. Part Two encompasses the years 1918–1922 and describes Shklovsky's underground activities against the Bolsheviks,
his escape to the Ukraine and service under Hetman Skoropadsky,
and his joining the Reds to fight against General Wrangel in the
southern Ukraine.

Between campaigns Shklovsky played a seminal role in the astonishing intellectual life of Petrograd. As a leader of the futurists,
founder of Russian formalism, teacher of the Serapion Brothers,
and influential member of LEF,[6] he exerted a powerful influence on
his own generation and on many of the young writers who eventually became major figures of the Soviet period. The formalist
critics Boris Eikhenbaum and Yury Tynyanov began their brilliant
careers mainly by enlarging upon Shklovsky's insights. Tynyanov's
later excursions into the historical novel, which laid the foundations
for that genre during the Soviet period, also bear the mark of his
influence. Five of the Serapion Brothers—Kaverin, Slonimsky,
Zoshchenko, Ivanov, and Lunts—began their careers with works
constructed to Shklovsky's specifications. Even Konstantin Fedin,
the most conservative of the Serapion Brothers, could not avoid
Shklovsky's influence, as his most famous novel, *Goroda i gody*
(Cities and Years), 1924, testifies. Yury Olesha's *Zavist'* (Envy),
1927, one of the masterpieces of the Soviet period, unquestionably
reflects the influence of Shklovsky.

A Sentimental Journey contains fascinating portraits of the artists and writers whom Shklovsky knew during those years—not
only the Serapion Brothers, but also Gorky, Blok, Gumilyov, Mandelstam, and many others. Throughout the unbroken sequence of
world war, revolution, and civil war, these men feverishly pursued
their trades. While battles raged on the outskirts of Petrograd,
they met in icy, sometimes flooded rooms to argue abstruse questions of literary style and structure. After showing the members of
Opoyaz how novels are assembled, Shklovsky would return to his

---

[6] LEF was an alignment of formalists and futurists organized by Mayakovsky in 1923; Shklovsky joined the group when he returned from Berlin.
Their announced intention was to battle the resurgence of conservative literary tendencies and to insist on the creation of a new documentary literature. The group and its magazine of the same name ceased to exist in 1925
only to reappear briefly as New LEF in 1927.

unit and show his students there the more mundane techniques involved in assembling armored cars.

As a soldier, Shklovsky was able to observe the mood of the Petrograd garrison and the sequence of events which led, almost by accident, to the February revolution. Between the revolutions, he served on the Petrograd Soviet as a representative of his army unit and then as commissar of the Austrian front. In this capacity, he was intimately involved in the newly created committees empowered to offset the authority of the officers; he reports in detail on the process by which the Provisional Government decided to launch an offensive on the Austrian front in June 1917, and on the revolt led by General Kornilov against the government. Disillusioned by his experiences at the front, Shklovsky returned to Petrograd and was transferred as commissar to the Russian army of occupation in Persia. He describes the dissident nationalities barely held in check by the hated Russian troops and the chaos that followed the withdrawal of those troops after the October revolution.

When Shklovsky returned from Persia, he joined an underground organization plotting to restore the Constituent Assembly, recently dispersed by the Bolsheviks. Threatened with arrest, he fled to Saratov and then to Kiev, which was occupied by the Germans and ruled by their puppet leader, Hetman Skoropadsky. When the Germans withdrew and Petlyura came to power, Shklovsky returned to Petrograd. He arrived in January 1919 and, with the help of Gorky, was exonerated of complicity in the Socialist Revolutionary terrorist activities of the summer of 1918.

In Petrograd, Shklovsky found his futurist friends Mayakovsky and Brik cooperating with the Bolsheviks and insisting on the artist's obligation to the new society. Calling himself a right-wing futurist, he objected to this alliance and rebuked them with his famous statement: "Art has always been free of life; its flag has never reflected the color of the flag over the city fortress."[7] Despite these differences of opinion, however, Shklovsky, Brik, and Mayakovsky formed a makeshift publishing enterprise which they called IMO—*Iskusstvo molodykh* (Art of the Young), which published editions of Mayakovsky and the third anthology of articles by members of Opoyaz.

[7] Viktor B. Shklovskii, "Ullia, Ullia, Marsiane," *Iskusstvo kommuny* [Art of the Commune], vol. 17 (March 30, 1919); reprinted in Shklovsky's *Khod konia* [Knight's Move] (Moscow-Berlin, 1923), p. 39.

By May 1919, the civil war had created impossible hardships in Petrograd, so Shklovsky and his wife decided to take refuge in the Ukraine. When illness prevented Shklovsky from leaving, his wife and her sister went to Kherson without him. Before he could join them, the White army commanded by General Denikin captured Kharkov and Kiev and severed connections between Petrograd and the south. Forced to remain in Petrograd, Shklovsky spent the summer writing his first book of memoirs, *Revolution and the Front*,[8] which later became Part One of *A Sentimental Journey*. During the fall and winter, he lectured on literary theory at the Translators' Studio, part of the network of organizations created by Gorky to provide work for the starving intelligentsia. Here he met Evgeny Zamyatin, who supervised translations of Anglo-American literature and who shared Shklovsky's assumptions about the nature and function of literature.[9] Among their students were Mikhail Zoshchenko, Lev Lunts, Nikolai Nikitin, Vladimir Pozner, Elizaveta Polonskaya, and Mikhail Slonimsky, who eventually formed the nucleus of the writers' workshop called the Serapion Brothers.

By the spring of 1920, Denikin had been repulsed. Shklovsky, with Gorky's help, obtained a travel permit and journeyed to the Kherson area to escort his wife back to Petrograd. Before he and his wife could leave, however, they were trapped by the new offensive that General Wrangel launched against the Red Army in June. Shklovsky joined the Reds and worked as a demolition man until a bomb exploded in his hands and he had to be evacuated back to Petrograd.

In the fall of 1920, Shklovsky and his wife moved into the House of Arts, now the center of the active literary life of the city. There he renewed his ties with Zamyatin and the young students from the Translators' Studio. Joined by Ilya Gruzdyov, Veniamin Kaverin, Vsevolod Ivanov, Konstantin Fedin, and Nikolai Tikhonov, the group officially organized in February 1921, calling themselves the Serapion Brothers. Throughout 1921, Shklovsky and Zamyatin met with the members every Saturday and criticized their manuscripts. Shklovsky imparted to them all the theories of literature that he had elaborated at the meetings of Opoyaz—especially the

[8] *Revoliutsiia i front* (Petrograd, 1921).

[9] The roles played by Shklovsky, Gorky, and Zamyatin in the formation and development of the Serapion Brothers are discussed in my article "Gor'kij, Šklovskii and the Serapion Brothers," *SEEJ*, 12 (1968): 1–13.

primacy of form and the necessity for innovation, principles which he illustrated by the work of Laurence Sterne. The increasingly experimental nature of the prose of the Serapion Brothers displeased Gorky, with his more traditional views, but he continued to give them his protection and advice. By the end of 1921, all Petrograd was exclaiming over the talent of the group, which had clearly inaugurated a new era of Russian prose.

In October 1921, Gorky, less and less successful in winning concessions for the intelligentsia from Lenin, left the Soviet Union. After his departure, the Serapion Brothers were evicted from the House of Arts. In February 1922 the Cheka began to arrest members of the Socialist Revolutionary party, and Shklovsky, facing imminent arrest, fled to Finland. There, on May 20, he began writing the second part of *A Sentimental Journey*, which he completed ten days later in Berlin.[10]

A Sentimental Journey was published in Berlin in 1923.[11] It actually consists of three separate books: *Revolution and the Front*, written by Shklovsky in the summer of 1919 and published in 1921; *Epilogue: End of the Book "Revolution and the Front,"* written in the latter part of 1921 and published early in 1922;[12] and "Writing Desk," written in May 1922. To make *A Sentimental Journey*, Shklovsky used *Revolution and the Front* as Part One, added "Writing Desk" as Part Two, divided *Epilogue* into two sections and spliced them into "Writing Desk."

When *A Sentimental Journey* appeared, it was hailed by the formalist critics Boris Eikhenbaum and Yury Tynyanov as the start of a promising new trend in the Russian novel.[13] The genre, they asserted, had been in a state of crisis since the deaths of Dostoevsky, Turgenev, and Tolstoy. The subject matter and techniques of those masters no longer suited the postrevolutionary era; the genre required total renewal.

A Sentimental Journey suggested a possible resolution of this crisis. It dispensed with traditional concerns of the nineteenth-

[10] *Gamburgskii schet* [Hamburg Account] (Leningrad, 1928), p. 97.

[11] *Sentimental'noe puteshestvie* (Moscow-Berlin, 1923; 2d ed. abr., Leningrad, 1924; 3d ed. abr., Moscow, 1929).

[12] Viktor B. Shklovskii and Lazar' Zervandov, *Epilog: Konets knigi "Revoliutsiia i front"* (Petrograd, 1922).

[13] See especially Eikhenbaum, "V poiskakh zhanra" [In Search of a Genre], *Russkii sovremennik* [The Russian Contemporary], no. 3 (1924): pp. 228–231; also Tynianov, "Literaturnoe segodnia" [Literary Today], *Russkii sovremennik*, no. 1 (1924): pp. 291–306.

century Russian novel: psychological analysis, the fictional hero, romantic intrigue, and lyrical nature descriptions. In Eikhenbaum's opinion, this new novel relinquished the usual neat and artificial plot; instead, it simply presented a set of the author's observations and experiences, with no particular effort to subordinate them to some overall scheme. It thus satisfied the new craving of the Russian public for facts, seen in the popularity of memoirs, letters, journals, and biographies. Indeed, Shklovsky's determination to incorporate factual material into the genre explains the long technical descriptions of hand grenades, printing presses, and motors included in *A Sentimental Journey.*

In the literary criticism that Shklovsky wrote between 1914 and 1923, he maintained that the techniques employed by the nineteenth-century Russian realists and by the symbolists had ceased to elicit perception. Readers tended to glide swiftly and blindly over a smooth and familiar verbal surface; consequently, their ability to perceive had to be revived by the use of distortion, achieved by the techniques that Shklovsky called *ostranenie* (estrangement) and *zatrudnennaia forma* (impeded form). "Estrangement" refers to any literary device that renders the familiar unfamiliar; it includes striking images and unusual points of view. "Impeded form" revives the reader's perception by presenting the familiar objects of the real world in verbal designs of great intricacy. The author places his verbal units in complex relationships to one another in order to retard the reader's progress and compel his attention.

Shklovsky's concern for perceptible forms, initiated by futurism, was intensified by the influences of Andrei Bely, Vasily Rozanov, and Laurence Sterne. In his *Theory of Prose*, 1925, Shklovsky included major critical studies of these three writers.[14] They provided ideal illustrations of the theories that he had developed out of his work on futurist poetry; they also exerted a lasting influence on his own techniques of style and composition.

As the title suggests, it is Sterne who presided over the creation of *A Sentimental Journey*—not only through his book by that title, but especially through his *Tristram Shandy*, which is the focus of Shklovsky's study in *Theory of Prose*. Shklovsky subjects the factual material of his memoirs to Sterne's intricate formal apparatus;

---

[14] *O teorii prozy* (Moscow-Leningrad, 1925; 2d ed. supp., Moscow, 1929). The article on Bely appears only in the second edition.

like Sterne, he uses an extended journey as his chief organizing principle. The journeys described by the two authors, however, differ markedly. Sterne, in his *A Sentimental Journey*, describes the leisurely travels of a sensitive gentleman through France and Italy. Shklovsky describes the travels of a bewildered intellectual through Russia, Persia, the Ukraine, and the Caucasus—all convulsed by violence and cruelty of every variety. Sterne's hero reacts to his experiences with pious and coy comments on the fallibility of human nature; Shklovsky's hero reacts with exclamations of grief and anger or with bitter irony. This enormous difference between the two journeys provides one source of the irony that suffuses Shklovsky's book.

This irony has several sources. It derives from the author's ostensible acceptance of the patently unacceptable, as in the scene where a soldier shows mercy to a baby by killing it slowly. It derives from the author's constant intrusions into the narrative to add a disrespectful comment or an offhand reference to the literary device he has just been using—the technique that Shklovsky calls *obnazhenie priema* (baring the device). For instance, after describing how some peasants killed a tax collector, Shklovsky says, "You'll tell me that this doesn't fit in here. So what! I should carry all this in my soul?" After a lengthy criticism of bureaucracy and Bolshevism, he suddenly announces: "This whole digression is built on the device which in my 'poetics' is called retardation."

The primary source of Shklovsky's irony, however, is the tension between actual events and the narrator's detached view of them—a type of estrangement. Violence is screened through the sensibility of a detached observer. Shklovsky's description of the death of his brother Nikolai, for example, is a triumph of understatement.

Periodically the tone shifts from ironic to lyrical. Objective recitals of violence conclude with deeply felt emotional passages, where Shklovsky expresses his nostalgia for Petrograd or his despair in the face of events over which he has no control. These lyrical passages, organized into digressions and leitmotifs, provide sharp contrasts to the general ironic tone.

The shifts in tone, usually abrupt, give Shklovsky's style a cryptic, contradictory quality, as in the following example:

My friend Aga Petros! We will meet again sometime here in the East, for the East now begins in Pskov, but before it began in Verzhbolovo; now it goes uninterruptedly through India to Borneo, Sumatra and Java—as far as the duck-billed platypus in Australia!

But the English colonials have put the platypus in a jar of alcohol and made Australia part of the West.

No, never again will I see Aga Petros, since I will die on Nevsky Prospekt across from the Kazan Cathedral.

So I wrote in Petersburg. Now the place ordained for my death has changed: I will die in the flying coffin of the Berlin subway.

This apostrophe sustains an elevated lyrical tone until the phrase "duck-billed platypus," which abruptly breaks the tone with an incongruous lexical choice (a departure from the other terms of the series). The subsequent paragraph intensifies the contrast by expanding the incongruous phrase. The third paragraph abruptly reverses the thought of the first paragraph. The fourth paragraph reverses the thought of the third paragraph and shifts the narrator's point of view in time and place. It is really a vagrant footnote, which Shklovsky inserted in the original version of *Epilogue* when he assembled *A Sentimental Journey* in Berlin. By that time, he had fully assimilated Sterne's techniques and he sought maximum formal complexity.

"Writing Desk," Part Two of *A Sentimental Journey*, shows most clearly the influence of Sterne. When Shklovsky wrote Part One in 1919, he had not yet wholly evolved his distinctive Sternian manner. His primary aim was to provide an objective chronicle of the events in which he participated. In order to present these events with a minimum of distortion, he avoided complicated formal techniques. In "Writing Desk," however, he launches a massive assault on formal cohesiveness in which he violates the norms of literary language and composition systematically. Abrupt and frequent shifts in language levels and compositional planes break the narrative into a series of loosely strung, nearly autonomous segments.

Shklovsky creates this rough verbal surface in a variety of ways —by parenthetical comments, impudent asides to the reader, interjections, puns, rhetorical questions, colloquialisms, and typographical divisions. At various points in the narrative, for example, he inserts the date at which he wrote that section and describes the circumstances under which he wrote it. At one point he inserts a roman numeral III: there is no I or II nor does the III mark the beginning of a new section. Equally deceptive is the use of paragraphs, for the indentations do not usually set off segments of related material; instead, Shklovsky resorts to the one-sentence paragraph, which became his trademark, or he assembles incongruous ideas in the same paragraph.

The studied nonchalance and staccato transitions which dominate the style of "Writing Desk" also prevail in its narrative structure. Shklovsky persistently interrupts the narrative with digressions of every conceivable kind: apostrophes, soliloquies, anecdotes, epitaphs, his family tree, Zervandov's manuscript, an essay on Russian formalism, even an ambivalent evaluation of Gorky, itself interrupted by digressions on Finland, Bolshevism, and friends in Petrograd.

Digressions occur in such profusion that they obscure the fundamental narrative axis—Shklovsky's adventures. The action is retarded by these digressions, which usually provide sharp contrasts in tone, theme, and time to the contexts in which they are imbedded. They are used not only to expand references in the narrative axis on a chronological plane parallel to it, but also to shuttle backward and forward in time.

The digression on Gorky illustrates Shklovsky's use of chronological displacement. In the midst of describing events that took place in November–December 1919, he abruptly announces: "I've decided to tell in this spot about Aleksei Maksimovich Peshkov—Maksim Gorky." He soon shifts to nostalgic reminiscences of 1921; then, at the end of the digression, he explicitly returns the time to 1920. In 1920, while fighting against Wrangel along the Dnieper, Shklovsky met a Jewish student named Brachmann, whom the soldiers cruelly tormented. The time then shifts, by association, to a parallel situation in Persia, 1917: Russian soldiers were tormenting a cat while its Persian owner stood by helplessly and wondered how to save it. This same part of the narrative contains Shklovsky's genealogy, the logical opening sequence for a book of memoirs. Placed at this juncture, it throws the narrative generations back in time.

The manner in which Shklovsky spliced *Epilogue* into "Writing Desk" sheds further light on his compositional techniques. After describing the last event of "Writing Desk," his escape to Finland in May of 1922—the event with which the book should logically end—Shklovsky returns to events of 1921 and tells about his publishing activities during that year. At this point, he inserts a portion of *Epilogue* (pages 245–266 in *A Sentimental Journey*) telling how he accidentally met his friend Lazar Zervandov in Petrograd. This segment also includes Zervandov's manuscript, which shifts the scene to Persia in 1918. Then Shklovsky returns to "Writing Desk" with his description of the Serapion Brothers, which returns the action to Petrograd in 1921. After this segment, he uses the last part of *Epilogue* as an epilogue to *A Sentimental Journey* (pages 272–276). In other words, Shklovsky divided *Epilogue* into two pieces and inserted between them the block of material about the Serapion Brothers in order to increase the segmentation of the narrative.

The meeting with Zervandov motivates a condensed recapitulation of materials treated in "Revolution and the Front"—the Persian episode. Following this recapitulation, Shklovsky relates, nominally in the words of Zervandov, what happened in Persia after the Russian troops withdrew; then he repeats Zervandov's story by inserting the manuscript that Zervandov supposedly wrote at his request. These two versions of the story overlap, but not entirely, since additional information is contained in the manuscript. Mainly the two versions give Shklovsky the opportunity to be "untidy" and to play with contrasting points of view and styles. In particular, he is parodying the traditional literary device of the conveniently discovered manuscript.

The preceding discussion has stressed the disjointed, polychromatic quality of the narrative. *A Sentimental Journey* does create a first impression of stylistic and compositional anarchy, but Shklovsky repudiated only the traditional methods of unifying a work of literature. In *A Sentimental Journey* he offsets his disruptive devices with an intricate system of leitmotifs, recurrent images, and interlocking cross-references.

Sometimes one word, frequently repeated, holds together an otherwise loosely organized segment. Such verbal clamps give cohesion to anecdotes and digressions. The words "despair" and "died," for instance, bind together the epitaph to Blok.

Frequently, by almost ritual repetition or by a particularly vivid anecdote, Shklovsky establishes a phrase firmly in the mind of the reader. He then uses this phrase without further explanation several pages later in a different context. Such a phrase, enriched with the connotations of its first appearance, permits the author to gain a highly evocative effect with a minimum of words. Early in "Writing Desk," for example, Shklovsky tells that many of the intelligentsia survived the revolution by making chocolate. Two pages later, he gains an ironic effect by a brief reference to this earlier anecdote: "We wanted to shoot. To break glass. We wanted to fight. I didn't know how to make chocolate."

Shklovsky uses this same device in the epitaph to his brother Nikolai. In that passage is the laconic sentence, "Only he didn't believe that the Bolsheviks could resurrect a Russia consumed in fire." This sentence echoes an earlier digression on Bolshevism, in which Shklovsky mentions the folk tale about the devil's apprentice who learned how to rejuvenate an old man by first burning him up and then restoring him as a young man. The apprentice succeeded in burning the old man, but failed to learn how to revive him. Using the word "miracle" as a verbal clamp, Shklovsky draws a parallel between the devil's apprentice and the Bolsheviks, who succeeded in consuming Russia in fire but could not revive her. Shklovsky evokes all the implications of this folk tale with one sentence lodged in the epitaph to his brother.

Some of these key phrases run throughout "Writing Desk" as leitmotifs and refrains. Shklovsky develops these in two ways. Sometimes he imbeds in the narrative an anecdote, a digression, or a passage of direct exposition and then echoes key phrases from these segments throughout the remainder of the book for their evocative and ironic effects. In other cases he postpones the exposition. A provocative phrase, a conclusion, or an effect without causes is abruptly stated, then left dangling as the narrative resumes. Eventually he illuminates the significance of the phrase with an explanation, then repeats the phrase, which now has a different resonance.

The leitmotif of "the falling stone," for example, is extensively developed at the beginning of "Writing Desk" and then repeated throughout the remainder of the book. The title "Writing Desk" itself, emblematic of the profession that sustained Shklovsky throughout his adventures, appears periodically, as Shklovsky tells the reader about the variety of makeshift desks that he employs in his travels. The previously quoted passage about the duck-billed platypus contains impressionistic phrases about East and West that also occur in variations throughout the book.

Two other leitmotifs—nightmare and escape—illustrate Shklovsky's technique of using postponed exposition. The nightmare of the exploding bomb first appears in "Writing Desk," when Shklovsky interrupts a character sketch of a friend to say, "At night I often dream that a bomb is exploding in my hands. That happened to me once." With no further explanation, he continues the narrative. Thirty-eight pages later, he explains that he was wounded by a bomb while fighting against Wrangel. Subsequently, he repeats the motif again.

The leitmotif of escape is developed in the same way. While telling about the entrance of Petlyura into Kiev in the fall of 1918, he interrupts the segment to remark:

In 1922, when I was escaping across the ice from Russia to Finland, I met a lady in a fishing shanty on the ice; we continued on together. When we got to shore and the Finns arrested us, she couldn't say enough good things about Finland, of which she had seen about two square yards.

This sentence does not relate to its context. Only after nearly eighty pages does Shklovsky finally tell the reader about his impending arrest and the need to escape from Petrograd. After the explanation, he sounds the motif again as a coda: "It was on just such a warm night that I walked away with my sledge from the lighted windows of my apartment."

These leitmotifs unify the book. Yet Shklovsky does not insert them in the interstices of the narrative, but squarely in the center of other segments—digressions, anecdotes—where they function as disruptive wedges. In the following passage, for example, he uses the leitmotif of "the falling stone" to interrupt an anecdote about a nurse:

A captured Red Army nurse was raped. The Polish officers infected her with syphilis. She was sleeping with them.

She infected them, then poisoned herself with morphine. She left a note: "I became a prostitute to infect the Poles."

But I am an art theoretician. I am a falling stone and, looking down, I know what motivation is!

I don't believe the note.

And even if I believe it, what's it to me, pray tell, that the Polish officers were infected?

Here the leitmotif, imbued with self-directed irony, contrasts sharply with the detached tone of the anecdote and intensifies the reversal which follows. The nurse's patriotism is impugned; the author's expected sympathy turns into skepticism; and the anecdote acquires the paradoxical flavor characteristic of the book.

The last few pages of *A Sentimental Journey*, replete with "bared devices," show the author in Berlin, where he sits at his latest writing desk and concludes that he will end his book by combining the motifs of both parts. Accordingly, the book ends with a reprise of several motifs of "the journey"—travel, crusade, escape, and exile—couched in the form of an apostrophe to Dr. Shedd, the American missionary in Persia.

Shklovsky remained in Berlin less than two years. In 1923 he described his unhappy experiences as an exile in his experimental epistolary novel entitled *Zoo, or Letters Not about Love*.[15] With the help of Gorky and Mayakovsky, he obtained an amnesty in the fall of 1923 and returned to settle in Moscow, which has been his home since that time.

Upon returning to Russia, Shklovsky immediately renewed his contacts with the Serapion Brothers and joined LEF, Mayakovsky's new alliance of futurists and formalists. He also continued his work in film theory and criticism, which he had begun in Berlin with an article on the art of Charlie Chaplin. After his return to the Soviet Union in 1923, he worked closely with the great directors of the twenties—Eisenstein, Pudovkin, and Dovzhenko. During the twenties, more than a dozen films were made from his scenarios.

Then steadily mounting opposition from the Marxist critics and the proletarian writers' organizations forced Shklovsky to re-evaluate the doctrines of Opoyaz. The prospect of abandoning the work of the formalists brought on a profound spiritual crisis, which is recorded in his autobiography, *The Third Factory*.[16] In this book he clings defiantly to the tenets of Opoyaz even as he sketches the tentative outlines of new positions.

In his work of the late twenties, partially collected in *Hamburg Account*, 1928, Shklovsky finally admitted in principle the relevance of social norms to literature; but he continued to deny the existence of a causal relationship and to view literature primarily as form, an intransigence that did not escape his detractors. His writings of the period also show a new impulse toward simplicity. In-

---

[15] *Zoo ili pis'ma ne o liubvi* (Moscow-Berlin, 1923; 2d ed. rev. and supp., Leningrad, 1924; 3d ed. rev., Leningrad, 1929; 4th ed. rev. in *Zhili-byli*).
[16] *Tret'ia fabrika* (Moscow, 1926).

voking his theory of perception, and extending a tendency already present in *A Sentimental Journey*, he asserted that the new Russian reading public had ceased to respond to long, intricate forms and now preferred unadorned "factography." The intricate, experimental forms made fashionable by the futurists, Opoyaz, and the Serapion Brothers tended to distort factual material. Accordingly, Shklovsky relinquished the "bared," disjointed devices of Laurence Sterne, with their coefficient of irony. Now he studied and practiced short, simple forms that would permit maximum orientation on the message. He led the exploration and refinement of such genres as the newspaper article, the feuilleton, and the sketch, forms that became prominent during the thirties. Out of these genres, he expected a new Russian literature to develop.

After 1930, when the regime no longer permitted art to fly its own flag, Shklovsky made more drastic changes in his approach to literature. He dutifully recited and nominally heeded the official formulas required during the Stalinist era, but he never completely surrendered his early positions. In fact, his valuable memoirs of the twenties, entitled *Mayakovsky*, call to mind *A Sentimental Journey* and *Zoo*.[17]

Since 1930, Shklovsky has produced thousands of articles, dozens of books, and more than ten new scenarios. As he recently wrote:

I did not die in the thirties and lost neither my talent nor my significance in Soviet art.

In this connection, let me relate a folk tale which Yury Olesha once told me:

A beetle was in love with a caterpillar. Once when he went to call, he found her not breathing and wrapped in a shroud. Then a butterfly flew out of the cocoon. The beetle hated the butterfly and most of the time he probably wrote articles about her caterpillar period. But he later saw with his own eyes that she was the very same caterpillar.[18]

The quality of the books published by Shklovsky since Stalin's death does testify to his survival. These include *Pro and Contra: Remarks on Dostoevsky* (1957), *Artistic Prose: Reflections and Critiques* (1959), *Lev Tolstoy* (1963), *Once upon a Time*

---

[17] *O Maiakovskom* (Moscow, 1940; 2d. ed. in *Zhili-byli*).
[18] Letter to R. Sheldon from Shklovsky, Moscow, November 19, 1963.

(1964), and *Tales on Prose* (1966).[19] These books have attracted a wide following both in the Soviet Union and in the West.

When conditions in the Soviet Union permit an objective assessment of early twentieth-century Russian culture, Viktor Shklovsky will be recognized as one of its pivotal figures. The brilliant achievements of the twenties in poetry, prose, theater, cinema, and criticism owe much to the rebellion that he led against hackneyed language and forms in all the arts.

POSTSCRIPT, 1984

Shklovsky continues to reside in Moscow and to write books. His book *Bowstring: On the Dissimilarity of the Similar* (1970 and 1974), was described by the reviewer in *TLS* as "the champagne of criticism." Since then, there has been a book on Eisenstein (1973 and 1976), and a book on plot, *The Energy of Delusion* (1981). Shklovsky celebrated his ninetieth birthday in 1983 by publishing a new version of his classic *Theory of Prose.*

More recently, in *The Literary Gazette* for February 15, 1984, he reported that he had been leafing through the American bibliography of his work and marveling anew at the ingeniously vitriolic titles that his enemies had found for their endless attacks on him and his work. This reflection, in turn, led him to contemplate the prospect of his death and to wonder what would be said about him after his death:

Throughout our life, we are writing one book. Our thoughts and words move from page to page; the pages are bound together and enclosed—shielded— between covers.

Though I would say that books are only the temporary custodians of our thoughts. And not necessarily the best. A thought placed on a page is like a butterfly on a pin. It is fixed in place—glazed, as it were. As if that were the end and there would be no continuation.

But books do not end. Art is endless. Does anyone really believe that the death of Don Quixote was the end of *Don Quixote?* It was only the beginning of his long journey through world literature.

There are now more than fifty books and more than two dozen screenplays. The mark made by Shklovsky is indelible. And his journey is only just beginning.

---

[19] *Za i protiv: Zametki o Dostoevskom* (Moscow, 1957); *Khudozhestvennaia proza: Razmyshleniia i razbory* (Moscow, 1959; 2d ed., Moscow, 1961); *Lev Tolstoi* (Moscow, 1963; 2d ed. rev., Moscow, 1967); *Zhili-byli* (Moscow, 1964; 2d ed. rev. and supp., Moscow, 1966); *Povesti o proze* (2 vols.; Moscow, 1966).

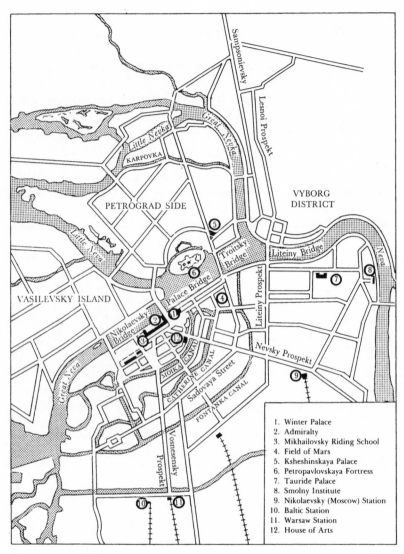

Petrograd, 1917

1. Winter Palace
2. Admiralty
3. Mikhailovsky Riding School
4. Field of Mars
5. Ksheshinskaya Palace
6. Petropavlovskaya Fortress
7. Tauride Palace
8. Smolny Institute
9. Nikolaevsky (Moscow) Station
10. Baltic Station
11. Warsaw Station
12. House of Arts

Driving Nails with a Samovar:
A Historical Introduction

"A new heroic era has opened in the life of
the word. The word is flesh and bread. It
shares the fate of bread and flesh: suffering."
OSIP MANDELSTAM

SHKLOVSKY'S *A Sentimental Journey* is a book about
war, revolution, and civil war. It is also a book about art,
especially modern art, and about the ways an artist has of handling
his materials. Sincerity in art, Shklovsky tells us, is less a question
of good intentions than of craftsmanship. Its opposite is not artifice,
but ineptitude. Far from eschewing "devices," sincerity takes them
seriously—which may, of course, mean playing with them, or bending them to new and unforeseen uses, adapting them to new meanings, sometimes by displacing meaning through a shift in style,
sometimes (as in parody) by making the hitherto hidden function
and use of devices all too visible, so that device and meaning play
upon and enrich each other and take from each other a constantly
renewable and ever-changing life.

This stylistic credo comes at us in a memoir of events so mo-
mentous that they have been called, by Alexander Kerensky, "the
turning point of history!" Nor did these events glide past a Shklovsky hiding remotely in an ivory tower. He was in the thick of them.
Active on four fronts, he was twice wounded and close to death.
The memoir conveys not the remoteness but the immediacy of
these events, in a style that is, at its best, as transparent, com-
pressed, staccato and intense as Hemingway's.

It begins on the eve of the February revolution in the barracks
of the Petrograd garrison, which was to play a crucial role in that
and the subsequent October revolution. Instead of analyzing the
grand alignments of national and international politics, he writes
about being restricted to barracks, about boredom, and about
streetcars. The front he will describe when, in the course of the
narrative, he gets there; diplomacy as it impinges on him—the
"cursed Allies" and their policy of annexations, to which he re-

peatedly refers. He focuses on what happened to him, on what he did, on how he felt about what he did. But he also plays with the structure of the reader's expectations about all this. Hence the deliberately fragmentary nature of the memoir.

Concerning their experiences in war, as Tolstoy noted, all men lie, some with the most honest intentions. The distance between the common traditional, usually exalted, expectations as to "what war is all about" and the actual experience is enormous. The pressure to conform exerted on those who have been through the experience by those who have only the expectations is great indeed. The pressure of the warrior's own unfulfilled expectations is even greater. Shklovsky, however, begins to talk about war and revolution by analyzing the "folklore of streetcars," the account of the Grand Duchess in disguise. The legend, he shows, expresses feelings about experience, not the experience itself. To be understood, it must be examined in terms of its devices. Already Shklovsky is leading the reader (and himself, too) out of the box of common expectations about war. This very unsentimental *Sentimental Journey* is, among other things, a sentimental education. As he writes, the events he records are still very close—in this respect, the book is more like a diary than a memoir, yet a diary that is most carefully and reflectively composed—and their excruciating impact still resonates. Shklovsky wants us to feel both the impact and the resonance. He is after the manner of Stendhal and Tolstoy, not that of Henri Barbusse, or the radical journalist Lembich, whose dispatches bore "as much resemblance to the truth as clouds to cymbals."

Russian literature is rich in memoirs. The richness is understandable. Russian history has alternated between periods of far-reaching and cataclysmic change and those of intensive resistance to change by means of organized repression of a brutal and violent kind. Hence the impulse to construct bridges, joining past to future, private experience to public catastrophe, public need to private dilemma, and one generation to another. As Ehrenburg has written, Russia has need of memoirs.

Given a great autobiographic and "confessional" tradition going back to the seventeenth-century Old Believer martyr Avvakum, it is not surprising that much of nineteenth-century Russian fiction should use the device of the memoir or the diary, from Lermontov's *A Hero of Our Time* to all the stories and novels variously translated as "notes," "sketches," or "diary" from the Russian *zapiski*. Reciprocally, autobiographies and memoirs were fictionalized, not in the sense that they became more haphazard with the truth, but rather that they used the devices of fiction, sustained narrative, psychologized landscape, dialogue, metaphor, sometimes even fictionalized names (but not necessarily) in so systematic and self-conscious a manner as to seem more "re-creation" than "record." In this vein, I might mention Dostoevsky's *Notes from the House of the Dead*, Aksakov's *Years of Childhood*, Tolstoy's trilogy on childhood, boyhood and youth, Gorky's *Autobiography*, and that rather special work of Gorky's that Shklovsky singles out for admiration, the *Literary Reminiscences*.

One might call *A Sentimental Journey*, like these, a kind of "nonfiction novel," to use the phrase that Truman Capote has made fashionable. It contains, in addition to the story of its own composition, its own esthetic—hence the references, implicit and explicit, to Cervantes and Sterne and Tolstoy, and to the literary theories of "formalism," that brilliant school of New Critics of which Shklovsky was a founder.

Early in his memoir, Shklovsky cites an encounter with Sukhanov (N. Himmer), that other great memoirist of the revolution. They had previously confronted each other in an argument about literature. Sukhanov, a Menshevik and a Marxist, has thought of Shklovsky, a formalist, as an "art for art's sake" man, a creature of the ivory tower. Suddenly, he runs into him, an armored car commander, in the thick of things. Sukhanov, a leader of the Soviet, but very much the detached intellectual, fiercely analytic about events when he is home at his desk but a little remote from them in the street, is surprised, a mite shaken, and Shklovsky notes this with characteristic irony.

Shklovsky's memoir, though it describes a number of the same events as Sukhanov's, could not be more different from it. In matters of political analysis, he cannot begin to compare with his Menshevik contemporary, who, against an assured (perhaps over-assured) grasp of the surge of history, measures particular events, personalities, tactics, policies. Shklovsky, on the other hand, although he insists that everything that happens is rational and can be understood, never really shows the hang of that reason, and most of what he writes cries out against it. Hegel and his Marxist heirs are certainly among the authors parodied. But even the metaphors used to convey a sense of something vast and monstrous and out of control are not without irony: "We were all being swept along by a river and the whole of wisdom consisted in yielding to its current." Or, "The masses were moving like spawning herring or carp, obeying their instinct." Or, this delicious description of the very vehicles over which Shklovsky presumably had command: "And throughout the city rushed the muses and furies of the February revolution—trucks and automobiles piled high and spilling over with soldiers, not knowing where they were going or where they would get gasoline, giving the impression of sounding the tocsin throughout the whole city."

If the monsters and muses that Shklovsky conjures up are a little playful, the "rationality" of the situation is nevertheless that it is beyond anyone's control and beyond even the control of reason to grasp. "The rusty iron hoops binding the masses of Russia grew taut." The situation is summed up but not explained. "The barracks had lost faith in the old order." These grand summary statements punctuate the *Journey*, along with epic similes and metaphors that suddenly command great sweeps of territory, as though Shklovsky were marking the high points of his road and asking us to look out over the countryside from there. A taut element of gallows humor, which always emphasizes the elemental, slips into these metaphors—as, for instance, the description of the migration of spotted rats which precedes the account of Russian troops moving out of Persia, as though Shklovsky were wryly noting that in the great panoramas of history, in the most rational and seemingly deliberate activities of mind, there is the force of instinct, by no means accidental and not necessarily stupid or ugly as may first appear, but of enormous and unreckoned force, unaccounted for and perhaps unaccountable.

Civilization itself finds its greatest apotheosis in the memoir in the person of Dr. Shedd, the American consul in Persia, who, against all reason, certainly against all reckoning of the balance of forces in favor of success, riding through the gorges and over the bluffs of the rugged East in his absurd fringed surrey (that symbol of nineteenth-century America), tried to save the lives of children in a region where the lives of children had never counted before.

Shklovsky is not interested in the rational surface of explanation, but in something deeper and bigger. Unlike Sukhanov, he has no ready-formed world view against which to measure events. He has no ideology. He would seem to have been associated with the Socialist Revolutionary party, though he never mentions this explicitly. There is an element of self-justification in the memoir, to be sure. He seems anxious to convince the Bolsheviks that although he was not one of them, he belonged to the same revolution and did nothing deliberately to undermine it. Not that in any sense he bootlicks. On the contrary, with a certain bravado, he joshes at the Bolsheviks and relates them in a rather belittling way to the times—instead of picturing them as they would have liked to see themselves, masters over the times. Nevertheless, he is not without anxiety over establishing revolutionary credentials and over dissociating himself from whatever counterrevolutionary connections he might have been accused of. Fundamentally, however, he is not trying to make a political point, and he is more concerned with the breakdown of ideologies under the impact of cataclysmic events than he is in attempting to fashion out of these events a coherent and rational system.

Like so much of the creative literature that came out of the First World War, from Ezra Pound's "Hugh Selwyn Mauberley" to the anonymous English *Her Privates We* to Céline's nihilist *Journey to the End of the Night*, Shklovsky's memoir is an account of disillusionment and disenchantment. With a kind of retrospective wonder, he records the shocks and traumas of his experience of war and revolution—his "first dead horse," the rumors of machine guns on rooftops, the first man he saw "jockeying for power" —relics of the days when he, as he puts it from the distance of 1919, "still believed in words." His disenchantment is not merely with the values of bourgeois civilization—Ezra Pound's "old bitch gone in the teeth"—but with the ideals of revolutionary democracy as well, for under the impact of war, revolution and counterrevolution, democratic socialism began to recede into the same painfully shimmering and dissolving mirage as democratic liberalism.

The number of casualties, the carnage and destruction, the area of irredeemable collapse—these were on an even vaster scale in the First World War than in the Second, and that first *Materialschlacht*, that battle of technology and equipment, was unprecedented. In the surrounding disintegration of hopes and values, art, and especially modern art, emerged as a new value. We are too accustomed to see the modernist movements of the 1920's—futurism, dadaism, surrealism—as part of the nihilism and cultural despair engendered by the war. In their way, these movements were trying to save what they could. In so many of the best works of poetry, fiction and reminiscence that deal with the First World War, art is the only value left. This was not merely because art had not been compromised by the hypocrisy of war propaganda, but rather because art had never submitted to bourgeois standards at all, had never really been a part of the moral code of its civilization. Indeed, modern art had been in active revolt against that moral code, against all forms of prescriptive morality, for at least about two decades before the war broke out. Modernism began with Ibsen and Nietzsche. Kandinsky painted his first "abstractions" about 1911. After 1914, landscapes and groups began to compose themselves in a manner weirdly confirmative of modern painting—fragmentary, deliberately distorted, with unexpected juxtapositions, dislocations and imbalances. The war seemed merely to confirm the truth of modern art. What Ibsen and Nietzsche had been trying to say suddenly became clear.

"I am a falling stone," writes Shklovsky, using a line of Spinoza's as one of his leitmotifs. In cataclysm, the individual is helpless. "No matter how hard I tried to direct events . . . they went their own way. I changed nothing." There is, of course, a small note of special pleading here, but one should not exaggerate its importance. Shklovsky is always contrasting the skill and intelligence of the individual, the ability to "make do," the capacity to improvise, to discover new uses for old materials, to join the most inappropriate objects in the most unexpected and imponderable projects, to make automobiles out of junk, bombs out of odd parts, and to drive nails with a samovar, all the skills and occasions of individual courage, with the stupidity of states, the decrepitude of ideals, the falling apart of armies and empires, the obesity and unresponsiveness in general of the herd. As for himself, he is "a stone which falls and can, at the same time, light a lantern to observe its own course." He makes himself into a case study for posterity.

This rather special, detached intelligence, this double consciousness, which at the same time participates directly in an action and remotely but meticulously observes its own participation, although the image and motif are from Spinoza, has been identified in the literature of the First World War, especially by German writers, as the distinguishing frame of mind of the front-line fighter, the product of his war experience. Ernst Juenger, the most talented of the German war writers, saw a kind of spiritual kinship between the *Frontkaempfer* and the modern industrial worker. Both were reduced to functions in an enormous process of which they were aware but which they could not hope fully to comprehend or encompass. Depersonalized, they became cogs in a vast machine, yet cogs which, in order to function, required a high degree of technique, imagination, intelligence, courage—all, human qualities that depend precisely on a high degree of personal development. Both responded to this contradiction with a kind of controlled schizophrenia—a capacity to participate in an experience and remain detached at the same time; aloof, looking down upon their own engagements much as an ikon saint looks down from heaven on the scene of his own martyrdom. Not quite like the saint perhaps, for they do not contemplate ultimate meanings, but merely the event itself. On their own pain and suffering they look with a technical eye, outside all morality, interested in the "what" and the "how," but scarcely in the "why" of things. And of the two, the front-line fighter is made of sterner, of more decisive stuff. He is the man of the future, the modern man par excellence.

Juenger's *Kriegserlebnis* became a part of the German politics of the 1920's that attempted to establish a solidarity of those who had been in the trenches, against the "rear," the civilians who had "betrayed" Germany. Shklovsky's memoir scarcely lends itself to such purposes. Yet his description and evaluation of the "double consciousness" produced by the war experience bear a striking resemblance to Juenger's, as indeed to much of the best writing that dealt with the great war that brought the nineteenth century to an end. By "nineteenth century" I mean a certain conjunction of hopes and aspirations: the bourgeoisie and democracy, civilization and the state—a conjunction already badly cracked by the events of 1848.

The revolutions of 1848 and their aftermath separated the bourgeoisie from the working class and from those intellectuals who identified themselves with the working class. Socialism, liberalism and nationalism, which had been, until 1848, closely intertwined ideological movements, after 1848 began to go increasingly separate ways—although their intermingling had been deep and was by no means without consequence for later history. The power politics of the 1860's (by means of which Germany and Italy became modern states), and even more so the imperialist rivalry for colonies abroad of the 1890's, served to forge ties between the bourgeoisie and remnants of the former military officer class it had once opposed. Imperialism, as Schumpeter has shown, gave the officer class a new lease on life. Nationalism, which had been a broad, cosmopolitan movement in the days of Mazzini and Mickiewicz began to turn exclusive, antiliberal and antisocialist as the numerical nineteenth century came to an end. Yet the foundations of the nation-state remained: (1) "the sovereignty of the people," (2) a basically *territorial* identity and (3) the idea of equality before the law. Competition among the states in ventures of power politics and imperialism created in itself an incentive to draw larger and larger masses of the population, larger increments of energy and wealth, into the political arena. Yet imperialism was inevitably destructive of the very foundations of the nation-state.

Among the nineteenth-century nation-states, three vast, anomalous multinational empires persisted until the end of the First World War: Austria-Hungary, Russia, Turkey. Each had taken some measures to come to terms with capitalism, technology and the political structure of the nation-state: Austria through the formation of the dual monarchy, Russia through the Great Reforms, and Turkey through the revolution of the Young Turks. But the measures proved insufficient to weather the storm. These decadent empires had become enmeshed in the alliance systems of England and France on the one hand and Germany on the other. They were indispensable to the balance of power set up by these alliance systems; and yet, they endowed this balance with their own inherent instability.

If capitalism, technology and nationalism intensified and even transformed international rivalries, a widely held nineteenth-century prejudice had it that these forces, working together, created an antidote to international rivalry as well, in the form of an organized and increasingly self-conscious working class. As the right feared and the left hoped, the proletariat had no fatherland. On the very eve of the First World War, the Second International was meeting in Brussels; yet somehow on the issue of whether socialist representatives in the various parliaments should vote against war credits for their respective governments, the delegates could not agree. When the war broke out, they were still arguing. Most of them voted for war credits. It seemed that the proletariat had various fatherlands after all.

Nevertheless, a few socialists resisted. As the war went on, their influence increased. The handful of dissident socialists who attended the pacifist congresses in the neutral Swiss towns of Zimmerwald and Kienthal in the summer of 1915 and early 1916 found themselves with a larger and more attentive following as war-weariness spread. They called for fraternization of the armies, the conversion of international war into class war, a peace without annexations, the rejection of secret agreements and treaties, and they proclaimed the right of political self-determination of peoples on the basis of a diplomacy known to all and subject to popular scrutiny and criticism.

The class-war motif aside, the extent to which, once America entered the war, Wilsonian propaganda echoed the propaganda of the Zimmerwaldians (among whom Lenin was a prominent figure) is remarkable. The main impact on Europe of Wilsonian propaganda was to steal the thunder of the socialist left by proclaiming "the self-determination of peoples," "open covenants openly arrived at," and "peace without victory," while divorcing these slogans from the idea of class struggle.

If war-weariness enhanced the prestige and popular appeal of the Zimmerwaldians throughout Europe, it gave them a special stature indeed in exhausted, demoralized Russia. All the parties of the left in Russia manifested within themselves some support for the principles of Zimmerwald, but the only party that subscribed to these principles as a party was the Bolsheviks.

In February 1917, the tsarist regime collapsed. Almost nobody came to its defense. For a few brief months, backward, repressed Imperial Russia became the freest democracy in Europe. This astonishing freedom flourished under very unstable circumstances, however; two mutually wary centers of power and authority in the capital were sizing each other up—the Provisional Government and the Soviet. The question of whom, if anyone, the armies would obey hung in the air like a big red balloon. The armies had not yet begun to dissolve, but the Soviet's Order Number One, establishing army committees as checks over the officers, immediately called discipline into question. Before Lenin's arrival at the Finland Station in Petrograd in April 1917, the Bolsheviks could claim only a small minority of delegates to the Soviet. Their willingness to countenance and even to hasten the dissolution of the armies, their support of the spontaneous peasant seizure of land from the landowners, their recognition of the Soviet and not the Provisional Government as the legitimate source of revolutionary authority, after Lenin's arrival, seemed to many demagogic, a kind of unprincipled "pushing" of those already formidable forces among the masses working for chaos and collapse.

Among the political parties, the Bolsheviks were not only the readiest to identify themselves with disintegrative forces on the grass-roots level, but as the most formidably disciplined and best organized of the revolutionary parties, the only one that could give shape and an effective direction to what others referred to derisively as *chern'*—the rabble. Party discipline and organization had always distinguished the Bolsheviks from other parties of the left. In 1903, Lenin had split the Russian Social Democratic (Marxist) party into its Bolshevik and Menshevik wings precisely over the issue of party organization. At the time, leaders of the left who otherwise respected Lenin, and certainly thought him "one of them," were puzzled by his fanaticism on this issue. To them, organization and discipline were secondary issues. To Lenin, they were precisely the central issue confronting a revolutionary Marxist party in tsarist Russia. Discipline and organization permitted the Bolsheviks to assume leadership and even a certain representative stature in the midst of fantastic disintegration and disruption without themselves being overwhelmed by the disintegration itself. Later, many of the left-wing leaders called the Bolshevik emergence and victory an accident, brought about merely by the strain of war on an incompletely industrialized country. Yet if it was an accident, it has surely proved to be the most stable accident in the modern history of Europe.

Shklovsky was a Socialist Revolutionary. He is reticent about his political beliefs and commitments, but it is clear that he disagrees with the Bolsheviks on a number of points, especially the war. As a revolutionary he argues that the hoped-for revolution in Germany can be brought about not by capitulation, but only by the successful completion of the war. While he rails against the Allies for clinging to discredited war aims, and against Russian liberals like Milyukov who for all their obeisance to democracy seem incapable of renouncing annexations, he warily exposes what seem to him the false hopes the Bolsheviks invest in fraternization.

Fraternization is to the advantage of the German general staff, as long as that sense of order which keeps an army an army remains sufficiently intact so that, when German officers issue orders,

German soldiers obey them. Under such circumstances, it can only hasten the dissolution of the Russian army, which is in any case already dissolving. He has seen a German staff directive to that effect in Czernowitz. Revolutionary Russia, with its armies intact, could bring revolution to Germany. So long as the tide of victory was with the Germans, however, fraternization at the front could only prove disastrous for the revolution.

There is, in Shklovsky's statements about the war, something that suggests he is preparing a case before an imagined revolutionary tribunal, exculpating himself from charges of counterrevolutionary chauvinism. More interesting is the other "case" he also prepares—the case study for posterity. He touches implicitly on the delicate matter of what makes a unit a unit, an army an army, a people a people and not just a random collection of wills and appetites. Whether he regards the Austrian-German army in the picturesque little towns of Galicia in the summer of 1917 (only a *shade* more willing to obey orders than the Russians) or whether he reflects on the curious creed-communities, the tribal alignments and age-old hatreds of the Kurds and Aissors, a world in which the military power had never been interwoven with the cultural mystique, the presumed civilizing mission, or the specific territorial identity of the nation-state, he manages to convey his sense of something elusive and crucially important, the basis of both group and individual identity, the forms and devices by means of which human sensibility engages the world as a self.

Not that, in his narrative, he discounts what Marxists would call "the economic base." His account of being entertained by a Persian "socialist" who has servants strew the floor with rose petals —a scene made to order for Shklovsky's sense of the ironic and the incongruous—would be evidence enough to the contrary, and it is scarcely unique. Nevertheless, as he half ironically puts it, "I'm not a socialist, I'm a Freudian." This remark is followed by his extraordinary statement that the Bolsheviks, in Russia's time of crisis, had been "dreamed up"—one of the most striking metaphors in the book: "They [the masses] escaped into Bolshevism the way a man hides from life in a psychosis." It is an analogy between the private and the public psyche that has resonance throughout the *Journey.*

As the Bolsheviks stepped into Russia's dream, the Socialist Revolutionaries receded. After having won a majority of seats to the Constituent Assembly, they saw the Assembly dismissed and dispersed by a handful of troops under the command of the Bolsheviks before it could meet. The left wing of the Socialist Revolutionary party continued to support the Bolsheviks. They left the Bolshevik government only in the summer of 1918, indignant over the idea of capitulating to the Germans.

A young Russian intellectual of Shklovsky's generation almost inevitably belonged to one of the left-wing political parties. His recruitment by a particular party might well have been accidental, and there was a good deal of "overlapping" among the parties, both in terms of ideology and in terms of temperament. Yet the character of the individual and the character of the party to which he belonged were in closer touch, and political affiliation indicated more about a man's temperament, than elsewhere. Before February 1917, all the parties of the left—and one might even say all political parties as such—were not merely oppositionist, but to greater or lesser degree, bearing both the stamp of their origins and the manner of their treatment at the hands of the regime, underground parties. The underground mentality was part of the distinctive flavor of Russian politics.

All the major political parties were parties of intellectuals. Aspiring to become mass parties, to some extent they succeeded. Their support was both broad and shallow—that is to say, extremely insecure. Their individual situations were fraught with contradictions.

The Kadets were liberals. They didn't want to be revolutionary at all; yet they were regarded as such by the regime, and forced into comradeship and rapport with their wilder brethren of the left. It was difficult indeed to behave like an Anglo-French parliamentary party and at the same time like an underground conspiracy. Pavel Milyukov, leader of the Kadets, saw himself as a European statesman. A brilliant historian and a shrewd politician, he nevertheless was blinded by the European image of statesmanship, which also destroyed his party. In the face of military disaster, he refused to renounce or even significantly to modify Russia's commitments to her Allies. This was in part because they were Allies (France and England, after all, whose parliamentary example Milyukov hoped to follow), in part because the image of a European statesman could not do without at least a touch of "blood and iron." Perhaps Milyukov really believed that the Russian army would fight for "Tsargrad," the tinsel creation of a tsarist imperial ideology Milyukov himself despised. In any case, while the Russian armies dissolved, Milyukov was insisting on the right to annex Constantinople. Yet at the same time he saw himself as the leader of the democratic upsurge.

The Mensheviks were Marxists. Unlike the Bolsheviks, they were an "open" party. They were both Marxists and pluralists. Although they called themselves revolutionaries, they tended to think of the genuine socialist revolution as something for the rather distant future. Their brand of Marxism seemed to lend to events a certain inevitability and cultivated in them a certain fatalism and passivity toward history. Their Marxism persuaded them that, as a "bourgeois-liberal" regime, the Provisional Government should have their support but not their participation. They were in the curious situation of being revolutionaries who didn't want to rush things. On the other hand, the Menshevik tradition of tolerance and respect for grass-roots, "spontaneous" movements gave the party a kind of "federative" tendency, a willingness to join up with, and a reluctance to take over, such movements. This "federative" tendency accounts for the Menshevik success in Georgia, where the party became identified with Georgian nationalism, as well as the indefiniteness of the party's relationship to the Provisional Government.

Although the Socialist Revolutionaries were as much a party of intellectuals as any of the others, they nevertheless aspired to a special relationship to the peasantry and hence to the great majority of the Russian people. Founded by Viktor Chernov and others in 1902, the party reincarnated many of the values of the Russian populism of the 1860's and 1870's, but with a mass appeal and on a mass base of support unknown before.

The main burden of Russian populism was a mystique of "the people" (*narod*), identified above all with the peasantry, that involved a sense of guilt and a sense of *oblige* on the part of intellectuals toward the people, but at the same time an exaltation of the Russian peasant as having something very special to teach intellectuals, and indeed the world. To some degree, *narodnichestvo* influenced all the parties; and it should be added that the Marxism of the 1890's and the polemics of the Marxists with the populists had not left the old populism unchanged. Nevertheless, the Socialist Revolutionaries saw themselves as, and indeed were, the heirs of Russian populism.

Franco Venturi has given a very thorough account of populism, its creed, its mood, its origins and fate, in his *Roots of Revolution*. Here I will only sum up some of its outstanding features. First and foremost was a faith in the Russian peasant, which was at the same time a kind of confidence in the "instinctive" life of the masses: that the Russian peasant offered the world an education in socialism and brotherhood in the specific form of the *mir*, or village commune. At the same time, the populists acknowledged that the peasant and his institutions existed under barbaric conditions, and held that they must be liberated from the system of economic exploitation and social subservience to which they were linked. The populists saw themselves as the agents of liberation, upon whom rested an enormous responsibility—to "go to the people," and, if we may touch slightly on Shklovsky's metaphor, somewhat as the sick and incomplete ego to the forces of the id in psychoanalysis, back to the source of life and energy; to be made whole again, but at the same time to give form and shape to the energizing forces, to "civilize" them.

The populists wanted at the same time to follow piously the logic of the people's own spontaneous development and to endow it with skills, with science, and with consciousness, form and sensibility. They were not lacking in respect for European civilization, especially science; yet this was coupled with a contempt for the bourgeoisie, the *juste milieu*, compromise, and that whole complex of bourgeois contemptibilities that the Russians call *poshlost'*, or aggressive and self-satisfied mediocrity. The tsarist state was held in contempt and the populists were determined to overthrow it, yet reluctant to sacrifice the people merely for the creation of a legal-bourgeois regime with its parliamentary gamesmanship masking continued exploitation. Here we see a certain anarchist streak, including the justification and use of terror, both as defense against the political police and as a tactic in its own right—and along with terror, an emphasis on conspiratorial organization that so often, paradoxically, accompanies anarchist tendencies.

In the years between the assassination of Alexander II and the emergence of the Socialist Revolutionary party, the populists, like all Russian intellectuals, had gone to school to Marx. In the process, they overcame their aversion to industrialization and developed a sense of the importance of a legal order. In the expansion of political activity that took place from the turn of the century on, the Socialist Revolutionaries became the largest political party, the most powerful "vote-getter," if one may use that inappropriately American phrase, in Russia. But they never abandoned terror as a political instrument. The party was even more loosely organized and contained an even wider spectrum of opinions than the Kadets or the Mensheviks. It also included a tightly organized Battle Organization in which intellectual adventurers like Savinkov won their spurs. In spite of its use of terror and the Battle Organization, the Socialist Revolutionaries were more a mood and an attitude than an ideological party.

Although Shklovsky was in, and in a sense really of, the party, he was certainly not a party man. Throughout the *Journey*, he contrasts the obesity of the herd with the intelligence and inventiveness of individuals. He caricatures the hysterical emotionality, often characteristic of the party, in the person of Kerensky, the former political lawyer turned hapless statesman. And in the matter that is closest to Shklovsky—literature, and the interpretation of literature—he excoriates such *narodnik* "saints" as Belinsky, Chernyshevsky, Mikhailovsky and Ivanov-Razumnik, along with the entire liberal-radical tradition of literary criticism and scholarship in Russia, which he accuses of having confused "the history of liberalism in Russia with the history of Russian literature." Opposed to these, he singles out for praise the solitary and politically dubious figure of Rozanov, with his extraordinary sense of the interplay between style and meaning and his Nietzschean affirmation, in all areas of life, of the primacy of the esthetic. There is also Shklovsky's portrait of Filonenko, Savinkov's right-hand man, commissar of the Rumanian front and later commissar at general-staff headquarters, would-be intellectual (proud of his French pronunciation), amateur astrologer, implicated in the Kornilov affair and other disasters, adventurer and opportunist.

In the summer of 1918, in protest against the negotiations the Bolsheviks were carrying on with the Germans at Brest-Litovsk, the Left-wing Socialist Revolutionaries withdrew from the coalition they had entered with the Bolsheviks. Savinkov, along with Filonenko, tried to organize a revolt. There was also an outbreak of terrorism. The German ambassador, Mirbach, was killed. So were two prominent Bolsheviks, Uritsky and Volodarsky. Lenin himself was gravely wounded in August. From this time on, the Bolsheviks held power alone.

At the end of the Civil War in 1921, the Bolsheviks had sixty-four prominent Socialist Revolutionaries in prison. They were brought to trial in the summer of 1922, amidst much publicity. Since Shklovsky was implicated in the trial, and since in a way it provided the occasion for the writing of the second part of his memoir, a brief account of the issues involved might well be in order.

The Bolsheviks had no intention of relinquishing their hold on power. Their claim to "revolutionary legitimacy" was that they were the party of the revolution, they alone had fought the revolution through to victory. They suppressed not their merely ideological opponents but those who had acted against them and thus against the revolution. Thus it made considerable difference whether Socialist Revolutionary terrorists had acted as individuals, or on orders from their party. Of the SR's in prison, few could be accused of particular terrorist acts; but all were prominent in the party leadership.

The trial was a matter of some delicacy abroad as well as at home. The Soviet Union was diplomatically isolated, and it was both an economic and a political necessity for the Bolsheviks to break out of that isolation. In western Europe, they sought to resume contact with the social-democratic parties of the Second International, even at the same time as they brought the Third (Communist) International under intensive cultivation. The socialist parties of Europe could hardly accuse the Bolsheviks of being, merely, revolutionary. They accused them instead of being undemocratic, of acting dictatorially not only against the counter-revolution, but against their fellow-revolutionists. Bukharin, in Berlin, tried to assure the socialists that the impending trial would not only be open, but thoroughly legal. The Belgian socialist Vandervelde even went to Moscow under the impression that he would be allowed to act as counsel for the accused. He was soon disappointed, and left.

As part of the preparation for the trial, a man who called himself Grigory Semyonov (his real name was probably Vasiliev)—a Socialist Revolutionary who had recanted, possibly he had been an *agent provocateur* for some time—published a pamphlet in Berlin (a Russian publishing house supported by the Soviet government brought it out in January 1922) in which he claimed that the terrorist acts of the summer of 1918 had been more than the indignant outbursts of individuals, but basic party policy, thus justifying the Bolsheviks in their dissolution of the Socialist Revolutionary party.[1] Semyonov also testified at the trial. He was an old SR. He had helped Kerensky escape from Gatchina in 1917. His word carried weight. Under the impact of his testimony, a number of the accused renounced their affiliation with the party. Among others, Semyonov in his pamphlet had implicated Shklovsky, and it was word of this that prompted Shklovsky, who thought at the time that he had (through Gorky and others) made his peace with the Bolsheviks, to look to his skin and disappear over the border.

Fourteen of the accused received suspended death sentences at the trial. Actually, it was the first of the "show trials," an ominous if relatively mild precursor of the grim dramas of the mid-1930's. Bukharin, himself to appear as the accused in one of the later trials, played the miserable role of prosecutor, even though it was he who had left Vandervelde with the impression that the accused would be permitted foreign counsel. Instead of foreign counsel, the accused found themselves confronted with the testimony against them of a number of distinguished revolutionaries from abroad. Lenin thought the trial a bad performance, not on moral grounds, of course, but tactically.

Shklovsky's timely escape spared him the humiliation of prison and public recantation. If there is a "confessional" element in his memoir, it is nevertheless absolutely dignified and honest; the cutting portrait of Filonenko might serve sufficiently as a prototype of the adventurer elevated beyond his talents by revolutionary upheaval, a type by no means limited to the Socialist Revolutionary party alone.

Still, Shklovsky's attachment to the SR's was not entirely accidental. I refer not merely to the fact that a number of his relatives belonged to the party—Isaak Vladimirovich Shklovsky, for instance, who, under the pseudonym "Dioneo," flourished as a journalist and commentator on political affairs. While "Dioneo" in England was writing bitter pamphlets against the Bolsheviks, Shklovsky was trying to reach some inner and outer *modus vivendi* with the party of Lenin. But as a young man, "Dioneo" spent four years in political exile in Siberia. After his return, he wrote a book

---

[1] G. Semyonov, *Voennaia i boevaia rabota partii Esera za 1917–1919 gg.* (Berlin, 1922).

on the Yakuts, which appeared in Russian in 1895 and in English translation in 1916.[2] While his literary talent is dimmer than his nephew's, "Dioneo" too shows a very special kind of feeling for the forms and observances, the rituals and customs, of life at the grass roots—for the semipermeable membrane that separates form and chaos. Not only does Shklovsky have, as T. E. Lawrence had for the Arab world, a vivid sense of the human possibilities of those peoples inhabiting the region between Lake Van and Lake Urmia, but he has as well—something that Lawrence, the Puritan and the Manichee, could never quite attain—a deep and intimate sense of identification with them.

Shklovsky's account of the Russian campaign in Persia is the most extraordinary part of his memoir, and not merely because it is a unique account of a historic venture in exotic territory. True, the exotic nature of the enterprise is highlighted in a number of ways, not least by the references to Xenophon, yet in the *Anabasis* the country and its people are seen merely as so many obstacles to be overcome.

"I am a man of the East," Shklovsky writes, and repeats, allowing the refrain to gather force from the narrative. In European literature, the East has traditionally been the place of escape from humdrum, the eye-opener, the place of adventure. From there, it is a brief span to the place of disillusionment and disenchantment where expectations and illusions are put to the test and found wanting—hence, the place from which things at home are seen as different from what they were originally assumed to be, because the expectations they generated are seen to be absurd. The East as the place where perspective is gained and values are reversed or transvalued has figured especially prominently in late romantic English literature, from Richard Burton to Lawrence Durrell.

In Russian literature, Shklovsky had as his particular and peculiar predecessor a lonely and almost forgotten genius, Konstantin Leontiev. For many years, Leontiev served as a Russian diplomat in the Turkish Mediterranean. Like the English and French romantics, he was impressed with the variety, the antiquity, the contrasts, the energy, the interlocking layered quality, the bewildering traces of contrasting past civilizations, the color, the vitality, the instability, the unreliability, the extreme cruelty, and

[2] *In Far Northeast Siberia* (London, 1916).

the severe contrasts of asceticism and sensuality, the sheer raw material available to feed the imagination. Unlike his western European counterparts, however, Leontiev saw the East as the place where Russian values were fulfilled rather than reversed; the source of all Russian values, for Leontiev, was Orthodoxy, and the possibility of Orthodoxy in the East was a new kind of community very different from the western European power-state. Shklovsky does not exactly share Leontiev's "Byzantinism," but I believe that Leontiev, who was also, incidentally a precursor of formalism in literary criticism, has influenced him in many ways.

The West represents, for Shklovsky, a relatively stable political order identified with large, coherent geographical territories, the subtle elaboration of political forms and hierarchies, law and the rule of law, the cultivation of practicality and the art of com- promise, sobriety, responsibility, organizational and technological skill, the pre-eminently political and practical virtues. The East is the visible and dramatic graveyard of empires. In the East, it is impossible to take politics seriously; and yet, this lack of serious- ness in politics is part of the terrible vulnerability of the area, its openness to invasion and conquest. A condottiere who can slap an army together and hold it together for a few weeks can conquer an empire. Conquerors sweep through vast stretches of territory, a new empire is proclaimed, it lasts "a day or two" and collapses. The collapse of overarching power leaves the incredibly complex mix- ture of tribes, religions, the remnants and traces of past migrations of peoples, the dislocated and displaced clans of past conquests released once more to turn against each other, long-smoldering past hatreds flaring, in a land where no power lasts and no grievance is ever forgotten or forgiven.

The East is the graveyard of empires and the birthplace of religions. After two centuries of exposure to the depredations of Europe, the new secular European religion of nationalism (from the turn of the century on) was beginning to push roots down into the craggy soil. The Young Turks came to power in 1908. Ataturk defied the Allies and with Bolshevik help created an independent, new and "national" Turkey by 1922. In 1908, the British and the Russians could still divide Persia between them, but by 1918, Reza Shah Pahlevi, trained among the Persian Cossacks of the Russian Colonel Stolder, gathered some national fragments around him, seized power and laid the foundations of the new Iran. Working with the Aramaic-speaking Syrian Christians of the Lake Urmia region, Shklovsky, in the land of Prester John, has a haunting sense of possible unities, potential centers of force.

"I am a man of the East," writes Shklovsky, meaning that he is particularly vulnerable and helpless, a falling stone, like Spinoza, a Jew subject to pogroms, unprovoked and irrational, against which there is no recourse. He takes to the East because "there is no anti-Semitism," because the Aissors speak Aramaic and remind him of old, submerged kinships. His father was Jewish, he tells us, failing to mention that his Jewish father was also a Christian convert; but he does dwell with a certain esthetic pleasure on the simple, direct, personal blood-line religion of the Aissors and their leader Mar Shimun, who claims descent from "the brother of our Lord."

The Russian soldiers in Persia make pogroms, and for Shklovsky the pogrom turns into a nightmare of running away. Amazingly, his Aissor friends turn up again in Petrograd, with an epic tale of the last days of Mar Shimun, and Shklovsky splices the story of Lazar Zervandov into an account of Petrograd in which he is dealing particularly with the literary life of the city and of Russia, the new movements, the new possibilities, particularly the Serapion Brothers, some of whom are in part his disciples. Zervandov is also a man of the East, also a falling stone, also a stone that illumines the course as he falls. Zervandov is an epic hero, turned by hard times and displacement into a bootblack in the streets of Petrograd. But a bootblack in Petrograd who is an epic hero also transforms Petrograd.

"For now the East begins in Pskov." Russia, which had been struggling toward modernity through the organization of technology and the nation-state, had relapsed into regional quarrels; in the Ukraine, where the Civil War raged back and forth over the railroad lines and where many of the major cities changed hands a dozen times in four years, in the Caucasus and in Siberia, the Bolsheviks were well on their way to putting the pieces back together. They brought to their task the heroic pose of leather jackets and the real organization and discipline of shock brigades, an absolute confidence in the power of the will, a faith in plans and a rhetoric of planning along with an enormously willful future-consciousness.

Shklovsky is skeptical. The man of the East has learned, however, to retain a certain faith through his skepticism. Among the fragments of forms and devices that is the wreckage of a civilization, the civilized man goes about looking for bits and pieces that he can use. He uses them for the needs of the moment, and in so doing he changes them, but the needs also change. To be a formalist is a little like being an Aissor bootblack in Petrograd. It does not mean to worship form and device as such. It means to make do. It means to keep alive, internally and externally, by making do, by driving nails with a samovar if necessary, and watching what the samovar does to the nails and the nails to the samovar, noting it wryly in appropriate sentences. What is to be respected is not the form but the spirit of improvisation that finds it—and, in excess of reason, uses it with skill, zest and originality.

SIDNEY MONAS

Austin, Texas
September 1969

VIKTOR SHKLOVSKY

A Sentimental Journey

Memoirs, 1917–1922

Map of Europe during World War I, with a detailed map of Galicia

TO LUSYA

Part One

REVOLUTION AND THE FRONT

$\mathcal{B}$EFORE the revolution, I worked as an instructor in a reserve armored division, which made me one of the more privileged soldiers.

I'll never forget the terrible sense of oppression that weighed on me and my brother, who was serving as a headquarters clerk.

I remember running furtively down the streets after eight o'clock at night and being restricted to the barracks for three months, but most of all I remember the streetcars.

The whole city had been turned into a military camp. The military police were called "semishniki,"[1] because they apparently got two kopeks for every man they arrested; they regularly hunted us down, cornered us in courtyards and threw us in the guardhouse. The reason for this "war" was that the soldiers crowded the streetcars and refused to pay for the ride.

The officers considered this a question of honor. We, the common soldiers, answered them with mute, vindictive sabotage.

This may be childish, but I'm convinced that restriction to the barracks, where men torn from their duties rotted on bunks with nothing to do, the dreariness of the barracks, the dull despair and resentment of the soldiers at being hunted down in the streets—all this stirred up the Petersburg garrison more than the constant reversals in the war and the persistent rumors of "treason."[2]

A special folklore, pitiful and characteristic, developed around streetcar themes. For example: a nurse is riding with some wounded men; a general starts bothering the wounded men and insults the nurse; she throws off her cape and stands before him in the uniform of a grand duchess. That's how they told it—"in the uniform." The general gets down on his knees and begs forgive-

7

ness, but she doesn't forgive him. As you see, the folklore was still completely monarchistic.

This story is sometimes set in Warsaw, sometimes in Petersburg.

They used to tell how a Cossack once killed a general. The general had tried to throw him off a streetcar and, in the process, ripped off his military decorations. Apparently such a streetcar killing really did happen in St. Pete, but I think the general was added for an epic effect: in those days, generals weren't riding streetcars yet—except the poor, retired ones.

No one was disseminating propaganda in the units—at least no one in my unit, where I was with the soldiers from five or six in the morning until late at night. I'm speaking about party propaganda. But even in its absence, the revolution was somehow an established fact. Everyone knew it would come, only it was expected after the war.

There was no one to disseminate propaganda in the units; there were few party members and those few were workers, who had almost no contact with the soldiers. Intellectuals, in the most primitive sense of the word—that is, anyone with some sort of education, even two years of secondary school—were promoted to officers and behaved, at least in the Petersburg garrison, no better and perhaps worse than the career officers. The second lieutenants weren't popular—especially those in the rear, who fought tooth and nail to stay in the reserve battalion. The soldiers used to sing about them:

> Before he spaded in a garden.
> Now we bow and beg his pardon.

Many of these men were guilty only of having too easily succumbed to the well-entrenched discipline of their military training. Later on, many of them sincerely devoted themselves to the cause of the revolution—indeed, they succumbed to its influence just as easily as they had previously toed the mark.

The story about Rasputin was widely circulated. I don't like this story. The manner in which it was told exposed the moral decay of the people. Later, the revolutionary pamphlets—all those "Adventures of Grishka"—and the success of this type of literature proved to me that, for large numbers of the common people, Rasputin had become a peculiar sort of folk hero—something like Vanka the Steward.[3]

But for various reasons—some of which simply frayed nerves and created the occasion for an outburst, while others acted internally, slowly changing the psyche of the people—the rusty iron hoops binding the masses of Russia grew taut.

The food supplies of the city continued to dwindle. By the standards of that time, the situation was bad. A shortage of bread made itself felt; lines appeared at the bakeries. At the Obvodny Canal, people had already begun to break into the shops. Those lucky enough to get bread carried it home, holding it tightly in their hands and looking at it lovingly.

Bread was bought from the soldiers. The crusts and scraps which, along with the sour smell of servitude, had been the trademark of the barracks now disappeared.

The cry for bread rang out under the windows and at the gates of the barracks, already carelessly guarded by the sentries, who let their comrades go out whenever they wanted to.

The barracks had lost faith in the old order. Pressed by the cruel, but already wavering, hand of the authorities, they began to ferment. At this time, a regular soldier—in fact, any soldier from the age of twenty-two to twenty-five—was a rarity. They had been savagely and senselessly slaughtered in the war.

Regular noncommissioned officers had been poured into the front lines as common soldiers and had perished in Prussia near Lvov and during the famous "strategic withdrawal," when the Russian army paved the whole countryside with its corpses. The Petersburg soldier of those days was either a dissatisfied peasant or a dissatisfied city-dweller.

These men were not even dressed in their new gray overcoats, but just hastily wrapped in them, then lumped into crowds, bands and gangs and called reserve battalions.

In essence, the barracks became simply brick pens to which more and more red and green draft notices drove ever-increasing herds of raw humanity.

The numerical proportion of officers to rank-and-file soldiers was in all probability no higher than that of overseers to slaves on the old-time galleys.

And outside the walls of the barracks, rumors circulated that the workers were "getting ready to demonstrate," that on February 18[4] workers from Kolpino "would march on the State Duma."

There were few ties between the workers and the rank-and-file soldiers, who were recruited either from the peasants or the petty bourgeoisie, but all these circumstances were conspiring to make some kind of explosion possible.

I remember the days before that explosion. The far-fetched conversations of the instructor-drivers about how nice it would be to steal an armored car, fire at the police and then ditch the armored car somewhere at the edge of town and leave a note on it: "Deliver to the Mikhailovsky Riding School." One very characteristic detail: concern about the vehicle remained. Evidently the men still lacked confidence in their ability to overthrow the old order. They only wanted to stir up a little trouble. But they had resented the police for a long time—mainly because the police were exempt from duty at the front.

I remember about two weeks before the revolution, our unit (about two hundred men) was marching along, hooting at a squad of policemen and shouting, "Dirty cops, dirty cops."

In the last days of February, people were literally hurling themselves at the police. The squads of Cossacks that were sent out into the street touched no one: they rode along laughing good-naturedly. This greatly heightened the rebellious mood of the crowd. On Nevsky Prospekt there was some shooting; several people were killed. A dead horse lay for a long time not far from the corner of Liteiny Prospekt. I still remember it. It was unusual then.

On Znamenskaya Square, a Cossack killed a police officer who had struck a woman demonstrator with his saber.

Indecisive patrols stood around in the streets. I remember an embarrassed machine-gun detachment with small machine guns on wheels (manufactured by Sokolov), with machine-gun belts in the packs of the horses—evidently some kind of equestrian machine-gun brigade. They stationed themselves at the corner of Basseinaya Street and Baskovaya Street. The machine gun, equally embarrassed, hugged the pavement like some little animal. The crowd clustered around it, not attacking or using their hands, but somehow pressing with their shoulders.

On Vladimirsky Prospekt were patrols from the Semyonovsky Regiment, which had the reputation of Cain.[5]

The patrols stood around indecisively: "Don't worry about us.

We feel like everybody else." The enormous coercion machine man-ufactured by the government was spinning its wheels. That night the Volhynian Regiment could hold fast no longer. By prior agree-ment, the men rushed for their rifles on the command of "Evening Prayer," broke into the supply room, took cartridges, ran out into the street and persuaded several small units in the vicinity to join them. They set out patrols in the area of their barracks—in the Liteiny district. Incidentally, the Volhynians broke open our guardhouse, which was next to their barracks. The freed prisoners returned to their former units. Our officers chose to be neutral; they too shared the very special conservative views of *The Evening Times*.[6] The barracks seethed and waited for the moment when someone would come and let them out into the street. Our officers said, "Do what you think best."

In the streets in my area, people in civvies were rushing out of doorways in small groups and taking weapons away from the officers.

Despite scattered gunfire, many people stood around in door-ways—even women and children. They looked as if they were waiting for a wedding or a magnificent funeral.

Three or four days before this, we had been ordered to render our vehicles inoperable. In our garage the volunteer engineer Be-linkin gave the removed parts to the soldiers who worked in his garage. But the armored cars of our garage were transferred to the Mikhailovsky Riding School. I went to the riding school, which was already full of people making off with automobiles. There were not enough parts for the armored cars. It seemed to me of primary importance to get the Lanchester cannon car back in operation. We had spare parts at the drivers' school, so I went there. Despite the commotion the men on duty were still at their posts. That surprised me at the time. Later on in Kiev, at the end of 1918, when I incited an armored division against the hetman, I noticed that almost all the soldiers claimed they were "on duty" and I was no longer surprised.

They liked me very much at the school. A soldier who opened the door for me asked, "You, Viktor Borisovich, are you for the people?" Getting a positive answer, he began to kiss me. We all kissed a lot in those days. They gave me the parts and even promised not to say who took them. I went back to my unit. To this day, I don't know if someone came to get the men or if they broke up and dispersed of their own accord. Men were milling around in the barracks. I took two experienced foremen from the garage, Gnutov and Bliznyakov, got some tools and went with them to repair the car. All this was in the afternoon, two or three hours after the revolt of the Volhynians—the first day.

I don't understand how so many events could have been packed into that day.

We towed the armored car to a garage on Kovenskaya Street, where we occupied the building, tore out the telephones and began to repair the car. We worked on it until evening. It turned out that water had been poured into the gas tank and had frozen. We had to chop out the ice and dry the tank with rags.

During a break, I ran over to see a writer I knew.[7]

It was crowded and hot in his rooms; the table was piled high with food; the tobacco smoke was like a wall. Some people were playing cards and they played for two more days without setting foot outside the door.

Later this same man very quickly and very sincerely became a staunch Bolshevik. Almost everyone who had been sitting around that table became a Communist.

And even now I remember so clearly their supercilious irony toward the "disturbance in the streets!"

Even before all this, a strike had been called in the city. The streetcars weren't running. All the cab-drivers who didn't join the strike were prevented from working. On the corner of Sadovaya Street and Nevsky Prospekt, I ran into an assistant professor I knew—an extremely talented and extremely foolish man formerly associated with the "academicians"—largely, it seems, at drinking bouts. He was shouting and commanding a group which was stopping cars. He was sober, but completely beside himself.

The uprising had already enveloped the area around the State Duma. The proximity of the various barracks to the Tauride Palace and, to a lesser extent, the memory of the speeches given there made the Duma the center of the uprising.

Apparently the first detachment was led to the Duma by Comrade Linde, later killed by the soldiers of the Special Army, in which he was a commissar. This is the same Linde who would lead the demonstration of the Finland Regiment in April and try to arrest the Provisional Government after Milyukov's famous note.

Our armored car rushed pellmell through the city. The dark streets were alive with people, standing around in small groups. They said that the police were shooting here and there.

They had been standing on the Sampsonievsky Bridge, had seen some policemen, but the police hadn't succeeded in shooting at them: they had all scattered. In some places people were already breaking into wine cellars. My group wanted to take some of the wine that was being handed out, but when I said that they shouldn't, they didn't argue.

At the same time, the armored cars from Dvoryanskaya Street had also sallied forth with Comrades Anardovich and Ogonians in charge. They immediately occupied the Petersburg side of town and headed toward the Duma. I don't know who told us that we should go to the Duma too.

An armored car, apparently a Garford, was already stationed at the approach to the Duma.

At the entrance to the Duma, I ran into an old army comrade, L., a volunteer—then already a second lieutenant in the artillery. We exchanged kisses. Everything was fine. We were all being swept along by a river and the whole of wisdom consisted in yielding to its current.

Night came. Chaos reigned in the Tauride Palace. Weapons were being brought; people were trailing in; provisions that had been requisitioned somewhere were being hauled around; bags were being stacked in a room near the entrance. Prisoners were already being brought in. At the Duma, some young lady gave her sanction to my post as commander of the car and even issued an order. I did have shells for the cannon. I don't know where I got them—apparently at the riding school. Naturally, I didn't carry out any orders—as a matter of fact, no one was carrying them out.

Wrapped in my fur coat, I slept for an hour or two behind a column. At the Duma, I ran into Sukhanov. I knew him from the editorial board of *Annals*,[8] from the literature department, to which I contributed (book reviews). But at a meeting of the staff I had given a report on literary theory in which I discussed art as pure form and argued vehemently with the Marxists. That, in all probability, is why Sukhanov was surprised to see me. He couldn't comprehend my presence at an armed uprising. And in my political naïveté, I was surprised to see him—I had no idea that political groupings had already been formed. Of course, at that moment they still had no influence on events. The masses were moving like spawning herring or carp, obeying their instinct.

That night Lieutenant D., commander of the armored motor pools, was arrested and brought in.

The men who brought him in were a little unsure of themselves. The arrested man addressed me reproachfully: "What's the matter? Didn't Captain Sokolikhin treat you right? Is that why you turned against him?" I replied that I had nothing against Captain Sokolikhin.

Half an hour later the lieutenant emerged, happy. The Military Commission of the State Duma had commissioned him, as one of the first "converts" among the officers in the motorized units, to organize the whole motorized operation in Petersburg.

This man, shrewd and, in his own way, intelligent, had a thirst for position, if not for power. Later he went over to the Anarchist Communists. I've dwelled on him because he was the first man I saw jockeying for position. Later on, I saw hordes of such people.

Early in the morning we drove into the city again. Someone gave me a military assignment and even an artilleryman as guide. I lost the guide, or he lost me, and I plunged into the jubilant turmoil of an insurgent people. I drove toward the Preobrazhensky Barracks, on Millionaya Street. Someone said that the men of the Preobrazhensky Regiment were resisting.

We drove up. It was a wonderful, blue, sunny morning. With a joyous volley of shots, the insurgent Preobrazhensky soldiers ran out of the barracks in new overcoats with very bright red tabs on their lapels.

There were pockets of resistance. Apparently, the training units from a battalion of combat engineers and from the Moscow Regiment fired on the crowd. The Cyclist Battalion on Lesnoi Prospekt held out quite a long time. I think this happened because only workers went to get them; when these units didn't see any soldiers, they were afraid to join.

The Fiat armored cars sent against them demolished a corner of the wooden barracks along with the men in it.

That night one of our armored-car crew, Fyodor Bogdanov, was killed. Riding in an open armored car, he was ambushed by some policemen with the only properly placed machine gun—in the window of a cellar (and not on a roof, from which a machine gun only sputters, since its fire doesn't have the proper trajectory).

Bogdanov's body doesn't lie in the Field of Mars: his relatives took the corpse somewhere outside the city.

Now about machine guns on roofs.[9] For practically two weeks, I was continually being called on to knock them out. Usually, when it seemed that they were shooting from a window, we would begin to shoot wildly at the house with our rifles and the dust rising from where our bullets hit the plaster was taken for return fire. I'm convinced that most of those killed during the February revolution were killed by our own bullets simply falling on us from above.

My company combed almost the whole Vladimirsky, Kuznechny, Yamskoi and Nikolaevsky area and I haven't a single scrap of evidence to indicate that there were machine guns on the roofs.

I might add that we fired into the air all the time, even with the cannons. A great many gunners visited my car. I especially remember the first one. After being wounded in the arm, he had stayed by his cannon. He was a security policeman from the barracks on Kirochnaya Street. He said that the security police had been among the first to go over to the insurgents' side. And all the gunners begged me for permission to shoot in order to show that we even had cannons; they stood on Nevsky Prospekt and shot into the air.

That day I spent most of the time on duty at Nikolaevsky Station. No one was guarding the station. I suggested (into thin air, since there was no one to suggest anything to) that we occupy the top floors of the Severnaya and Znamenskaya Hotels so that we could keep the whole station covered, but we lacked the necessary forces. If you posted a guard from among the soldiers running in and out, the guard either left or stood there without being relieved until he passed out. The officers in charge—at least they seemed to be in charge—were a one-armed student and an ancient naval officer in what seemed to be the uniform of an ensign. He was completely worn out. Trains kept arriving with troops from somewhere, going somewhere. We would ride up to them in the armored car with four or five infantrymen and the exhausted ensign would say to the troops' officers:

"The city is in the hands of the insurgent people. Do you wish to join the insurgent people?" Men and horses gawked at us from the cars. The officers would answer evasively that they were just passing through. The soldiers just looked at us and we never knew whether or not they would climb down from the high railroad cars. Armored cars with drivers we knew arrived to help. They would stay awhile, then drive off.

And throughout the city rushed the muses and furies of the February revolution—trucks and automobiles piled high and spilling over with soldiers, not knowing where they were going or where they would get gasoline, giving the impression of sounding the tocsin throughout the whole city.

They rushed around, circling and buzzing like bees.

It was the slaughter of the innocent cars. The countless automobile schools, in order to fill the motorized companies, had been cranking out hordes of drivers with half an hour's training. And now these half-trained characters gleefully fell upon the vehicles.

The city resounded with crashes. I don't know how many collisions I saw during those days. In a word, all my students learned to drive in two days.

Later on, the city was jammed with automobiles simply left by the wayside.

We were fed at food stations, where they concocted an incredibly rich fare out of geese, sausage, and whatever else turned up.

I was happy with these crowds. It was like Easter—a joyous, naïve, disorderly carnival paradise.

By this time almost everyone was armed with weapons taken from the officers or, for the most part, from the arsenals. There were plenty of weapons. They went from hand to hand and were not sold but freely passed around. There were many fine Colts.

In no sense did we represent a fighting force, but somehow we didn't think about that. There were nights of panic when we expected troops to attack from somewhere. But the Petersburg garrison kept growing larger and larger. Men came pulling machine guns on ropes or carrying them stacked like firewood in a truck; the soldiers of the machine-gun regiments and schools of Strelna and Oranienbaum arrived draped with cartridge belts.

In the vicinity of Strelna, an advance party of foot soldiers met some colonel riding in an automobile. The colonel looked a little like Nicholas. He was greeted with stormy, frenzied enthusiasm until the mistake was cleared up.

The machine guns that arrived in St. Pete were inoperable. The great bulk of them, for example, had no stuffing boxes and it was impossible to pour water into them. There were more than enough of them, but the quantity did not increase our fighting strength. I remember how the machine guns around the Baltic and Warsaw Stations were placed literally at every step. Of course, such an arrangement would have made it extremely awkward to shoot. But fighting strength was not important. It gradually became clear that now there was no enemy in insurgent St. Pete. The officers had come over to the side of the insurgents; the Mikhailovsky Artillery Institute arrived in formation. A little later, the First Reserve Regiment and its officers joined us. One very energetic volunteer, a Jewish engineer, who had actually been directing our school for a year and a half, flushed all our officers out of their apartments. The officers met. They even got the division commander. By then, no fewer than three temporary commanders had spent some time with us, but as soon as they had received their papers from the State Duma, they disappeared somewhere.

The officers met. They hesitantly decided to join the insurgents, even to offer resistance to the government troops. The Provisional Government had already come into existence. To distinguish themselves from the noninsurgents, they decided to wear red bands on their sleeves. At first they wanted raspberry ones. Military units in the true sense of the word did not exist at that time. Meals were not even being prepared. The units were scattered. The Mikhailovsky Riding School was occupied. The vehicles had scattered in all directions.

Our unit was in somewhat better shape. The platoons took turns being on duty and appeared when summoned, even at night.

The patrols posted began to pick up the automobiles that were running aimlessly around the city and to collect them in the unit compound. In this way, many vehicles were saved. But the starting mechanisms had already been removed from the abandoned and frozen vehicles. These dropped sharply in price after the revolution.

Because of the strange assortment of weapons, the unit took on the motley appearance of an outfit of high-school students.

Two films of that time have been preserved. One of them depicts the feeding of pigeons in our unit compound; the other, a unit stepping out in full military regalia, with an Austin armored car at the head and soldiers brandishing officers' swords at the rear.

Things didn't go too badly for our officers. Everyone liked our commander, Captain Sokolikhin, because he hadn't pushed the unit and diligently concerned himself with getting boots for the men. On the first day of the revolution, he was given a driver's coat with no epaulets and an armed guard of five men so that strangers wouldn't hurt him. Another officer got to keep his weapon because it was a rifle of St. George, awarded for extreme bravery. The election of new officers began. The motor-pool unit registered a protest against the old division commander. Intrigues began and jockeying for position, with the help of the soldiers.

And all the time, troops kept coming to the Tauride Palace. The pavement all but collapsed from the trampling of feet, and the air glittered constantly with the color red.

The Soviet was already in session, but Order No. 1[10] still hadn't been issued and Rodzyanko was still popular in the units. Yet the Soviet bristled with guns, shouts and strife.

For many units coming to the Tauride Palace, the speeches of Chkheidze and others were the first revolutionary speeches they had heard.

What did they think about the war? It seems to me they believed that it would end of its own accord. This belief was general when the summons to the peoples of the whole world was issued. I remember that those arriving from the Monzun position said that there they had already made a pact with the Germans: neither we nor they were to shoot. In general, an Easter mood prevailed; everything was going well and it was believed that this was only the beginning of everything good.

Order No. 1 was brought to the riding school and distributed in the ranks during a review. The soldiers started replying "Hello, mister colonel!" and they brought it off very well, very amiably. I think that Order No. 1—though apparently it anticipated events, since there were as yet no committees in the units—was timely and indispensable. It was impossible to hold the units together only with officers just back from a long absence. Although committees are completely impossible in an army—even less possible than elected officers—still they were the only thing that somehow or other held the army together.

The worst thing about the committees was that in no time at all they lost contact with those who had elected them. And the delegates to the Soviet did not show up in their units for months at a time. The soldiers were left completely ignorant of what was happening in the Soviets. The only thing that helped matters was the immense faith, not yet squandered, in the "personal" representation of the soldiers. The first Soviet was made up mainly of volunteers and soldiers from the intelligentsia, which, of course, contributed to the lack of contact.

On the other hand, almost no one in the barracks was working; the intelligentsia were in flight; there was almost no one willing to work in the area of education. In the Combat-Engineers' Battalion —the Sixth, I think—out of several hundred volunteers fewer than ten signed the list of those agreeing to work in schools to promote literacy. The vast majority of them saw the revolution as a chance to take some extra leave. In our unit, platoon leaders and foremen made up the council. It had a businesslike quality.

And regiment after regiment kept passing through the Hall of Catherine in the Tauride Palace. The placards still said, "Allegiance to the Provisional Government" and even "War to the Final Victory." But we could no longer wage war. However, I'm speaking now only about the Petersburg garrison. The enormous reserve units—as many as several tens of thousands—were no longer sending troops to the front and at the same time had nothing to do in the city, since they lacked the weapons necessary to defend the revolution. They were simply rotting in their barracks. No one had as yet spoken the words "Peace at any cost"; Lenin had not yet arrived; the Bolsheviks were still saying we should stand by with rifles. But there was no longer any garrison: there was only a depot full of soldiers. The flame of revolution was still flickering among the masses. It was not the hot flame of burning coke, however, but the feeble fire made by alcohol poured over wood—consuming itself without yet igniting the wood.

Kerensky was such a fire. The first time I saw Kerensky, he was in hysterics. It was after an article directed against him in *Izvestia;* he ran into the Soldiers' Section of the Soviet to ask whether they believed in him. He hurled garbled phrases and, in truth, seemed to flicker with long, dry, crackling sparks.

With the harassed face of a man whose days are already numbered, he shouted and finally, in complete exhaustion, fell into a chair. That made a terrible impression.

Another time I saw Kerensky when I had already been made a commissar. I was to get him for a conference and caught up with him at the Naval Academy. I found his gray Locomobile and, while waiting, began to converse with the driver.

"They'll carry him out right away," said the driver. And sure enough, within a few minutes, they carried him through the door of the building. He was sitting in his usual tired posture in a chair raised high above the crowd. I got into the car next to him and started to talk. With dry, bloodless lips, with an emaciated and puffy face, he weakly clasped his hands together and said in a raspy voice, "The important thing is will and perseverance." He seemed to me like a man already at the end of his rope, a man who knew that he was already doomed.

I'm hastening to finish writing about what everyone knows and hurrying to get to the front.

How did I wind up at the front? Lenin arrived. There were Bolsheviks in the motor pools of the division; they offered Lenin an armored car for the trip from the station to the Kshesinskaya Palace, which our unit had taken over for quarters. A certain part of the division was decisively for the Bolsheviks. I was then on the division committee and, with my school, represented the wing of the division that wanted to continue the war.

Here I should introduce a new personage—Maksimilian Filonenko. At one time he had been commander of the armored motor pools, where he conducted himself grandly and more or less humanely; later he voluntarily went to the front. There he was unsuccessful, was somehow overlooked, took offense and did his utmost to leave.

He arrived in St. Pete when the revolution was already over and dug in. What was happening there interested him far more than a modest position at the front.

He was a small man in his military jacket, with short-clipped hair and a rather large, round head, which made him slightly resemble a kitten. An engineer by education, he knew four or five foreign languages, but was especially pleased with his French pronunciation. He was the son of an important engineer and had repeatedly held responsible positions in shipbuilding plants and invariably left after botching the job. He had good mental faculties, but not an iota of talent.

A first-class student wanting to be a genius. I didn't know him intimately: he liked me and was a good comrade. But he had for a goal—his goal, his star—only himself. There was, however, no star in his heaven and he sought one in vain.

At first he began to come to the division committee as a guest; in a Russia devoid of qualified men, among committee members already as apathetic as fish, he seemed absolutely brilliant. Later he began to take work at the behest of some company or other, most often of the armored motor pools, where they valued him for his previous service and took a lot from him that they wouldn't have tolerated from anyone else. In the gloomy assembling departments, where monstrous machines were standing, and in the carbon monoxide of exhaust fumes, people were scaling vehicles—the same people who, after the July insurrection,[11] would abandon their vehicles at the first sign of trouble. Carefully and intelligently, with all kinds of intricate flourishes, Filonenko spun his dialectical web. Later he figured out a way to become senior officer in a service unit. When he was recalled to the front, he didn't want to go. He had been involved in a scandal there, as I found out later —a flogged soldier. There he was a dead man. Here, however, he had calculated the correct "angle of attack" and, like an airplane, was preparing for the takeoff.

From the division committee, he received a fantastic mandate— to serve on the Soviet of Deputies not as the representative of a unit, but as a representative of the committee itself. It was, of course, not the strangest mandate in the Soviet. I once met there a rather talented Jewish violoncellist, Ch., who had earlier served in the orchestra of the Preobrazhensky Regiment. He was now representing the Don Cossacks.

In the Soviet, Filonenko made several successful speeches in opposition to Zinoviev; at the garrison meeting, after the April demonstration of the Finland Regiment, he defended the idea of a coalition ministry.

He had one big asset—he had contour, definiteness and a strong will. And it was clear that he would play some role. At this time, he was loyal in the highest degree to the Soviet. But he needed a gimmick. Such a gimmick was his proposal to send to the front commissars who would personally take part in the fighting. He made this proposal to me and Comrade Anardovich. I agreed. I was restless and itched for something definite to do and Filonenko struck me as a sensible man and the right sort for the revolution.

Now about Anardovich. Comrade Anardovich, later a commissar in the Special Army, had been wounded on the barricades in 1905. An orthodox SR, he had influence in the motor pools and led sixteen or seventeen armored cars into battle at a time when the comrades who eventually became quite leftist had not yet managed to goad themselves into action at all. This hook-nosed man with the energetic face was touchingly simple and elemental. He wrote verses under the influence of Nadson, believed in the first Soviet like a village priest in his prayerbook, and was wholeheartedly and unwaveringly devoted to the revolution. His favorite expression was "clear and simple." He could talk without stopping for three or four hours and nothing got the better of him. He managed the masses superbly, as I later saw for myself. He had absolutely no fear of a crowd and confidently opposed its pressure with his decisiveness.

I dwell on him, by the way, because Anardovich was really the only true worker among the war commissars—a worker fresh from his lathe.

The proposal was to send to the army men personally obligated to take part in the war as living proof of the Russian democracy's intention to stay in the war.[12] It was brought before the division committee and accepted by it. All the non-Bolshevik members agreed to go. I remember how I stood with lowered head and heavy heart. My sensation was like that of a worker who catches his sleeve in a machine and feels himself being dragged in: he still resists, but his heart has already surrendered to the inevitability of death. I was third on the list of those to be sent to the front: Filonenko, Anardovich, Shklovsky.

Up until the last days of October, the division continued to regard us as its envoys, taking our mandate from them. I regarded it that way myself. Filonenko, however, quickly cut his ties with the division that had helped him move ahead.

Now began the long, drawn-out, complicated business of getting our commission through the always amenable Provisional Government and through the not-so-amenable (but generally ignorant of its own best interests) Executive Committee of the Duma—the respected Fabius Cunctator Academy.

And the Executive Committee had absolutely no idea what to do with the army. Having opposed itself to the Provisional Government—or, more exactly, having dreamed up the Provisional Government and opposed it to itself—it could neither take action nor not take action. All real authority was in its hands, but what it had in mind, no one knew. The army failed to understand this complicated and profoundly socialistic situation: it demanded authority, orders.

Hordes of people from various units had come running to Chkheidze's Executive Committee of the Soviet demanding orders; therefore the Executive Committee was already receptive to the idea of a double-mandate commissariat.

When I recall this situation, Filonenko seems to me to have been the organizer of the War Commissariat. He quickly passed from the idea of people who would set an example to the idea of people who would give orders—to the idea of a commissar.

Why did the Military Commission of the Executive Committee come up with Filonenko as a candidate? I think because of the complete dearth of qualified people. It had to shut its eyes and let him through. Apparently he had once been an SR, but had dropped his ties with the party before the revolution. His candidacy was accepted; Anardovich went as his aide, the engineer Tsipkevich went as another aide. Tsipkevich had been in the RSR, but was now essentially "not interested in politics." I haven't spoken about Tsipkevich yet. I'll speak of him later. Eventually I saw for myself the enormous talent Tsipkevich had for organizing things.

He had been a production engineer and organizer. The revolution upset him with its tendency to disrupt plans and schedules; he wanted to regulate it like an engine or a railroad. I was sent in charge of agitation.

Now I will answer the question why I went to the front, why I considered it necessary to launch an offensive and why I fought in that offensive.

I was for the offensive because I considered the revolution itself for the offensive. According to my conviction at that time, an offensive was possible. We either had to take the offensive or stick our bayonets in the ground and go whistling home. I didn't believe in fraternization and I was right. My mistake was in forgetting that one should never launch an offensive with a siren behind him —a democratic government with a bourgeois tail. One should never fight with a fight going on in the rear. An offensive, in my opinion, was imperative because a victory by the troops of the republic would have led to a revolution in Germany. That revolution would have been more fun than the one pressured by revanchism.[13] We had to attack while we still had an army, but we needed a homogeneous government able to implement a minimum program quickly.

And one more thing—the Allies, damn them, would not give their consent to our definition of a peace "without annexations and reparations"; and these words, bandied about in the newspapers—I know how sacred they were to every soldier, whose feet were rotting in the water of the trenches, whose neck was gnawed by lice. These words were truly sacred to the barefoot soldiers.

Those who repudiated them are guilty of blood, filth and callousness. Oh, if we could only have unfurled before the June regiments the holy banner of a just war, I wouldn't want to cry over your graves now, my poor comrades!

But I've betrayed myself—I don't want to be a critic of events: I only want to leave material for the critics.

I'm telling about events and making of myself a case study for posterity.

And so—we set off.

I was sorry to part with my unit and our school, which we had brought to a degree of perfection unheard of in Russia. My unit stayed behind, rotting along with the rest of the revolutionary garrison. Just a touch slower than the other units. My outfit hadn't raided their supply room.

Now one more recollection of Petersburg.

The subcouncil of the Soldiers' Section, opposing Lenin in its very proper newspaper, published a resolution to the effect that it considered Lenin's propaganda every bit as harmful as the counter-revolutionary propaganda. Lenin came to explain himself to the council. It was a day full of turmoil. The hall filled with council members. The volunteer Zavadie presided. Lenin spoke his piece with elemental force, rolling his thought like an enormous cobble-stone. When he spoke of how simple it was to build a Socialist revolution, he swept all doubts before him like a wild boar tram-pling through the reeds.

While he was speaking, the hall agreed with him and something like desperation ran through it. I remember a bearded soldier shouting at the subcouncil—"Bourgeois dogs! Mama's boys!" and, at the same time, demanding "Chkheidze as chairman, Chkheidze!" It's a little hard to imagine what was going on in that soldier's head.

Lieber argued with Lenin. He spoke extremely well and animatedly. But his words flew like chaff, instead of falling like seeds. I left for the front with the sensation that a blind, powerful force was trampling everything before it. It was in the early days of June. We had already celebrated the first May Day of our revolution. The whole city was living it. The streets seethed with impromptu meetings. Private life seemed pallid. And that's when I left and fell into another world.

Five of us went: Filonenko, Tsipkevich, Anardovich, I and, as secretary, a cheerful and very capable man from Odessa, Comrade Vonsky.

We arrived in Kiev. In Kiev, the Soviet of Soldiers' Deputies was fighting with deserters and Ukrainians. There wasn't hide or hair of a Soviet of Workers' Deputies since there were no major factories in Kiev except an arsenal and the Greter plant.

A yellow-and-azure flag flew over the city. Ukrainian soldiers were protecting the Duma and there were meetings in the streets: Russians were arguing with Ukrainians, while the Jews were sulking and waiting to be beaten up.

It was a nasty situation: the troops sent through Kiev turned into Ukrainians in Kiev and sat tight.

We proceeded farther. On the other side of Kiev, the train began to reflect the proximity of the front. Huge numbers of people were heaped on the roofs of the cars like fruit in decorative baskets. All the spaces between the cars were occupied. Our small car, desperately jolting along at the rear of the train, overflowed with people.

We arrived at Kamenets-Podolsk; the Iskomityuz—the Executive Committee of the Southwestern Front—was located there in the high-school building. Here we met the previously appointed commissar Moiseenko; his senior aide was Linde. These men were already tired. The revolution had completely worn them down.

They started talking about Savinkov. Savinkov gave orders in the army as if he had real authority. He received people on certain days and took upon himself the initiative for action. Moiseenko regarded himself as only a consultant to the committee and thought that just as soon as the committees got stronger, the commissar would become expendable. It wasn't likely that the commissar would ever become expendable to the Iskomityuz. Volunteers, rather timid teachers who had accidentally wound up in the service, doctors—all these were people who never sought their own advantage, but still were very ill equipped to cope with the storm of revolution. The makeup of the committee was haphazard. The masses had chosen men who weren't compromised and at the same time could speak out and act. Every reasonably well-educated man who was not also an officer almost automatically went from committee to committee and ended up in a committee at the front.

That explains the great number of Jews on the committees, since, out of the entire intelligentsia, only the Jewish intellectuals were common soldiers at the moment of revolution.

In general, the committee members were people with no ready answers, people who recognized the impossibility of building anything with their own strength; therefore they were inclined toward a holding operation. They were afraid of what was happening on the home front. The home front wasn't bound hand and foot by the Germans, from whom there was no more escape at the front than from atmospheric pressure. What was happening in the rear shook the front, disrupted it and threw into confusion the enormous factory called an army.

In such a factory, everyone usually does very little; but if he stops doing that little, the result becomes disastrous.

At this time, talks about an offensive were going on. The offensive seemed every bit as inevitable as the onset of night after day—and not because Kerensky wanted it, though to the soldiers Kerensky did embody the fervor of the revolution—but because everyone felt that you can't mobilize the nation's men, tear them away from their jobs and then leave them standing around shaking their fists. The army had either to fight or to disperse; for the time being, it decided to fight.

Everyone knew that there would somehow be an offensive even if everyone said:

"But I don't want to fight!"

The committees also contained party members—supporters of the Bund, SR's and Mensheviks. The last, for the most part, of the Plekhanov variety. Bolsheviks had not yet appeared on the committees. Now and then, some soldier not belonging to the intelligentsia-Socialist group would manage to get on a committee and this "beast from the lower depths" would speak gloomy words, confused but comprehensible. These men called themselves Bolsheviks. Most of them wanted mainly to save their own hides; that is, they weren't inclined toward self-sacrifice and were therefore impossible at the front, where all were victims. If you were to try to define their true essence, you might most accurately call them Stirnerites. They already had influence among the soldiers, but were not respected. Bolshevism made its appearance among the masses later, out of desperation, as a verbal justification for the refusal even to continue the war. I'm speaking about war Bolshevism.

But for the time being, the regiments were held together by their naïve revolutionary ideology, by the "Marseillaise," by the red banner and especially by the great momentum of such a huge accumulation of men as an army; they were held together by the residues and habits of everyday army life.

Those who represented the compromised status of the revolutionary army were the committees, especially the supreme committees. The task of the committee members was, above all, the preservation of the army. How to preserve it they didn't know, and they waited for the storm and feared it and didn't know whether to struggle against it. They themselves couldn't define the nature of this storm; therefore they were timid and tried just to preserve the army, which, even though compromised, was still capable of continuing the war.

The offensive hung in the air, just as the expectation of the Bolshevik coup did later on. We were hurrying toward the front.

Our automobile wheeled down the road past an old Turkish fortress and left Kamenets behind, surrounded by its beautiful ring of water. The road unwound in sweeping curves as it climbed the steep hills. A high, narrow bridge hung over the river. I knew this road. I had wrecked a car on it once; this time I fell asleep on the floor of the car.

We drove at breakneck speed; by morning we were already in Czernowitz. This white city in the foothills, resembling Kiev a little, but very Polish and a brisk trade center, was the location for the headquarters and committee of the Eighth Army. The commander of the army was General Kornilov.

We were assigned a fine apartment that had escaped being plundered. I eagerly picked up a local war bulletin. It looked very funny. You could gather from it that the main question now was the struggle of the Czernowitz garrison committee with the Arkom (the army committee) because of a request for reinforcements from the front. The political alignment was home-grown and a bit makeshift: the Kadets supported the platform of the Petersburg Soviet, so there were Zimmerwald Kadets,[14] Bolsheviks in favor of continuing the war, Mensheviks with the land-reform program of the SR's and—to top it off—Socialist Individualists.

Later on, I realized that all these groups meant nothing in the army—neither the small-time ones nor the other kind. Moral authority was held by the Petersburg Soviet, not by any of the parties. Everyone recognized the Soviet, believed in it, followed it. True, it was standing still; consequently, everyone who followed it had gone on past.

We didn't stay long in Czernowitz. Filonenko gave his first public address here and we had our first falling-out. He arrived at the army committee and gave the troops a briefing in which he touched mainly on external policies and painted a glowing picture of the relations between the Allies and revolutionary Russia. It was so irresponsible and, in fact, so detrimental even from a practical standpoint—because you can't fool a man forever—that I sent him a note pointing out the folly of such statements. Then he abruptly changed the subject and launched a frenzied attack on the bourgeoisie and on the idea of not being able to get along without them. All this was done very vividly and clearly; it struck the committee as a revelation—a complete clarification of the issue. But the committee at this moment was not concerned primarily with information.

Everyone knew that there would be an offensive and the representatives of the units sent around a questionnaire asking if their men were willing to fight. The answers were lacking in assurance. I remember one especially: "I don't know whether the field committees will fight, but the regimental committee will fight." But this was not the important thing. The men were complaining because the units were under strength, because each company was only forty strong, and because these forty men were barefoot and sick. Only the representative of the so-called "Savage Division," made up of mountaineers, answered with conviction: "We will fight anytime and against anyone." Kornilov cleared things up. His words amounted to this—that despite the units' being under strength, we had a fivefold advantage over the enemy at the point of the proposed attack and that our military objectives could be attained on the basis of the actual strength of the units. But some divisions were only nine hundred strong!

The apprehensions of the soldiers—that they would be assigned military objectives based not on the actual number of troops, but on the regulation strength of the unit—were not unfounded. I knew a case under the old regime when an infantry regiment (the Semyonovsky) was replaced at the front by a dismounted cavalry regiment about one-fifth its size.

One other general complaint was heard in all the speeches of the delegates and to this complaint, of course, Kornilov could say nothing—this was the complaint about being completely cut off from any signs of life. I already knew the front a little and I could imagine the anguish of the man in the trenches, where nothing was visible, not even the enemy—only snow in winter, blades of grass in summer.

At one session, a very detailed report was given about the strength of the army and its weapon supply. The only thing not designated was the point for the breakthrough, but everyone knew it would be Stanislau.

It was strange to hear the plan for the offensive discussed in such detail: at the meeting, more than a hundred men talked about roads, about the number of weapons. The democratic principle of discussion was carried here to the absurd, but we managed eventually to extend and elaborate this absurd. At Stanislau, right before the offensive, all members of the company committees representing the shock troops—the Nineteenth Corps—were gathered together and at this gathering they were still discussing the question: to attack or not to attack. This is not to mention the meetings right in the trenches—sometimes held a few dozen steps from the enemy. But that didn't seem strange to me then. I don't think that even Kornilov clearly understood the hopelessness of the situation. He was first and foremost a military man. A general charging into the fray with a revolver. He viewed the army as a good driver views his automobile. The most important thing to the driver is that the car runs, not who rides in it. Kornilov needed the army to fight. He was surprised at the strange methods used by the revolution to prepare the offensive. He still wanted to believe that it was possible to fight that way—just as a driver, trying a new fuel, very much wants the car to run as well as it does with gasoline and can get carried away with the idea of using carbide or turpentine.

This wasn't the first time I had met Kornilov. I had seen him during the April days when the Petersburg regiments were demonstrating against Milyukov. At that time he had called up to order some armored cars from our division. We had already unanimously resolved to place ourselves directly under the command of the Soviet. Therefore the resolution was "not to consider it under any circumstances." When I went to convey the news to him, Kornilov spoke very softly, obviously not understanding at all how it was that he, a commander, had no troops and wondering who needed him as a commander. He found it unpleasant to see me in the army; later he reconciled himself to me, but began to take me for a madman.

The army committee firmly believed in Kornilov at that moment. When he appeared after giving a report to the officers, he was welcomed enthusiastically. But no one liked "Kornilov's men." That's what they called the men of the first "Death Battalion," which was being formed in Czernowitz of volunteers—for the most part, men from the service units and company clerks who had decided to see some action.

I can testify that this battalion fought no worse than the best of the old regiments. But these shock battalions, already sewing the skull and crossbones on their sleeves, hurt the unity of the army and made the highly mistrustful soldiers fear that now certain special units were being created to act as policemen. The most loyal committee members were against the shock troops. They got on the soldiers' nerves; it was said of them that they received a big salary and had special privileges. I was unconditionally against the shock battalions, because to make them up, men with energy and enthusiasm, men of relatively high intelligence, were taken out of the regiment. What drove them from the regiments was the grief of seeing the army already beginning to decay. But they were even more needed in these regiments, like salt in corned beef.

On the committee, "Kornilov's men" were violently attacked; they justified themselves rather peevishly.

By the way, I remember the women's battalions. This idea was undoubtedly hatched on the home front and thought up expressly as an insult to the front.

I wandered around Czernowitz. A clean little town resembling Kiev. We ate very well there—in the European style, which is cleaner than ours. The soldiers hadn't pillaged the town; in the apartment where I bunked there were even some pillows, rugs and silver things around. The apartment was of the usual, rather plush, old-gentry type. The streetcars were running; people weren't hanging onto them and they paid for the ride. Reinforcements were leaving town for the front, although hardly any troops ever arrived from the rear; and when they did arrive, they badly demoralized the regiments. As far as the condition of the garrison went, the town was, all in all, not bad. But none of this depended on conscious will, which could not exist among men who had not yet truly gone through the revolution; in other words, all hung precariously on good intentions.

Filonenko and his secretary Vonsky, a cheerful, sturdy and, in his own way, good guy, very energetic and resourceful, remained in Czernowitz. Anardovich and I left for the front, where the offensive was supposed to begin at any moment. And so, for the fourth time, my automobile drove through the fields of Galicia with their Polish cemeteries, where the crosses are melodramatically huge in the Polish style, the Jewish painted tombstones overgrown with dry grass, the marble statues battered by the wind and rain. At the crossroads, the dear, blue, orthodox crucifixes of Galicia, with saints fastened to the diagonals of the crosses. With sharp turns, the road kept going along the same narrow but smooth way.

Sometimes we drove past clumps of trees; then the measured knock of the car was echoed in the trees by a sound that resembled the sound of a whip cracking through the leaves. We arrived at some dark little town. This was the headquarters of the corps which was assigned to make the breakthrough.

It was the Twelfth Corps. We were greeted by the chief of staff, who was dead-tired (it was night). He looked as if he had been working for a week, had not slept for a week and had a toothache besides. He didn't have a toothache, but he must have felt like a man with paralyzed legs ordered to jump or a man with frozen fingers ordered to pick up silver coins off a stone floor. He began to talk hopelessly about how the regiments refused to dig parallels—a parallel is a trench dug in front of the main trench and joined to it by a passageway; its purpose is to get closer to the enemy in order to minimize losses during an attack. Some vagabond regiment had just made its appearance in this area—without officers or transport, with only its field kitchen. It had detached itself from a nearby army and was homeward bound—and the offensive only a few days off. While he talked, in the next room, dimly lit with a kerosene lamp, telegraph machines feebly clicked and threw off blue sparks; narrow paper ribbons slowly crept out of the machines.

From headquarters, we waded through dark, deep mud over to see the commander of the corps, General Cheremisov. Cheremisov resembled Kornilov, also short with a yellow Mongolian face and slanted eyes, but somehow rounder, less dried up. He seemed smarter and more talented than Kornilov. He had been in this area during the previous offensive as chief of staff and had a really superb knowledge of Galicia and Bukovina. He instinctively liked the revolution and war because of the wide opportunities they gave him. Cheremisov was not afraid of the soldiers: I know for a fact that when one company decided to kill him and set up a mortar in front of his house, he came out to see what all the noise was and very calmly pointed out to the soldiers that it was improper to use the mortar in this position, since the explosion of the shell would destroy the neighboring houses. The soldiers agreed and took away the mortar. Cheremisov was not very put out, but he did indicate one thing that was certainly true: what upset the soldiers most of all was the clamor in the newspapers—the loud cries from the home front, "Attack! Attack!" At the moment in question, this is how things stood: in the area of Stanislau, we had concentrated up to seven hundred heavy guns; the buildup of this sector of the front had begun. Those regiments already assigned to sectors of the front consolidated their positions, and new units were poured in to fill the gaps in the line. Then came the first hitch. The Eleventh Division, which was in good condition, didn't want to go to the front, not because it was against the offensive—I hardly ever ran across direct repudiations of the war—but because it had been taken from another sector of the front; moreover, it had been promised a rest. The Sixty-first Division, I think (I don't remember the exact number; I know that it included the Kinburg Infantry Regiment), didn't want to dig parallels; some other division also wanted this and didn't want that. And the enemy in front of us had almost nothing—some barbed wire, machine guns and almost empty trenches. We decided to go without delay to Stanislau. We went at night. It was still a long way to the town, which was right in the line of trenches. But the front was already outlined by the uninterrupted flights of rockets, which the Germans burned in fear of a night attack. The cannons weren't firing, or at least we didn't hear them. The car noiselessly pursued the road, left it behind and rushed straight for those blue fires. We passed some quietly running, heavy vehicles of the ordnance depot, carrying shells. The stream of vehicles kept getting thicker, becoming solid as we drew nearer to the town. The drivers, tired from the lateness of the hour, sat silently on the jolting, heavy wagons; the horses pulled silently at the traces.

We reached the town. Stayed at a hotel—the Astoria, I think. The town of Stanislau had changed hands several times. The Russians and the Austrians had taken it from the right and from the left, then from the front and from the rear. This was already the third time I had entered it during the war and each time by a different road. It had been a prosperous town; the houses were still intact; the shooting had damaged them very little. The outlying area, as well as the gasworks, had suffered most of all. But this is not surprising: some of the small houses on the outskirts stood a few steps from the trenches. People were living in these houses. Our lines began just on the other side of the Bistritsa River. Everyone said this was an awkward disposition of the troops. It had been done this way so that that the dispatch could say: "Our troops have crossed the Bistritsa." The town was overflowing with troops.

The headquarters of nearly all the divisions of the Twelfth Corps, which at that time constituted nearly a whole army in itself, were crowded into the town. The members of the headquarters operations section lived in the hotel where I was staying. In the courtyard was a gun battery, on the roof an artillery observation point; below, in a Polish café doing a lively business, sat the officers; and in the air hung a two-colored haze, brown and bluish, from the shell-bursts of the Austrian shrapnel. At night you could hear the boom of our heavy guns; they resounded right in your ear, reflecting off the walls of the courtyard with a hollow sound—the same sound you make when you throw a large ball with all your strength against a stone floor.

Stanislau was the only place at the front where I had occasion to sleep on a bed—with real blankets and sheets. I didn't stay long in Stanislau this time. I was summoned to the Aleksandropol Regiment, which occupied a rather unusual position.

The enemy forces stood facing our troops on a round, wooded mountain called Kosmachka. Our regiment was encamped on an-

other mountain. Between us and the German troops was a distance
of not less than two miles. There wasn't really a war going on
here. Planks had been thrown over the trenches and the trenches
themselves were half filled up. The men had fraternized long and
assiduously; the soldiers had been getting together in the villages
situated between the lines and here they had set up an exclusive,
neutral brothel. Even some of the officers took part in the fraternization—among them a brave and capable man, bearer of the Cross
of St. George and apparently once a student—one Captain Chinarov. I think that Chinarov was fundamentally an honest man, but
he was so incredibly muddled that when we occupied the village of
Rosulna, the inhabitants informed us that Chinarov had repeatedly
driven to Austrian headquarters, where he went on sprees with the
officers and accompanied them on trips behind the Austrian lines.

When we took Rosulna, we found in the Austrian headquarters
building a German manual on fraternization, published by German
headquarters on very good paper—in Leipzig, I think.

Chinarov had been arrested by Kornilov and was in the guardhouse with a certain second lieutenant K., who later turned out to
be an *agent provocateur* from Kazan.

I tried to get Chinarov out, because our conceptions of the
freedom of speech and action belonging to each individual citizen
were fantastically broad then. I didn't get Chinarov out. His regiment wanted him back, so I set off to calm the men down.

I drove a long time, apparently through the little town of
Nadworna. You could already begin to feel the Carpathians. The
road was paved with slabs of wood. Over it was placed something
on the order of triumphal arches decorated with fir boughs—a
technique of camouflaging roads borrowed from the Austrians.
First we stopped by corps headquarters (the Sixteenth Corps);
here a perplexed General Stogov met us. He understood nothing.
"All these Bolsheviks, Mensheviks," he complained to me, "I've
come to consider you all—excuse the expression—traitors." He
didn't hurt my feelings. It was very hard for him. His corps
consisted entirely of reserve divisions, with six or seven hundred
men in each, brought together out of several regiments during the
regrouping, when the divisions had shifted from four battalions to
three.

These hastily assembled units, with no traditions, with the
commanders quarreling among themselves, were, of course, very

bad. General Stogov was very fond of "his men" and it pained him that the soldiers were in such bad shape. He had no influence with the soldiers, though they knew and appreciated him.

After seeing Stogov, I went to division headquarters. There too everything was complete confusion. Although everyone knew that no military objective had been assigned to this corps, still it was strange to see troops in such a state; it was impossible to count on them even for simple garrison duty in the villages abandoned by the enemy.

I went to the regiment. I assembled the soldiers without organizing a rally, so as not to heat up the atmosphere, and simply talked to them in an ordinary voice. I said that Chinarov would be tried and that I couldn't return him to them. The soldiers obviously thought very highly of him and lost no time in giving me some false testimony about him.

But anyway the regiment quieted down a little simply from having unburdened themselves to an outsider. Later this regiment gave Filonenko and the army committee a lot of trouble. Finally it was disbanded.

From the Aleksandropol Regiment, I returned to Stanislau. There I was asked to go the the Kinburg Regiment. Things were also very bad in that regiment, which was stationed about a mile from Stanislau. These troops were in a battle zone and were refusing to dig parallels—consequently they were not preparing for the offensive. I set off again. This time it wasn't a trip but an automobile race the whole length of our positions. The Germans could see the road and kept it under fire. They were hitting all around the car, but it looked possible to get through and we got through.

We crossed the Bistritsa River and soon reached the regiment's position. We assembled the soldiers, using a dugout for the speakers' platform. One soldier said to me, "I don't want to die." With desperate energy, I spoke about the right of the revolution to our lives. I didn't despise words then, as I do now. Comrade Anardovich told me that my impassioned speech had made his hair stand on end. The audience was deciding the question of its own death, an immediate death, and the necessity of ordering men to renounce themselves, the silence of this sad crowd of thousands and the vague uneasiness caused by the proximity of the enemy stretched nerves to the breaking point.

After I got through, a short, very dirty soldier spoke—all decked out in his uniform. His talk was simple and to the point, about the most elementary things. From his words, I realized that he was among the half-dozen men who had decided the previous night to work up ahead of our trenches.

Later on, after the rally, I went up and started to talk to him. He turned out to be a Jew, an artist who had returned from abroad to enlist. This was almost saintliness. Neither the soldier in a service unit, nor the infantry officer, nor the commissar, nor any man who has an extra pair of boots and underwear can comprehend all the anguish of the common soldier, all the heaviness of his burden.

This Jewish intellectual carried the weight of the earth in his boots.

Then Anardovich spoke. He spoke convincingly; he was intoxicated through and through by the spirit of the Soviet; he was happy, not knowing how difficult and complicated our situation was. His convictions made him simple and convincing. All the commonplaces of all the speeches given at the Soviet were included in his hour-long speech. The revolution had engraved its norms on his soul. He was like an Orthodox Christian.

Afterwards we went down some dark narrow streets and again talked, this time to a dark, invisible crowd of men with shovels who didn't know whether to go or not to go.

We convinced the Kinburg Regiment.

We were spending the night somewhere at regimental headquarters. That same night, sleepy and rumpled like a soldier's overcoat, we drove on to talk to the Malmyzh Regiment.

More conversations. Here I encountered something new. A group of soldiers announced with a happy smile: "Don't talk to us; we don't understand anything; we're deaf as Mordvinians."[15] Afterwards, I guess, we went to the Urzhum Regiment. The hardest thing was having to appear everywhere as exponents of pure reason and at the same time operate in the places where conditions were the most serious.

The Urzhum Regiment—or whatever this regiment was called —was living in the trenches. The men wandered around in the narrow crevice of the trench. Two huge gray heaps of earth inclined toward each other; between them, seated in a hole, the men wearily bided their time. The regiment extended out over nearly half a mile. The men in the trenches were making them-

selves at home. Some were cooking rice kasha in their small field
messtins; others were digging themselves a hole for the night.

When you stuck your head out of the trench, what you saw was
blades of grass, what you heard was the occasional leisurely whistle of bullets.

Making the rounds, I talked to the soldiers; they sort of huddled
together.

Along the bottom of the trench, a narrow little stream ran under
the boards you walked on.

We followed its course. As the terrain descended, the walls got
damper, the soldiers gloomier.

Finally the trench broke off. We came out in a swamp. Only a
low wall made of bags of dirt and sod separated us from the
enemy.

A company consisting almost entirely of Ukrainians was sitting
there. It was impossible to stand—dangerous. The wall was too
low.

We felt the utter confusion of these men. It seemed to me that
they had been sitting that way the whole war.

I started to talk to them about the Ukraine. I had thought that
this was a major and important question. At least the people in
Kiev could talk of nothing else. They stopped me:

"Don't bother us with that!"

For these troops, the whole question of an independent or a de-
pendent Ukraine did not exist. They hastened to inform me that
they were for the commune. What they meant by that, I don't
know. Perhaps only communal pastures. The soldiers were talka-
tive; they were evidently overjoyed to talk to someone new, but
they didn't know they had to argue if they wanted the answer that
would instantly banish all their doubts.

The ability to ask questions is an important ability. A noncommissioned officer, obviously popular with his company, stood
among the sitting soldiers like a chairman and asked me:

"Our boys are upset. Is it true that Kerensky's a Socialist
Democrat instead of a Socialist Revolutionary? That's why they're
upset."

I answered his question. Although my answer did seem to dispel
his doubts, he wasn't satisfied with its brevity.

It seemed to me that the soldiers would listen to such a noncom,
who didn't understand anything himself and who couldn't be un-

derstood, and then they would say "So what" and go their own
ways.

I went over to the officers' meeting. "Our regiment is in poor
shape," said the officers, "bad, unreliable."

So it seemed to me. But what could be done?

They look at your hands and wait for a miracle. But I performed
no miracle—I left for Stanislau.

Back to the same town. Polish, secretly hostile. Clean, pillaged.
They told me that I had to go to the Eleventh Division. There,
things were still worse. This fresh, recently replenished division
didn't want to stay in the trenches. Sitting in trenches is generally
difficult, but here it was worse than usual. I took off. Everything
went wrong on the road. The tires blew out, the rims flew off, the
complete breakdown of the car seemed imminent, though the
driver clearly was trying to get us there no matter what. We made
it. First of all, if I'm not mistaken, to headquarters of the Forty-
first Yakut Regiment—a small Galician hut, rather clean and
brightly colored inside. The commander of the regiment reported
that his men categorically refused to fight. We called a rally. A
cart was placed in the middle of a field; felled birches and maples
were put around it; next to it, still unfaded, a red-and-gold banner.
Heat. The sun beat down. High in the air, a German plane
watched closely as the Russians got ready for the offensive. Anardovich spoke first—the usual speech, along the lines of *Izvestia*. He
spoke without a cap; the sun glared on his shaved head. Someone
in the crowd said, "That's right!" His neighbors jabbed him and
he shut up. The regiments knew nothing about freedom of speech;
they regarded themselves as a single voting entity. Those who
opposed the majority were beaten up. In the Malmyzh Regiment a
telegraph operator was beaten so unmercifully for a speech urging
continuation of the war that he crawled away on all fours.

I spoke after Anardovich finished. I have the strange habit of
always smiling when I talk. This irritates a crowd, especially when
it's in a menacing mood. "Laugh, you toothless wonder!" Then a
soldier got up; he spoke badly, but was no demagogue. His argu-
ments went like this: "In the first place, why not let the Germans
alone? Once you stir them up, they'll be hard to handle. In the
second place, why not let the Eleventh Division alone? We just got
out of the trenches and were promised a rest before moving out.
The general even said, 'Congratulations, comrades, on getting a

rest.'" We talked and got nowhere. We went to the next regiment. The same thing. The regiments stood fast and said they weren't going anywhere. We stopped by division headquarters. The company was staying at a large, fairly clean farmhouse. There we found the division commander, who felt guilty though he didn't know of what—also the chaplain, some staff members and some who were apparently members of the Simferopol Soviet. They had come to the front with presents for the troops and were astonished that all this was nothing like what they had expected. They too had been talking about the offensive and the troops had nearly beaten them to death. We joined this coalition and sadly ate dinner.

It was raining and we had left our overcoats back at the regiment. But the division had to be mobilized at all costs. The words "at all costs" were running through my brain so furiously that later on, in Persia, I felt that "Atallcosts" was one word and "Atallcos" a city in Kurdistan. We left to mobilize the division. Filonenko was summoned. Even before his arrival, we found out that the machine-gun, grenadier and engineer companies were in favor of carrying out the order, that they had even formed a separate camp and were keeping watch over the rest of the infantry. I should say that all the trained units of the army were for the offensive and, above all, for maintaining order and discipline. City people are more unselfish, but they have more imagination and can't conceive of an "Eleventh Division" or a "Fifth Company" as something autonomous. But what we needed was a division, not separate outfits. We assembled, via the regimental committee, all the leaders who disagreed with us. We told them that it was impossible to sit still and rot: we had to fight or disperse. The life of everyone who spoke was at stake. We promised to hold an inquest to find out why the Eleventh Division had been deceived— lured to the trenches with the promise of a rest. We all parted with broken hearts, very unhappy with each other. But, still, the Eleventh Division did "move out."

The first to get under way were the machine gunners, who moved out pulling their machine guns behind them, ready for the attack. That night a machine-gun company deserted from the regiment; the rest went after them to Stanislau, where they all remained, keeping each other guarded. But still the division had been mobilized. I bring in this story with such detail to show how problems of moderate difficulty were solved.

We arrived at Stanislau ahead of the Eleventh Division.

Here, in a movie theater, Filonenko organized a huge meeting of the delegates from all the regimental and company committees of the Twelfth Corps—the shock troops. It was unanimously decided to attack. Battle committees were chosen to assist the commanders; the rest of the committee members were to fight in the ranks. It may very well be that all the men who voted for this were mistaken, but their sacrifice was based on an honest mistake. They decided on death if it would only tear the noose of war from the neck of the revolution. While we were having troubles with the Twelfth Corps, things in the nearby corps were also a mess. News came that the Glukhov Regiment of the Seventy-ninth Division— I've forgotten its number, but I'll never forget its name—was in complete disarray. The officers had scattered; the regimental committee had been changed three times and no longer had the confidence of the soldiers; the committee members had been forbidden to talk in the barracks, so they had to hold their meetings on the street. In another regiment of the same division, the soldiers had mercilessly beaten the chairman of the regimental committee, Doctor Shur, an old member of the Bund; provocation by the police sent to the front was assumed. The beaten doctor had been placed under arrest. Filonenko went to rescue him, which he succeeded in doing without artillery or cavalry. Three of us went to the Glukhov Regiment—Filonenko, Anardovich and I—leaving Tsipkevich to organize the corps for the offensive. Tsipkevich was a superb organizer, having formerly worked in a workers' brigade, then in the Nikolaevsky ship-building yards and finally in the Eighth Army, where the committee members revered him.

His method of operation was as follows. In the evening the corps commander informed him of our army's objectives for the next day. That night Tsipkevich would assign sectors of the front to the committee members and send them off; the next day they would telegraph the results. They paid special attention to our troop movements and the flow of matériel. And while Tsipkevich was using his revolutionary methods to unsnarl bottlenecks on the railroad, we went to the Glukhov Regiment.

The Glukhov Regiment stood on our left flank in the Carpathians, not far from Kirlya-Baba. Even during the reign of Nicholas, this regiment had deserted their positions two or three times—or so they boasted. They were camped in a dismal, rainy, godforsaken place with no roads. The road kept climbing higher and higher; at times we could see below us villages and hills descending gradually into the valley.

Finally we came to the burned remains of two small towns, divided by a shallow but swift river. Dangling from the railroad bridge over the river was a tiny locomotive. The retreating troops had pushed it off the bridge and it still hung there. These little towns are called Kuty and Wiznitz; they stand right at the gates of the Carpathians. Farther on, the road went along a river, as is generally the case in the Carpathians. On the opposite side, a train was rolling slowly along the narrow-gauge tracks. An agonizing road. Steep inclines, log surfaces—the only thing able to withstand the rains of the Carpathians—all this combined to make our trip terribly difficult. Beside the road were slopes covered with the dark fur of gloomy spruce trees and occasionally an almost vertical field: it seemed that a man and horse could climb and plow such a steep slope only on all fours—and then only by clinging to the rocks with their teeth. From time to time we encountered old mountaineers in their short, bright-colored sheepskin coats, with black umbrellas in their hands. Squads of girls were repairing the road; they smiled readily at the car. It was raining; every few minutes, it would not exactly clear but sort of turn gray and the rain would stop. Halfway there, the car gave out completely; the tires were torn to shreds. It was dark. We forded the river and spent the night in a mountaineer's cabin. It looked like Peer Gynt's abode. In the morning we patched the tires somehow, stuffing one of them with moss. We finally arrived at the regiment. Headquarters was deserted. Some second lieutenant met us—a suspicious-looking type. No doubt he had conducted a campaign against the officers and committees and had joined up with the Muravyovs, as I would now say; then when everything started shaking and falling apart, he got cold feet. Now he had just one ambition—to go on leave. The regiment was unbearable. Its noncommissioned officers had almost all run off to join the shock troops. It had no bottom and no top.

The committee tried to talk us out of a rally, but we decided to call one anyway. There was a rostrum in the middle of the meadow. The soldiers assembled; an orchestra showed up. When the orchestra played the "Marseillaise," they all saluted. We got the impression that these men still had something—the regiment hadn't completely turned into mush. Life in the trenches over such a long period had worn the men down; many used sticks and walked with the practiced steps of blind men: they were suffering from ophthalmia. Worn out, cut off from Russia, they had formed their own republic. The machine-gun detachment was once again the exception. We conducted the rally. They listened restlessly, interrupting with shouts:

"Beat him up; he's a bourgeois dog; he's got pockets in his field shirt," or "How much are you getting from the bourgeois dogs?" I succeeded in finishing my speech, but while Filonenko was talking, a crowd under the leadership of a certain Lomakin ran up to the rostrum and grabbed us. They didn't beat us up, but shoved against us with shouts of "Come to stir us up, huh!" One soldier took off his boot and kept spinning around, showing his foot and shouting, "Our feet! The trenches have rotted our feet!" They had already decided to hang us—as simple as that—to hang us by the neck, but at this point Anardovich rescued us all. He began with a string of unspeakably vile curses. The soldiers were so taken aback that they calmed down. To him, a revolutionary for fifteen years, this mob seemed like a herd of swine gone berserk. He wasn't sorry for them or afraid. It's hard for me to reproduce his speech; I only know that, among other things, he said, "And even with a noose around my neck, I'll tell you you're scum." It worked. They put us on their shoulders and carried us to the car. But as we drove off, they threw several rocks at us.

Ultimately Anardovich got the regiment under control. He went by himself, ordered them to hand over their rifles, divided them into companies, separated out seventy men and sent them under guard (one Cossack) to Kornilov's battalion, where they said they were "reinforcements" and where they fought no worse than anyone else. The rest went with him.

They turned out no worse than the other regiments. All this, of course, came to no avail: we were trying to keep the individual regiments from disintegrating, but this disintegration was a rational process, like all that exists, and was taking place all over Russia.

From the Glukhov Regiment we went back to Stanislau via Kuty. There the artillery was already softening up the enemy for the offensive. Seven hundred cannons, well aimed, were leisurely battering the German trenches. For the gunners, this is cheerful, not difficult, work. You can eat, drink tea and then do some more shooting. It's not as unpleasant as shooting to repel an enemy attack. Our gunners shot remarkably well, considering that they didn't have the advantages of aerial reconnaissance. German aviation infinitely surpassed our own. I watched the bombardment from an attic—looking over the roof tiles of a tall house, since the special observation point was too full: at first, there had been two of them, but one was destroyed by an enemy shell. The observers had been killed; there were only shreds of flesh to bury.

What struck me about the bombardment of the enemy positions was the small amount of noise: the cannons didn't seem to roar, or else they didn't all roar at once. Fountains of dirt spurted up from the trenches of the enemy. From the height of the fountain, you could guess at the caliber of the shell. And in the air over Stanislau hung two-colored clouds from the explosions of Austrian shrapnel. About 1:00 p.m., on June 23, 1917, headquarters got word that the Kinburg Regiment had become restless and decided to attack without waiting for the complete destruction of the enemy barbed-wire entanglements. Our fire, still calm and deliberate, was directed at the enemy reserves. From the roof, I could see through binoculars small gray men running out of our trenches and crossing the field. At first our men appeared in separate sectors; then the winding line of our attacking troops stretched across the whole front. I wept on the roof.

We had already learned that the first charge went beyond three rows of enemy fortifications. The charge was superb and its success was being exploited. I climbed down from the roof and headed for the front. I walked along a road and across our trenches toward the Austrians. I crossed the Bistritsa. Here and there, along the sides of the road, were holes where our infantry had dug in during the attack. The Austrian trenches had been almost completely destroyed. It was amazing how well built they were. Our soldiers were scratching around in them looking for sugar. The committee members had succeeded in destroying the wine; otherwise, the soldiers would have gotten drunk. Now the second and third waves of the advancing Russians wearily crossed the field. Austrian weapons, overcoats, helmets were under foot everywhere. The enemy had not expected the assault, despite our long conversations about it. The commander of the Austrian artillery had been killed near a forty-centimeter gun. But not the whole front had moved forward: off to the left of the road, it sounded like sticks hitting each other—it was rifle and machine-gun fire. I reached headquarters of the Eleventh Division. They recognized me, but they had no time to attend to me: the sticks were hitting each other more and more often; the battle was beginning in earnest. I went to look at the Austrian trenches. Fine trenches—even armored turrets for observers!

Word came that the Austrians had been smashed all along the line; the cross fire had died down. I walked farther. Some armored cars, sent to pursue the enemy, had arrived from Stanislau. They were standing in front of a small bridge destroyed by the Austrians, while the drivers filled up the ditch. I ran into a friend here; he was killed in battle later the same day. I went on. The number of dead was small; the wounded kept streaming in, most of them ours, which meant that the enemy hadn't been encircled yet. Right there by the road, under a bush, lay a dead man; he lay still. Next to him, the soldiers were calmly having a breakfast of Austrian canned goods, setting the cans on the corpse.

Filonenko, very pleased about everything, caught up with me in his car. I got in. The German airplanes were flying low, very low, not at all afraid of our gun fire; I think they were armored. At times they dipped almost low enough to knock us off the road with their tails. Sometimes they threw out a red ribbon that hung vertically over our line to correct their artillery fire.

A shell fell in front of the radiator of our car; I think they had aimed at the cloud of dust. We wheeled into the whirlwind of sand and rocks raised by the explosion, just had time to shout and we were already through.

On the first day, the troops got as far as the Povelcha River, where they consolidated their position. When we got there, the troops' morale was excellent, even though during the advance the regiments had overlapped each other and everything was confused beyond belief. By evening, the first results of the advance were known: the enemy's front had been breached; we had advanced about six miles and captured two German divisions and more than three thousand machine guns.

I'm writing this after almost two years. Our offensive was on June 23, 1917 (old style), and I'm writing on Whitsunday 1919. The windows of the dacha where I'm living (Lakhta) jiggle from the muffled and distant cannon shots. Somewhere, someone—either

Finns or Belgians of some sort—is shooting some of "ours," also unknown to me.

The next day I went to the front again. The Povelcha had been crossed, with insignificant losses. I know that the Kamchatka Regiment, which I ran into, had lost only forty or fifty men.

We drove beyond the front line, left the car and walked on with the scouts.

In the course of the next two or three days, we often went with the scouts ahead of our line. The offensive was developing in an unusual way. Our light artillery led the attack, without even being supported; it hardly had time to set up its position and fire a few shots before it had to move on. Later the Austrians borrowed this procedure from us and, during engagements in the vicinity of Dolina, it became more than clear that their artillery faced our front line. But in those days the artillery would even move along ahead of the front line. After the artillery came the infantry, then the cavalry. There was no chance to use the Savage Division, apparently because of the rugged terrain. In general, it was a good deal worse than our regular cavalry, which was very good. Later it was the cavalry alone that covered our retreat. They were still regular soldiers. At that time their mood was almost chauvinistic. "We're for peace without annexations and reparations," they said, "and for war to the final victory." For the time being, however, it was the artillery that handled the pursuit of the enemy.

And in our rear the huge heavy supply columns of the advancing army rumbled along, slamming into each other in one continual din.

The difference between the thin line—more like a thread—of the Russian front and our huge overloaded rear was all too clear.

I remember one of our sorties. We went out at night. Vonsky went with me—a good man, very energetic, from Odessa; he had been able to get a large number of wounded out through Stanislau. Just ahead of us to the right was a burning village. The Austrians had set it on fire. The blaze made the night still darker. In the distance the withdrawing enemy was shooting toward the flames.

The soldiers were drawing water out of a well by fastening their mess gear to a telephone wire.

We went on into the dark.

The armored cars caught up with us. The drivers hailed us. One of them, an old student of mine, had recognized me. We decided to go with him in his narrow, single-turreted "Lanchester." It was hot and stuffy inside. The walls were covered with thick felt and plastered with portraits of Kerensky and pieces of red calico.

We drove on into a forest that was supposed to be thick with Austrian units. No one shot at us.

We stopped. Another burning village off to the side, beyond the forest. The enemy was shooting toward the forest. That meant they had already evacuated it. A stray shell fragment lit at our feet. Everyone began to talk in a whisper. The whole forest, the whole road, was littered with the heavy German helmets, distinguished by their visors and low neckguards. Rifles . . . shovels . . . rolls of wire were everywhere.

In the morning a car full of war correspondents overtook us. One of them was Lembich, from *The Russian Word*. I remember he was dying to get to the telegraph office in Stanislau so that he could send a dispatch based on third-hand information—bearing about as much resemblance to the truth as clouds to cymbals.

The next day we drove on. On the road we met an artillery officer with a map in his hands; he was looking for elevation 255 and nearly reduced to asking passers-by about it. He didn't know how to read maps. I don't know where he popped up from.

So, driving along as inconspicuously as possible, we reached Halicz. Halicz had just been occupied by a detachment of scouts, apparently from the Transamur Division—green piping—and by a platoon of armored cars, apparently from the Seventh Army. This dinky, godforsaken little town, which no one would have even noticed except for its vital strategic importance as a bridgehead, was deserted. The Germans had pulled out; the dynamited bridge looked like a sphinx in the desert. On the opposite bank we could see two of our scouts; they had either swum across the river or forded it. Far under the bridge the waves of the Dniester ran swiftly and indifferently past the war they had grown to hate.

There were about ten houses in the town. In one of them, about thirty men, counting our troops and the commissars (Tsipkevich and me). High on the nearby mountain rose the crumbling black walls of the castle of Daniil Galitsky. It was all just as I had seen it back in 1915 when I drove a car from Brod via Halicz to Lvov, Stanislau and Kolomea during a blizzard. This time, I had gone from Stanislau to Halicz. We had so changed our positions that when we found our old trenches, they faced the wrong way.

But there was something new in Halicz—the remarkable German fortifications.

The holes had been dug right into the base of a tall Galician mountain and then reinforced with a double wall of thick timbers. Huge vaults had been dug for the artillery shells and around all this were bowling alleys, showers and little shelters made from the white trunks of birch trees, with the bark left on.

Usually when the Germans abandon their positions, they leave them spick and span—even sweep the floors so that no papers of any kind will be left in the trash—for example, addressed envelopes, from which it might be possible to guess at the composition of the unit in question.

This time they had been in a hurry and left shells, as well as various unimportant bits of paper. They had carried off all the artillery. Our soldiers entertained themselves in the occupied town in the usual ways. They set off rockets, threw grenades, took equipment only to chuck it a few steps away. It was sunny and very peaceful. And quiet, as quiet as a spa in the fall when everyone has left.

We drove back. Past ravaged, burned-out villages, past forests no longer whispering, past chapels burning with the yellow flame of candles someone had lit, I drove into Stanislau.

Here I was told to go to the Sixteenth Corps, in the vicinity of Nadworna. There were hardly any enemy troops there—perhaps a few outposts on watch in the trenches or perhaps only watchdogs. The enemy was withdrawing, but still our reserve divisions couldn't make up their minds to advance, even though this Torricellian vacuum was sucking them in. I was sent to get the units moving. I set off again, saw General Stogov, who tried to hide the disgraceful condition of his units but, of course, couldn't. Kornilov had written him: "Occupy the village of Rosulna."

He answered: "The enemy is in the village of Rosulna."

Kornilov very pointedly telegraphed: "If the enemy is there, dislodge him."

But the troops weren't fighting and weren't dislodging anybody.

I got there. To intimidate our men, the Austrians had put one single cannon on the Kosmachka, that same round, wooded mountain I had seen from the Aleksandropol Regiment. It was shooting to the right, to the left, along the roads—wherever it supposed our headquarters to be and where, of course, it was. Our artillery was silent and for good reason. The men knew there was no enemy line in front of them. Shooting at the village was hard on people; shooting at the forest was hard on shells; so, for the sake of conscience, they shot only at the Kosmachka. In the field you could see a flame—a local, latter-day burning bush. Oil ignited in a borehole two years before was still burning.

We drove along the front. The Austrians had already pulled back and cleared out of their old trenches.

Good trenches, and dry, even though it was a swampy spot with a few groves of spruce—a regular Petersburg swamp. Little houses everywhere, everywhere the same little shelters made of birch with the bark intact.

I reached our front. While going through the forest, I kept running into stray soldiers with rifles, mostly young men. I asked, "Where are you off to?"

"I'm sick."

In other words, deserting from the front. What could you do with them? Even though you know it's useless, you say, "Go on back. This is disgraceful." They keep going. I finally got to the edge of the forest. Snatches of conversation. Here and there, small groups of men. The regimental commander was giving a report:

"Yesterday this company deserted; yesterday that one panicked and opened fire on its own men."

I called the committee together. The whole committee was on the front line, being used to plug up the holes. I went up to one company, making myself understood almost entirely by interjections: "Comrades, what's going on?"

"Nothing. We're staying put."

"Go to Rosulna!"

They began to explain that to get to Rosulna, you had to cross a field, and while you were crossing, they would cut you down from the Kosmachka. Frustration.

I took a rifle and a grenade. "Who's going with me to Rosulna?" One scout volunteered. We went through the fields, sometimes in the grass, sometimes in sparse patches of grain—rye, maybe. We got to the village; the road was deserted.

We walked into the first hut. Some terrified peasant women asked us in a whisper, "What's going on? Will you come soon?" We didn't say anything. A quiet blond boy about seven or eight invited us in his hard-to-understand Galician jargon to come and look at the Austrians. This time we crawled.

Standing in the river by a bridge, a small band of Austrians was throwing up a barbed-wire entanglement, a single-strand necklace on thin steel rods.

It was out of the question for one or two men to run them off. Frustration. I picked up various bits of paper left in the abandoned battery and set out straight across the field toward our men. When I got there, I left the scout and departed. I thought, let him tell it.

I advised them to bombard the "front" with artillery fire and to send armored cars into Rosulna; maybe then our infantry would tag along behind them.

These things were done and, with practically a knee in their backs, the troops plodded into Rosulna. In Rosulna they perked up a bit: they had bypassed the terrible Kosmachka, whose taking they thought would have caused such fantastic bloodshed (another famous mountain, Kirlya-Baba, had actually been paved with bones), but because of our delay, the Austrians had saved all their artillery.

It was in Rosulna that we found that German staff guide to fraternization. . . .

Was it worth bothering with such troops? Why didn't we understand that you can't fight with such crap at the front? Partly because we had no other way out of the war except a major victory over Germany, which was the only way, in our opinion, to stir up a revolution there. And, in fact, tanks did eventually crush Wilhelm's throne. We didn't dare see how impossible it was, so we proceeded to do the impossible.

Furthermore we knew that what lay in front of us was also not an army, but slop—distinctly worse than our Sixteenth Corps and a good deal more cowardly; but, alas, the Germans did, however approximately, follow orders.

And so we entered Rosulna.

I don't remember leaving Rosulna, but I do remember spending several days in front of a company of soldiers who had deserted their positions. I gave them hell. They were sorry and sweating. It was raining. I made up my mind to take this company back myself. The front was now about ten or fifteen miles from Rosulna.

With sticks in hand, we moved out in the rain through a tall, black, gloomy forest. We headed toward the village of Lodzjana.

We kept going. Sometimes the road was broken by a trench filled up with dirt. The dirt had settled and formed deep pits, in which the supply columns bogged down and floundered. No one bothered to climb out and put sandbags in the holes, although they lay around by the thousands since the breastwork for the trench had been made out of them.

A strange country. It can't even fix a road. And so thousands of wagons will come along and they will all bog down at the very same place, and thousands of horses will sweat a thousand times and so will three times that many thousands of men.

It was night when we reached the village of Lodzjana. More complaints. The unfortunate commanders of the reserve units were complaining. The units had been replenished with regular noncommissioned officers from the city; they conducted antiwar agitation with all the strength of their moderate intellects. But even these city troops were better than the "chickens," among whom were some gentlemen wanting to "prove themselves worthy" and to "atone." I reduced several noncoms to the ranks for desertion, though I didn't have the slightest authority to do so.

The troops' morale left something to be desired. During a relatively easy march, they had thrown away their overcoats. They were freezing, wrapping themselves up in blankets. At Lodzjana, I was told that the shock troops of the Seventy-fourth Division were refusing to move up to the front line.

For a shock battalion—even to me, who was already used to such things—this seemed like excessive cowardice. I went to see what was going on and immediately found myself in a crowd of exhausted and overwrought men. Then came their grievances. It turned out that the battalion consisted of regular soldiers and noncommissioned officers who had run away from the disintegration of their previous units. But even in their new unit they found the same disintegration—not from the reluctance of the soldiers to fight, but from their inability to organize. The battalion had no vehicles, had no cartridges for its Japanese rifles—in short, was unarmed, unless you consider the grenades picked up in the Austrian trenches. And it was being ordered to move up to the front line.

Through Vonsky, who had just arrived, I somehow got rifles

and cartridges, and sent the men into battle. Nearly the whole battalion was wiped out in one desperate charge.

I understand them. It was suicide.

I went to bed. That night the Ruthenian innkeeper got me up with a desperate wail: the soldiers were cutting down his unripened grain. I got up and spent the night running around in the dew. In the morning Kornilov arrived and ordered us to bring all the shells captured from the Austrians as soon as possible.

The front now ran along the edge of the village; the place was restless. During the day, the soldiers had killed two Jews; they said the Jews had been signaling. I'm convinced that wasn't the case. This combination of cowardice and spy-mania was unbearable. And all the same, this blood was somehow on my hands. The front had to be pushed forward. Our artillery was shooting more and more often, pushing back the Austrians, who didn't hold their ground very well. To our right, in the area of the Forty-second Division, where Anardovich was then, they would run even from shrapnel fire.

From the height of our village, you could see the Austrians evacuating the front-line area, dispatching train after train in the direction of Dolina, almost without a break. Obviously the evacuation was winding up. They were getting ready to surrender.

On the next day, a real battle broke out. It proceeded along either the Lomnitsa or the Povelcha River. We kept receiving the most vague and contradictory information, all kinds of military gibberish. I set out for the front. The forest was full of stray men. I found a regimental headquarters; there, too, they knew almost nothing. The battle proceeded in the forest; the units would fall back, then advance. There were no communications along the front. I went forward and crossed the river; the warm water immediately got into my boots and began to squeak and gurgle. After crossing a series of small glades, I came to a spruce forest, where bullets were whistling and ricocheting off the trees with a staccato whine.

While walking through the forest, I stumbled upon our line. Individual holes had been dug in the ground, still wet from the rain during the night, and the stumps torn roughly out of the ground showed their broken roots. There was water in the holes and tired, wet men were lying in the water. Two or three officers were hiding behind trees, but at least they were standing up. They obviously didn't know what they were supposed to do. The machine guns were firing without interruption and apparently to no avail. You could hear the ragged, nervous sound of rifle bullets. Various soldiers were grumbling about the officers.

"Why should they stay in the rear? Where they should be is about two hundred yards up ahead." Someone explained that the troops hadn't made up their minds whether to move forward. Some Hungarians were in front of them. The regiments to the right and left were already almost half a mile ahead. I turned to the soldiers:

"Move forward." They were silent. . . . It was so depressing in that forest, in that godforsaken corner of the revolutionary front. I picked up two Russian tin bombs lying by the head of some soldier and put them in my pocket; I picked up a rifle, stepped over our line and moved forward. The shots ahead of us had died down. I went about sixty steps, I guess—a ditch, a road, another ditch, and just beyond it were the Austrians. I almost stepped on them. I threw the bomb to the side; if I'd thrown it straight ahead, it would have gone over their heads. A yellow flame flared up with a muffled roar; I felt the concussion. . . . Time seemed to stand still. Sometimes during a storm, when lightning illuminates the clouds, they seem that still. . . .

And at that moment I heard a shout and our regiment ran forward, ran past me in a complete frenzy.

They couldn't stand it anymore; they came running.

I remember the charge. Everything around me seemed remote, sparse, strange and still.

I remember the yellow straps on the gray uniform of a German lieutenant. The lieutenant was the first to jump up in front of me; after a second of stupefaction, he rushed forward, turned and fell, tucking his knees under his chest as if he were looking for a place to lie down. The yellow strap crisscrossed his back. It wasn't I who killed him.

I ran past the enemy trenches and looked around: one of our soldiers, hastily removing the pack off a dead officer, suddenly fell beside him.

We were going into battle on a gray day, among the wet trees. Some German shouting "I give up" fell on his knees and put up his hands. One of our soldiers ran past, half turned and, aiming on the run, shot at him.

The troops ran faster than I did; I fell behind. I knew that you never attack standing at your full height, but we had lost our senses. Fatigue, hatred for the war and for ourselves kept us from thinking about self-preservation.

Somewhere off to the left in some elder bushes, a German machine gun opened up with a sporadic rattle.

Behind us appeared a group of Austrians, hurrying to surrender.

We made a running jump into a swiftly flowing creek, which almost bowled us over, and took care of some enemy troops trying to dig in on the opposite bank.

Then a deserted little village with chickens running around in the streets. One of the men tried to catch one. There were just a few of us left; most had been wiped out.

On the other side of the village, there was another barbed-wire entanglement; we reached it.

At that moment, we realized we had no more cartridges left. The regiment had shot them up while lying in the forest. I yelled, "Get down and dig in." We were already deep in enemy territory.

At that moment, I felt something warm in my side and I found myself being knocked to the ground. More accurately, I found myself lying on the ground. I jumped up and again yelled, "Dig in. The cartridges will be here soon."

I was shot through the stomach.

I felt that the main thing was to get out of there as fast as possible. Although I knew that a man wounded in the stomach should absolutely not budge for at least an hour or two, I started to crawl toward the rear. I wanted to get out from under the machine guns.

I didn't dream about Petersburg or the village of Lodzjana. Any place at all—even if only three steps away—seemed desirable to me.

I kept crawling and was happy. Streams flowed into rivers, the river flowed into the sea and I carried my burden.

I took off my belt and threw away the rifle, even though this is bad form for a wounded man.

A hundred steps from the battle, some soldier, wounded in the leg, gave me a bandage taken off a dead soldier and dressed my wound. There was little blood. Just a speck.

He and I crawled toward the creek, all the time speaking friendly words to each other.

It was a long, long way to Lodzjana.

On the other side of the creek were the stretcher-bearers with stretcher poles on their shoulders.

They assembled a stretcher, put me on it, covered me up, and the four of them carried me on their shoulders.

I was cold; I'd gotten soaked in those creeks. It was hard for the stretcher-bearers to walk, bracing their legs in the water of the swiftly flowing creek. I didn't think about anything. It was almost warm, but dark. It was evening.

When a wounded man is being carried on someone's shoulders, he lies on the sagging canvas and sees almost nothing but trees and sky. Everyone is carried beneath the sky.

We kept to paths because the roads were being bombarded by the Austrian artillery.

We arrived at a first-aid station.

It was jammed full of wounded men. The whole floor was covered. They put me by the entrance, but soon moved me: I was considered to be very seriously wounded.

The doctor came up. I told him to send Vonsky a telegram and tell him I had been wounded. He looked at the wound and said that the S-shaped lower intestine had been perforated.

"Do you smoke?" he asked.

"No."

"Have a smoke; it doesn't make any difference. Did you hiccough?"

"No."

"Well, maybe you won't die, but give me the address of your relatives."

In addition to the wound, I was in severe shock; my pulse was weak. They gave me an injection of camphor.

An orderly took off my wet boots and jacket and asked if he could have them. "I'll clean the blood off them and you don't need them anymore. . . ."

The first-aid station was being bombarded. The orderlies were hurrying to send all the wounded men to the rear. They put me and an officer, whose arm had been smashed from shoulder to wrist, on the bottom of an ammunition cart and sent us on our way.

We rode along. Everywhere we looked, we saw wounded men. The tired driver was cursing: "I'm going to dump you along here."

We threatened him: "Keep driving. We won't let ourselves be left in the road." I don't know how all this would have ended. The sky was already turning light. Morning was coming. Vonsky met us on the road with a car. As it happened, a motorcyclist had delivered my telegram to him at the Forty-second Division and had given him a lift on the same motorcycle. He put me and my companion in the car and took us to Nadworna.

I asked about the front. What was happening in the Forty-second Division was more or less the same as I had seen. The Austrians were weak and running even from shrapnel fire—in other words, from the merest trifles; but our units were moving apathetically, sluggishly, or else weren't moving at all.

Sometimes, though, our officers, telephone operators and combat engineers would put to flight an entire Austrian regiment. Doctors were going out to cut barbed wire and the units wouldn't cover them. All the untrained men of Russia were spinning their wheels.

We were brought to Nadworna. We were delivered, put on new stretchers (there were no beds) and ordered to wait. I was told that if I didn't develop peritonitis, I would live. I lay there weak, but already convinced I would live.

The hospital was still in good shape, run by a popular old doctor. Our orderlies didn't do any work, of course—didn't take care of the wounded and didn't clean up the horses.

Captured Austrians made the best orderlies. The Austrians valued above all the place where they were fed and well treated; then, too, they were more cultured and couldn't, simply didn't know how to, do bad work—just as a well-trained driver can't neglect his car. In the hospital I received a telegram from my division. They wrote that they felt I had accomplished my mission.

Later someone I knew from the first days of military service, a volunteer by the name of Dolgopolov, hunted me up. He had been wounded, too. His armored car had plugged up a hole in the front about a mile wide; in the process, a shell had fallen into its turret and made all the men deaf.

Dolgopolov's eardrums had been broken. He kept complaining that it itched inside his ear and couldn't be scratched. All the same, he didn't stay down: he went into battle almost every day. He was a real muscle man, with a strong neck but an already fractured soul.

Several weeks before, he had spent some time in Petersburg. He happened to know some people there connected with the journal *The New Life.*[16] At first, he argued with them; then they told him exactly why the war was being carried on in the interests of imperialists all over the world and they destroyed the whole psychology of this intellectual soldier who had refused to become an officer and who already had three St. George medals—this poor bastard with the twelve-inch neck.

It seemed to him that they were right; his eardrums itched, curved and pinched between the ossicles; his heart didn't catch on fire; it too somehow ached.

But I was still enjoying the fact of being alive.

About a week later, Filonenko and Kornilov came to see me. Kornilov brought a Cross of St. George, for which I was grateful, but somehow I couldn't bring myself to go through the whole ritual, which included a kiss of acceptance. Kornilov was somewhat disappointed. Filonenko was cheerful. He was on his way up. Now he was already a commissar of the Rumanian front. I found out from him about the debacle at Tarnopol, about what our troops did at Kalusz, about how the Bolsheviks had made their bid for power on the third and fifth of July and been ineffectively suppressed. I didn't guess the seriousness of these events right away.

But a few days later, the senior doctor came to see me; this lame, gray-bearded, slightly balmy native of Kronstadt announced that we were being evacuated right away.

The packing up began, grew ever more hurried until the evacuation gradually turned into a rout.

The enemy wasn't pressing us directly, but about two weeks before, in the region of Tarnopol, two regiments had simply left their positions, then a third; then still another didn't go where it was supposed to and the undermined front collapsed. The Germans had sent their cavalry into the breach; all it had to do was stand aside so as not to be trampled by fleeing Russians.

There's a certain children's game: you stand wooden blocks on end, one after another in a spiral, in such a way that when they fall, they hit each other; then you push one and havoc quickly runs through the whole spiral. The Seventh Army had pushed us. Our right flank was exposed.

Things were being collected ever more hurriedly. The district and city hospitals, being the most nervous, had already run away, leaving behind the large tents so valuable and necessary at the front.

The senior doctor flew into a rage and made the soldiers stay. Leaning on his crutch, he literally stood at the gate and refused to let any wagons leave empty. The third day of the evacuation was already drawing to a close.

They asked me if I could walk. I put my overcoat on over my underwear, then slippers, stopped a car, got in, and took off.

Our hospital pulled out after my departure. Since it was impossible to transport the most seriously wounded, they stayed behind with only the senior nurse, who cried when the vehicles left, but stayed. Someone had to stay. The straw thrown out of the hospital building was already burning; the hospital vans were circling the infirmary building, running over the garden so it wouldn't fall into the hands of the enemy.

The Austrian orderlies were carrying the wounded on their shoulders; they didn't want to be captured either—even by their own men. I drove through Nadworna. Sugar was being distributed —as much as you could take.

The supply depots were burning. Almost by force of arms, the wounded were fighting for places in the very last train, which was slowly pulling out . . . men on top of the cars, between the cars, men tying themselves under the cars . . . a tiny locomotive, straining every fiber, moving backward and forward, pulled at the long line of cars, about to burst asunder at any moment.

The infantry was on the move. The artillery, too. First-aid stations were replacing the hospitals. Artillery fire was again heard, the shells apparently landing not far away.

I tried to straighten out the columns of vehicles and to assign cargoes to the empty ones, but couldn't; I didn't feel well.

I was put in an overcrowded makeshift ambulance and carted to Kolomea.

Kolomea was packed. I went to headquarters and found Cheremisov, who was then already an army commander. He was composed, but agitated. He didn't recognize me, didn't even see me. He had other things on his mind.

I found somebody I knew, got in the commander's train and set off for Czernowitz. The headquarters telegraph operators were traveling in the same car, calmly playing guitars and carrying on their telegraphic conversations.

I didn't get to Czernowitz; the train stopped. Up ahead they were letting freight go through. I got off the train, hopped in a freight wagon and reached Czernowitz. There I went to the Kauffman Infirmary. Clean, quiet, organized—definitely a city place. They told me I had an infiltrate. This apparently means an internal hemorrhage. They said it was a serious case. I was lying down. It was quiet in the ward. A very young officer with a broken back was lying there embroidering with beads; he would never be able to stand up or even sit up.

The other wounded officers were reproaching me for what we had done to Russia.

Vonsky came. He had gone to Nadworna to look for me; he had a committee member with him, a quiet "teacher of the people," a Mordvinian.

They told me all about our retreat. The front had fallen apart; only our armored cars were holding back the Germans, only anti-aircraft guns mounted on the backs of trucks. The armored cars had been hanging on for sixteen hours. Halil Bek, my old friend, Caucasian, lieutenant colonel, twenty-six years old, who had a childlike faith in the Soviets then and had even stopped drinking after the proclamation about the evils of drunkenness, held out for five hours in a blown-up armored car, then was wounded for the twelfth time and carried out from under the debris. Later he went into battle again—this time with the infantry.

The Eleventh Cavalry Division held the Germans in a mounted and dismounted formation. None of the soldiers escaped intact; the division was practically wiped out.

Men caught up the falling army in their arms, put their heads under its weight. It was such a sad love. Somehow the hospital had become less quiet. I had the feeling that Czernowitz was being evacuated.

I asked to be given an attendant. And the first thing I knew, I was being transported to the hospital train, to the car for the seriously wounded.

The train slowly started to crawl along the front. We went seven miles in twenty-four hours. It was tormentingly tedious. . . .

I got off my stretcher, and my attendant and I slipped off the train. We rode for a while with the troops, then in hospital vans, then with the retreating artillery, lying on some badly arranged shells. In this way, along the incredibly beautiful road high above the rocky bank of the Dniester, I reached Kiev via Mogilev. From there on the floor of a train compartment to St. Pete. To the dear, stern city of the Russian revolution.

In St. Pete they put me into an infirmary again, but when they saw that I was alive, and obviously not about to die, they let me out.

I was like a soldier released from active duty.

Thus ended my first trip to the front. The first since the revolution. Now I'll stop talking about myself for a while and tell about the whole front.

I don't like Barbusse's book *Under Fire*—it's glossy and contrived. Writing about war is very difficult. Of all that I've read, the only thing I can remember as a plausible description of it are Stendhal's Waterloo and Tolstoy's battle scenes. To describe the mood of a front without resorting to false and artificial passages is just as hard. Never—not even while landing—would any aviator be able to hear words—even the most touching ones. Anyone who has flown at all knows it's impossible. Until I'm shown the statistics, I will never believe that there was so much fighting with bayonets on the western front or that it was possible to destroy a German foxhole with your hands and cave in the hole with your feet. I will never believe in this book, with its jumble of corpses, its end washed away by a flood and various conclusions.

So I will speak. I will try to relate how I understand everything that happened.

The Russian army was ruptured even before the revolution. Revolution, the Russian revolution, with the "maximalism of democratism" by the Provisional Government, freed the army from all constraints. There were no laws left in the army—not even rules. But there was a complement of trained men, capable of sacrifice, capable of holding the trenches. Even without constraints, a short war was possible—a blitzkrieg. It so happens that at the front the enemy is a reality: it's clear that if you go home, he'll come right behind you. In any army, three-fourths of the men don't fight; if there had been troops in this war that fought as well as men work for themselves, they could have not only attacked Germany, but gone across Germany into France. When the Roga-

tin Regiment, about four hundred strong, saw the Germans bayonet their commander right before their eyes, they went wild with
rage and slaughtered the entire German regiment to the last man.
The potential for this kind of fighting did exist, but two things
killed it. The first was the criminal, triple-damned, foul, ruthless
policies of the Allies. They wouldn't go along with our peace
conditions. They, no one but they, blew up Russia. Their refusal
allowed the so-called Internationalists to come to the fore. For an
explanation of their role, I'll cite a parallel. I'm not a Socialist—I'm
a Freudian.

A man is sleeping and he hears the doorbell ring. He knows that
he has to get up, but he doesn't want to. And so he invents a dream
and puts into it that sound, motivating it in another way—for
example, he may dream of church bells.

Russia invented the Bolsheviks as a motivation for desertion and
plunder; the Bolsheviks are not guilty of having been dreamed.

But who was ringing?

Perhaps World Revolution.

But not all had fallen asleep or not all could have the same
dream. To my description of the army, the following amendment
must be added. Mine was a killing occupation: I had to be in the
worst units during their worst moments. We did have entire
infantry divisions that were in good shape. I'll name the first that
comes to mind—well, for example, the Nineteenth. For that reason,
the Bolsheviks had to hamstring the army, which Krylenko succeeded in doing when he destroyed the apparatus of command and
its surrogate—the committees.

Why did the army take the offensive? Because it was an army.
For an army, it's no harder to take the offensive, no harder psycho-
logically than standing still. And an offensive is a less bloody
business than a retreat. The army, feeling its disintegration,
couldn't avoid using its strength in an all-out effort to end the war.
It was, after all, an army and therefore it took the offensive. The
offensive could have succeeded, but it didn't succeed because of
political circumstances. The units were already "falling asleep";
they escaped into Bolshevism the way a man hides from life in a
psychosis.

I will write more. I'll describe the Kornilov affair, as I know it,
and my session in Persia, but what I wrote just now I consider
important. I wrote it remembering the corpses I saw.

One word more. When you judge the Russian revolution, don't forget to weigh in the balance of sacrifice—a balance too light—the blood of those who accepted death among the cornfields of Galicia, the blood of my poor comrades.

The Kornilov Affair

I arrived in Petersburg weak, almost sick. I went to my unit. It was obviously in bad shape. Where there had been thirty cars, there were now five in working order.

I went to the Tauride Palace. Some armored cars were stationed there with the letters VSRSD[17] written on the green armor in red paint. I was asked to make a report to the Petrograd Soviet. I said something or other. I don't know whether they understood me. I wanted to say that the army was finished—not only because politics had become involved, but because once involved, they hadn't reshaped the situation completely.

The Bolsheviks were destroyed, utterly crushed. . . . But that didn't mean anything—they were building up again.

In St. Pete, I met Savinkov and Filonenko. Their main occupation was disdaining Kerensky.

After our rout-retreat, the army committees of the southwestern front, the front committee and the commissars convened in Kamenets-Podolsk. The conference was held in an atmosphere tainted by the crushing defeat. And despite the fact that the man who had called it, Savinkov, walked out in the middle of the conference, leaving Filonenko by himself, Kornilov was chosen supreme commander. This came about out of desperation. The way things subsequently worked out—as I understand it now—Filonenko, as supreme commissar under Kornilov, had to intimidate the Provisional Government with Kornilov, and not vice versa.

At that time, the government was holding all kinds of meetings, at which Kornilov gave speeches written for him by Filonenko.

It's not surprising that the content of these speeches and the accurate description of the collapse of the railroad transportation system reflected the hand and knowledge of an engineer.

62

All this was abetted by various war correspondents, who fanned the flames. One of them told Filonenko:

"I'm on your side, but if you're hanged, I'll get a really great story out of it."

The intimidation proceeded. The right wing of the Provisional Government intimidated the left. At the same time, still other intrigues were going on. Part of the commanders—as far as I know, a very small part—had much bigger plans than a simple "correction" of the government. Later I happened to see the little notes which the men of this faction had been writing back and forth. The commander of one army had been writing directly to the commander of a cavalry regiment that it was essential to detach the reliable officers and send them to General Headquarters for special training in bomb throwing. I think these throwers were being assembled in Mogilev, a few at a time from everywhere and, I think, unsuccessfully. In this way, the Kornilov revolt represented, on one hand, a reaction against the disintegration of the old army and, on the other, a juncture of two intrigues, which weren't exactly the same but closely interwoven and headed in the same direction. Kornilov was simply under the influence of the Black Hundreds, although they didn't have many of their own people at headquarters. Savinkov's group didn't want this "rebellion"; but they needed someone firm at the top, the incarnation of military urgency in the figure of Kornilov, but they miscalculated. I'm guessing that Filonenko exceeded his authority. Kerensky went into hysterics and Kornilov threw on the scales his own valor and three hundred of his Turkomans; on the other side of the scale lay the revolutionary momentum of 180 million people.

The scales began to tip.

The preparation for the Kornilov revolt had escaped me. I didn't notice it. At its peak I was lying in an infirmary and then I went to Kislovodsk for two weeks, where I lived in the country and at night looked down from the roof. Even here you could feel the Russian revolution, fantastic and terrible. In Pyatigorsk the soldiers were wearing unlaced boots and belts, not around their waists, but over one shoulder like sword-holders. I understood the reasons for this strange, slovenly costume. These men wanted everything to be different.

I didn't want to return to the front, but I had to. I tore myself away from the bazaar and the grapevines swarming with wasps, from the steep lane and the road made of native limestone. I tore myself away, returned to St. Pete and from there back to Mogilev-Podolsk, to my army. At that moment, all the commissars were gathered in Mogilev for a meeting with Kornilov. Anardovich had come from the Eighth Army, since Tsipkevich had transferred into the Ninth Army with Cheremisov; Filonenko was already chief commissar.

I arrived in Mogilev. The men at the railroad station recognized me and said, "Two telegrams have come over the wire." They showed them to me: it was Kornilov's telegram refusing to give up the title of supreme commander and ordering the army to recognize his authority; at the end of the telegram, he promised to raise the salaries of railroad men and telegraph operators. At the same time, a telegram from Kerensky had arrived declaring Kornilov a rebel.

Only the administrative branches of headquarters were in Mogilev; operations was in Lipkany. I could imagine what was happening in the army at that moment, or, more accurately, what would happen, what a wedge had been driven into it, and it was terrible to consider the possibility of headquarters acting out of turn.

I rushed to the direct wire.

"Have you received Kornilov's telegram? What do you think? Isn't all this provocation?"

They answered me: "Anything is possible now."

I got in touch with the Mogilev Soviet fast and proposed putting a guard on the telegraph office and the station. We got in touch with the army committee and decided to go to Lipkany. We got in two ambulances and took off. We were warned that there was a distinct possibility we would be arrested, but we didn't believe it and, of course, we were right. At the head of the army committee then was Comrade Erofeev, a gloomy SR, no longer young; he was a friend of the chairman of the army committee.

We drove all night on the Podolsk roads, as wide as a field, practically the equal of six Nevsky Prospekts in width. In the morning, we stopped at a village and found a peasant holding a copy of Kornilov's freshly printed proclamation. Where it came from, I don't know. We looked around, tried to find out, but got nowhere. It proved to me that the Kornilov revolt had either been organized by someone or was being exploited by someone organized.

We got to headquarters. There a telegram had just been received from Kornilov with an order to release all the radio-telegraph offices.

I countermanded the order, put a guard on the telegraph office and dispatched to every corps committee members empowered to act as corps commanders. We printed an order to the effect that army orders for the time being should be signed by me and the committee.

Haste was essential or this rumpus might provoke some kind of inappropriate action. The order came out lousy—worse than "No. 1." The question of the proper attitude toward commanders had been especially touchy in our army, which was more loyal to Kaledin than to Kornilov.

I sent a telegram to the effect that only I had the right to make arrests and suggested that anyone else who tried it did so at his own risk.

The army committee already had its own list of unreliable officers, which I think was accurate, but the committees wanted to replace these men with others more reliable. I didn't believe the new ones would be any more reliable.

I preferred not to tamper with the army. In any case, we so successfully laid the groundwork that when the commanders had to choose between carrying out the order of the supreme commander or that of the government, not one man stood up for Kornilov.

Later on, when the committee was taken over by the Bolsheviks, even they, though critical of the committee, recognized its contribution in putting down the Kornilov revolt. My contribution consisted in seeing that no one was killed and that the army, though deeply shaken, still did not utter that terrible panicky word—"betrayed by the officers."

The fate of our officers is deeply tragic. They were not children of the bourgeoisie and the gentry—at least most of them weren't. The officers, both qualitatively and quantitatively, constituted the entire sum of even slightly literate men in all of Russia. Anyone who could be promoted to an officer had been promoted. Whether these men were good or bad, there were no others and they should have been spared. A literate man not in an officer's uniform was a rarity; a clerk—a treasure. Sometimes an enormous troop train would arrive and there wouldn't be one literate man in the group —not even anyone to call the roll.

The Jews were an exception. Jews had not been promoted. I had not been promoted, because I was the son of a Jew and of half-Jewish blood. Therefore a very large part of the literate and more or less cultivated soldiers were Jews. And they were elected to the committees. What happened was this: about 40 per cent of those elected to the most responsible positions in the army were Jews and, at the same time, the army remained permeated with the most ingrained, irrational anti-Semitism and organized pogroms.

Now about the officers. These men, chosen on the principle of literacy, naturally bore the imprint of the old regime; they had been trained by it. But we all bore such an imprint. See how easily even the representatives of the proletarian "local authorities" revert to the old ways. For example, corporal punishment remained in force even during the dictatorship of the proletariat. In the province of Perm it was simply the general rule. Just as when the army ran after the breakthrough at Tarnopol, in order to stop those who were running, *ad hoc* committees made up of soldiers from the units that had stood fast caught the deserters; and, infuriated by the fact that this had happened on the Russian land, where the Volhynian villages were burning, they flogged the men. Neither the committee nor the commissar was to blame. The deserter was offered a choice of being shot or flogged. A monstrous sort of oath was invented by which he renounced his rights as a citizen and testified that what was being done to him was being done with his consent.

Russia's bones were crooked. The bones of the Russian officers were crooked. Russia's habits, her train of thought were part of them. But the officers welcomed the revolution. They too were exhausted by the war. In the trenches and out of the trenches, the plans of the imperialists were clear to everyone, even the generals. But the army, its downfall, filled the entire horizon. They had to save it, they had to sacrifice, they had to do their utmost. The best among them sacrificed and did their utmost—and there were many of them.

The position of the officer was, of course, more difficult than the position of the committee member: he had to give orders and he couldn't leave. "The Truth of the Trenches," not to mention the truthful newspaper *Pravda*, haunted him and pointed to him as the figure directly responsible for prolonging the war. And he had to stay there. The best of them stayed and they were the very ones who suffered the most after October. We were unable to win the allegiance of these men, exhausted by war, capable of faith in the revolution, capable of sacrifice, as they had demonstrated more than once. Such was the fate of all literate Russians who had the misfortune to be in that precinct where the sea foamed with blood —Russia.

No one in our army took the side of the supreme commander. Representatives from the Savage Division came from the Daghestan and Ossetian Regiment and said that they were for a democratic Russia and Kerensky. And they unanimously asked to have their regiments organized separately, since one of the Daghestanis had killed an Ossetian, or vice versa, and now they were blood enemies and taking turns killing each other. We complied with their request. Soon they were sent to the Caucasus on leave—unfortunately, not disarmed. Later it was these superbly armed men— each of them had two revolvers in addition to his rifle—who looted our trains and burned Cossack villages, preying on their own ancient lands.

A priest with a cross on the ribbon of St. George rode up on horseback; he represented the committee of some Cossack division. Things were calm in his group. Soon afterwards, a certain coolness set in between the committee and me. The committee wanted to carry out a whole program of reshuffling among the officers. They had their own candidates. I didn't agree with this system. I thought that the substitutes, several of whom were known to me, were unreliable and only more willing to please than the men being replaced.

The committee was mad at me, or perhaps only disappointed. They very gently told me that I still hadn't recovered from my wounds, that I was overtaxing myself.

Anardovich came over from Mogilev. He was morose and disillusioned with the Petrograd Soviet, which supported the war yet waxed indignant about the death penalty; he was also disillusioned with Filonenko, who had turned out to be "a rascal."

Anardovich had changed. In his poncho, tarpaulin cap and field jacket, he was no longer the same as I had known him. And he now had other habits—the habits of giving orders.

Anardovich didn't take over any duties, but he spent several days waiting for his assignment. He was transferred to the Special Army to take the place of Linde, commander of the first detachment to arrive at the Tauride Palace, leader of the Finland Regi-

ment in the days of its first demonstration against Milyukov—
Linde, now killed by the soldiers, pinned to the ground with a
bayonet through his neck.

I don't know what became of Anardovich after that. I never
heard anything more about him.

I was now alone. There was much to do. But the character of
the duties had changed. Life had become prosaic.

From every corner of the army, but mainly from the units in the
rear, thick "dossiers" made their way to me—about three fingers
thick, written in ink or simply in pencil. The usual type was
someone's complaint against someone else, about the theft of some
gear or rope. The dossiers kept coming, always getting thicker,
through all the committees and investigating commissions, finally
working their way up to me. I understood little that was in them. It
was hard for me. You call in the accused, chew him out, and he
leaves happy. Maybe he should have been hanged?

The problem of provisions and billeting was critical. And winter
was approaching. The large estates—several of them produced
more than half a million bushels of grain apiece—had been ruined.

Some soldiers carried on agitation among the peasants: "Don't
give us grain or we'll be able to fight for five more years."

A congress of assorted peasant committees was called, since the
Committees for the Exploitation of the Land hadn't been organized
yet. They got grain.

The single memory of several free hours, when I kept my
troubles at least at arm's length, is the memory of an automobile
trip to Jassy. I went with the quartermaster general to clear up the
situation at front-line headquarters. We drove through Batuszany,
where the headquarters of the Ninth Army was. Here, for the first
time, I saw the Rumanian troops. I knew about them only from
having heard for a long time that they were bad: the officers used
makeup and weren't ever at the front; the soldiers deserted. But
when I saw them, they had been retrained by French instructors
and they made a very good impression. I remember the way they
marched. I was used to the slow step of our infantry, so their
march produced the impression of almost a run, strong and sure.

Their relations with our troops were strained. . . .

The Ninth Army was commanded by Cheremisov. He had finally triumphed. Originally, after Kornilov became supreme commander, Kerensky had appointed Cheremisov commander of the

southwestern front without consulting Kornilov. Kornilov, offended, had telephoned Cheremisov and suggested that he decline the post which he had illegally accepted. Cheremisov replied that he would "defend his post with a bomb." As a result, both men threatened to resign. Filonenko reconciled them and Cheremisov was made commander of the Ninth Army. At that moment, the army committee was positively enamored of him.

Tsipkevich transferred with Cheremisov as commissar of the Ninth Army. But Tsipkevich had suffered a severe disappointment after Kalusz and his imperious nature kept him from getting along with the army committee. He sent in his resignation. I don't know where he went after that. He wanted to go abroad, to America. He said that only the Americans, as specialists in getting major enterprises back on their feet, could finish the war.

It was already night. The automobile drew transparent specks of dust into its white shaft of light; into the double white shaft of the headlights, it drew the road, which submissively sped by under the wheels. Ringing softly and distinctly, the carburetor sucked air; the car chattered; when solitary oaks rose up over the road, the noise of the motor resounding off them grew sharper—as if someone were shearing off the leaves with whistling blows of a whip. We flew on, drawn by the remote horizon. . . . We flew on, losing our way, rushing across the steppe, the wide, level steppe. . . .

Terrified rabbits, suddenly wrested from the darkness, stood frozen, startled by the pale shadow. But day had come. First came the dawn and, with a tiresome paw, it raked me once again into the business at hand.

The commissar of the Rumanian front wasn't there: he too had got stuck at General Headquarters. Incidentally, there were two commissars at the Rumanian front—one from the Provisional Government and one from the Soviet of Soldiers' and Workers' Deputies. It was the dual power incarnate. True, these men tried to work together in a friendly way. Only neither one of them was on the scene. Everything was being managed by some confused officer-in-charge. I found out from him that Shcherbachev—the commander of the front—had initially wanted to join Kornilov and had even prepared a telegram to that effect, but the men had held him back and talked him out of it. I don't know how true this was. The situation with the Rumanians was also critical. The king had sent Cheremisov an Order of Michael of the First Degree the size of your fist, but he was also regularly sending field headquarters a stack of complaints about nine feet thick.

Our troops wanted to stir up a revolution in Rumania and thought to do this in the simplest way, that is, "by pulling down the king." But we lacked the most important thing needed for a revolution in Rumania: prestige with the populace. We had no military prestige either: the Rumanians remembered our previous sneers at them and the way we had conducted ourselves almost like conquerors and they didn't forgive us our present weakness; we treated the populace too badly to have any prestige as revolutionaries, though not so badly as we treated many other nationalities—in particular, the Jews and the Persians.

I drove back.

I returned to Lipkany. Anardovich had left. A new commissar arrived—Comrade Vientsegolsky, former chairman of the army committee in the same army, a Pole who called himself a Socialist Individualist. Despite such an odd party allegiance, he was by no means a fool: he knew how to make men follow him.

He had his own ideas regarding the Eighth Army. In particular, regarding this whole quadrille of reshuffling officers. Perhaps a personal element entered in here—say, unconsciously personal. We met on friendly terms, since I had no doubt that I would be leaving. And I did leave.

The army committee was assembled for an account of Vientsegolsky's visit to Petersburg. He related that the Allies would not consent to peace, we could not fight and we could not make peace; it remained only to "knock on the doors of the Allies and plead."

At the same time, delegates to the Democratic Conference were elected.[18] All those who favored continuing the war were sent, although I proposed to send a proportional number of Bolsheviks. There were Bolsheviks on the army committee. They were men with a psychology of political sabotage, not class warfare. They had just one practical proposal: "to address an appeal to the peoples of the entire world."

I said something or other; now I don't remember what. I only remember that I left the meeting dead-tired, lay down on somebody's bed and slept a long time—a desperately long time, in some way consciously clinging to sleep, feeling that despair stood by the bed and that it would begin talking to me as soon as I opened my eyes.

I was chosen among others as a delegate to the Conference; they also sent Comrade Chairman of the Council Erofeev, a solid man with no idea of what to do, and the Mordvinian teacher and a Menshevik officer and someone else. I left with them, having decided to hunt up a new post for myself and not return.

Persia

I begin to write again. I was writing about despair. I'll go on. I arrived in Petersburg; the conference had begun.

The Bolsheviks were clearly winning. True, they were in the minority at the conference, but this was because various representatives of learned societies and others had been invited. The army committees were not Bolshevik, but I know how little contact these committees had with the masses. And the average soldier was worn out and saw no point to the war; he needed a change of government the way a mailman needs a change of shoes.

A worn-out Chkheidze conducted the meeting—a worn-out Chkheidze looking like an old merchant who's watching the utter ruin of his business and attempting to laugh. People talked and talked. The representative of the Latgals demanded the rights of self-determination for his people and we didn't even know where this people lived—in the environs of Petersburg, as it turned out.

The galleries of the theater were sagging under the weight of all these people.

Kerensky arrived—the sorcerer abandoned by his spirits. He hurled dry, rough words, trying to be inflamed and to inflame. Finally feeble hysterics broke out in the pit. People shouted and shouted. Kerensky's lips were dry and cracked.

Then there was the famous meeting regarding the coalition.

Was a coalition needed or not? One shrewd man proposed a coalition without the Kadets. He gave a long speech, incredibly boring.

We voted. The list of those abstaining was headed by shrewd old Chernov.

I voted against the coalition. I felt that a coalition government would fall apart. As it turned out, the appointment of capitalist ministers did ultimately contribute to the uprising of the Bolshevik regiments, which took so reluctantly to the streets.

But, of course, that's beside the point.

I was at the meeting of the division committee of my unit. A representative from the War Ministry and Chernov came to the meeting. Chernov had his say. Such speeches are fine for selling gingerbread to the poor or for sweet-talking a woman as you undress her.

M., the commissar of the division, was an incredibly slow-witted and panicky man (a sergeant); he thought of nothing but getting to be a second lieutenant. And he made it . . . just before October. He also had a way of saying something, then stopping in a daze and trying to comprehend what he'd been saying.

The meeting took place in our drivers' school, in the hall where we had fixed up an amphitheater for the students. In the upper rows, with their heads on the tables, sat some soldiers from one of the units. There were six of them; of these, three were too drunk to lift their heads.

And Chernov droned on, with trills and crescendos.

There was a commotion at the end of the meeting. The drunks were turned out. I went to the War Ministry at the Soviet and said I would go anywhere, only as far away as possible. I felt as if I were in a room where the lamps had been smoking for forty-eight hours.

At that time Verkhovsky was spinning his wheels in the War Ministry. You know how a car spins its wheels? A car gets its wheels in the mud or on ice and can't budge. The motor turns over, the car roars, the chains on the wheels clank and spew lumps of mud—and the car doesn't budge.

That's how General Verkhovsky was spinning his wheels. He was a decisive man with initiative, nerve and drive.

His idea to reduce the army to 40 per cent of its size was a daring thought. But to carry it out was impossible. The fabric of the country had deteriorated.

Oh, by the way! How many times I received from Kerensky the telegram: "Introduce iron discipline into army without delay and telegraph when implemented."

At the War Ministry, I had previously met a commissar who was leaving for Persia; he was a Menshevik named Task, a former chairman of the Kiev Soviet. I will write a lot about him. They let me go to Persia, although they did try to keep me. But frustration had driven me to the brink, as the moon draws a somnambulist to the roof. I got on a train and set out for Persia. Then it was very simple: five days to Tiflis without changing trains and from Tiflis to Tabriz two days, also without changing. I set out. In the vicinity of Mineralnye Vody, the Chechens were already wrecking trains. No matter, we got through.

Near Baku, I saw the Caspian Sea, a cold green not like any other sea. And camels, walking with their easy gait.

Some officers traveling with me were going to the Caucasian front.

One of them, wounded in the stomach by an explosive bullet and half-castrated by it, kept singing:

> Boiled chickies,
> Broiled chickies,
> Chi-ckies also
> Wants to live.
> How come you're boiled?
> How come you're broiled?

And so on. . . . He was about eighteen. He was by no means an educated man and he grieved the only way he knew how. And that's all.

And speaking of castration. I had been going to the hospital in Petersburg (they were taking X rays to figure out why my wound hadn't been fatal) and I saw an officer there. He too had been castrated by a wound. His fiancée had been coming to see him. She knew nothing. He hadn't been able to tell her when she came the first time and after that it kept getting harder and harder. And no one else would say anything. The wounded man asked the doctor to tell her and the doctor asked a nurse and the nurse wouldn't tell her.

And it wasn't so much the matter of telling her. The accident was simply too absurdly awful.

I arrived in Tiflis. A nice town, a poor man's Moscow. There was shooting in the streets; wildly enthusiastic Georgian troops were shooting into the air; they couldn't not shoot. The national character. I spent one night with the Georgian Futurists. Nice kids, more homesick for Moscow than "Chekhov's sisters."

The town was calm, not destroyed—true, they were eating bread made of corn—but the streetcars were still running and the people hadn't become savages yet.

I set off for Tabriz. The train climbed higher and higher.

Trees with dark-gold leaves clung to the mountains. The stream below was either following us or running toward us. The train kept climbing higher, writhing from the effort.

In Aleksandropol we hitched on to another train and were off to Dzhulfa. We arrived—a solitary station. The turbid Araxes River ran along the foot of a mountain. On the other bank, small houses made of clay, with flat roofs; to me they seemed like houses with no roofs at all. It was night.

I'm writing on July 22, 1919. When I arrived from Moscow on the nineteenth of this month and brought some bread (ten pounds) to a close friend, this man began to weep—he wasn't used to bread.

That's how it was—the houses had lost their roofs, the people had somewhat lost their heads, but they had long since grown accustomed to this state of affairs.

Our car was once again uncoupled. Then a new train was made up, all together about four or five cars with two locomotives, one in front and one in back.

We crossed a bridge, were perfunctorily inspected by customs (Persian customs officials, who were afraid of us), and the train, forcing itself, straining every fiber, began again to scramble up the heights.

Now on all sides was no longer the reddish-gold forest, but instead only red mountains and red ledges set off by snow, the snow on the peaks very close to us. The train, straining every fiber, at times almost came to a complete stop—it seemed that we would roll back down at any moment.

On all sides was desert. Only the water in an irrigation channel leading to someone's fields from the very top of the mountains ran swiftly toward us, trying to hurl itself out of its banks.

Here and there gardens could be seen below, marking the infrequent oases. The stations were deserted. We had reached the top. You felt that it was high, but that was all right—it was flat.

We ate in the Regional Union[19] at the Sufian station. From there the train was going to Tabriz, but I had to get to Urmia, where army headquarters was. Or, more exactly, the headquarters of the Seventh Detached Cavalry Corps, as our Persian army was called.

I changed trains and very quickly arrived in Sharafkhaneh.

Here I saw something unbelievable. A desert salt marsh. It was an enormous, smooth inland sea, clearly dead. Long jetties on piles extended into the water. Several good-sized black barges were being loaded with something or other.

But strangest of all, there were no houses along the shore, no people in sight.

Only the desert. And deserted warehouses. Goods lying about. Rolls of barbed wire. Several granaries. A dozen cars standing on the tracks. But the port was dead. This is the main port of Lake Urmia, a place supposedly with a tremendous future. You couldn't see the opposite shore. But to the left was an island called Shahi: the shahs used to hunt there.

I stayed all night there in the plywood cottage of the Regional Union. I left in the morning. The same sea and below the same piles blanched by the salt. An uncanny silence. The warehouses were being guarded by Turkish prisoners. They were more reliable. There were two ways of getting across the lake: either in a barge towed by a launch or simply in the launch, if it were an urgent matter. All together, there were about half a dozen steamboats on the lake; one of them, the *Admiral*, was rather large— about the same size as the steamboats that go between Kronstadt and Petersburg—but with an internal-combustion engine. The steamboats had been brought from the Caspian Sea and assembled here.

I set out for Urmia in a small launch. It was about thirty-five or forty miles.

Flamingos were flying over the lake, turning pink as they flew up. The undersides of their wings are pink. The boat chugged along and cut the still, smooth waves.

A fleet had been dragged to this salt lake, which had always been deserted—deserted during the reign of the Chaldeans, during the reign of the Assyrians, always marginal; now a fleet, piles driven in, birds frightened away and all for the sake of war.

The corps supply officer traveling with me related how hard it was to feed our army. "Up to the lake, it's not so bad—the railroad, then reloading on barges. The barges really help out; in some of them, you can carry as much as five hundred tons right up to the landing piers. There are five of them on the lake; then reloading on horse or ox transport, then in the mountains reloading on camels, mules or donkeys—and so on, every foot of the way."

And so practically every camel, horse, donkey and bull in the Caucasus and Turkestan had been driven into Persia. But we didn't succeed in getting them back out.

There were about sixty thousand of us in northern Persia— about five thousand at the front, with the rest in units to handle transport and protect the routes; the route from the front to Sharafkhaneh, 240 miles, had to be protected and, as a result, the army was starving.

The launch pulled up to the pier. . . . The cliffs were no longer red, but gray. . . . It was deserted: only one small clay house in sight. This was Gelenzhik.

We stepped out on shore. It was desolate, like standing in front of a blank wall.

Children were wandering around almost naked, in rags reduced to tattered threads.

I didn't want to wait for a car; I requested horses, picked out some men, and we began to clatter over the rocks to Urmia.

The road broke away from the salt marsh and went across fields enclosed with clay walls. Lombardy poplars stuck out in the fields like factory smokestacks, their branches seeming to swaddle the trunk.

We rode for quite a while along an unbroken clay steppe, past shabby cemeteries with markers made of pieces of rock stood on end. Then we turned into a brick gate and rode into the city of Urmia. Red mountains were visible beyond the city wall; the sky was far above; snow sparkled on the mountains. We came to a gray wall, went through a door and followed a narrow corridor into a small courtyard. Huge grapevines with gnarled trunks, strong and thick, climbed up the walls, making a green net over the entire courtyard. At the end of the courtyard stood a one-story house with enormous windows covered with calico. I went through the dark vestibule into a room.

White walls. The ceiling was made of beams placed a foot apart. Thin boards had been placed between the beams, and woven mats were attached to these boards.

The room was flooded with diffused light passing through the calico.

Here I met Task and one other old acquaintance, a certain L., who was panicked: he had come to the East and had expected an East as gaily colored as a peacock's tail; instead he saw an East of clay and straw, and war in all its nakedness. Nowhere was the inner lining of war, its predatory essence, so clear as in the crevices of Persia. There was no enemy. There were Turks off somewhere, but they were separated from us by impenetrable passes, where a camel would flounder in snow up to his nostrils. Only with inconceivable effort could the Turks get through to us, as in fact they had done in 1914.[20]

But that's beside the point. The point was Persia, which had already been occupied by Russian troops for ten years.[21]

We had gone to a foreign country, occupied it, added to its gloom and violence our violence, laughed at its laws, hampered its trade, refused to let it open any factories and supported the shah.[22] And for this purpose, we kept troops—kept them there even after the revolution. It was imperialism—what's more, Russian imperialism, which is to say, stupid imperialism. We had built a railroad to Persia, set up a fleet on Lake Urmia, built a colossal number of roads in the valleys, laid roads through passes where since the time of Adam there had been nothing but donkey trails, where the Kurds had been able to pass through the most impossible spots only by building bonfires and afterwards practically gouging out the heated rock with their fingernails.

A lot of money was spent in Persia. And it was all useless, like teaching a pig to waltz. We squeezed and choked, but found the corpse inedible.

The February revolution had not improved the situation in Persia. To begin with, we were entangled in all kinds of treaties with England: Persia was one part of the intended prey. Moreover, the revolution, while in general warding off the threat of Persia's being absorbed by us, had replaced one slow-witted, but organized, tyrannical government with several petty offshoots of the Russian tyrannical will. The subjects of the tyrannical government were themselves tyrants. If there had been a flood in Persia and it had fallen my lot to be Noah—to build an ark and to save the pure and honest, passively honest and actively honest people, I would not have had to build a big tub.

L. and I went to take a look at the town. The whole town was paved. The story of this pavement is as follows:

A certain general had ordered the Persians to pave the streets. Any property owner who refused was nailed by the ear to the door of his own house.

So naturally the town was paved. Facing the streets were the same clay walls, about the height of two men. There were low doors in the walls—no gates at all. Several mosques with low minarets and cupolas made of tiles. On one of the minarets, a stork had built her nest. This sacred bird is never disturbed. Water runs swiftly through all the streets in irrigation ditches. At the crossroads are graveyards—dusty, shabby and small. The gravestones —simply pieces of rock stood on end. Few people on the streets. Persian women, covered with black shawls, occasionally went by. The edges of rough soldiers' underpants stuck out from under their shawls. Some Persian men were walking around. We saw some Aissors. Small donkeys, with loads of brick on their backs, were trotting down the street; the driver would shout, "Khabardār."[23] They were carrying material for repairing the bazaar after a pogrom. When the drivers wanted to force the donkey to turn a little, they would jump off and push against his side. We were on our way to the bazaar. There were more and more people on the streets. The clay walls gave way to stalls, selling everything from gaily decorated cradles to dried, very sweet grapes and almonds. There was the entrance to the bazaar, which consisted of numerous tunnels under pointed arches pierced with holes. Along the sides, the stalls were almost empty. In the row specializing in fabrics, almost all the doors to the shops were of fresh wood that hadn't darkened yet. There had been a major pogrom here. The owners of the pottery stalls were sitting there matching the broken pieces left after the pogrom and fastening them together with cement and small iron braces. There were few wares, no imports and they were afraid to display what they did have. The hoofs of the donkeys bringing bricks faintly clattered. One row was occupied by shoemakers. They were making boots right on the spot. In the large deep stalls at the back of the bazaar, men were twisting wool into cord and, with a round stone as model, making caps that widened at the top like mitres. Down another lane, each artisan was manipulating a small hammer and a piece of oak to make a black design on a rough red and blue cloth. A whole beehive, but the clay debris still not cleaned up were everywhere.

We watched them cooking over coals heated up with a wicker fan, baking lavash, a thin, cardboard-like bread which they make by spreading dough on the inside walls of the oven; then we went home.

That same night, L. left for St. Pete. Task left for the front. I was left alone. Our troops were the only force in Persia and I was supposed to be in charge.

And now it's July 30, 1919, and I'm writing while on guard with a rifle between my legs. It doesn't get in my way. I think I'm just as powerless now as I was then, but now I don't have any responsibility. Now I'll tell what kind of country it was that I found myself in.

Azerbaijan and part of Kurdistan were the areas occupied by our troops. A mixed population. Persians, Armenians, Tatars, Kurds, Nestorian Aissors and Jews made up the population. None of these tribes had gotten along together since time immemorial. When the Russians came, this changed: it got still worse.

The day after my arrival, I went to get acquainted with the army committee. It made a very painful impression on me. Absolutely ignorant men who had no idea what to do. The chairman had first been Comrade Stepanians, an Armenian; he had been a poor chairman and made a hopeless muddle of the committee's affairs.

Then they had elected Geobbekian, afterwards a friend of the chairman of the regional soviet. This one was worse. With him you never knew what would happen from one minute to the next; in one and the same speech, he could back the Kadets and the Bolsheviks.

He had an amusing way of stopping a speaker in the middle of his talk and saying, "I'll explain it to you, comrade," and then he'd talk a blue streak for an hour. So he was the only one who ever talked. But we had to do something about the Constituent Assembly. Elections had to be held in an incredibly scattered army of small detachments. The soldier chosen chairman of the elections committee, a Tolstoyan, unexpectedly turned out to be a capable man.

But the rest of the committee—may they forgive me for the bad memory—busied themselves organizing amateur theatricals.

I suppose this was understandable. Life was so boring—no newspapers, no women, just the reticence of the Persian population. Well, as a result, a sort of summer-stock theater had been formed with an incredibly summer-stock repertory.

The troupe performed in a large clay barn, dark and poorly equipped—more poorly than the convicts' theater in Dostoevsky's *The House of the Dead*. It was a vaudeville repertory. The soldiers flocked in. Its organizers were planning to take their show out on the road.

But in this quiet city with its clay walls and perpetually closed doors, things were not going well.

The nights rumbled with gunshots. The soldiers liked to shoot into the air. They got drunk; wine was obtained from the Aissors and the Jews and perhaps even from the Moslems.

In the frontier town of Ushnuiyeh, there was a pogrom; everything was smashed and pillaged. Task went out there to investigate; he managed to find one company that had accidentally not taken part in the pogrom and, with its help, recovered the spoils; as punishment, the regiment was left on duty at this post.

There was no fighting anywhere.

We were getting ready for the elections. The army committees were re-elected. The army was getting weaker and deteriorating.

Persia suffered as usual.

The power of the shah is insignificant in Persia. He does distribute all the land and all the land in the country is his land, but these are only words. Actually the khans agree to recognize themselves as his vassals.

I won't attempt to explain this strange system, which has long since outlived its usefulness but still persists. Apparently the khans lease out the villages. Or else a strong, armed man living in the village systematically plunders it and gives a share to the khans.

The peasants are serfs in the sense that they are in the hands of a master as long as they live on his land. It's up to them to get water from the high mountains by digging irrigation ditches, so they stand up to their knees in the swiftly flowing water and roast in the sun. There's a lot of emigration: people go to Baku, to Turkestan, wherever they can—anywhere they can eat.

In the cities live the merchants, rich and, in a manner of speaking, educated; their children are taught in the French mission schools. They too have their own villages. The emergence of a bourgeoisie did not do away with serfdom.

Apparently, however, the khans already have heirs. Merchants and Armenians made the Persian revolution. It was the revolution of a minority. Detachments of thirty to forty men ranged at will over the whole country. The present governor of Urmia himself had been in such a detachment along with some local millionaires, the Manusurians brothers.

The Persians had a constitution, which they said was more

liberal than Switzerland's. The governor of Urmia was a revolutionary—that is, a participant in the Persian revolution. He too had his own villages and serfs. True, there were Persian Cossacks in Persia, units serving the shah that were recruited from among the Persians and commanded by our instructors.

The Persian Cossacks—to be more accurate, the men who used them for their own purposes—were almost universally hated by the populace. They, however, took orders not from the governor, but from the Russian government.

Now it seemed that they took orders from no one.

During our withdrawal they tried to attack us.

Of course, no one obeyed the governor. He requested from us ten Kuban Cossacks who "would obey him." The Kurdish khans didn't obey him since they were stronger: each of them had several dozen horsemen and one of them, Sinko, had a large detachment. This was one of the mistakes of Russian diplomacy. Grand Duke Nikolai Nikolaevich, in that epoch when he was building himself a palace in the Lenkoran Valley and plotting to create a Cossack army in Armenia, decided to win one of the Kurdish chieftains over to the Russian side. The choice fell on Sinko, khan of a tribe living in the vicinity of the Kuchin Pass, which connected the district of Khoi-Dilman with the district of Urmia. Sinko was given rifles and even machine guns, which made him a constant threat to us. He helped massacre Christians and ultimately laughed at us, saying, "My hundred and forty horsemen are driving out your regiment."

The Armenians didn't obey, either, though they were loyal, but loyal because they were the aristocracy in Persia. They had a strong organization called "Dashnaktsution." It may be that in the Caucasus the "Dashnaktsution" was a Socialist party like our SR's, but in Persia it was a powerful society for self-defense.

The Aissors, Nestorian Christians, were also a kind of independent state. They considered themselves direct descendants of the ancient Assyrians and spoke the Aramaic language. One branch of them had originally settled in the environs of Urmia. At one time they had occupied the whole region. The Kurds had gradually exterminated them. Now their number had been replenished by the mountain Ashurite Aissors, a savage people who had lived from time immemorial in the very center of Kurdistan—around Dzhelamerok, in the Van Province of Turkey. The Jacobites, a tribe related to them, lived in the vicinity of Mosul.

Each family lived in the mountains under the leadership of a malik, or chieftain; each village was governed by a priest; all the maliks were under the command of the Patriarch of the East and India, Mar Shimun, a black-eyed, ruddy, gray-haired Aissor. The patriarch's order is hereditary and passes from uncle to nephew. Legend traces the origin of the patriarchs from Simon, the brother of the Lord.

The Nestorians had a glorious past. When the orthodox believers drove them out of Syria in the seventh century, they crossed the mountains and came to Persia, where they were joyfully welcomed as enemies of Byzantium. Here they stimulated literary activity and spread their influence to Siberia, India and especially to Turkestan. They were even in China, where to this day there are several completely assimilated Nestorian families.

Tamerlane drove them to the mountains of Kurdistan; that's where they were living now like savages. They're black-haired, semitic-looking and ruddy-complexioned.

Nestorian missionaries used to get as far as India; whole Christian colonies appeared there. They passed through Siberia in the north; in the east they got as far as Japan. The writing which they invented was the basis of the Mongolian alphabet and apparently of the Korean. Perhaps they were the nation of Prester John, whose help the Crusaders had been expecting. Now they were a small tribe, driven into these mountains, which are indicated simply with blank spots even on the most detailed German maps. The Turks whittled away the tribe, but it continued to hold its ground. Their main village was Oramar. But Oramar had been occupied by the Kurds since 1914. The Russian troops used the Aissors as a special militia; when they withdrew in 1914 and left the Aissors behind, their fate was terrible. Doctor Shedd, head of the American mission, told me that more than forty thousand of them were massacred, stacked on pyres and burned. Those who survived took sanctuary in the American mission. But the Persians added iron filings to their bread and they died in droves. In 1916 a reconnaissance detachment of Russian Cossacks and the special Aissor militia of Aga Petros Elov decided to recapture Oramar, located in the heart of enemy territory more than 150 miles away. The road was difficult. The mules couldn't carry in any of the mountain ordnance. The Aissors carried it in on their shoulders. The cavalry made out as best they could; the Aissors kept to the peaks of the mountains, because the idea of mountain warfare is to occupy the commanding heights. I recommend a comparison with the description of the way the Carduchi waged war (Xenophon, Book 4).

Oramar was flanked, captured and sacked. The horses were fed with grapes, the donkeys with millet. Mar Shimun and the bishops —they were wearing turbans wrapped around their red fezzes— had attacked with bayonets and cut down the prisoners. Our Urmian consul, Nikitin, had gone on the expedition and, by the way, he told me that in an area once occupied by the Aissors, but now by the Kurds, he had found a small stone temple with no windows or decorations. It was called the Temple of Mary Mem. The Kurds hadn't destroyed this temple. Moreover, they had even spared the Christian relatives of the temple priests. This was explained by the fact that, according to legend, under this temple had been imprisoned a Great Serpent, which would come out if the temple were destroyed. Once in the lifetime of every guardian of the temple, the Serpent would show itself, but the present guardian of the temple hadn't seen it yet.

The exiled Aissors lived, starved, plundered, aroused the burning hatred of the Persians. They visited the bazaars dressed in small felt caps, multicolored vests and wide pants made from scraps of calico and tied above the ankles with ropes. The Christian religion, which bound the Aissors together, had long since grown slack and subsisted only as another means of differentiating them from the Moslems.

There were religious missions in Urmia—Russian, German, French, American; they all pursued the souls of the poor Nestorians and, of course, played politics. The missions meddled in government matters and they too constituted a sort of separate state. Each mission extended protection to its new converts. Because of this, there were some who changed their faith two or three times. In one family practically all the Christian denominations were represented.

The French mission in Urmia had a strange appearance. A large monastery with columns, men in black soutanes and round caps with pompons. It was the largest building in town.

The Russian mission, built, incidentally, on land illegally taken from private owners, looked like a large new monastery, with its red-brick walls. During my stay in Persia, the mission had already begun to decline: the bishop had left; its influence had waned.

All these organizations worked among the Urmian Aissors; the mountain Ashurite Aissors were harder to convert.

The Aissors had been living in the vicinity of Urmia for a long time: they had appeared here no later than the seventh century. But in our time, their relations with the Persians had become severely strained. The main reason was the Aissors' participation in the war. They had a guerrilla band which fought on our side. Christianity bound them to us, as well as their respect for the Allies. In their own way, the Aissors are an energetic people: many of them had gone to America, where an Aissorian journal is even published. I remember someone pointed out to me an Aissor walking down the street in his national costume—patchwork pants and rawhide shoes—and said that he was a doctor of philosophy from an American university.

It was these fantastic people who had their own guerrilla band, men terrible in their thousand-year hatred of the Kurds and the Persians. The leader of this guerrilla band was a certain Aga Petros Elov, a black-haired man with a low forehead, curly hair and a broad, barrel-like chest. His striped pants and formal double-breasted jacket with red piping made him look like a telegraph operator. Elov had a colorful past. The consul showed me a printed résumé on him in a secret official publication of the Ministry of Foreign Affairs. I don't know it by heart, but I'm quoting rather accurately from memory:

"Aga Petros Elov is the party who was in such-and-such a year the Turkish consul in Urmia; in such-and-such a year he governed a certain locality in Turkey and ruined the populace with exorbitant taxes; while residing in America, he was sentenced to a term of hard labor in Philadelphia. At the present time, he sides with Russia and is our unofficial dragoman. His services are to be used with extreme caution."

Aga Petros and his guerrilla band had rendered us great services in the campaign against Oramar. I accidentally saved his life a few days after my arrival in Urmia. Drunken soldiers of the Third Frontier Regiment had arrested him in the street and were threatening to bayonet him. I got him away from them by saying that I was arresting him; then I took him to my apartment. He spoke good French and English and bad Russian.

We didn't feed his band; we gave them nothing but rifles and cartridges. And even the rifles supplied were mediocre—the three-shot French Lebel without muzzle rings. You can burn your hand with this kind of rifle if you aren't careful how you pick it up after shooting. This guerrilla band damaged the relations between the

Persians and the Aissors, which had already been essentially bad. But in any case, Aga Petros was a daring and, in his own way, an honest man. This is the kind of thing that happened to him: Several years previously, before starting to serve the Russians, he was summoned before the Persian governor of Urmia on some charge. He handled this matter by arresting the governor himself and forcing the khans to recognize him, the Aga, as governor. The shah summoned Petros to come before him, but he didn't go, wisely believing that home is best; instead, he summoned the shah. Finally, the shah persuaded him to resign by sending him a medal. That's the kind of man this unofficial dragoman was. And I've forgotten something else: he wasn't a malik—the chieftain of ancient times—but one of the maliks, a man named Hamu, worked for him. Mar Shimun's faction looked down on Petros, considering him an upstart.

The third segment of the population—second in numbers—were the Kurds. In peaceful times they lived on the border between Turkey and Persia. More accurately, Turkey and Persia bordered on the lands where they lived. Part of them were Turkish citizens, part Persian. All together, there are about two million Kurds. In the 1880's they had tried to set up an independent state. The initiative came from the Persian Kurds. But the cultural level of the Kurds makes it impossible for them to set up a strong organization. To this day, they live as clans. With extensive cattle-raising and some farming, they live very well during peaceful times. Our soldiers used to say the Kurds were "richer than Cossacks."

But now they were completely ruined, suffering terribly from the war. Above all, from the fact that the war had closed their nomadic routes.

Formerly they had driven their cattle into Mesopotamia in the winter and in the summer moved into the mountains to escape the heat.

The war had closed the routes. Part of the herd stayed in the valleys and died from the heat; part was lost in the mountains.

Moreover, the Russians came to Kurdistan already hating the Kurds—a hatred inherited from the Armenians and understandable in them.

The formula "The Kurd is the enemy" deprived the peaceful Kurds, and even their children, of the protection afforded by the laws of war.

The general who took Solozhbulak (I've forgotten his name) proudly called himself "the exterminator of the Kurds."

With all their valor, the Kurds couldn't offer resistance to us. They still live not even as tribes, but as scattered clans.

After the February revolution, there was an important movement among the Kurds toward a covenant between the free Kurds and free Russia. There were all kinds of meetings and they sent men to us for negotiations.

The envoys returned saying: "The Russians are free, but they understand freedom only in the Russian way."

I know how cruel the Kurds are, but the East in general is cruel. Thirty years before, around Dzhelamerok, the Aissors had skinned alive several Englishmen, who had antagonized them by imprudently copying down inscriptions. And I didn't even see the Kurds during the time when they were slaughtering the Persians, cutting off the enemy's genitals and stuffing them into his mouth. I saw them when they had been dispersed and bored Russians were killing them for lack of anything better to do. The Kurds were dying of hunger and eating coal and clay in the vicinity of Solozhbulak, once all abloom.

The Kurds were also living wretchedly in the valleys of Mergevar and Tevgevar.

No, not at all. They had been driven out of these valleys, which they once inhabited as a rich tribe with 200,000 sheep and 40,000 cattle. The Transbaikal Cossacks had settled there. In the army committee, they were referred to as the "yellow peril" and not just because of the yellow stripes on their pants. Broad-faced, very swarthy, they rode ponies that could live literally on roots; the Transbaikal Cossacks were valiant and cruel, like the Huns.

However, without knowing much about the Huns, I think that the cruelty of the Transbaikal Cossacks was more absent-minded.

One Persian told me, "When they slash with their sabers, they probably don't realize they're using sabers. They think they're using whips."

I had a chance to experience the intransigence of these Cossacks first-hand.

I was driving into Gerdyk, our outpost in Mergevar.

A broad valley. On a knoll, a destroyed Kurdish fortification. Beside it, stumps, a lot of stumps. From high, high on the mountain fell a waterfall, shattering into dust.

On the other side of the valley, a jet of water the width of a barrel came gushing out of the mountain. Silence. Not a soul in sight. At night jackals howled. Foxes, gray foxes, caught trout from the bank of the river.

I had come to ask these Cossacks not to hinder us from returning the Kurds to their homes, where they might be able to live off the millet which had been sown and had not yet completely crumbled.

I spoke to them about the children wandering around our camps, about the fact that we were leaving anyway. And got nowhere.

In the geographical entity known as Russia live all kinds of . . . people.

By the way, this whole valley apparently belonged to an Armenian—Manusurians; and its khan also belonged to him.

That's how the Kurds were perishing in Persia. The Persians themselves were hostile to them because of religious differences. The Persians were Shiites, followers of Ali; the Kurds were Sunnites. These Moslem sects got along together like Catholics and Protestants (during the era of the Huguenots).

The position of the Kurds in Turkey was not much better. The Turks used them as fighting material, maintaining them as irregular units, not on food allotments, but on grass.

All these tribes—Persians, Kurds, Aissors, Armenians—hated each other. From time to time, out of a feeling of self-preservation, the desire to make peace would appear.

In my time, even a holiday, "Reconciliation of the Nations," was declared. The most eminent representatives of each national group assembled and swore to end internecine war. It was even touching: they all exchanged kisses. They had left their weapons at the entrance.

I don't know where they got the weapons: we had supposedly disarmed the populace.

In honor of this occasion, everyone decided to wear a special green-and-white rosette.

All this was brought off very seriously, slyly and naïvely. Irony hadn't been introduced into their relations as yet.

What struck me about the holiday were the mullahs with their red beards and deliberate, stately movements. They move more gracefully than Europeans.

Russian authority was represented in Persia by the consul, the commander of the army, the commissar, the committees, each official in charge of an outpost, many of whom subjected the populace to extortion, and, in addition, by every soldier with a rifle.

Urmia was restless. Shooting was heard every night—one of the signs that there was no longer any discipline in the garrison. Dull, humdrum complaints trailed in from all sides. The army was quietly rotting. I was miserable in the East, just as Gogol had been miserable in Palestine waiting at the dreary station in Nazareth for the rain to stop. The main complaint had to do with fodder. Huge convoys were going hungry. The hay stored somewhere in the mountains near Diza had been carelessly stored, or too cunningly. We didn't get it out in time. There weren't enough ropes and the Kurdish Khan Sinko provided no means of transport. Fall had begun. The springs began to run and the hay was ruined. Task spent a long time looking into this incident, picked fights with everybody, but didn't find the guilty party. The reserve supply of fodder was in the Khoi-Dilman region. This was a rich area, but the location was inconvenient—on the right flank of our front. *Sumna*—a straw that has been crushed and bound at the time of threshing in special Persian threshing machines—as well as alfalfa and hay, was stored in rather large quantities, but it had to be pressed and the work detail stationed at Dilman sabotaged the pressing operation, pressed the fodder wrong and broke the presses. The loaders worked half-heartedly, as did the hungry men of the convoy.

In Bana, on our left flank, the horses ate oak leaves and bark and gnawed at fences; whole herds of horses died. And cavalry units predominated in our army. The ability to work declined markedly. The army committee sent inspectors to all the harbors —it did little good. The situation was complicated by the fact that the loading and freighting crews at many harbors consisted of German colonists, who had strongly Germanophile sentiments about the war.

The hired crews of Persians could have helped out, but the populace persuaded them to quit work and not help the Russians. The loss of horses was taken very hard by our cavalry, which consisted of Cossacks, men riding their own horses—in other words, sentimental about them.

To add to all this, the army was faced with a currency problem, which soon became critical.

To make everything that follows more clear, I'll say a few

words about Persian money—"doggies," as the soldiers called it. They called Persian money "doggies" because it bore the picture of a lion.

The monetary unit was the kran—a silver coin which had previously been worth about thirty kopeks.

The five-kran piece was called a half-toman. It was bigger around than our ruble and had been coined at the Petersburg mint. The five-kran piece was worth from one ruble, fifty kopeks, up to one ruble, eighty kopeks.

After we stopped importing goods into Persia, the exchange value of the ruble fell; it was decided to pay our troops in Persian currency, figuring the half-toman at one ruble, eighty kopeks.

Being paid in the local currency would have worked decidedly to the troops' advantage. But we didn't have enough silver for such a payroll. This idea was talked about, then forgotten, but the ruble continued to drop. In the Kuchin Pass, I saw with my own eyes trains of donkeys whose *khordzhiny* (saddle bags) were crammed with Russian bank notes. They weren't a very precious commodity. The matter was complicated by the fact that the units in the rear were being paid in Persian currency.

The problem got worse. Everyone took an interest; consequently it was impossible to approach the problem rationally.

The Third Frontier Regiment was especially insistent. It was an enormous regiment consisting of four battalions. Finally, with difficulty, enough silver was obtained for a partial payment; for the remaining sum, in line with Task's suggestion, savings-deposit booklets were given out in which the sum still owing was entered as a credit. Then a new difficulty arose. It's impossible to imagine anything more capricious than the rate of exchange in Persia. Small silver coins had one rate of exchange, rubles another. Even gold had its own rate of exchange—not according to weight, but according to where it was minted, so that one weight of gold in Turkish lira was worth much more than the same weight in Russian pieces. Small Russian banknotes had their own rate of exchange. Hundred-ruble notes and five-hundred-ruble notes had still another rate of exchange, the thousand-ruble note showing the Duma another, the "kerenkas,"[24] just issued by the Provisional Government, still another. Moreover, the rate for the Russian ruble would change literally twice a day, depending on the latest information telegraphed from Tabriz. No need to say that the Russian bank in Tabriz wouldn't take Russian money. The situation got to be such that at each change in value, the soldier felt that he'd been cheated—and, in fact, he had been.

The minute the silver was handed out, the soldiers all rushed to change it into rubles, which they would take back to Russia. The bankers (*sarafs*) would momentarily inflate the ruble by fifteen kopeks (shai) and more, and the soldiers, feeling resentful, would stage a series of pogroms. The pogroms, however, were constant.

I'll describe one of them. For a long time, there had been rumors in Urmia that there would be a pogrom. Some Jewish soldier warned a compatriot in the bazaar about it. One morning in winter, when snow lay on the stones, I went out for a while. The irrigation ditches were frozen. The wretched Persian beggars, nearly naked Kurds from devastated areas, were huddling almost frozen against the walls. There was hardly anyone on the streets. A Persian I knew ran by and shouted at me:

"They're looting the bazaar!"

I lived across from headquarters, so I rushed to the commander, Prince Vadbolsky. He confirmed my news. Vadbolsky was a daring and honest man. Now he lost his head. Who could be sent to put down the pogrom? There were no disciplined units! Each would only join the looters. The Transbaikal Cossacks could be called from the outskirts of the city, but everyone knew the risk of throwing wood on the fire. The Kubans could be sent—Kubans didn't loot, at least in Persia—but they maintained a shrewd neutrality of the Khokhol-Caucasian variety and wouldn't interfere with the looting.[25] More than anything, they were afraid to spoil their relations with the infantry. Their maximum program was to get back home. I raced to the army committee. It was meeting in full strength and deliberating on ways of combatting hypothetical pogroms. No one wanted to do anything about a real pogrom. Everyone was afraid, and particularly dreadful was the thought of driving off the marauders with weapons. But meanwhile the army committee, together with the town regimental council, would have made up a group of about 150—a force to reckon with. I told the committee members that I would go by myself. Task was away.

I went to the bazaar. Several men were clustered around the entrance. Two or three scared Persian police and a few French officers observing everything with an air of calm, disdainful amazement. Soldiers came running past, bent over, carrying all kinds of

stuff in their arms and dropping it. The bazaar itself was dark with
dust and there was the constant cry—ow, ow, ow—as in a bathhouse. A blind animal rage swept over me. I picked up a board and
with a shout ran down the dark tunnel hitting all comers. The
broken shutters of the stores hung on their hinges. Men were
rummaging in the interiors of the dark stalls, jerking out long
strips of material like intestines. Beggars were snatching the pieces
and hiding them.

They were robbing the shoemakers. Tools, shoe trees, pieces of
leather, assorted slippers of yellow leather littered the ground.

Several Persians squatting in front of their stalls as the intrud-
ers broke in were wailing in high, wild voices and gouging their
faces. The bazaar thundered from the blows of rocks against the
doors, hollow as drums. The dust raised by the vandals made you
want to cough and spit up your insides. Ahead of me, I drove a
mob as reckless and blind as I was myself.

Most of the men were in the carpet section. One of them, in a
leather jacket, very tall and stocky, was breaking down a sturdy
door with a crowbar. I rushed over to him and clumsily hit him. He
recoiled, but didn't run—instead he threw his crowbar at me. I
caught the blow on the shoulder and immediately, automatically,
began to shoot point-blank at him, time after time, without hitting
him. By doing this, I broke some unwritten law of pogroms.

These thugs weren't armed with rifles and therefore it was all
right for me to hit them with a board, but not all right to shoot.

At the sound of shots, men came running.

This happened at a point where the tunnels intersected. I started
to run, which didn't demonstrate a lot of valor.

And it all seemed like a dream. I used to have a similar nightmare—I'm running down a low, narrow corridor with white walls
which turn into a ceiling. A little like the corridors of the Aleksan-
drinsky Theater, only five times lower and narrower. Everywhere
doors and more doors. An even white light and, from behind, the
sounds of pursuit. I run and hide behind a door.

I remembered and relived that nightmare again while awake in
the gray tunnels of the Urmian bazaar.

Behind me, people were running and shouting. At the bend, the
tunnels converged from two sides like arrows; a mob was running
down each one. I pulled off the fur jacket I was wearing and flung
it behind me.

I even managed to take the documents out of the pocket.

The two waves turned and met at my jacket and seized it, temporarily forgetting about me.

I gained a few steps and rushed toward a narrow passageway. Three or four men started to run after me.

I fired without looking back. They disappeared. I sprang out of the bazaar.

It was cold. Snow was falling and melting. The pavement glistened; a wet lantern hung on its bracket just as in Petersburg.

The bazaar rumbled.

I went around the bazaar and returned again to the exit.

The broad-faced Transbaikal Cossacks had arrived. The plane of their temples makes an angle with the plane of their faces—but just barely. I don't know how their heads got to be so round.

They stood there and calmly filled their saddlebags with the cloth that was strewn about—the shabby rough Persian calico. . . .

I ordered them to leave.

The Kubans arrived on foot. The appearance of these calm men in black fur coats who weren't taking part in the pogrom, who were just walking past these thugs with a half-derisive, half-condescending grin, somewhat abated the pogrom.

The Persians were offering no resistance: they knew that if they killed or wounded even one soldier, the pogrom would spread to the town.

A detachment of Aissors arrived; they had heard that I'd been killed.

They couldn't be allowed in, nor could the Dashnaks: we couldn't embroil them with our troops.

Finally, the committee members arrived—with no weapons, of course.

They too thought that I'd been killed.

We picked up boards and went along the passageways driving out the men. They had already been looting for about four hours.

We ran down the tunnels, dragging the soldiers out of the stalls, throwing them out of there, kicking them—despite the fact that the marauders were sometimes in the majority.

And the committee, of course, believed in procedures that were strictly democratic.

I remember . . . the dust in the air. The din of doors being beaten down. A kind, once very honest and daring committee member stood on the high, wide cornice running along the stalls and shouted:

"Comrades, what are you doing! Is this really the way to fight capitalism? Capitalism has to be fought efficiently!"

And sometimes three or four men would gather around one whose shirt was bulging with objects and excitedly babble, "Get rid of it. What are you going to do with that junk? Get rid of it."

It was strange. A man would be running with a dagger in his hand and wild eyes; you caught him, shook him and he had: two gilded frames, two boots for the left foot and several handfuls of currants.

Incidentally, Prince Vadbolsky was right when he told me, "Seventy-five per cent of the soldiers are passively honest, but they're also neutral."

Two soldiers were leading one of these "neutrals"—holding his arms, while he shouted hysterically:

"They're looting. A disgrace . . . I'm a Bolshevik . . . disgrace . . . I don't believe you."

But all the same, the passive majority looked on the pogrom as a bit of harmless mischief.

We barricaded all but one of the entrances and drove everyone out of the bazaar.

That night, details went around and confiscated the loot. The men were all in an ugly mood: "It's wrong to loot. But it's all right to harass the troops?"

The soldiers felt very sorry for me. What a bad deal for a man to lose a fur coat because of some Persians! The coat is expensive. And the man is all right. They looked everywhere for the coat.

Ushnuiyeh, Sharafkhaneh, and many other places were plundered in about the same way—and two or three times.

Dilman was plundered later—during the withdrawal of our troops to Russia; however, it wasn't the departing troops who plundered it, but the town garrison. The town was divided into sectors; each company pillaged its own sector. To be able to see better, they set the town on fire.

The town of Khoi was plundered by the troops passing through it on their way to Dzhulfa during the evacuation of Persia.

Tabriz wasn't plundered. The bazaar at Tabriz has goods from all over the world; it's a big city with goods lying about in piles.

It's so big and intricate that when the merchants themselves go into an unfamiliar section, they take along a beggar for a guide.

Looters went into the bazaar several times, but they didn't come back out. . . . They got separated in there and, in all probability, were torn to pieces.

Tabriz wasn't sacked.

But the fate of the Kurdish city on Turkish territory, the fate of rich Solozhbulak, once a notable trading center on the caravan route, was sad. It was plundered right up to the roofs, that is, completely leveled; although no one plunders clay walls, without roofs they dissolve in the rain and only the baseboards remain. The roofs were removed and sold.

I haven't spoken yet about how Petersburg kept us informed. They were always sending us some communiqué on the Democratic Conference.

I remember being called at night. You went down a narrow lane, entered the courtyard, covered over with almost bare grapevines, and into the telegraph office. One wall, as is generally the case in Persia, was made of glass (it had been calico, but we put in glass without any putty); it was dark outside the windows.

You walked up to the direct-line apparatus to Tiflis. Glowing in the darkness, the plummet of the regulator goes around; the weight on the mechanism slowly drops. Something clicks; a tape with words on it creeps out.

Sometimes the apparatus gets off the track and starts printing t-t-t-t-rrrrr-vvv . . . .

Some sort of gibberish comes creeping out of the apparatus like white macaroni. You interrupt it: "What's happening there? What are the Bolsheviks up to? . . . Send underwear for the troops, currency . . . ."

The apparatus quietly tears along: "ter . . . ter . . . ter . . . Tereshchenko speaking . . . the democracy . . . ." The white tapeworm creeps along. . . .

Tereshchenko crept through the apparatus until October. . . .

Then confusion, a communication about the coup, about how the front and the Ukrainian National Assembly "insisted on the point of view of the Provisional Government" . . . then the staggering telegram from the postal clerks that they were being driven out . . . then a communication about Kerensky's capture of Petrograd . . . then . . . the tape from Russia broke off like that telegram in

Wells' novel that the immortal inventor of Cavorite sent from the moon.[26]

We were left alone.

The army committee passed a strongly worded resolution about the Bolsheviks. It was a joint session of the army committee and the regimental committees; only one member of the army committee spoke out for the Bolsheviks—and that was apparently Comrade Novomysky. He said, "Comrades, we don't have either cloth or leather. How can we fight?" He was a good man, who later on helped us a lot. But I think he left his faith in the people behind in Persia.

Task and I were left high and dry in the army—commissars of a nonexistent government.

Now about Task.

Efrem Task was an old party worker, a Menshevik. His specialty in the party had been the installation of underground presses.

Enterprises of this type require enormous self-control and Task had it.

He had spent a lot of time in prisons and had escaped many times, and his whole life was dominated by one thought—he was a typical professional revolutionary in the best and purest sense of that word.

For me, a dilettante, it was simply terrifying to see such persistence and dedication to an idea. He had one defect—the quick temper of a man who has been tortured a lot; therefore he wasn't good at working directly with the masses.

But he had mastered all the techniques of conferences, resolutions and all the organized experience that lies behind these techniques.

After the sharply worded resolution that the army committee had passed, after the telegram about the armistice, in a situation where the troops were Russian, the government was Transcaucasian and the soldiers wanted to go home, it was incredibly difficult to continue as before. The simplest thing of all was to leave. The commissar in the adjacent army had been arrested. We weren't bothered.

Task called a conference; he knew how to get the men's attention and to attract a large attendance.

Even the Bolsheviks came to the conference; they made up about a third of the group; I remember only one name—Baburishvili.

We had to reach some kind of understanding.

At that time, the Constituent Assembly still hadn't been dissolved; we agreed on the Constituent Assembly and on recognition of the Transcaucasian government, on the condition, however, that one of its tasks should be to fight against Kaledin, the representative of Russian reaction. The armistice was recognized as an established fact—there had already been a telegram about it from front headquarters—but we decided to wait for the end of negotiations. In any case, the mechanism of the army had been preserved.

At this time, I was called to Solozhbulak.

We learned by telegram that there had been a pogrom in Solozhbulak; moreover, disorders were breaking out on the question of organizing national cadres: the Georgians in one infantry division had been sent to the rear for organization into some sort of national regiment; the remaining Russians also went to the rear. Simultaneously, we received a telegram from the front to the effect that the Afan column of the Grozny Regiment had decided to move to the rear; it was notifying us so that we might take suitable measures to safeguard the discarded supplies.

I left that night. The high walls of the American mission flashed by, then the house of the Russian Colonel Stolder, commander of the Persian Cossacks.

Stolder's home was in the country; the windows were lit from within by the bright light of kerosene lamps.

Our Talbot glided into the beautiful moonlit Persian night. The moon seemed very high. The sky, the Persian sky, hovered gently overhead. It was an ethereal, spacious sky.

Someone had set fire to a top-heavy old willow, of the kind that grow along all the roads here; it was burning on the other side of the ditch. A tree, precious in these parts, was burning. For a Moslem, it's a good deed to dig a well or plant a tree. One of our men passing by had set fire to it.

The fire, just barely visible, was quietly licking the edges of old cracks, disturbing the blue tranquility of the night and its sharp, blue-gray shadows.

All around, for dozens of acres, vines lay on the parched gray earth. The vineyards extended as far as the eye could see, like our

Russian fields. We drove on, fording rivers, driving past the high arches of steep, half-destroyed Persian bridges.

The road started to climb. Now the land around was studded with the edges of small rocks, black and white under an avalanche of moonlight.

Then the shadows turned gray; the wind began to blow; the sun rose. We had descended again and were driving along the shore of Lake Urmia. By morning we were in Haidarabad.

Nomads' tents, half buried in the ground, stood among the rocks, as well as several dugouts, whose long sloping roofs could be seen in a dozen places.

A gray building suggesting the European tropics, made out of gray unbaked brick. A huge iron barge was unloading at the pier. On the shore lay heaps of rails fastened together with iron ties.

A horse-drawn, narrow-gauge railroad was to run from there to the Ranandus Gorge in the direction of Mosul. I suspect that the rails proved useful to the Turks.

And that is Haidarabad in its entirety.

Under a small lean-to completely open on all sides, some beggars were warming themselves at a fire of dry grass.

By then we took the war in stride; it chafed no more than the boots we wore. We looked at these beggars calmly, the way we looked at a wall, the way we looked at all of Persia, and now at the death throes of Russia.

It was very cold. In my field jacket, put on over a heavy shirt and sweater, with a felt cloak over my poncho, I was freezing. The Kurds were almost naked.

For some, their only clothing consisted of a strange-looking felt cape; it was cut in such a way that it stuck up on their shoulders like the imploring stumps of a man with no arms.

We were used to beggars now. Children about five years old wandered all around the camps with nothing but a black rag for a shirt. Their eyes festered and swarmed with flies.

Hunched over, with the mechanical gesture of a tired animal, they picked through the garbage looking for something edible. At night they gathered at the mess halls and got warm. A few of them, mainly the older ones, were taken into the companies as helpers; the others died as quietly and slowly as only the infinitely steadfast human being can die.

We drove out of Haidarabad on newly constructed roads, where we passed Persians and Kurds shuffling along under the supervision of our combat engineers; we also drove through salt marshes. At one point the car started to spin its wheels; we got out of this salt swamp only by putting dry grass under the wheels.

All along the road, we saw ravaged villages.

I had seen a lot of destruction. I saw the incinerated villages of Galicia and houses reduced to pulp, but I wasn't prepared for the sight of the Persian ruins.

When you take the roof off a house built of clay and straw, the house simply turns into a pile of clay.

And the road went on, endless, like the war—all military roads are dead ends.

In the salt marshes, I came across herds of horses. As I've already written, we didn't have enough fodder; there was no point in keeping the horses that had lost their strength. It didn't pay to feed them and no one had enough pity to kill them, so they were driven out to pasture on the bare steppe. They were slowly dying. And I drove past.

Apropos of pity. The following scene was described to me. There's a Cossack. In front of him lies a naked baby, abandoned by the Kurds. The Cossack wants to kill it. He hits it once and stops to think, hits it again and stops to think.

They tell him: "Finish it off."

And he: "I can't—I feel sorry for it."

I arrived in Solozhbulak. A small town in a hollow. At one time it had been famous for its fur coats decorated with gold.

The pogrom was over: everything was picked clean.

I went to the army committee, assembled the regimental committees and started to talk.

They angrily answered me that the Kurds were enemies. "The Kurd is the enemy"—that's the byword of the Russian soldier in Persia. And right there they thought it over and said that they weren't for the pogrom.

I found out some strange things. Except for the Kubans and one medical company, everyone had joined in the pillaging—one and all.

Serving in our supply trains—apparently as volunteers—were some Molokans, with their three-horse teams.

There are the following associations: Molokans, Dukhobors, White Arabia, Mysticism, then something else. . . . Well, even these Molokans joined in the pillaging. The gunners pillaged, too.

During the pogrom, the division commander locked himself in his house and wouldn't come out.

Then, too, let's not overlook some customs of the Persian-Kurdish pogroms in this story.

When the pillaging began, the Kurds—Solozhbulak was a Kurdish town—would take their wives out on the roofs, not taking any of their things with them and leaving the city completely at the mercy of the looters. This way they avoided rape—not always, of course.

The grief and shame of the pogroms lay like dust on my soul and "sorrow, like a troop of Negroes, bloodied my heart." (This is the second part of a phrase from some Persian poem.)

I don't want to weep alone, so I'll say something else too painful to hide.

One soldier argued energetically before the army committee that it was wrong to take things from people when they were starving.

It should be said that our army, in contrast to some of the corps in the Caucasus, did not go hungry: at least one and a half pounds of bread and plenty of mutton were issued every day. The outposts guarding the passes were an exception.

One soldier, dispatched to look for provisions, brought back samples of the Kurds' starvation bread. The bread was made out of coal and clay, with a very small amount of acorns added.

No one wanted to listen to him.

You can imagine how the Kurds hated our requisitioning parties —all the more since many divisions simply helped themselves; no records were kept.

The Kurds surrounded one such party. The commander, Ivanov by name, defended himself for a long time with a saber before they cut off his head and gave it to the children to play with.

And the children played with it for three weeks.

Thus did the Kurdish tribe. And the Russian tribe set upon the Kurds a punitive squadron which exacted for the heads of the dead a recompense in cattle and ravaged the guilty villages, as well as several that were not guilty.

Men I knew told me that when our troops burst into a village, the women would smear their faces, breasts and body from knees to waist with excrement to save themselves from rape. The soldiers wiped them off with rags and raped them.

I assembled the garrison at a meeting outside the town and tried to get them to denounce the principle of the pogrom, but to tell the truth, I got nowhere.

The crowd kept interrupting me. "Wild beasts have lived here since time immemorial; we were brought here—and we've turned into wild beasts. Why are we here?"

And I would tell them that they wouldn't be here long, but that they would pay for the blood they had spilled and it would be hard to return home across that blood.

And who was to blame? Those who sent them there and also the already half-forgotten, but unexpiated, crime of war.

I wandered around town. On one corner, several soldiers were having a little fun, kicking a cat up in the air with a kerosene can tied to its tail.

A long row of Kurds were sitting on their haunches, waiting for our doctor to see them. Now and then women would appear on the streets. Their faces weren't covered. Tall, slender, handsome Kurds would pass by in turbans turned up into a peaked cap with a black tassel. Their shirts were tied with wide belts made of a long, long piece of material.

And all around—havoc: some dirty rags, disdained by the marauders, littered the ground.

A Kurdish boy sat in the street and sang:

> The night is dark and I can't see,
> Marusya, come along with me.

A man was dying in broad daylight, writhing and twisting; his bare back and shoulder blades were terrible. People walking by stepped over him.

That night I sent Task a panicky telegram:

"Have inspected Kurdistan units. In the name of revolution and humanity, demand withdrawal of troops."

This telegram didn't go over too well—apparently, it's naïve and funny to demand the withdrawal of troops in the name of humanity. But I was right.

We were leaving anyway and keeping the troops in Kurdistan

was useless. It would have been better to withdraw the troops than do what was done—put the troops in the position of having to flee, leaving even their supplies behind.

I don't want to seem smarter than I am, so I'll simply say what I think.

All our shrewd and far-sighted policies were for nothing. If, instead of trying to make history, we had simply tried to consider ourselves responsible for the separate events that make up history, then perhaps this wouldn't have turned out so ludicrously.

A man should worry less about history and more about his own biography.

I left Solozhbulak and set out for Afan along the bank of a stream.

I kept seeing the same things on the road: ravaged villages and dead people. I counted eight bodies.

I've seen a lot of corpses in my lifetime, but these struck me by their everyday appearance. They hadn't been killed in the war. No, they had been killed like dogs by someone wanting to test his rifle.

The driver drove carefully, now and then exclaiming, "There, that looks like a dead donkey; no, it's another man." It was hard on him; he had drivers' nerves. Drivers are nervous.

After that, I saw three more bodies, all laid out with their feet touching by someone following the Kurdish custom of using corpses as roadside decorations. On the face of one corpse, a cat was sitting, all bristled up, awkwardly gnawing at the cheeks with its small mouth. . . .

But then we passed an artillery unit—a mountain battery coming from Solozhbulak to relieve some other unit. Strong mules were carrying the artfully packed cannons. From all corners of this pack, Kurdish utensils and rags were sticking out—spoils from the pogrom at Solozhbulak.

So I passed along the battery, reviewing the troops entrusted to me.

I arrived in Afan.

A narrow cleft in the mountains had been made slightly wider. Two nomads' tents, two or three wooden huts, dugouts, a stream, a herd of reddish-brown sheep. Bare mountains all around. And on the other side of the mountains, the Kurds.

On top of the mountains, our defensive fortifications.

I had a talk with the regimental commander. As far as I

remember, he was a man highly respected by the soldiers. He told me that the soldiers' hostility toward the Kurds had reached such a point that they, or anyway some of them, had burned—I don't remember whether dead or alive—three Kurds, peaceful workers from this area. And now, as a result, they feared the Kurds even more.

By the way, part of the regiment had voted for the SR's; the other part voted for the Bolsheviks. I don't remember the exact tallies.

I went to the regiment and said to the men, "Comrades, in driving over here, I saw eight bodies along the road. Why are you killing people?"

Someone answered me, "You counted wrong. There are more than that."

I said to him, "I don't have the authority to give orders and I don't want to beg; I'm telling you that no matter what resolutions you pass, you're not leaving here until you're told. The road is long; if you want to, go at your own risk—without barges—go on and try it. The general withdrawal will begin soon."

And I left. I don't know whether because of me or on their own account, but they did wait for the general rout.

And I went back to Urmia, inspecting the Kuban units along the way. Their horses were in such a state that you could hardly imagine even leading them. They were supposed to leave in the first wave, so that we could move the fodder to the rear. I arrived in Urmia. Here I was told that the demobilization had already begun on the order of Przhevalsky (commander of front-line headquarters); soldiers over thirty years of age were being released.

And in the meantime, strange as it may seem, some who had been away on leave actually returned, saying that things were bad in Russia, very bad.

A Cossack, tall as a beanstalk, with his small head completely shaved, arrived from Kiev, from the Cossack Legislative Assembly. He was a commissar of the Cossack troops.

Russia was beginning to break down into its primary factors. We gave the Cossack a hostile reception. But he wasn't put out: he sat with us, drank his tea with small bites of sugar and thought his own thoughts.

I think his mission was to speed up the evacuation of the Kubans.

The Kubans were in a hurry to get home. I remember the day that one unit stationed in the city departed. They engaged musicians, got a pitcher of wine and did Cossack dances for two hours without stopping.

Then, with some difficulty, they mounted their horses and rode away, seemingly sober.

Some Persians stood across the way and watched fondly.

Even the sailors of the Black Sea fleet had taken part in the Dilman pogrom.

Already headquarters was being guarded only by Aissors. By this time, all that remained of the Army of the Caucasus were the various headquarters companies.

Bolsheviks had appeared on the army council—Baburishvili, some dentist and a sailor named Saltykov.

The flotilla had been hopeless as far as work was concerned, but was vital for the withdrawal.

It was teeming with intrigues. One officer, Khatchikov, won a group over to his side by proposing to unite all the ships into one flotilla—that is, add to the military ships those attached to the railroad and the Regional Union and then stay in Persia and set up a private shipping company.

However, until they could get organized, he proposed that they start hauling currants and dried fruit back and forth along with the military cargos.

And all the while, the evacuation was proceeding—the whole thing simply amounted to seizure of the ships.

Naturally, this little arrangement would have made Khatchikov immeasurably rich, since there is gold in Persia.

To implement this intention, Khatchikov managed to get himself elected commander of the flotilla, though in our army the elective principle still didn't exist.

We fought this scheme as hard as we could, even appointed commissions; but the flotilla committee ruled that he didn't come under our jurisdiction, which was limited to dry land.

We appealed the case to the Central Caspian Committee, which recalled Saltykov and Khatchikov.

According to the information I received from the commissar of the Baltic Fleet, Penkaitis, Khatchikov eventually helped hand over our Caspian fleet to the English.

This way, his natural bent for commerce and industry found a suitable outlet.

And the troops were leaving. It had been assumed that headquarters would be transferred to the other shore of the lake, where it would be on the railroad line, but this would have been impossible to do without accelerating the pace of the troops toward the rear.

Because of the withdrawal, the problem of currency exchange again became critical. The withdrawing Transbaikal Cossacks arrested the new chairman of the army committee, who had been elected at the army conference; that was Comrade Tatiev, a very honest man who devoutly believed in world revolution.

These Cossacks demanded that their currency be exchanged at a rate of nine shahis for one ruble. They rushed to the governor and, by threatening the bankers with sticks, he got the exchange. Tatiev was released.

⚓

The armistice didn't present much of a problem on our front. We had almost no contact with the enemy. Winter had swept the Turks and us from the mountains into the valleys. Outposts were maintained only at a few points.

The condition of the Turkish army was poor. All they had to eat was fried wheat. They weren't even considering an offensive. The Petrograd government had already concluded an armistice with the Turks.

It was necessary to make this state of affairs official and we received an order to that effect from the regional soviet.

An airplane was dispatched to the Turks to drop proclamations suggesting that we begin negotiations. In addition, we sent a radiogram. The main problem, in general, was to negotiate a line of demarcation.

The Turks answered us with a radio communication in German and proposed that we go to Mosul for negotiations.

Those sent were Colonel Ern, Task and Saltykov, whom the army committee was willing to send anywhere, only as far away as possible.

I didn't like Saltykov, with his self-assurance and cockiness.

I stayed with Tatiev to manage the army. I had the same feeling I'd had when wrestling. You're grappling with a man many times stronger than you are. You have him in a bear hug and you're still holding your own, but your heart has already surrendered. You're holding your own, but you aren't breathing.

And the brakes had to be applied.

It was easier for Tatiev. He had received a telegram that we got by accident about how Russia's peace offer had been received in Berlin—a telegram now forgotten about the tears of joy in the streets—so he told me in his soft voice with a Georgian accent: "You'll see. Our revolution will save the world."

I'm now writing at midnight on August 9.

Hungary has fallen. The banker is raking our stake from the table.

My head aches; I want to sleep all the time. I'm suffering from severe anemia. If I suddenly stand up from my chair now, my head will start spinning and I'll fall.

I can write only at night. I know what that means. The oil has burned up and, by nighttime, when all my strength is gone, the wick burns. . . .

This is how I lived.

I woke up in the morning in a small white room. It was freezing cold. The heat had escaped through the panes of the window, installed without any putty. But the sun was shining. I fed the small iron stove with poplar logs; it got warm, cozy, and smelled of resin.

It was the best moment of the day.

I got up and opened a pile of telegrams—all about one thing: the disintegration that demanded immediate withdrawal and prevented it.

Individual units were already rushing to Dzhulfa, trying to get to Russia as fast as possible.

A bottleneck developed. The escaping soldiers seized the trains bringing us provisions, threw off their cargo, boarded them and turned them back toward Russia.

The Dilman work detail had fled.

I cursed the tracks along which they were traveling and delayed them.

We were carrying on various negotiations with the local Persian community.

Here's a characteristic instance of the cunning simple-minded-ness of the Persian.

When our men were going to Mosul for the negotiations, the Persian governor proposed that the negotiations be held in Urmia instead and, rather hesitantly but seriously, he said that Persia, for its part, demanded Baghdad, which had once belonged to them. Unfortunately, we weren't in a position to hand over Baghdad. The Aissors were convinced that Task would either be killed in Mosul or sent to Constantinople as a hostage.

In the meantime, we waited for Task and visited the Persians.

One time I was invited to visit a local democrat, Arshan Dama-yuneh. We walked through several courtyards. A servant with a lantern accompanied us, bowing continually. Servants were stand-ing along the walls of the last passageway in crude shoes and shabby, semimilitary Persian uniforms, throwing flowers under our feet.

We entered the rooms.

The blinding light of many lamps with dual wicks (in Persia you hardly ever see any other kind) hurt our eyes: we were no longer used to bright lights. Carpets of many colors covered the walls.

Guests in evening dress, with dazzling white shirt fronts and small, black Persian caps, were sitting around conversing with officers from the French mission, who wore tight gray uniforms of good clean broadcloth.

From the ceiling hung a chandelier with candles—a crystal chandelier—decorated with glass spheres silvered on the inside.

The brand-new white calico tablecloths crackled and showed the trademarks and labels that they still bore.

We, the committee members—all the soldiers and I—arrived dirty, disheveled, tired and, above all, guilty.

Dinner began. Somewhere outside, an enormous local orchestra struck up "Homesickness"[27] on their lutes.

There was fine china and crystal on the table. There's a lot of fine china in Persia.

Either Shustov or Saradjev cognac, watery sour milk and courses without end.

Speeches were given. . . . The governor crinkled his eyes in a friendly way and said, "Chox, chox jakshi."[28] The translator, an Armenian Dashnaktsation, was nice, though a little insane (he was proud of having been in a group armed with bombs that had once occupied the Ottoman Bank to force a guarantee of Armenia's independence; the group had been coaxed out of there with its valises and bombs only by the false guarantees of France). This translator gave a free translation of the speeches, liberally inserting all his own thoughts and hopes and choking with delight.

My neighbor translated for me the program of the party which called itself Socialist Democratic.

Its first point was: "Serfdom is not to be abolished." I checked this translation with someone else; it turned out to be exact.

A program for doing away with pauperism followed.

I stood up with a glass in my hand. Looking at the sleeve of my frayed field jacket, I started to speak, interrupting the speech with long pauses in which the translator babbled.

I spoke first about how we wanted nothing for Persia but its good fortune and how, despite all our pogroms, we respected the country more than anyone.

At the end, I lost my temper and wished Persia a social revolution.

The lutes were playing "Homesickness."

Another evening I went to the home of Aga Petros for a dinner party, to celebrate Mar Shimun's being awarded the Order of St. Vladimir.

To get to the home of Petros, you had to go through long passageways; each passageway ended at a clay building, in which the way led out the rear door, then turned.

You don't take a house like this by surprise.

At the last door, there was a flock of ducks and geese. You find this at the house of almost every Persian.

The metallic cackle of birds had at first awakened me almost every night.

There was no garden in the courtyard of Petros.

It was night. High on the wall, huddled from the cold, sat a peacock. The heavy, magnificent tail even in the moonlight stood out sharply against the whitish clay.

Only Aissors had been invited.

The servants, in colored socks, went to and fro without a sound.

A breeze made sails of the calico at the windows.

Vadbolsky arrived. In general, he lived like a hermit and went nowhere.

Vadbolsky conducted the ceremony with casual deference and awarded the decoration "with trembling hands."

In his own way, he knew the East well and was respected there.

The patriarch, with his ruddy face, was deeply moved; his eyes were shining; his hair was strangely gray, a completely silver gray and he was only twenty-six years old.

Later on, the Kurd Sinko lured him into a trap and killed him.

There were stacks of rifles in the hall.

They had been taken away from the Aissors as soon as they arrived at the house.

Everyone was preoccupied.

I'm writing so much about the Aissors because I considered it possible to make them into a significant force.

More accurately—I saw no other possibilities for creating such a force.

In addition, we were obligated to save these people, who had cast their lot with Russia.

It's interesting how legends are created.

Petros, or some orthodox priest—an Aissor—the one who was apparently always attending some reception at the governor's with the manner of a wandering monk, said that we shouldn't get mad at the Aissors, "the poor devils"; he told me:

"You know, our women went to Vadbolsky and said to him— 'we'll give you our husbands, only order us to be killed: anything, but don't leave us at the mercy of the Persians.' "

Of course, no one went to Vadbolsky with these words, but everyone was thinking them and hearing them said.

The Armenians and the Aissors made us the following proposition: They asked us to leave two Russian regiments as a nucleus around which national militias could be built. But where could we get two regiments?

However, we could give them weapons and instructors.

We had extra weapons. And many of the officers and sergeants stayed on as instructors, expecting nothing good for themselves in Russia.

I was in favor of a rapid, frantically rapid, mobilization.

Russian troops handed over their weapons very reluctantly, but I knew a way.

All that had to be done was to give leaves to a whole detachment

—for instance, the detachment assigned to the weapons depot. They would leave and you could take the weapons.

Incidentally, about weapons. The soldiers were firmly convinced that there was an order requiring them to take their rifles when they left Persia. It was said that the soldiers would not be let into Russia without their rifles.

The regional soviet itself, to my repeated inquiries for permission to release the soldiers with weapons, replied with an order to disarm the demobilized men. But how to disarm them?

Considering that the rifles would be carried off anyway, I proposed that we allow this, but write into the documents of each soldier that he was carrying a rifle of such-and-such number and so many cartridges, which he would be obliged to register at his local soviet.

I wanted to do this in order to discourage the selling of rifles.

A rifle—especially a Russian one—is a treasure in the East. At the beginning of our retreat, the Persians gave two to three thousand rubles for a rifle; for a cartridge, they paid three rubles in the bazaar; for the same cartridge, they gave a bottle of cognac at the Kangarlu station.

For the sake of comparison, consider the price of the women abducted from Persia and from the Caucasus by our soldiers.

In Feodosia, for example, a woman cost fifteen rubles used and forty rubles unused, and she was yours forever.

So why not sell a rifle!

Even the cannons were sold. But, after all, this doesn't surprise anyone now.

I wasn't allowed to register the rifles carried off, but was ordered to oppose it.

In any case, it was possible to get weapons for the national militia.

Comrade Stepanians organized the Armenian units; he had been chairman of the army committee and then an aide-de-camp to the commissar.

On first acquaintance, Stepanians gave the impression of not being a very cultured man.

He had been born in Russia and apparently had few connections with the local Armenians.

But I saw him grow in stature when the question of defending his people arose. I was amazed at his decisiveness and authority.

The Armenians have the same thing that you find only among the Jews—national discipline.

The Dashnaktsations made themselves as comfortable in the home of Manusurians as in their own.

The host himself held the reins of Stepanians' horse.

When the Armenian deserters had to be found, the following announcement was posted: "You, Armenian deserters, are ordered to appear by such-and-such a date; those not appearing will be killed by such-and-such a date."

And, of course, those who didn't appear would be killed by their closest relatives.

Because of this mobilization, friction developed between Mar Shimun and Petros.

But in the end, they made it up by having Petros become Mar Shimun's chief of staff.

Petros was upset. "This is war—you can't defend Urmia and not Gerdyk!" But our troops had already pulled out of Gerdyk. He sent a dozen of his own men there.

Our men were pulling out, discarding supplies, discarding weapons and sugar—an enormous amount of sugar.

We were returning to Kurdistan all that we had pillaged.

I wanted to turn over our supply depots to the newly organized troops—the things which we couldn't take along.

They could have hauled them off somehow. And then this equipment would have stayed in the hands of our friends.

By the way, because of this mobilization, I finally had a falling out with Task when he returned.

He said that the mobilization, especially when done so hastily, would lead to adventures of the Prince Wied variety. I was very let down, since I saw no other alternatives.

Task was oriented to Russia, to getting our army out and home in one piece—if possible. My orientation was local.

If there had been only one person close to me, if I had not, in addition, wanted to get back to libraries, I would have gone nowhere: I would have stayed put in the East.

One other characteristic reconciled me to the East—the absence of anti-Semitism.

In the army they were already saying that Shklovsky was . . . a yid, as I was informed by a member of the profession, a Jewish officer just graduated from the military academy.

In Persia, and apparently in Turkey, Jews are not attacked.

Here they speak in a language that apparently comes from the Aramaic, while the Jews in the Russian Caucasus speak in some sort of Tatar dialect.

When the English took Jerusalem,[29] a delegation of Aissors came to me bringing ten pounds of sugar and some Oramar currants and this is what they said.

But first just a few words. There was tea on the table because the arriving guests had to be served something:

"Our people and your people will once again live together side by side. True, we once destroyed Solomon's temple, but later we raised it up again."

That's what they said—considering themselves descendants of the Assyrians and me a Jew.

Actually, they were mistaken—I'm not all Jew and they're not descendants of the Assyrians.

By blood, they're Semitic—Arameans.

But the sense of uninterrupted tradition in their conversation was characteristic—a distinctive feature of the peoples here.

Urmia was restless. Drunken soldiers were walking around, shooting into the air at night, carrying in their blood the germs of another pogrom.

One night, just at dawn, a Persian ran into my room; two soldiers were chasing him with rifles—they were drunk.

I had to take a revolver and personally escort him to his house.

There were strange stories. One morning while Task was still away at the negotiations in Mosul, some barefoot men in filthy clothes came to see us—two or three of them had rifles.

"Who are you?"

"We're prisoners from the stockade."

"Well, who let you out?"

"We just left."

And the guards said, "The prisoners decided to come and see you, so how could we stop them?"

Among the prisoners were some condemned to hard labor.

They did have something to complain about. It was filthy in the stockades, so filthy that the prisoners would break the windows in the winter and then it was cold without the glass. There was no place to bathe and no clean underwear. They were held a long, long time without questioning—months.

The next day we went to check the list of prisoners. It turned out that anyone who felt like it did the arresting: the judge advocate, security, the unit commanders, the commanding officer and the army committee.

And you can say without exaggerating that the men arrested were forgotten. Not out of cruelty, but out of general confusion and a lack of concern for people.

The Kurds were kept apart. They were put in a cellar. It was called the Kurdish cellar. It was a dismal, gray room with a strong smell. The Kurds kept in it were charged, for the most part, with espionage.

Some of the Kurds had children; obviously, they had no place to go, so they sat with their fathers in the hole. What surprised me most of all was why the prisoners didn't leave.

I know for sure that it wouldn't have occurred to the guards to shoot.

But they didn't leave. Obviously some sense of propriety still remained.

⟨✵⟩

The results of the elections for the Constituent Assembly held in our Persian army were about as follows: the SR slate received two-thirds of the votes: the Bolsheviks, one-third; the Mensheviks and Kadets received a few dozen each.

The insignificant number of votes received by the Kadets stems from the fact that all the men in small units of two or three hundred know each other; and if an officer had voted for the Kadets, he would have been open to the charge of being a Kadet and this, in those times, was not without danger.

⟨✵⟩

I keep describing misery and more misery. And I'm sick of it.

In all the hundreds of thousands of soldiers in our army, couldn't there have just possibly have been something good, something worthwhile?

There was. But the condition of our army—the total disillusionment, the deep despondency, the willingness to resort even to sabotage if only to end the war—all this brought out the worst, not the best, side of the men.

Of course, it's not the Russian people who are to blame—at least they're not the main culprits.

I think that any army put in that situation at that moment would have behaved the same way.

We had posted special commissars at the landing piers. Men to keep their eye on the troop embarkation. These men didn't run away, though it was very hard for them.

The medical unit worked pretty well.

In every unit, there were men who did some job that they considered to be for the common good.

But the army, lacking the instinct of self-preservation that a nation has, was sick, and sick people rarely put their best foot forward.

One thing that can be mentioned is the good attitude of the soldiers toward each other—they weren't like wolves with each other.

But the most important thing is that the men waited their turn, usually with patience, and put up with the situation when in fact there was no longer anything to hold them back.

Even on the road, this patience lasted, withstanding everything in the name of the word "home."

But I've gotten off the track.

I ordered all the wine in town to be destroyed. Technically I had the right—though this was of very little interest to me—because the year before we had forbidden the production of wine. . . .

A special commission made up of Persians and members of our committee destroyed the wine.

When the wine in the main wine cellar, belonging to a certain Dzhaparidzeh, was destroyed, the water in the ditch ran pink and a huge crowd fixedly eyed the scarlet stream running out from under the wall of the big, ugly gray house.

The destruction of the wine didn't take place without misunderstandings.

This place smelled too much of wine and money.

The drunkenness tapered off, but didn't disappear. Wine was hauled in from the other side of the lake.

Meanwhile, famine stalked the land.

It had already become commonplace to see people dying in the street.

People were fighting over the garbage thrown out of the headquarters mess hall.

At dinnertime, hungry children gathered in our compound.

One morning when I got up and opened the street door, some-thing soft fell to the side. I stooped down and looked. . . . Some-one had left a dead baby at my door.

I think it was a complaint.

Delegations of women kept coming to ask the consul for help. But what could he do? He was the consul of a nonexistent govern-ment; he might as well have been consul in the land of blue antelopes.

Condemned to watch, I watched as the Persians gave alms to their beggars—two raisins or one almond.

The American mission did more—actually it was the only source of food for the populace.

Caravans of camels loaded with silver were often received by Doctor Shedd, a gray-haired old man—head of the mission.

I don't know how much we Russians were to blame for the famine.

In all probability, we were responsible to the extent that the war created a class of refugees. We also hindered the cultivation of the fields by driving out the inhabitants and, what is more important, by upsetting the irrigation system.

All the fields here produce a harvest only when irrigated.

The fields are divided into sections and then inundated a section at a time.

The water is apportioned according to a strict order, established and strictly regulated by local customs.

Under the influence of individual landowners, acting in their own interests or sometimes thinking to serve justice, our troops tampered with this arrangement.

As a result, part of the fields went without water.

In addition, it was apparently a bad year in general.

To make matters worse, we requisitioned their barley—wheat we imported from Russia—and did nothing to provide for the populace.

The English would have acted differently: they would have found bread and fed those who were starving.

However, the Persians preferred us to the English.

"You pillage; the English suck."

By this time, some units in our army no longer recognized the authority of the army committee or, for that matter, my authority, the source of which wasn't clear even to me.

Tabriz had seceded and was attempting to organize its own army congress. Then Khoi seceded and proclaimed itself autonomous, but quickly reconsidered.

At least, I received a telegram from there about the pogroms.

The withdrawal was supposed to be carried out in the following way: part of the troops were to go on foot to Dzhulfa and part from Solozhbulak along the right shore of the lake, more or less from Urmia to Tabriz. The units that left first were supposed to wait at prearranged places and guard the road while the last groups passed through.

In this way, the road was supposed to be protected all the way to Petrovsk.

Such a movement is called "to advance in waves."

Naturally, nothing worked out.

Already the first regiments dispatched were rushing to get as far as possible from Persia.

A great many wanted to get to Stavropol Province.

One division got through relatively well—I've forgotten its number. It went in march formation, with the wagons in the middle, and got through without losing a single man.

Those individual men who had left on the orders demobilizing all men over thirty years of age naturally tried to get as far away as possible. And they took the railroad cars intended for us. Our cars had special brakes, but they took them in the vicinity of Rostov.

Only four cars were left standing at the siding from Sharafkhaneh to Sufian.

And the units of what was apparently the Fourth Corps of the Caucasian Army were moving toward Dzhulfa.

The cars bringing us provisions were seized.

Headquarters was still functioning, if half-heartedly. But then why should they take heart?

To our complete surprise, Stepanians' wife arrived in Urmia with their child. She brought newspapers with her. She was a typical Russian female student. She brought with her an atmosphere of a rather philistine, optimistic Bolshevism. But somehow she didn't bring it off too convincingly.

The main thing was missing—revolutionary zeal. Perhaps I was mistaken; perhaps I'm mistaken now. All I saw was the slump, the abatement of energy.

The revolution was going downhill, not uphill.

And it made little difference what was causing this decline.

But if we had been asked then, "Who are you for—Kaledin, Kornilov or the Bolsheviks?," Task and I would have chosen the Bolsheviks.

However, in a certain comedy, the harlequin was asked, "Do you prefer to be hanged or quartered?"

He answered, "I prefer soup."

Task still hadn't come. Once we got a radiogram from Ern which set out the Turks' terms for the armistice. Ern asked for Vadbolsky's approval. He replied: Sign!

Then Task came—on horseback, as I recall. The dissolution of the army had taken its toll of automobiles: no car had been sent for him.

The Turks had conducted him as far as Sheikhin-Gerusin, from where he went by foot along a telegraph line whose poles had been chopped down for firewood; only the four rows of wire stretched out in the dust.

The Turks noticed that we had sent no one for our own men. We no longer even pretended that we were an army.

I'll pass along some excerpts of Task's story.

To go through peace negotiations from the position of weakness is a rough business.

When our delegates were on their way to the Turks, the latter met them in a pass.

To the Turks, peace is happiness. They embraced our men and laughed with joy.

The Turkish soldiers, thin and ragged, looked at our delegates and smiled. . . .

They went by way of the famous Ranandus Gorge, the route we would have taken in attacking Mosul.

This is a deep and precipitous gorge. At one point, a waterfall drops from the very brink of the mountain wall. The water shatters against the rocks and shoots up in a geyser with clouds of foam.

On the way, they stopped briefly in Ardebil, a circular town with high walls. There's one street in town—the square in the center.

They came into Mesopotamia and began to encounter herds of horses, gaunt and sway-backed. The car had to maneuver between dead horses.

They drove into Mosul. The Germans, masters at that time of

both us and the Turks, received the delegates coldly and, without further ado, proposed that they sign the armistice agreement, which stipulated, among other conditions, the immediate evacuation of Persia.

Naturally, we had to evacuate Persia and we knew that we would, but we didn't want to do it in response to a German order.

Unfortunately, I don't remember all the German conditions.

You could piece it together from the Tiflis newspapers. I think the archives of our headquarters were lost.

You could get all the details from the German newspapers or from Efrem Task.

The representative of the Turks—and a most amiable representative at that—was Halim Pasha.

Halim Pasha's fame in the East is enormous. It was this very same Halim Pasha who, during the evacuation of Erzurum, buried four hundred Armenian babies alive.

I think in Turkish they call this "slamming the door."

And the negotiations had to be conducted with this man, quite nice to all appearances.

The Turks were overjoyed about the peace. Halim Pasha spoke bitterly of how they had had to fight for ten years.

By the way, Task was at his house for a reception.

A Jewish doctor was sitting on the floor, playing on something like a zither and singing.

In the most pathetic spots, Halim Pasha would join in, snapping his fingers and taking the singer a glass of vodka.

The singer would kiss the master's hand.

Halim Pasha spoke enthusiastically about the annulment of debts: "That's very fine, I like that, we don't want to pay either."

There were Russian prisoners in town, cowed and cringing at the sight of a German soldier.

Our men tried to talk to them. Some of them leaned toward a monarchy, the others timidly toward a republic. . . .

When the truce envoys were getting ready to return home, women who had been abducted from Armenia forced their way through to them, grabbed their horses by the legs and tails and shouted, "Take us with you; kill us." But the men silently left. . . .

Our men had to endure Brest before Brest.[30]

I told Task that I was leaving. He didn't object.

The Aissors were very sad; for me, too, leaving was hard, but I thought I might be able to do something in St. Pete; and I would have had to stay for good, since I didn't want to go with the army. The end was already in sight.

And it was the end of December.

⁂

In the year seventeen hundred something or other, probably during the reign of Catherine the First—it doesn't matter to them —spotted rats from the steppes of Central Asia gathered into herds, legions, swarms, and migrated to Europe.

They moved in a broad even mass. Birds of prey from all over the world hovered over them. Thousands perished; millions perished; hundreds of millions kept going.

They reached the Volga, hurled themselves into the water and swam across. The river swept them downstream; the entire Volga as far as Astrakhan was dark with their bodies; but they crossed the river and entered Europe.

Then they dispersed and became invisible as they occupied every square foot.

I joined a small herd and got in a barge at Gelenzhik.

A tired soldier—the commanding officer—recognized me and began relating what one regiment had just endured in making its way to Gelenzhik.

The soldiers sitting in the barge wanted to throw the boxes of cartridges overboard, saying they got in their way and weren't needed anyway. They were talked out of it with some difficulty.

The iron barge was full. The men were lying there, not talking much, waiting for the launch.

The launch came, hitched on to us and pulled. We left.

I was sitting on deck.

Gelenzhik was left behind. The motor roared.

A lantern was lit; its reflection swung in the water.

We arrived at Sharafkhaneh. Here the men going to Russia were already piling up from all the ports on the lake.

On the siding stood four railroad cars, so packed that the springs were sagging and buckling.

I climbed on without looking. It was a passenger car, but shabby.

No one knew when the train would leave.

The men started to talk to me. Soldiers from a reconnaissance platoon of one of the regiments. I knew these men: they were famous for their daring in raiding sheep.

This detachment consisted of pardoned criminals. I knew how they had carried one of their seriously wounded comrades out from under fire.

We talked quietly about the Kurds and for the last time I heard the words: "the Kurd is the enemy."

It was getting light. Heavy pigeons were moving around on the roof: more and more passengers kept climbing on.

Daylight. The voice of the man in charge of loading the train was heard: "Comrades, you're going to certain death. It's impossible to overload the cars like that. Climb down, comrades!"

We were as deaf as Mordvinians.

Finally, a locomotive pulled up and we started to move.

We went as far as Sufian, submissively being jostled and taking it.

We had to change trains at Sufian. The food station of the Regional Union was still functioning.

A train was made up out of freight cars. The brake cars had long since been taken.

We started up and the cars began to make more and more noise, pressing against each other, constantly gathering momentum, bumping together as if trying to jump over each other.

Everyone sat watching his pack.

The milestones flashing by in quick succession rhymed the road. The locomotive whistled perplexedly.

On this downgrade, the terrible downgrade to Dzhulfa, there had been many accidents. Once a train had jumped the tracks on a curve and the cars piled on top of each other made a mountain sixty feet high.

We got to Dzhulfa.

Here the wave of men coming from the Fourth Corps merged with our wave. This mass of men waited for a train.

A train arrived. We didn't go at each other tooth and nail, no. We packed ourselves into the cars like briquettes.

The nervous excitement accompanying all these migrations made everyone patient.

In the vicinity of Aleksandropol, either a tunnel or a wire scraped off the men riding on the roof.

Here our wave merged with those coming from Sarikamish.

A rat that has gone all across Asia hasn't much to say. It doesn't even know whether it's the same rat that left home.

In Aleksandropol, a lot of the soldiers were getting into empty cars going to Sarikamish and Erzurum in order to get to Russia via the front.

The station was intact. The iron lines of the tracks had a hypnotic effect: the station was already out of our minds.

I ran into some soldiers who knew me and got on the train with them.

I went as far as Tiflis, or, more accurately, to Naftlug (an intermediate point). They wouldn't let us out in Tiflis, fearing a pogrom.

I went on foot to the city.

Tiflis was living through harrowing days. The frontiers were rapidly being exposed, leaving the city unprotected.

An invasion by the Turks was becoming yesterday's danger; our soldiers were today's danger. People were rushing around.

On one hand, special medical commissions were releasing to a man all the Russian soldiers in the garrison; on the other hand, the newspapers, which, of course, didn't reach the front, were asking the soldiers to stay at their positions until the arrival of their own national forces.

And the front was wide open, as bare of soldiers as the Tauride garden of leaves on a windy fall day.

Nationalism—Armenian, Georgian, Moslem, even Ukrainian—was blossoming on all the streets in the magnificent colors of bright caps and pants, as well as in the newspapers—in chauvinistic articles.

The only nationalism not in view was Great Russian; it took the form of vindictive sabotage.

I remember seeing a Russian cook in the street; she was looking at some troops or, more accurately, a detachment in bright-colored uniforms that was marching down the street and she said:

"So, you let the Russians do your fighting for you; now try it yourselves."

The formation of the Transcaucasian government, as I had

already seen at the front, greatly increased the eagerness of the soldiers to get home, giving them a new motive.

And this government was being formed out of desperation, not out of joy.

In their dealings with the Bolsheviks, the local people tried to adopt Bolshevik methods.

When it turned out that the Bolsheviks had more than half the votes at the conference concerning the front, the conference split down the middle and the minority was recognized by the Caucasian government as the only legal party.

But, of course, a conference concerning the front held by an army passing through carried no weight.

The organization of the national troops went like this.

The city was overflowing with officers.

Even in Kiev during the time of Skoropadsky, I never saw so many silver epaulettes.

Cadres of soldiers were put together with difficulty. It was especially hard with the Georgians.

The only Georgian troops really prepared to fight were the units of the Red Guard, organized out of cadres of Mensheviks.

In any case, the Armenian troops—really a hastily assembled militia—lost the fortress of Erzurum with startling speed.

Things were complicated by the fact that there were a lot of unsettled questions between the Armenians and the Georgians.

It was almost impossible to define the border between their territories.

At the same time, units of Moslems—posing a threat to everyone —were being organized and these men were in superb fighting condition.

They were eyed disapprovingly, but nothing could be done.

The Caucasus was in the process of self-determination.

The show "Russia" was over; everyone was hurrying to get his coat and hat.[31]

The Georgian Military Road was in the hands of the Ingushians and Ossetians, who were seizing automobiles and making a collection of them.

The Circassians had descended from the mountains and were attacking the Terek Cossacks, who had been on their land for a hundred years.

Grozny was besieged.

Men were descending from the Derbent Mountains on Petrovsk. The Tatars were eying the Baku railroad, for the time being still protected by regular Moslem units.

In Elisavetpol, and wherever else it was possible, Tatars were slaughtering Armenians. Armenians were slaughtering Tatars.

Someone slaughtered the Russian immigrants on the Mugan Steppe.

The Russian center in Tiflis, a small shabby center, had wanted to send boxcars of weapons to the Mugan.

But the Ukrainians, who had their own detachment in Tiflis, declared that 75 per cent of the settlers in the Mugan were Ukrainians and that if the Russians sent them weapons, it would be an act of aggression, interfering in the sovereignty of an independent country. They confiscated the boxcars and kept them from leaving.

The Mugan immigrants were slaughtered without hindrance, to such an extent that there's no longer any question of establishing their nationality—even by plebiscite.

The attitude toward the Russian troops passing through was the following. At first, they weren't touched.

Sometimes the Moslems stopped trains and demanded that the Armenians be handed over. Sometimes battles took place because of this.

Then rumors from Persia—our men's shooting from the railroad cars and our obvious weakness whetted appetites. Train wrecks were already being staged to get at the Russian troops.

But first I'll finish telling about how our troops got out of Persia. In December or at the end of November 1918, I was in Kiev serving with Hetman Skoropadsky's troops, which ended by my taking an armored car and a machine-gun truck over to the Red Army. But about this and the strange skirmishes on the Kreshchatik, and about much else that is strange, more anon.

In a word, I found Task there in Kiev. He was lying in an unheated apartment and hardly able to talk: he was suffering from a severe case of tonsillitis.

He despised both the followers of Petlyura and the followers of the hetman. It was strange to see such an energetic man not at work.

This is what he told me.

Headquarters had been moved to the railroad track.

While our troops were pulling out of Urmia, the Persian Cossacks attacked us. Some of the inhabitants took part in the battle. The Aissors fought on our side. Aga Petros put cannons on Jewish Mountain and destroyed a section of the town. The Persian Cossacks were slaughtered, during which time their commander, Stolder, and his daughter were killed; Stolder's son-in-law shot himself.

Our troops in the mountains, now demobilized, with an elected commander and the regiments reduced to shambles, were surrounded by the Kurds. In the vicinity of Wolf Gate, some wagons were burning. From their light, you could see how the attackers would pick up the rifle of one of our dead soldiers and fight over it among themselves.

When the sun came up, the whole area was littered with bodies.

There was nothing to burn, so our troops soaked underwear and rugs with oil and burned them.

A few words about underwear. At one time we had asked the corps supply officer—practically with tears in our eyes—to get underwear for the army. The need was extremely critical. They answered us: No. They were completely out.

And then when we got to the supply depots, we found underwear. We asked, "What's this?"

"It's the emergency reserve."

It was an emergency reserve of inertia.

It was now being burned.

There was flour and butter. There was iron, torn off the roofs of houses; pancakes were cooked on these sheets.

There were no boxcars—the sides and roofs had been torn off the platforms.

There were no locomotives. Task himself went to Aleksandropol after them with two companies of soldiers. There he was given about eight or ten.

It was time to go back. The soldiers said, "We're not going."

"What do you mean you're not going! Your comrades are waiting."

"We're not going."

The engineers said they would try to get through without an escort.

The locomotives started to whistle; the soldiers stood in a

gloomy formation. The locomotives started up; suddenly someone yelled "Get in" and right away a lot of voices: "Get in! . . . Get in!"—and the whole crowd rushed toward the slowly moving loco- motives.

The locomotives were delivered.

At this time, there was a new misfortune. Several boxcars full of dynamite had been thrown into the Araxes River; then somebody threw a bomb in the same place to stun fish. There was a terrible explosion.

The explosion obliterated several hundred men—and so few only by chance: the high, steep banks of the river absorbed the main impact.

A few days later, Task went on a scouting mission in a boxcar attached to a locomotive.

The Kurds staged a wreck. They staged wrecks very often, despite the fact that the Russians took hostages from the adjacent villages.

Task's compartment was demolished and he suffered a concus- sion. Soon he came to and was carried to a station, but it turned out that he had lost the ability to speak.

The troops went on without him.

He didn't dare travel under the sign of the Red Cross, so he hired a guide to lead him on the circular route through the moun- tainous part of Armenia.

In these mountains, our men were expecting the Kurds to at- tack. Armenians, under the command of noncommissioned officers who had returned from the front, were holding the regular out- posts. They received Task very suspiciously and conducted him under escort to a village.

The village consisted of peasant huts half dug into the wall of a mountain. They arranged for our men to spend the night in one of these huts. Lambs were keeping warm in the same building; in the corner was a woman in labor.

After a series of harrowing experiences going through about 180 miles of mountains, Task came out at the railroad track again, having gone fewer than eighteen miles as the crow flies.

Here he was intercepted by some Tatars, but the translator of the detachment, a teacher, let him go through and he came once again to the Armenian positions.

Thus transpired and thus ended the Russian anabasis, or rather katabasis—the withdrawal of several tens of thousands of men, traveling exactly like the companions of Xenophon along the routes of Kurdistan and, moreover, also traveling with elected leaders.

Whether or not the Kurds are descendants of Xenophon's Carduchi, their customs have remained the same.

But the spirit of warriors that force their way home changes. Perhaps everything can be explained by the fact that Xenophon's warriors were warriors by profession and ours—soldiers of misfortune.

One more story, quite short.

About three weeks ago, on the train from Petrograd to Moscow, I ran into a soldier from our Persian army.

He told me another detail about the explosion.

After the explosion, our soldiers, surrounded by enemies, were waiting for a train to come for them; while waiting, they busied themselves by picking up and putting together the shattered pieces of their comrades' bodies.

They picked up pieces for a long time.

Naturally, some of the pieces got mixed up.

One officer went up to the long row of corpses.

The last body had been put together out of the leftover pieces.

It had the torso of a large man. Someone had added a small head; on the chest were small arms of different sizes, both left.

The officer looked for a rather long time; then he sat on the ground and burst out laughing . . . laughing . . . laughing. . . .

In Tiflis—I'm returning to my trip—a crime was committed.

An armored train, dispatched to disarm some soldiers, killed several thousand with machine-gun fire.

This armored train continued on its way, becoming somehow autonomous; it was accused of many killings.

I wedged my way into a railroad car and went to Baku.

The whole station had been literally smashed to bits.

It had obviously been pounded long and violently.

There was no water at the station.

We saw signs of train wrecks rather often.

I'm remembering now another road: the caravan route through the Kuchin Pass to Dilman.

This route passed through the territory of Sinko, the Kurdish khan. . . .

I was going there at night in a car. Both sides of the road were littered with bones.

Two or three skeletons still had a few pieces of bloody meat on them.

Wolves' eyes glittered in the headlights very close to the ground.

Three pairs of eyes, side by side. One pair higher, another lower. Always in groups of three. The wolves were content.

On the way back, the car broke down near Dilman by the cliff where there's a bas-relief depicting some horsemen, evidently from the epoch of the Seleucidae.

Out of sheer stubbornness, I continued on foot. The moon was already out. The caravans didn't travel at night there, afraid of being plundered.

I walked the whole road listening to a stream, sometimes climbing above it, sometimes walking in the water.

I walked along, remembering the pictures of caravan routes in children's books.

It was just like that: these routes are marked only by the bones of horses and camels.

That's how the route of our troops was marked.

Overturned wagons lined the route at even intervals.

The officers were already traveling without their insignia.

I traveled from Baku on the roof of a railroad car. It was cold and uncomfortable, even though I was glued to an air vent.

Near the station of Khasavyurt,[32] we were told that all the watering stations had been destroyed.

We poured water into the locomotive with our mess gear.

The stationmaster was worn out, in the middle of nowhere, stunned by this constant stream of men traveling by in every direction.

He told us, "A train just went through in the direction of Chervonnaya" (maybe I'm mistaken about the name). "Go on if you want to, but I don't advise it."

Naturally, we went on. I managed to get inside the car this time. We covered about twelve miles. Outside the windows—a blizzard. It was dark in the cars.

Suddenly a shock.

Bags, boxes, everything went flying, but not on the floor—on our heads: the entire floor was covered with a mosaic of men.

The train had stopped.

Almost everyone in the car sat still, afraid of losing his place.

I climbed out of the car and asked, "What's happened?"

They said—a collision.

It turned out that another train had been going along ahead of us.

It had run out of something—wood, I guess. The engineer had left the train and gone to a station.

The conductor had forgotten to put out a lantern.

We had piled into the end cars.

In front of our locomotive lay a random heap of boards and wheels sticking up.

You could hear a horse's plaintive neigh; someone was moaning.

Everyone rushed up to the locomotive: "Is the engine all right?"

Steam was coming out of the engine; it was making gutteral noises.

The second thought was to clear the track and go, go.

Before us lay five double-axle cars, completely smashed.

An enormous American freight car, with an iron frame, hadn't been smashed, just upended. You could see a light in it.

We asked, "Everybody all right?"

"Everybody's all right—just one smashed skull."

The track had to be cleared.

And all these men, individual men—who would be in charge?

We stood and looked.

The conductor came to the rescue. He started to give orders.

We got some rope from the Cossacks riding in the forward train and started to pull the cars off to the side. In clearing the track, we only bothered about one of the two routes—the route home.

Only a few worked, but they worked hard. The wheels were set back on the tracks with one jerk.

By swinging on the upended car, we pulled it down on its side. The wounded were pulled out from under the debris.

By that time, a locomotive had pulled up to the forward train and it started to move.

We tried ours. It screeched, but moved.

A whistle. We went back to our cars. In the darkness, the men were sitting motionless. "Are we going?"

"We're going."

By morning, we were at the Chervonnaya station.

That's where the Cossack villages begin.

On the platform you could see—white bread.

All around, like bushy trees, towered columns of smoke.

Burning Circassian villages; Cossack villages burning.

Gray-haired Cossacks, with Berdan rifles on their shoulders, were going through the cars asking for our cartridges and rifles.

The young men hadn't come back yet; the villages were almost unarmed.

True, not long before, the Cossacks had raided some Circassian village and taken cattle, but now they were being raided.

They were calling for volunteers to stay and help them. They were offering twenty-five rubles a day.

Two or three men stayed.

When our mountain artillery had passed through a few days before, the Chechens were attacking the Cossack villages.

The populace begged the battery on their knees to lay over and drive away the enemy with their guns. But the men were in a hurry.

And we too kept going. Hardly anyone had any weapons.

We went on. By day pillars of smoke, by night pillars of fire encircled us. Russia was burning.

Petrovsk, Derbent, then more Cossack villages.

Russia was burning. We were fleeing.

Our group split up around Rostov, at Tikhoretskaya: some went on foot along the Don to Tsaritsyn; others went directly on the train.

We traveled quietly through the territory of the Don Cossacks. We huddled together in the stations. Some Kadets inspected our soldiers. They were selling a newspaper in which the receipts for millions of German marks were printed; the signatures—Zinoviev, Gorky, Lenin.[33]

We got through. We heard shooting at Kozlov. Someone was shooting at someone else. We didn't get out of the train. We were fleeing.

The stationmaster, who had been beaten up several times, wouldn't give us a locomotive, so we took one. An engineer in our group volunteered to run it. He kept complaining that he didn't know the lay of the land.

We set out—and we made it. Great is the god of fugitives.

We rode into Moscow. Was this Moscow?

A mountain of snow. Cold. Silence. The walls gaping with black shell holes, pocked with fine bullet holes.

I hurried on to Petersburg.

It was January. I climbed out of the train and walked through the familiar railroad station.

In front of the station towered mountains of snow and ice.

It was quiet, ominous, muffled.

You can't escape your destiny; I had returned to Petersburg.

I'll stop writing. Today is August 19, 1919.

Yesterday, in a raid on Kronstadt, the English sank the cruiser *Memory of Azov*.

And it's not over yet.

Part Two

WRITING
DESK

I' M starting to write on May 20, 1922, in Raivola (Finland). Of course, I'm not sorry that I kissed and ate and saw the sun. I'm sorry that no matter how hard I tried to direct events, they went their own way. I'm sorry that I fought in Galicia, that I got mixed up with armored cars in Petersburg, that I fought along the Dnieper. I changed nothing. And now, as I sit by the window and look at the spring, which goes past me without asking what weather it should arrange for tomorrow—which doesn't need my permission, perhaps because I'm not from around here—I'm thinking that I should have probably let the revolution go past me in the same way.

When you fall like a stone, you don't need to think; when you think, you don't need to fall. I confused two occupations.

The forces moving me were external to me.

The forces moving others were external to them.

I am only a falling stone.

A stone that falls and can, at the same time, light a lantern to observe its own course.[34]

. . . .

In the middle of January 1918, I returned to Petersburg from northern Persia. What I did in Persia has already been described in the book *Revolution and the Front*.

My first impression: the way people fell upon the white bread I had brought with me.

Then: the way the city had grown quiet.

Like after an explosion, when it's all over, when everything's blown up.

Like a man whose insides have been torn out by an explosion, but he keeps on talking.

Imagine a group of such men.

They sit and talk. What else are they to do—howl?

Petersburg made this impression on me in 1918.

The Constituent Assembly had been dissolved.

There was no front. In general, everything was wide open.

And there was no regular life of any kind, only wreckage.

I hadn't seen the October revolution; I hadn't seen the explosion, if there was an explosion.

I fell right into the hole.

And then Grigory Semyonov sent someone to see me.

I had seen Semyonov before at the Smolny Institute.

He was a small man, usually dressed in a badly fitting field shirt and wide pants; he had a rather sloping forehead, wore glasses on his small nose and was, in general, a small man. He talked in a treble, but soberly. His treble was convincing. He had a short upper lip.

He was a dull man and good at politics. He had no skill with words. For instance, he'd see you with a woman and ask, "Is this your girl friend?" He was somehow not real, like the office jargon: "paper subject to dispatch." I don't know whether this is comprehensible. If it isn't, go talk to Semyonov yourself. He won't turn your stomach.

Well, so a man came to me and said:

"Organize an armored outfit for us. We've been completely smashed. Now we're picking up the pieces."

He was right about being smashed.

The units hadn't turned out to demonstrate in favor of the Constituent Assembly.

Only one small squad of fifteen men had shown up with a placard: "The men of the listening posts welcome the Constituent Assembly."

Meanwhile, for many months an armored division consisting of ten cars had been creeping toward Petersburg.

It had been creeping along cautiously, step by step, with only one thought—to be in Petersburg by the time the Constituent Assembly was convened.

I hadn't worked in this division. In our division it was possible to get armored cars. But there were no men; there was no one to call them out.

And it somehow happened that the armored cars in which men

were waiting simply hadn't turned up. The men had talked a little and argued a little, but no one ever got around to giving the order.

A placard had been hanging over the street—"Long live the Constituent Assembly." Some men carrying a similar placard got as far as the corner of Kirochnaya Street and Liteiny Prospekt.

At that point, they were shot at. They didn't shoot back; they threw down their placard and ran.

The yardkeepers later made broom handles out of the sticks from the placard.

All this happened without me and I'm writing about it from other people's words.

But I did see the broom handles—the very ones made from the placard.

When I arrived in St. Pete, I joined a commission whose name I don't remember. It was supposed to be responsible for the protection of antiquities and it was located in the Winter Palace.[35]

That was where Lunacharsky received people.

I was sent to the palace of Nikolai Mikhailovich, where a red-haired young man named Comrade Lozimir had set up housekeeping.

The platoon on duty was armed with swords from Damascus; Persian miniatures lay on the floor. In the corner, I found an icon depicting the Emperor Paul as the Archangel Michael. It was apparently the work of Borovikovsky.

It had been rolled up in a newspaper and tied with string.

But there was less looting than usual. Troops who have occupied an enemy city and are billeted in apartments like to use the abandoned property in their own way: to stuff a broken window with a good rug or to use a chair for kindling wood.

There were a lot of men running around in the Winter Palace. And sometimes it was completely empty. That meant that things were going badly for the Bolsheviks. The intellectuals were not cooperating, were selling newspapers in the streets, were chopping ice.

Were looking for work.

At one point, they were all making chocolate.

But at first, they merely fried everything fryable in cocoa butter, which was sold right from the factories. Later on, they learned how to make chocolate. They sold pastries. They opened cafés—at least, the richer ones did. All this came later, not until spring.

The main thing, however, is that it was terrible.

Anyway, some men came to me and said, "We're getting ready to start a revolt. We have the necessary forces. Get us an armored division."

I was introduced to the man formerly in charge of the armored division that had come to St. Pete.

The soldiers in my unit liked me a lot. The narrowness of my political horizon, my constant concern that everything be made right immediately, my tactics, as opposed to strategy—all this made me comprehensible to the soldiers.

In the drivers' school, I had been an instructor, had been with the troops from seven in the morning till four in the afternoon and we had been on good terms. Now I handed in my resignation to Lunacharsky in a very solemn manner, which probably surprised him, and began to organize an armored division. Actually, seizing armored cars presented no problem. All you had to do was have your own men attached to the cars—preferably, one for each car but, in any case, a man who could refuel and start the cars and get them ready. Then you just went and took the cars.

The armored cars had already been seized more than once.

They were seized during the February revolution. The Bolsheviks seized them during the July insurrection. That time, it was our drivers who got them back from the Bolsheviks by showing up in a tin-plated armored car that was used for training purposes. They were scared to death.

The Bolsheviks seized the armored cars again during the October revolution, when everyone was confused and neutral.

The "right-wing" units were supposed to seize the armored cars before the revolt of the military cadets three days after the revolution, but the cadets, acting on their own, had beaten them to it.

Our unit from the drivers' school, under the command of Feldenkreitser, had headed for the Mikhailovsky Riding School in a truck, but got there half an hour late.

So, all things considered, our enterprise was technically feasible.

I went to see my old drivers, who were everywhere the cars were —at the Mikhailovsky Riding School, at the skating rink on Kamennoostrovsky Prospekt and at the armored motor pools. Later on, the Bolsheviks kept shifting the cars from place to place—for instance, for a while they concentrated them at the Petropavlovskaya Fortress; but our men stayed with their cars. If they were removed, we sent other men.

The fact is that there were very few Bolsheviks among the drivers—almost none; consequently, the first commissars in the armored units had been brought in from outside, or chosen from among the metalworkers, or even the janitors.

A driver is a worker, but a special kind of worker. He's a loner, not part of the herd. Running a powerful armored car makes him impulsive. The car's forty to sixty horsepower makes an adventurer out of a man. Drivers are the heirs of the cavalry. Moreover, many of my drivers fiercely loved Russia and nothing more than Russia. Consequently, I always had my own men in the armored units.

We continued our "encirclement of the garages"—that is, we would rent apartments around a garage so that we could gather in small groups, then come out inconspicuously and get into the garage.

What more were we planning to do?

We wanted to shoot. To break glass. We wanted to fight.

I didn't know how to make chocolate.

Besides, the drivers didn't like the type of commissar that was beginning to appear. They drove them around and hated them.

They wanted to shoot.

Things were not going so well in the other units of the organization. The old army no longer existed.

While I was serving on the Winter Palace Commission, I went among the regiments to collect items taken from museums.

Most of the men in the regiments had pilfered things and then cleared out. Some organization—Filonenko was the only member I knew—was sending its own men to replace them.

These were the Volhynian and Preobrazhensky Regiments and some other that I've forgotten. The Semyonovsky Regiment was a special case. Someone unknown to me was infiltrating it so skillfully that the men weren't even disarmed before they went over to Yudenich's side.

The organization that I belonged to didn't consider itself affiliated with any party; this was constantly emphasized. It was rather the remnants of the committee for the defense of the Constituent Assembly, so the men in it were there by mandate of the units rather than the parties. Semyonov especially emphasized the non-party nature of the organization.

The infiltration of the regiments was going rather well.

When the Bolsheviks demanded that the regiments hand over their weapons, they refused.

The Bolsheviks came during the night.

The regiments had not been kept together. Each one had been broken up, with one battalion here, another there. They didn't all sleep in the barracks. A lot of them went home to sleep: it was more peaceful. The Bolshevik units apparently made their first move against the Volhynians.

The sentry shouted, "To arms," but there was no armed resistance.

Were the units that disarmed the Volhynians actually Bolshevik?

That reminds me of a sentence we once had to translate from Latin into Russian: "Were not the birds that saved Rome geese?"

But perhaps those units actually weren't Bolshevik. At least the drivers of the armored car sent against the Volhynians were anything but Bolshevik. The Volhynian and Preobrazhensky Regiments were dispersed. Before leaving, the Volhynians blew up their barracks. The last of the old army was now liquidated.

The Bolsheviks began to establish the Red Army while they were disarming the Red Guard. Our organization decided to infiltrate its own men into the Red Army. It was decided to send two kinds of men: those who were tough and smart and would gain the confidence of the high command, as well as the respect of their comrades, and those who would constantly gripe and undermine the morale of the units with their complaints.

It was very cleverly worked out.

But unfortunately there was no one to send.

We did manage to get some men on the staff.

That way, they knew what was going on in the Red Army, but they weren't able to do anything about it. It's true that we did have one artillery unit. But I didn't know what the contacts were: I was too involved with the armored cars. We were waiting for a demonstration, which was repeatedly put off. I remember one of the deadlines—May 1, 1918. Then another deadline was set: there was supposed to be a strike organized by a group of designated men.

The strike never came off.

But we would meet in apartments on the various nights designated for the demonstration, drink tea, look over our revolvers and send aides to the garages.

I think it would be easier for a woman to get her baby halfway out and then not give birth than it was for us to do that.

It's terribly hard to hold men on such a course: they deteriorate, lose hope.

Deadlines came and went.

I think that by this time the organization had almost no one it could count on. There were about twenty men among the workers. There were units that were supposed to join us, but we all knew— except for those moments when we didn't want to know—that it was awfully unlikely.

Working in a conspiracy is nasty, ugly, subterranean, dirty work. Men meet underground and, in the darkness, don't even know whom they're meeting.

I should mention that we had nothing to do with Savinkov's men.

At that time, we came in contact with various anonymous organizations "recognizing the Constituent Assembly," as well as with the commanders of isolated units who said that their men would go against the Bolsheviks. Once we ran across a division trained in laying mines; they were part of the "sailor" opposition to the Bolsheviks.

These men were linked among themselves by a naval organization and apparently made contact with us through the workers of a plant across from which they were docked. Naturally, they could demonstrate just as well as the armored cars, but the Bolsheviks had succeeded in disarming them. As it turned out, the unit sent to disarm them couldn't pull the bolts out of the cannons, simply didn't know how. Instead, they started to beat the breech end of the gun with sledge hammers. In other words, these men weren't sailors. The Bolsheviks hadn't found the sailors reliable enough to send on such a mission. The Bolsheviks were very weak, too, but the ship was listing on their side.

The Bolsheviks were strong in that their goal was definite and simple.

The Red Army hardly existed yet, but its mores were already taking shape.

This was the time that came after that period when discipline had been totally lacking in the army. Men had been hired to serve.

Now the units were attached directly to the nearest soviet.

In general, it was a time of local power and local terror.

People were killed on the spot.

In one of the Red Army units on the Petrograd side of town, a boy stole some boots from one of his comrades.

They caught him and sentenced him to be shot.

He didn't believe it. He got upset and cried, but not much. Mostly out of propriety. He thought they were just trying to scare him and wanted to oblige.

They took him out into a lycée garden and shot him.

Then they put the body in a cab, sent along another soldier to keep him company, as if he were drunk, and dispatched the cab to the mortuary of the Petropavlovskaya Hospital.

The men who did that without the slightest animosity were dreadful and timely for Russia.

They continued a tradition of mob rule, like the mobs that used to throw thieves into the Fontanka Canal.

One soldier talked to me about mob rule.

He said, "That's when a dead man talks."

"What do you mean, a dead man talks?"

"Well, a man who's shortly going to be dead talks."

You can see how irreversible it was.

At that time, I was summoned to the Cheka, because Filonenko had stopped by to see me.

I don't like Filonenko now and I didn't like him then, but I remember when we were at the front, I slept in the car with my head on his shoulder. This nervous, unpleasant and unreliable man was living in Petersburg under an assumed name, or under several assumed names.

He was being followed and they were right at his heels.

He dropped in on me, ate with me and drank my coffee. The next day, about eight members of the Cheka were standing in front of my house.

I said hello to them whenever I went out. They replied.

I was summoned to the Cheka and interrogated by Otto.

They asked if I knew Filonenko. I said I did and admitted that he periodically dropped in on me.

They asked me why. I said for information about the signs of the zodiac. Strange as it may sound, that was the truth.

Filonenko was fascinated by astrology.

The interrogator suggested that I give some testimony about myself.

I told him about Persia. He listened, his assistant listened, and so did another prisoner who had been brought in for questioning.

They let me go. I'm a professional raconteur.

They arrested my father, but soon let him go. He was held all together about two months.

Meanwhile, the situation had changed. At first, the revolution had been miraculously self-confident. Then came the Treaty of Brest.

I waited for a miracle more than once. And the Bolsheviks believe in miracles.

They even perform miracles, but miracles are hard to perform.

You remember the folk tale about the devil who could make an old man young again? First he consumes the man in fire; then he restores him to life rejuvenated.

Then the devil's apprentice tries to perform the miracle. He's able to consume the man in fire, but he can't rejuvenate him.

When the Bolsheviks left the front wide open without signing the peace treaty, they were hoping for a miracle, but the man consumed in fire didn't rise from the dead.

And the Germans walked through the open front.

Before signing the Treaty of Brest, the Bolsheviks sent telegrams to all the major soviets to ask whether they should sign the treaty.

They all answered no. Vladivostok[36] was especially emphatic. This had the appearance of irony.

The treaty was signed.

Evidently the Bolsheviks had inquired out of curiosity.

The miracle hadn't come off and they already realized it.

It's interesting to note that when the Germans were already attacking unarmed Russia, a meeting was held at the Narodny Dom and Zinoviev pleaded with the remnants of several armed regiments to stand up for their "native land." He didn't even add the word "socialist."

They were naïve, the Bolsheviks. They overestimated the

strength of Russian traditions. They believed in the "old guard." They thought that the men loved "Mother Russia."

But she didn't exist.

And now, when they're making concessions and multiplying the number of shopkeepers, they've only changed the object of their faith. They still believe in miracles.

And today, if you walk out on Nevsky Prospekt, on the streets of lovely Petrograd, with its blue sky, on the streets of Petrograd, where the grass is so green, when you see these men today—the new men who were summoned to perform a miracle—you'll also see that all they've done is open cafés.

On the corner of Grebetskaya and Pushkarskaya Streets, a riddled streetcar pole is still standing.

If you don't believe that there was a revolution, go and put your hand in the wound. It's wide. The pole was pierced by a three-inch shell.

And all the same, if nothing's left of Russia but its borders, if it exists only as a spatial concept, if it's totally leveled, I know one thing—there is no guilt and there are no guilty.

And I am guilty only of not having let life go past me like the weather; I am guilty of having had too little faith in miracles. There are men among us who wanted to finish the revolution on its second day.

We didn't believe in miracles.

There are no miracles and faith alone doesn't produce them.

And, like a closed circle, everything returned to its former place.

Only the "places" no longer existed.

My comrades, the drivers, wanted to fight the Germans in Petersburg, on Nevsky Prospekt.

But the situation had changed.

The Soviet of People's Commissars had moved to Moscow. It was believed that the center of gravity for our work should also be transferred either there or to the Volga region.

But I couldn't go there, since my organization wasn't transportable.

By that time, I was involved with the armored cars again.

In my work, I happened to meet a certain officer. I don't know where he is now.

He had wonderful, clear eyes.

He had been terribly wounded. He was missing a piece of skull; his arms and legs had been shot up and had knitted badly.

In the thick of battle (I think it was 1916), he once found himself chasing an armored train with an armored car, which isn't proper, since "by and large," as the Bolsheviks say, an armored train is more powerful than a car. The armored train started to retreat, which isn't proper either.

In hot pursuit, the car drove onto the station platform, but here it came under fire from several gun batteries. Then the driver crashed through the wide doors of the station buffet, drove his heavy car through the tables, crashed through the back door, drove down the stairs and escaped across the square after mowing down a cavalry detachment.

He had a military background, but he understood a lot and, incidentally, had an excellent feeling for art—that is, he knew whether a thing was good or not.

We became good friends. He was a very fine and honest man.

In one building that he was responsible for, a frame for a Garford armored car turned up. It had been junked. We then took some pieces of junked armored cars from several garages and used them to repair our own.

The drivers even managed to relieve the enemy of a three-inch cannon with its bolt still intact, two machine guns, shells and cartridge belts. This was no easy matter, since the shells were heavy and you had to carry them under your coat or jacket two at a time and watch that they didn't hit against each other or clang.

This is how we got the bolt. A pintsized driver came up to me. He took a fork out of his pocket (I don't know its technical name, but it's the thing that expels the spent cartridge from the gun barrel), gave it to me and asked, "Viktor, is that the bolt?"

"No," I said.

"Well, what about this?" He sucked in his belly and, from behind his leather belt, pulled out a huge, heavy piece. It was the bolt. How he had managed to suck in that entire bolt, I'll never know.

We put together the armored car and even rode around the compound in it, but we didn't put it into action, even though, with the experience of our unit, we could easily have seized any garage.

We repaired the car openly, in broad daylight; that's why we didn't get caught.

In other words, I couldn't leave.

Then came our downfall. An organization can't exist for years on end; in time, of course, it collapses.

But we were so reckless that we even called meetings of the whole organization, complete with speeches and debates.

The "Red Army section" of the organization was arrested on Nikolaevskaya Street. Forged documents were found in a hassock.

By that time, Semyonov had already left for the Volga region.

They arrested Lepper, in whose notebook they found all the names and addresses written in code, which the Cheka cracked in two hours.

My brother was arrested at work (in the Red Army).

I escaped and settled on the outskirts of the city, not in a room but a corner.

I was issued a passport at the commissariat on one of the unit forms.

By that time, our organization had veered somewhat to the right. We had allied ourselves with N. S.; V. Ignatiev played an important role.

The organization was splitting up: some left for Arkhangelsk via Vologda, others for the Volga region.

I suggested capturing the prison, but they said it was impossible.

I was living in Chornaya Rechka in the apartment of a gardener.

It was a time of famine. I had little to eat myself, but there was no time to think of that.

The gardener's family was living on linden leaves and vegetable greens. An old schoolteacher was living in a tiny separate room of the same apartment. I found out about her existence only when they came to take away her body. She had died of hunger.

A lot of people were dying of hunger then. There's no reason to think it's a quick death.

A man can find in his situation all kinds of nuances.

I remember how surprised I was in Persia that the homeless Kurds lived around the walls of the city, picking out places in the wall where there was a slight hollow, even if only a few inches.

Evidently it seemed warmer to them there.

And when a man's starving, he lives that way—continually fretting, wondering which is tastier, boiled greens or linden leaves. He even gets excited about these problems and, gradually becoming immersed in such nuances, he dies.

There was cholera in St. Pete then, but people weren't being eaten yet.

True, there was talk about some postman who ate his wife, but I don't know whether that's true or not.

It was quiet, sunny and hungry—very hungry.

In the morning we drank coffee made out of rye. Sugar was being sold on the street for seventy-five kopeks a chunk.

You could drink a cup of coffee either without milk or without sugar: there wasn't enough money for both.

Rye cookies were also being sold on the street. We ate soup made of oats. The oats were steamed in a pot, then run through a meat grinder—"through the machine," as they used to say—several times. It was hard work. Afterwards, they were put through a sieve and you got soup made from oat flour. When it's being cooked, you have to be careful or it will boil over like milk.

Before the oats were ground, the black specks had to be fished out. I don't know what they were—evidently the seeds of some weed.

For this operation, the oats were spread out on the table and the whole family picked the refuse out of it. So you wound up fussing with oats all day.

Potato peels were used to make a very tasteless gruel, as thin as Persian bread. Everyone was issued anywhere from an eighth- to a quarter-pound of bread a day. Sometimes herring was issued.

Before you ate this herring, you were advised to cut off the extremities—the head and tail. They had already spoiled.

Our organization wasn't setting deadlines anymore. Somewhere in the east, the Czechs were advancing.[37] Rebellion raged in Yaroslavl.[38] Where we were, it was quiet.

I still hadn't disbanded my friends.

It was easy for us to stick together, since we had split into half a dozen detachments of five to ten men each, linked by bonds of "friendship and kinship." There was nothing to do. I remember once I was asked to get hold of a car, evidently for purposes of expropriation. Semyonov made the request.

I told one of the drivers about it.

He went to some nearby garage, picked out a car, cranked it up, got in and drove away.

But the expropriation didn't take place.

The fate of that driver was strange. He was living in the apartment of an old, completely faded woman. She took care of him and fed him compote. Consequently, he married her.

Marriage to an old woman was the fate of many men who lived adventurously. I saw dozens of examples.

I always felt sorry for them. We even recognized the problem and warned each other—"Don't eat compote."

This showed a kind of fatigue or a craving for peace and quiet.

Adventurism generally ends in corruption.

I remember seeing one of my students after I returned from Persia.

"What are you doing now?"

"Robbing houses, sir. If you'll indicate apartments for us to rob, we'll give you ten per cent."

Strictly a business proposition.

He was eventually shot.

He'd been a pretty good driver.

Hardly anyone was above a little thing like requisitioning alcohol, that is, petty thievery of various kinds. The laws had been repealed and everything was being revised.

Of course, not everyone indulged in crime.

I knew drivers who stayed with their cars, took nothing except kerosene for their cars and loved Russia deeply; they didn't sleep nights for thinking about her.

These men were usually married to young women and had children.

And, needless to say, the drivers had no monopoly on corruption.

One time I dropped in on a friend of mine, K.

He told me the following: "You know, some acquaintances just came by to see me. They were asking for a crowbar. I asked how long a one they needed. They showed me with their hands—not too long. Well, then, I just told them that what they needed was a jimmy. I asked what they needed a jimmy for. They said to crack a safe."

And so some cracked safes, some headed east to join Wrangel

and Denikin, others were shot and still others hated the Bolsheviks with a hatred so salty that it kept them from spoiling.

Quite a few people went over to the Bolsheviks.

I'm speaking now about the revolutionary crowd—those who generally carry out orders, not those who give them.

But I was sitting in Chornaya Rechka writing a work on the theme "The Connection between Plot Devices and General Stylistic Devices."[39] I wrote on a small round table, holding the reference books on my knees.

Then the organization sent for me and said I should go to Saratov. I was given a ticket.

I could stay in St. Pete only at great risk. The Bolsheviks were looking for me. I left.

I left K. behind and also the man who had previously been in charge of the division. K. wasn't arrested and later on, when he was discovered with an armored car, he successfully escaped to the south.

He said that it was essential to press for nationalization of the mines in the Don Basin. But all the same, the officers there inducted him into the White Army.

I don't know what kind of welcome he got from Denikin in the Volunteer Army.

I left.

The drivers dispersed. Eventually, I lost track of them.

My comrades who had been arrested were shot. My brother was shot. He was not a rightist. He loved the revolution a thousand times more than three-fourths of the "Red commanders."

Only he didn't believe that the Bolsheviks could resurrect a Russia consumed in fire. He left two children. The Volunteer Army was unacceptable to him because it stood for returning Russia to the past.

Why did he fight?

I haven't said the most important thing.

We had heroes.

And you and I are people. So I'm writing what kind of people we were.

They killed my brother after the killing of Uritsky.

They shot him on the firing range at Okhta.

The soldiers of his own regiment shot him. The officer who killed him told me.

Later, specialists did the killing.

The regiment stayed on duty.

My brother was outwardly calm. He died valiantly.

His name was Nikolai. He was twenty-seven years old.

The worst thing about being shot is that they take off the dead man's boots and jacket—that is, they make him take them off before he's killed.

May 20, 1922.

I continue writing.

It's been a long time since I've written so much. It's as if I were getting ready to die. Frustration and a red sun. It's late afternoon.

I went to Moscow. We had a hideout on Syromyatniki Street. It was soon discovered.

In Moscow, I saw Lidia Konoplyova, a blonde with pink cheeks and a Vologodskian accent. Even then, she was already veering to the left. Incidentally, she said that in the village where she taught, the peasants would recognize the Bolsheviks.

I don't know anything about the killing of Volodarsky. That was organized by Semyonov on his own hook. I found out who killed him only in March of 1922 from Semyonov's testimony.[40]

I went to Saratov—with false documents. A lot of people with documents of this kind were being picked up.

The organization in Saratov was affiliated with the SR's.

Its main job was to send people to Samara.

But there were evidently plans for a local insurrection.

I got to Saratov and spent most of my time in a maze of hideouts, which were different for every day of the week.

This didn't keep the Bolsheviks from discovering them with the help of an informer.

Quite a few people were living in Saratov.

The military organization was being directed by some half-crazy man, whose name I've forgotten. I know that he later went to Samara and was killed by Kolchak's soldiers during the uprising.[41]

We lived conspiratorially, but very naïvely—practically all of us in one room.

I didn't have to live in that cellar since there were already so many people jammed into it.

Instead, they settled me in an insane asylum about four miles from Saratov.

It was a quiet place, surrounded by a large, unfenced garden, which was lit with lanterns.

I lived there for quite a while.

Sometimes—I don't remember why—I slept in a haystack near Saratov.

The hay tickles and right away you take on a distinctly rustic appearance.

And at night you wake up and look around, you climb up a little higher, toward the sky, black with stars, and you think about the absurdity of life.

Absurdities tend to have the appearance of logic, but not in a field under the stars.

The Austrian prisoners were being sent home while I was in Saratov. Many of them didn't want to go. They'd already become accustomed to Russian women. Their women cried.

There were revolts in the villages all around us; that is, the peasants wouldn't hand over their grain. Then the Red Army men would come in trucks.

Every village revolted by itself. The committee in Saratov also sat by itself.

The room was in a cellar.

The leaders lived elsewhere.

We would go out of town to a certain mountain for meetings, but one time we set out only to discover that we were all traveling on the same streetcar.

The town was deserted, but there was a lot of bread. The Red Army men went around in wide-brimmed hats and were afraid of their own uniforms.

That is to say, the Red Army men were afraid of their hats because they thought that if they had to retreat from Samara, the hats would make them too conspicuous.

The Volga was deserted. From the cliff, you could see sand and the different hues of the water. The shops along the riverbank were deserted.

I felt useless in Saratov, so they soon sent me to Atkarsk.

Atkarsk is a small town, nothing above one story: two stone buildings—the old city hall and the high school.

The town's divided into two sections, one of which is called the "plowing section"—its inhabitants plow.

In other words, it's only half a town.

And across from the building occupied by the soviet—the old high school—stood cannons, which they shot at the "plowing" side of town during "peasant revolts."

The streets weren't paved.

The houses were roofed with boards. Bread was fifty kopeks a pound. You could identify people from Petersburg by the fact that they ate bread right in the street.

All the shops in the bazaar were closed. A few women were selling small pears. Some nondescript man was showing a cyclorama, "The Adventures of Grishka."

In the middle of town, there was a dense garden where people strolled in the evenings.

And in the middle of the garden, there was a small pavilion with a Soviet dining room. You could eat there, but not with knives and forks—with your fingers.

Meat was served—even beer. The waiter hadn't taken a bath since the beginning of World War I.

There were stacks of grain on the "plowing" side of town.

There was plenty to eat in town, but it was vile. The vegetable oil was awful.

And the whole town dressed alike—in a bluish cloth with white stripes. That's all that was issued.

And everything possible had been requisitioned—right down to the teaspoons.

Everything was terribly bare. It had probably always been that way. Previously, though, people had lived a little better.

I settled there. They gave me a room at the shoemaker's, across from the soviet.

The shoemaker had previously worked with his two sons in his own shop in the bazaar, but he had been arrested as a representative of the bourgeoisie. They held him a while until it got ludicrous; then they let him go, but forbade him to work for himself.

So he lived as best he could.

Thanks to my connections, I got a job as agent for the exploitation of supplies "unfit as presently constituted," that is, unable to be used for their intended purpose.

These supplies consisted of old boots, pants, scrap iron and various other rubbish.

I was supposed to receive this rubbish, sort it out and send it on to Saratov. However, I suggested organizing a repair shop right in Atkarsk.

I was given whole granaries filled to the brim with old boots and assorted rags.

I hired my landlord and his sons, took on several other men, and we went to work.

As strange as it may seem, the work interested me.

I lived with the shoemakers, separated from them only by a partition with cracks in it. I slept on a wooden couch and at night the bedbugs attacked me until I was covered with blood.

But somehow I didn't notice it. It was the landlord who called attention to it and moved me from the couch to the counter.

I already considered myself a shoemaker.

Sometimes I was summoned to the local Cheka, which checked all newcomers practically every day.

They would question me item by item: who are you, what did you do before the war, during the war, between February and October, and so on.

According to my passport, I was a machinist. They would question me about my speciality—for instance, they asked me to name the parts of a lathe.

I knew them then. I held my own very convincingly.

It's pleasant to lose yourself. To forget your name, slip out of your old habits. To think up some other man and consider yourself him. If it had not been for my writing desk, for my work, I would never again have become Viktor Shklovsky. I was writing a book, *Plot as a Stylistic Phenomenon.*[42] To transport the books I needed for references, I had unbound them and divided them into small parcels.

I had to write on a window sill.

Looking more closely at my—false—passport, I found in the column concerning change of family situation a black stamp with the inscription that so-and-so had died in the Obukhovskaya Hospital on such-and-such a date. I could imagine an interesting conversation between the Cheka and me:

"Are you so-and-so?"

"Yes."

"And why are you already dead?"

Now "seventy-pounders" were arriving in town. These were office and factory workers that the Soviet had permitted to come to the country and take home seventy pounds of flour each. Such permission was given.

These men overran the countryside.

Then the permission was revoked.

One man shot himself. He couldn't live without flour.

One officer came to see me who had escaped from Yaroslavl with his wife. Both he and his wife were wounded and were concealing their wounds.

After the revolt, he had gone to Moscow and lived in the bushes next to the Church of the Saviour.

He ate a lot of bread and was absolutely pale.

He said that Yaroslavl was defending itself desperately.

I went to eat in the aforementioned garden in town, where dinner was served to authorized personnel.

There were no forks. You ate with your fingers. A dinner with meat.

There was a high-school student there from the Lentovskaya high school. I made friends with him. He was complaining that there were too few Socialists in their high school.

He was about seventeen and had been going out with a punitive expedition.

Now he was in trouble.

Near the town of Balanda, he had shot an extra thirteen men and his superiors were mad at him.

He had decided to look for another job.

Scouts from the other bank of the Volga were crossing to our side and, in the process, accidentally took Volsk when the Red Army soldiers fled.

One unit fled from Atkarsk because the men had been scared by a storm.

They grabbed their things and fled to a ravine.

The scouts, however, couldn't attack Saratov, since there were only fifteen of them.

The Don Cossacks were attacking from the other side of the Volga, but they were poorly armed. People crossing from that side said that in many cases all the Whites had for ammunition were the blank cartridges with grapeshot used for target practice. At least, that's what the Red Army men told me.

Everything was very unstable.

Someone was saying that the Cossacks were rattling sticks to simulate gunfire.

Armored cars were helping to put down the revolts, but I couldn't make contact with them.

None of my students was there.

It was in Atkarsk that I found out about the attempt on Lenin's life and the killing of Uritsky.[43]

This was followed by a raid on our organization in Saratov. Everyone was arrested.

I found out about this accidentally after I got there. All the same, I decided to stop by an apartment where I knew I could get a new passport.

I considered mine damaged.

I arrived. It was awfully quiet. The maid opened the door.

A big hedgehog was walking around, making a lot of noise with its paws. Its owner had been taken away. I don't know whether he ever saw his hedgehog again.

I continued my search, got hold of a passport, hopped on the streetcar and, within the hour, left for Atkarsk on an oil train.

There I gathered up my books, which I'd been using to write the article "The Connection between Plot Devices and General Stylistic Devices," and mailed them to Petersburg. This article is like Kipling's story about the whale—"the suspenders, please don't forget the suspenders!"[44]

Then I left for Moscow.

I was absurdly dressed. In a poncho, a sailor's shirt and a Red Army soldier's hat.

My friends said that I was simply begging to be arrested.

I rode in a van with some sailors from Baku and some refugees carrying ten sacks full of rusk. That was all they had.

I reached Moscow, where the news about the arrests was confirmed. I decided to go to the Ukraine.

In Moscow my money and papers were stolen while I was buying hair dye.

I went to a friend's place (he had nothing to do with politics) and dyed my hair. It came out violet. We laughed a lot about that. I had to shave. I couldn't spend the night there.

I went to see someone else. He led me into his archives, locked the door and said:

"If there's a search tonight, just rustle and tell them you're paper."

In Moscow, I gave a short report on the theme "The Plot in Poetry."

In Moscow, I saw Lidia Konoplyova again, the blonde with pink cheeks. She was dissatisfied and said that the party's policies were incorrect, that the people weren't behind the Bolsheviks. I also saw an old woman, who told me over and over, "And what are we doing! Nothing's working out!" On the next day, they were both arrested.

The Saratov organization was subverted by informers. Semyonov was arrested in a Moscow café by the Pokrovsky Gate. He fired back at the men making the arrest. He carried a big Mauser everywhere he went. They took him to prison. In the compound, he pulled out another big Mauser, shot and wounded the informer.

He was tried and then amnestied.

I headed for the Ukraine.

A lot of people were going. Everyone in Kursk was working. You could stop any old woman on the street and chances are she had been working in some commissariat. In Kursk, I got our hideouts mixed up and gave some people a scare.

At Kursk or Oryol, I changed trains for Lgov. We got as far as Zhelobovka, where everyone got off the train and went the rest of the way to the Ukraine on foot.

We walked out in the open. A lot of people were going, all of them with bundles on their backs.

Some soldiers were coming toward us. They stopped me and a short Jew in an unusually long overcoat.

"Follow us!"

We followed, but they led us not toward the station, but into a field.

We came to a hollow. It was quiet. The wind wasn't blowing.

I was wearing a leather jacket with a little hole over the stomach that had been made by a bullet during the war.

I often felt that little hole with my finger.

The leather jacket was worn out. I had worked under all kinds of cars in it.

Over it I was wearing a short jacket made out of an old soldier's overcoat, then a sweater.

They told me to take off my clothes.

One of the soldiers looked at me thoughtfully and said, "You're disguised, comrade. You definitely have money on you!"

I pulled out my money and showed it to him. All I had on me was five hundred tsarist rubles.

"No, I don't mean those. You've got big money on you, either glued into the tops of your boots or. . . ."

While examining my things, he explained to me in detail the ways people hide their money.

He looked at me with real respect and said, "Why don't you tell me where you've hidden your money? I'm interested."

I said, "I've got no money."

"Well, in that case, get dressed."

I got dressed and he examined the Jew; then he unfolded my things, but without much interest, and he said:

"Well, there's nothing at all in your things. I know that no one keeps anything in his things. They keep it all on their person."

Then he laid out all the things, mine and the Jew's, and took what he wanted. All very quietly and calmly—it wasn't even offensive. Simply as if he were in a store.

He took some of my money and the jacket with the little hole in it.

It was quiet in that hollow. I talked to the soldier about the Third International. Our conversation was just getting started when he removed my boots. I talked about the Ukraine. He escorted us part of the way.

We ran into another soldier on the way, but our escort told him we had already been "examined." He pointed to some poplars in the field and told us to walk toward them.

It was raining and I was walking through a plowed field. I lost my traveling companion and wandered for a long time. There were men plowing in the distance. That surprised me.

Now I know how vital it is to keep plowing even between two fronts, even under the bullets. And now I'm not even surprised at those who keep throwing themselves into the thick of things.

I reached a barbed-wire entanglement with a German soldier behind it.

How hard it was to go up to that German!

I mustered all the German words I knew and said them to the

sentry. He let me through and I found myself in a small village crammed with refugees and goods—the village of Korenevo.

There were plenty of yellow rolls, red sausages and blue sugar lumps in this village.

In one of the huts we gathered around a samovar. I and some officer who had escaped barefoot from Russia drank tea with sugar in it and ate rolls.

All the analogies to a mess of pottage I know myself.[45] No prompting please!

When I got to Kharkov, I stayed a while with relatives.

In Kharkov, I saw my oldest brother, Doctor Evgeny Shklovsky.

He was dead within the year.

He had been in charge of a hospital train. Men attacked the train and started killing the wounded.

He tried to explain that this was forbidden. Once before the revolution he had succeeded in stopping a cholera riot in the town of Ostrov. Here that was impossible. He was beaten unmercifully, stripped, locked in an empty boxcar and taken along.

The orderly gave him a coat.

He was taken to Kharkov, where he sent a note to our relatives.

They looked for him a long time along the tracks. They found him and got him to a hospital, where he died from the beatings, fully conscious. He felt his own pulse stopping.

He cried hard before dying.

Either the Whites or the Reds killed him.

I don't remember which—I really don't remember. But his death was unjust.

He died at the age of thirty-five. He had been exiled as a youth and had escaped. He graduated from an architectural college in Paris.

When he returned to Russia, he became a doctor. He was a successful surgeon and worked in the Otto Clinic.

One day I went to the railroad station and decided to go to Kiev for a few days. I left from the station without telling anyone.

Kiev was full of people. The bourgeoisie and intelligentsia of Russia were wintering there.

I never saw so many officers in my life.

The Kreshchatik constantly glittered with medals of Vladimir and St. George.

The city hummed with activity; there were a lot of restaurants.

I saw a beggar pull a piece of bread out of his sack and offer it to a cabby's horse.

The horse turned it down.

It was the time when the entire Russian bourgeoisie was assembled in the Ukraine, when the Ukraine was occupied by Germans; but the Germans hadn't quite picked it clean.

Three-colored flags were flying in the streets. These were the headquarters for the volunteer units of Kirpichov and Count Keller and some other outfit called "Our Homeland."

On one of the streets hung a flag that no one had seen before. I believe it was yellow and black; in the window there were portraits of Nicholas and Alexandra. This was the embassy of the Astrakhan Army.

The troops of Hetman Skoropadsky were scarcely to be seen, although once a day detachments of Russian officers went by for the changing of the guard at the hetman's palace. They had a special uniform with a small cockade and narrow epaulettes.

The Germans stood at their posts in the enormous boots with thick wooden soles that had been especially made for the guards.

While I ran around, winter came.

It was a Russian city. There were absolutely no Ukrainians in sight.

Russian newspapers were published. I remember *The Kievan Idea* and something on the order of *Day* and *The Devil's Pepper Shaker*.

The Kievan Idea, of course, had existed before, but now it was overshadowed by *The Devil's Pepper Shaker*, run by Pyotr Pilsky and Ilya Vasilevsky (ne-Bukva).

I think that even now they're still publishing *The Devil's Pepper Shaker* somewhere.

There was a bar of sorts—"One-Eyed Jimmie's"—and in it sat Agnivtsev and Lev Nikulin, who later became director of the political section of the Baltic Fleet and is now a member of the Afghanistan legation.

Here I met several members of the SR party, who at that time were connected with the Union for the Rebirth of Russia, the head of which was Stankevich.

The Germans were on their way out. You could feel it in the air that they'd been defeated by the Allies.

In other words, Skoropadsky was also doomed and, because of this, steps had to be taken.

Petlyura's men were moving in from the countryside.

But the Union for the Rebirth of Russia—and, in fact, all of Russian Kiev except the Bolsheviks—was constrained by the will of the Allies.

In Kiev the will of the Allies was embodied in the person of the French consul, who was apparently in Odessa. His name was Hénaud.

Hénaud didn't want any changes to take place in the political situation of the Ukraine.

There was already a revolution going on in Germany. In Kiev the Germans were forming soviets—true, right-wing ones—and getting ready to leave.

Trains loaded with bacon and sugar were already leaving the Ukraine for Germany. The cars belonging to the Russian army—those wonderful Packards—were also being taken to Germany.

The withdrawal of the Germans was by no means a rout.

There were the following forces in the Ukraine: in Kiev, Skoropadsky, supported by the Russian officers. They didn't know themselves why they were supporting him, but that's what Hénaud had ordered.

All around Kiev was Petlyura, with an entire army.

In Kiev were the Germans, who had been ordered by the French to support Skoropadsky.

At least, this is how it looked from the sidelines.

Also in Kiev was the municipal duma, supported by a group of Russian Socialists who were in league with some local workers.

They wanted to stage a democratic revolution, but Hénaud wouldn't allow it.

And on the horizon, promising to "crush us all," loomed the hungry Bolsheviks.

I was asked on this occasion to enlist in the armored division. First I went to the fortress, to Skoropadsky's unit.

There, being a new arrival from Russia, I was asked whether the Bolsheviks would fight. One second lieutenant was interested in knowing whether the Bolsheviks' horses were shod or not.

I left the fortress by a bridge and I don't remember why I was laughing.

Some khokhol passing by stopped and looked at me; with real admiration, he said: "There goes a sly yid for you. He's just fleeced someone and he's laughing about it." There was only admiration in his voice—not a trace of anti-Semitism.

But I didn't serve Skoropadsky directly: I chose the Fourth Armored Division.

The whole unit was Russian. The same kind of drivers, only these leaned more toward the Bolsheviks. Bolshevism thrives in foreign climes.

You heard only Russian spoken in that unit.

They gave me a good welcome and put me to work repairing cars.

Several officers came into the unit when I did and for the same reason.

Petlyura's men had already surrounded the city. Their artillery kept up a constant bombardment and at night you could see the shell bursts.

It was winter. Children were going down all the slopes on toboggans.

I ran across some acquaintances in Kiev. Some were nervous; others were already used to everything. They spoke about the terror during the previous coups.

Worst of all were the Ukrainians. They generally shot Bolsheviks as Russians and Russians as Bolsheviks.

One artist I knew (Davidova) told me that the husband and two brothers of the woman living with her had been shot in their garden (the Ukrainians generally did their shooting in gardens).

She went to claim her dead, but was forbidden to bury them.

She carried the bodies to Davidova's apartment, put them on the couch and spent three days with them like that.

Petlyura's men were coming. The Russian officers fought them without knowing why. The Germans had been ordered to prevent fighting.

And the windows in Kiev were broken. More often than not, there was plywood in the windows rather than glass.

Kiev was to change hands ten more times.

Meanwhile, the cafés functioned as usual and in one theater the soothsayer and clairvoyant Armand Duclos gave a performance.

I attended the performance.

He guessed names that were written on a piece of paper and handed to his assistant. But everyone was most interested in his predictions. I remember the questions. They were all the same type.

Many asked, "Is my furniture in Petersburg still all right?"

"I see, yes, I see it—your furniture," he said to each, as he lurched about the stage in his blindfold; "it's all right."

Once he was asked, "Will the Bolsheviks come to Kiev?"

Duclos promised that they wouldn't.

I met him later in Petersburg—and it was quite funny!—he was serving as a clairvoyant in the cultural and educational section of a Red Army unit and was receiving a food allotment from the Red Army.

I didn't attend his performances there, so I don't know what they asked him about. But I do know this: "The wind blows from the East, the wind blows from the West, and on its circuits the wind returns."[46]

And in this strange daily life, as strong as the sculptured peaks of Gaul, as long as a bread line, what was most strange of all was that we were equally interested in rolls and life. Everything that remained in the soul seemed of equal importance; all things were equal.

Just as water containing ice can be no warmer than 32 degrees, so the soldiers of the armored division were fundamentally Bolsheviks and they despised themselves for serving the hetman.

And I couldn't seem to explain to them what the Constituent Assembly was.

I had one comrade—I won't hide it—he was a Jew. He had been educated as an artist—that is, strictly speaking, not educated.

He had lived in Helsingfors with the sailors and had deserted from the tsar's service, but then I'm very sorry I fought for Lloyd George in June.

Anyway, this artist became a Bolshevik in the province of Perm and collected taxes.

And he said: "All I can say about what we did is that it was worse than the Inquisition." When the peasants caught one of his assistants, they covered him with boards and rolled an iron keg full of kerosene over the boards until he died.

You'll tell me that this doesn't fit in here. So what! I should carry all this in my soul?

But I'll give you something that does fit.

When Skoropadsky's government was on its last legs, when he himself had already fled to Berlin, his empty palace was still being guarded.

A few words about Skoropadsky.

Skoropadsky was elected hetman.

He was then living in Kiev, at the end of an ordinary stairway, in an ordinary apartment.

Once some man climbed up the stairway looking for someone and he rang at Skoropadsky's apartment by mistake. The cleaning woman opened the door.

The man asked:

"Does so-and-so live here?"

The cleaning woman calmly answered:

"No, this is the tsar's house."

And she closed the door.

And that doesn't mean anything either.

So during the last days of Skoropadsky (he was no longer there; he had fled to Berlin, but he was still being guarded), the Whites caught a Ukrainian by the name of Ivanov (a student). These Whites themselves were students—at least the officers were.

They caught him, interrogated him and beat him with ramrods until he died.

They decided against a coup, since they were afraid of pitting Russians against Russians. There were quite a few SR's in Kiev, but the party was in a stupor and not at all happy about its ties with the Union for the Rebirth of Russia.

These ties were living out their last days.

And in the Fourth Armored Division, the soldiers considered me a Bolshevik, even though I told them clearly and precisely what I was.

The armored cars were being taken away from us and sent to the front, which was at first far off in Korosten, then just outside the city and finally right in the city on the Podol.

I put sugar in the hetman's cars.

Here's how it's done: the sugar, either granular or in chunks, is put in the gas tank; it melts and goes along with the gas into the carburetor (a finely calibrated opening, through which the gas mixture passes into the combustion chamber).

Because of the drop in temperature caused by evaporation, the sugar congeals and plugs up the opening.

You can blow out the carburetor with an air pump, but it will clog up again.

But all the same, the cars kept leaving and soon they were all at the Lukyanovsky Barracks, outside our reach.

The men were very well fed and drank vodka.

But at night shell bursts flashed all around the city.

The Union for the Rebirth of Russia had its own unit on the Kreshchatik, but it wasn't kept up to strength and, in general, behaved with more than a little indecisiveness.

The officers and students were mobilized.

Some students were shot and killed at the university for some reason.

The hetman's men found out about Grigoriev's treachery, but all the same they kept believing in something, mainly in outside help from the French.

More deadlines. Finally the decision that the municipal duma would convene and we would support it.

That night I called the unit together, but despite the shell bursts around the city, only fifteen men would follow me. The rest said they had to stay on duty.

There were no armored cars. They were at headquarters on Lukyanovskaya Street.

I commandeered a truck and put some machine guns on it. Bunchuzhny (the sergeant major) tried to alert headquarters, but I tore out the telephone line.

We drove to the Kreshchatik, where the military branch of the Union was supposed to be. No one. But I did find out that volunteers were already on their way to arrest us.

I went to the barracks, where our outfits were. One Latvian fellow was sitting there. His men were ready to go, but he didn't know what to do. At the same time, our men occupied the Lukyanovsky Barracks and put the headquarters staff under arrest.

But we didn't know about this.

The fact is that the duma didn't convene: it had decided not to. And our headquarters had dispersed without telling us beforehand. I looked in all the apartments. There was no one anywhere. I let the men go and headed for the Greter plant on Borshchegovka Street. There sat the workers. They wanted to march on the city, but they were arguing about slogans. So there was no performance, though the orchestra was all ready.

During the afternoon, Petlyura entered the city.

The following men had been handling the work of our organization in Kiev: one strongly right-wing man who looked like a dictator in his high jackboots, one very old man and one Ukrainian, who later became a Bolshevik.

Petlyura's men entered the city in formation.

They had artillery. The soldiers spoke Russian with each other. The townspeople gathered in droves and said loudly, for everyone to hear: "The hetman's men told us they were just gangs. Gangs indeed—it's a real army." This was said in Russian and out of loyalty.

The poor souls, they tried so hard to be enthusiastic.

In 1922, when I was escaping across the ice from Russia to Finland, I met a lady in a fishing shanty on the ice; we continued on together. When we got to shore and the Finns arrested us, she couldn't say enough good things about Finland, of which she had seen about two square yards.

But there is a worse grief, the grief that comes when a man has been tortured so long that he's already "crazed," that is, already out of his mind. They used to use the term "crazed" to describe a man tortured on the rack. The man is being tortured. All around him is only the cold, hard wood of the rack; but the hands of the executioner or his assistant, though hard, are warm and human.

And the man on the rack rubs his cheek against those warm hands which hold him to inflict the torture.

That is my nightmare.

Petlyura's men entered the city. There turned out to be a lot of Ukrainians in the city. I had met them before, working as regimental clerks, etc.

I'm not making fun of the Ukrainians, although, in the bottom of our hearts, we people of Russian background are hostile to any "dialect." How we made fun of the Ukrainian language! A hundred times I heard, "Samoper poper na mordopisniu," which means: "The automobile drove to the photograph." We don't like what isn't our own. Turgenev's "Grae, grae, voropae" weren't inspired by love, either.[47]

But Petlyura was like a national hero—the clerks' hero. Our own clerks approved of him. The Ukrainians entered the city, occupied it, apparently didn't loot and began to decorate the city. They hung out French and English coats-of-arms and eagerly waited for the Allies to send ambassadors. But the soldiers did disarm the volunteers and took their French armored helmets for themselves.

The volunteers were imprisoned in the Pedagogical Museum. Then someone threw a bomb. Dynamite had been stored there and a terrific explosion took place. A lot of men were killed and the glass broken in nearby houses flew all over.

I spent several days in the unit.

We had new officers, among them Bunchuzhny, who had turned out to be a Ukrainian after all.

They told me that they were awfully afraid of the Bolsheviks. What they didn't know was that their own troops were in sympathy with the Bolsheviks.

The troops flowed along like water, seeking a political channel, and the direction was toward Moscow. Meanwhile, the process of Ukrainization went forward.

During those days, all the hard signs in Kiev perished.

The order was given to change all the billboards to Ukrainian.

Not everyone knew the language. We in the units and the Ukrainians sent in from outside talked about technical matters in Russian, occasionally adding a Ukrainian word or two.

Once again it was "Grae, grae, voropae."

There's a mess of pottage for you!

All the billboards had to be changed to Ukrainian in one day.

It's easily done. All you had to do was change the hard sign into a soft sign, and one kind of *i* into another kind.

People worked around the clock. There were ladders everywhere.

The billboards were changed. The hard signs had been put up during Skoropadsky's regime.

I guess I forgot to write about how we lived. I lived in a lawyer's bathroom, and when I couldn't stay there, I settled in an apartment which people had once used for hiding; now people arrived there bearing various tidings, but they were charged about five rubles a night. Still, you could sleep. Hardly anyone had any money. I was still getting paid by my unit. Hardly anyone had an extra shirt.

And no one could figure out where the lice were coming from—such big ones!

The company was very fine. I remember one red-bearded former minister from Belorussia. I don't know his name; we just called him Belorussia. He was a very fine man.

The Union got on everyone's nerves. The party viewed its own military organization with serious misgivings and the military organization felt the same way about the party.

People with any kind of connections joined the police force. Things were now serious, since gangs of marauders armed with machine guns were prowling the streets.

I attempted to work on a newspaper, but Pyotr Pilsky took it upon himself to correct my first review article. I took offense and wouldn't let him print it.

It was at the newspaper office that I found out about the way Kolchak disbanded the National Conference in Ufa.[48]

I was informed of this by a plump woman, the wife of the publisher, who added, "That's right, they ran the others out. Serves them right. Good for the Bolsheviks!"

I fell on the floor in a faint. Completely out. For the first and only time in my life, I fainted. I hadn't realized that the fate of the Constituent Assembly meant so much to me.

By this time, the party had veered sharply to the left. You'd be walking down the Kreshchatik and you'd meet a comrade.

"What's new?"

He'd answer: "Well, I've decided to recognize the Soviet regime!" And so joyfully.

There was more than one occasion when the civil war in Russia could have been stopped. Of course, this can be blamed on the Bolsheviks. But they weren't invented—they were discovered.

At one of our meetings, the right wing said: "Let's try our hand at cultural work." In party jargon, this meant the same as the army command, "Stand in place and smoke, if you want to."

The "jig" was up. It was "curtains." You had to do something, so you did something with no causal connection or, to put it in our philological terminology, something of another semantic norm.

And I delivered a speech. My course isn't clear; I'm not quick to catch on. I too am of another semantic norm—I'm like a samovar used to drive nails.

I said: "Let's recognize this triple-damned Soviet regime! Like at the judgment of Solomon, let's not demand half the baby. Let's give up the baby to strangers; only let him live!"

They shouted at me, "He'll die; they'll kill him."

But what could I do? In this game, I could see only one move at a time.

The party repudiated its military organization. Herman proposed that the organization be renamed the Union for the Defense of the Constituent Assembly; with that, he collected a few men and left for Odessa.

Others intended to head for the Don and fight with Krasnov.

But I intended to head for Russia, to my dear, stern Petersburg.

Most people just fretted.

The Dardanelles were wide open. The Whites were waiting for the French; they believed in the Allies.

And they didn't believe, but a man with property has to believe in something.

It was said that the French had already landed in Odessa and blocked off part of the city with chairs. Those chairs marked the territory of a new French colony and not even cats could get through.

It was said that the French had a violet ray with which they could blind all the Bolsheviks. Boris Mirsky wrote an article about this violet ray called "The Sick Beauty." The beauty was the old world, which needed to be cured with a violet ray.

The Bolsheviks had never struck such terror as they did then. A somber draft was blowing out of somber, empty Russia.

It was said that the English had already landed in Baku a herd of apes trained in all the rules of warfare. The people who said this weren't sick. It was said that you couldn't propagandize these apes, that they went into battle completely without fear and that they would defeat the Bolsheviks.

People held their hands about two feet off the ground to indicate the size of these apes. They said that when Baku was taken, one of these apes was killed and it was buried with a band playing Scottish military music and the Scots cried.

That's because the instructors of the ape legions were Scottish.

A somber draft was blowing out of Russia. The somber spot called Russia was growing. The "sick beauty" was delirious.

People were heading for Constantinople.

If I don't tell it here, then where else can I tell this fact?

When I had first arrived in Kiev, I stopped in to see a manufacturer. He was in tobacco—you could call him a tobacco magnate.

This man had furniture in Petersburg and I had been asked to tell him that his furniture had disappeared.

I stopped to see this man. On the table were marmalade and pastry and cakes and rolls, candy and chocolate, and children at the table, and clean underwear and a wife, and no one had been shot.

Also sitting there was a certain famous Russian humorist.

This humorist said, "There will be no order in Russia until

every home, every back yard and every apartment contains a Bolshevik with his throat cut."

The tobacco magnate was calm. His money was in a foreign bank. He said, "Do you know how much a woman working in my factory at Vilna made?" The humorist didn't know. "Five kopeks a day and, you know, I'm not surprised that they rebelled." (Or maybe he said, "I'm not surprised that they were dissatisfied." I don't remember his exact words.)

This man wasn't sick.

So the Germans were selling knickknacks on the streets, but they were hauling bacon and grain out of the Ukraine, not to mention our cars, which I knew at sight: the Packards and the Locomobiles.

The Germans' trains were guarded by sentries in long fur coats with sheepskin collars.

I remembered that when the Germans were withdrawing during the war, they never forgot to sweep the floors of their offices before they left.

I was invited to the home of a certain lady. She had found out that I was leaving. This lady lived in a room full of rugs and antique mahogany furniture. Both she and the furniture looked pretty good to me. She was heading for Constantinople; her husband lived in Petersburg.

She asked me to take some money to Russia—about seven thousand, I guess. That was real money then.

It's hard not to be well dressed.

"During the war," I was young and loved cars, but when you're walking down Nevsky Prospekt, and it's spring, and the women are already lightly and beautifully dressed in their spring outfits— when spring comes and everywhere women, women, then it's hard to walk down the street dirty.

It was hard even in Kiev to walk among well-dressed people with car chains on your shoulders. I love silk stockings. But in Petersburg, the dear and stern, it wasn't hard. When you carried a big black bag, even with firewood in it, you were only proud to be strong. But there are silk stockings in Petersburg now.

This woman embarrassed me. I took her money, drilled a hole in a heavy spoon and in the handle of a knife, and put the thousand-ruble notes in them.

Now the whole question was how to go. I spent a few more days in Kiev, greeted the New Year in the black, empty building of the municipal duma, ate sausage, but drank no vodka.

On the street, I ran into a prisoner of war coming from Germany. I exchanged clothes and documents with him (they consisted of one sheet of paper) and decided that now it was possible to go.

I went to say good-by to an artist friend. She looked me over and said, "It's not bad, but don't look anyone in the eye or you'll be recognized."

And so I blended into the hungry, dirty army of POW's.

Those coming from Austria were dressed in various nondescript military castoffs; those coming from Germany in uniforms with a yellow stripe on the sleeve and sometimes on the pants.

The prisoners from Germany were even more emaciated than those from Austria.

I attempted to spend the night in a wooden barracks.

It was strange to see some of the soldiers urinating right on the bunks.

All around, you heard the kind of conversations that were engendered by this infinitely wretched way of life. You heard conversations about whorehouses.

They said in all seriousness that in Kiev, Tereshchenko had set up a whorehouse for the prisoners, with nurses wearing white smocks in attendance. And first of all, they washed you.

And these weren't cynical conversations, but just dreams about a clean whorehouse. They looked for these houses all over Kiev, believed in them and asked each other for the address.

I ought to say that, generally speaking, the least cynical thing I heard in the army about women were these words: "No matter how good the chow is, if there aren't any broads around, something's still missing."

Another excerpt from POW folklore is the story about how a prisoner returning to Russia runs into his wife, who's going in the other direction with a Hungarian prisoner.

First of all, the soldier takes the Hungarian's gold watch—this is obviously an epic image—then he undresses him and takes away his fine clothing, then he takes his suitcases and finally he kills him.

But he takes his wife back to Russia, saying to his traveling companions, "I'll find out who she sold my stuff to, then I'll kill her."

This story was composed outside Russia. It's purely legendary, which is clear from the fact that all the prices for the cattle sold by the woman are based on prewar norms.

We set out.

In dress and every other way, I was just like the POW's. The only difference was the wool sweater under my jacket and the leather boots on my feet.

We spent a long time riding around the Ukraine. The Germans kept taking our locomotives. We were silent. I never saw such downtrodden men as those prisoners.

We slept in the railroad cars. The next morning, it turned out that several men had frozen to death. The stoves had been removed from the cars, so, instead of a stovepipe, there was a hole in the roof and there were holes in the floor. We made trivets out of bricks and covered them with pieces of metal from the undercarriage of the car. We burned dried weeds. They gave us thin soup to eat on the journey, but there were no bowls.

I was surprised to see some of the prisoners take off their shoes, which had wooden soles, and use them as bowls.

We got to the border. Here we were told that we had to walk about ten miles to get to the Russian train.

We walked along, wooden shoes clattering. We stopped in at some huts, where they gave us something to eat and asked whether this was all of us. Many had relatives who'd been taken prisoner, or "perhaps" had been.

If I were to wind up on an uninhabited island, I'd become not Robinson Crusoe, but an ape. That's what my wife said about me. I never heard a truer definition. It wasn't hard for me.

I have the capacity to flow, to change, even to become ice or steam. I can fit into any kind of shoes. I went along with the others.

I gave my neighbor a wool blanket, in which I'd been wrapping myself.

We had arrived. Russia.

A train was waiting—armored, with a red inscription "Death to the bourgeois dogs." The letters stuck out as if they were climbing into the air, but the armored train itself was moth-eaten and empty-looking.

The train was waiting. We climbed in. It was cold. A group of disabled veterans carrying bags was going with us. At that time, disabled veterans were permitted to haul provisions, which gave them a sort of pension. They climbed in; they scrambled over the edge on their bellies and crawled into our trivet-heated cars. These disabled veterans with their bags and the POW's were traveling along the black rails toward Russia. Russia put plus signs between both groups and between much else and it all added up to Bolsheviks. We were on our way.

We were given dried fish, but no bread. We gnawed at it. Bacon and the feeling of being full were only memories.

The POW's didn't talk, didn't ask any questions. When we got there, we would find out.

Included in the train were cars full of coffins, with the black inscription, hastily scrawled in tar:

RETURN COFFINS

When men died, they were taken as far as Kursk and buried. But the coffins went back. These boxes could be used again.

We came to some station and saw a passenger train. It was absolutely packed. People were climbing in the windows, which is risky: someone's likely to remove your boots while you're climbing in.

I started out riding between the cars: there were a lot of men on top of the cars, too. Russia flowed by slowly, like cobbler's wax.

I worked myself like a corkscrew into one of the cars. I kept twisting and finally wedged myself in. Then I sat there and scratched.

A man was sitting across from me. He asked some questions. I answered. He said, "How did you sink to such a level? I could understand it in somebody else, but not in you."

I kept my mouth shut.

"And I," he said, "know who you are!"

"Who am I?"

"You're one of the Petersburg metalworkers, probably from the Vyborg side of town."

With genuine enthusiasm, I said, "How did you guess?"

"It's my specialty. I'm from the Kursk Cheka."

He wasn't kidding—the fur coat and gold watch—but he wasn't too squeamish about me; he put me at ease.

We traveled on.

Then another wave of POW's. We were already past Kursk. Some soldier urinated on my bag from up above and I had about twenty pounds of sugar in it. A lot of the prisoners were carrying sugar.

That night we arrived in Moscow. The city was dark. Books were being burned at the railroad station and all around were big signs with gold letters. We walked through the city at night. It was terrifying—completely deserted.

We came to some lane and spent the night on bunks.

On one wall was a big sign depicting a man with lice on his collar and under his arms. I looked at it very attentively.

The next morning, I was issued papers in the name of Iosif Vilenchik, summer pants, a sort of double-breasted jacket, underwear, a spoonful of sugar and one yellow kerenka worth twenty rubles.

I went to see a philologist friend of mine. He was overjoyed to see me and gave me a place to sleep. He wasn't afraid of lice, though he hadn't caught typhus yet.

He caught it later and was so sick he forgot his own name.

We sat and talked, stoking the fire with shelves from the bookcase, a chest removed from under a butterfly collection, and window frames.

I went by to see Krylenko and gave him a letter from his sister in Kiev (I had known her in Kiev).

I told him that there were no victors, but that there had to be peace.

He agreed, but he said that they were the victors and that the state of emergency would soon be over. I went to see Krylenko's mother. She lived in a garden on the Ostozhenko side of town.

I returned to the barracks and left for Petersburg with a group of POW's. We went on the train.

I took off my cap in the car. I have a striking head, which was bald even then, with a very prominent forehead.

I took off my cap and lay down on an upper berth. Some other men who weren't POW's came into the car. We swore at them. I have a loud voice.

I climbed down and sat on the bench. It was a third-class coach, not heated, and it was rather well lit.

And suddenly a man in a white collar sitting across from me turned to me and said, "I know you. You're Shklovsky."

I looked and saw on his chest a piece of blue material. That was the badge that the Cheka agents had worn when they stood around my apartment. And I recognized this man's face. He had usually stood on the corner.

Even now as I write, my heart's in my throat. And I remember very well the little blue ribbon, though I never heard anyone mention a Cheka uniform.

I replied, "I'm Vilenchik. I just got out of a German camp. I don't know you. You see my comrades? I lived with them in the prison camps for three years."

The POW's didn't understand what was going on. They thought it was a question of their right to be traveling. Someone up above absent-mindedly said, "He's one of us. Let him alone."

The car was made of wood and well lit. It began to seem a little close in there.

I said to the agent, "Look, now that we're acquainted, let's have some tea. I've got sugar."

I climbed up, got my bag, put it down, took out the tea kettle, went into the next compartment for some boiling water and, without a second thought, walked through the car and out onto the rear platform.

On the platform, I put the tea kettle down, stepped on the landing, jumped off and started to run, painfully banging my feet on the railroad ties.

If an express had been coming, it would have flattened me.

I saw the tail light of the train disappear.

It was snowing a little. I'd left my overcoat on the train. On one side of the rails it was snowing so hard you couldn't see a thing. On the other side I saw a road.

I followed the road. This happened around Klin.

I walked until I came to a village. I knocked. They let me in. I said that I had missed the train, that I worked in Austria as a civilian and that I wanted to buy a jacket made of good, light sheepskin. They sold it for 250 rubles.

I also bought some boots, for which I handed over my sweater; it was instantly put on top the stove to drive out the lice. I had a lot of them.

Then I drank some tea. The tea was made out of birch sap and had no taste or smell, only color. You could boil this sap for a year without making it any worse.

I hired a horse and by morning had made it to the next station for Moscow.

At the station, I boarded a local train, went as far as Petrovsk-Razumovsky, then got to Moscow on another train.

Gorky was in Moscow and I knew him from having worked on his publications *The New Life* and *Annals*.

I went to see Aleksei Maksimovich Gorky. He wrote a letter to Yakov Sverdlov. Sverdlov didn't keep me in the waiting room. He led me into a big room with a real rug on the floor.

Yakov Sverdlov turned out to be a young man; he was wearing a jacket and leather trousers.

This was during the time when the Ufa Conference was breaking up and Volsky's group was appearing.[49] Sverdlov received me without suspicion. I told him I wasn't a White and he didn't interrogate me. He gave me a letter on an official form of the Central Executive Committee and in the letter he asked that the Shklovsky case be closed.

Before I left Moscow, I ran into Larisa Reisner. She welcomed me and asked if I couldn't help her get Fyodor Raskolnikov out of Revel. I was introduced to some member of the Revolutionary War Council.

I was used to being in motion and I had no quarrel with the Bolsheviks, so I agreed to attack Revel with armored cars and attempt to take the prison.

This enterprise never came off because the sailors who were supposed to go with me went off in every which way, but mostly to Yamburg for pork. Some of them had typhus.

The English eventually traded Fyodor Raskolnikov for something or other.

Meanwhile, I went to Petersburg with Reisner on some sort of fantastic mandate that she had signed.

She was then Commissar of General Naval Headquarters.

While he was working on my case, Gorky finally wrangled a promise from the Central Committee to release the former grand dukes. He believed that the terror was over and that the grand dukes could work with him on the antiquarian commission.

But he was tricked. On the very night when I was going to Moscow, the grand dukes were shot by the Petersburg Cheka.

When Nikolai Mikhailovich was shot, he was holding a kitten in his arms.

I arrived in Petersburg and went to see Elena Stasova at the Smolny Institute. She worked for the Cheka and was handling my case. I went to her office and gave her the note from Sverdlov. Stasova is a thin, very intellectual-looking blonde. Good-looking. She told me that I was under arrest and that Yakov Sverdlov's note carried no weight, since the Cheka was autonomous. She said something like this: "Both Sverdlov and I are party members. He can't give me orders."

I said that I wasn't afraid of her and asked her not to try to intimidate me. Stasova then very kindly and efficiently explained that she wasn't intimidating me, just arresting me. But she didn't arrest me. She let me go without insisting on my arrest and she advised me not to come back to her office, but to telephone her. I walked out with sweat running down my back. I called her a day later and she told me my case was closed. All in a very satisfied voice.

In short, the Cheka wanted to arrest me in 1922 for something I did in 1918, without taking into account that my case had been closed by the amnesty granted at the Saratov proceedings and by my own personal appearance before Stasova. I couldn't give evidence against my former comrades. That is not my specialty.

At the beginning of 1919, then, I turned up in St. Pete. It was an ominous, primitive time. I saw how sledges were invented.

At first, people simply dragged their bags and things along the sidewalk; then they started to tie a piece of wood to their bags. By the end of the winter, sledges had been invented.

It was worse with houses. The city wasn't designed for this new way of life. It was impossible to build new houses. And no one knew how to build igloos.

At first, the old-fashioned furnaces were kept going with furniture; then people just stopped using them. Instead, they moved into the kitchen. Everything was now divided into two categories: combustible and noncombustible. During the period from 1920 to 1922, a new type of abode was constructed.

This consisted of a small room with a small pot-bellied stove. Little tin boxes hung from the joints of the stovepipes to catch the tar.

Food was cooked on these stoves.

Life was wretched during this "period of transition."

People slept in their coats, covered with rugs. People who lived in houses with central heating died in droves.

They froze to death—whole apartments of them.

Almost everyone sat around at home in his coat. You tied a rope around the bottom of the coat to keep in the warmth.

We didn't know yet that you have to eat fats to live. We ate only potatoes and bread—bread with particular greediness. Wounds don't heal without fats. Scratch your hand and the hand rots and the rag on the wound rots.

We wounded ourselves with implacable axes. We had little interest in women. We were impotent; the women had stopped menstruating.

Love affairs began later. Everything was as bare and open as a watch with its back off. Women slept with men because they were living in the same apartment. Girls with thick braids surrendered themselves at five-thirty in the afternoon because the streetcars stopped running at six.

Everything had its own time.

A friend of mine, a man who they said at the university had all the signs of genius, lived in the middle of his old room between four chairs covered with a tarpaulin and some rugs. He crawled in there, warmed the air with his breath and lived. And he installed electricity there. That's where he wrote his work on the similarities between the Malayan language and the Japanese. As far as politics went, he was a Communist.

The water mains burst and the toilets froze. It's terrible when a man has to relieve himself on the street. A dear friend of mine, not the one who lived under the rugs, said he envied the dogs: they had no shame.

It was cold. People burned books in their stoves. They lingered in the dark "House of Writers" to escape the freezing cold and ate scraps from other people's plates.

Once it turned bitter cold—extraordinarily cold. It had apparently never been so cold. It was like a deluge.

People were freezing to death, were dying.

But then a warm, humid wind began to blow and the warm air hit the walls of the houses, frozen through and through, and turned them silver. The whole city was silver now; previously only the Aleksandrovsky Column had been silver.

The walls of the few rooms that were heated in the houses showed up from the street as occasional dark patches on the silver. It was 45 degrees at my place. People came to get warm and to sleep on the floor around the stove. Shortly before, I had broken up a shed for wood. Some of my old students from the drivers' school had invited me to the dismemberment. They also put iron runners on my sledge. They were living by means of stolen kerosene.

And so the thaw began. I went out on the street. A warm western wind.

I saw my friend coming, swathed in a hood, a rug and something else. He was pulling a sledge and in the sledge, bundle within bundle, sat his little girl.

I stopped him and said, "Boris, it's warm out." He couldn't tell the difference anymore.

I went to get warm and to eat at Grzhebin's house. While I was there, the State Publishing House sent Grzhebin a letter from Merezhkovsky in which he asked the revolutionary government (Soviet) to support him (Merezhkovsky), "a man who had always been for the Revolution," by buying his collected works. His collected works, however, he had already sold to Grzhebin. Yury Annenkov and Mikhail Slonimsky also read this letter. I'm capable of selling the same manuscript to two publishers, but I wouldn't have written such a letter.

People were dying and the corpses were being hauled on sleds. The corpses were being left in deserted apartments. Funerals were too expensive.

Once I paid a visit to some old friends. They were living in a house on a very aristocratic street. First they would burn the furniture, then the floor boards, and then they would move into the next apartment. Rather like the slash-and-burn school of agriculture.

There was no one in the house but them.

In Moscow there was more food, but it was colder and more crowded.

A certain military unit was living in one Moscow house. Two stories had been assigned to the men, but they didn't use them. First they settled on the lower story and burned up everything; then they moved to the upper, cut a hole through to the lower apartment, locked the lower apartment and used the hole as a toilet.

This enterprise functioned for a year.

It wasn't so much swinishness as the use of things from a new point of view, and weakness.

Without being shod like a horse, without cleats of some kind, it's hard to stand up on the damned ice.

There's a roaring in your ears, you're half-dead from the strain and you fall down. But your head keeps thinking by itself about "The Connection between Plot Devices and General Stylistic Devices." "Please don't forget the suspenders." I was just finishing my article then. Boris was finishing his.[50] Osip Brik had finished his article on "sound repetitions." In 1919 the "IMO" Publishing House published our booklet *Poetics*—fifteen printer's signatures, with forty thousand characters per signature.

We held meetings. Once we met in a room that was flooded. We sat on the backs of chairs. Sometimes we met in the dark. Sergei Bondi would come noisily into the dark entranceway with two huge wooden boxes tied together by a rope. The rope cut into his shoulder.

Somebody lit a match. His face, young and bearded, was the face of Christ taken down from the cross.

We worked from 1917 to 1922. We created a scientific school and rolled a rock up the mountain.

My wife (I got married in 1919 or 1920 and took my wife's name, Kordi, but I didn't stick to it: I sign my name Shklovsky) lived on the Petersburg side of town.

It was very far.

We decided to move closer to the center of town.

A young Communist invited us to move into his apartment.

He lived on Znamenskaya Street.

He was the son of a lawyer who owned some mines near Rostov-on-the-Don.

His father had died after the October coup. His uncle had shot himself. He left a note: "The damn Bolsheviks."

Now he lived all by himself. He was a fine and honest boy. I liked the mahogany writing desk in his room.

We shared the housekeeping tasks. We ate bread when there was some, and we ate horsemeat. We sold our things. It was easier for me to sell my things than it was for him. I had fewer qualms. When it was cold, I went around his apartment with an ax and chopped up the furniture, which pained him.

Yudenich had launched his attack. Communists were being mobilized and sent to the front.

When the Bashkirs were fleeing, he threw bombs at them.

He was wounded in the shoulder during an attack.

He was sent to the infirmary. The wound wouldn't heal because of his fat deficiency.

Finally, it began to knit.

He was sent to the front again, only this time the front was a place not far from Petersburg. Somewhere around Lembolov.

The Greens were attacking. Then he was transferred still closer to Petersburg.

He was staying at headquarters. He caught typhus. He lay in a barracks. Water dripped onto the roof. Some of the sick men were insane. They crawled around under the beds and raved.

The boy's heart kept stopping.

His heart kept stopping and he had to have an injection of camphor. There wasn't any camphor.

A nurse was making the rounds of the infirmary. The boy was handsome, a tennis-player type with a broad chest. She gave him a camphor injection, the last, the very last ampule in the infirmary. He got well.

Finland was stirring.[51] A supreme effort had to be made.

Trotsky shouted, "Comrades, let us make the supreme effort!"

The Communist went back to the front. There was snow. Snow and spruce, or pines. One time he and a comrade were riding their horses through the snow, riding, riding.

Then he stopped, got off his horse and sat on a rock. Sitting on a rock signifies despair in the epic (see A. Veselovsky, volume 3). He sat on a real rock and started to weep. He'd been riding with a comrade.

His comrade jumped on his horse and rode full-tilt to the apartment for some cocaine.

The supreme effort had to be made. The Communist was taken and sent to the front against Poland.[52]

At first, his group advanced. Then they were cut off. He was taken prisoner. He managed to get rid of his Cheka papers. (He was a Cheka agent.)

They found the papers, but the photograph had been so damaged that they didn't recognize the Communist.

The prisoners were beaten and then they decided to shoot them

the next morning. During the night, some Jews, members of the
Bund who were guarding the prisoners, let them go. They escaped
and were taken prisoner by another unit.

This time, they were beaten, but not shot.

They were taken captive and held in various prisons for a year.
And during this year, the soldiers never said that he was an agent
for the Cheka.

I have to write that.

When the other prisoners walked past his cell, they slipped him
cans of food from behind their backs and said, "Take it, comrade."

The soldiers and the officers fed him. The Poles beat him
terribly, especially on the calves of the leg. They say that marks
don't show on the calves of the leg.

It was cold. His toes were frostbitten. They amputated his toes.

A captured Red Army nurse was raped. The Polish officers
infected her with syphilis. She was sleeping with them.

She infected them, then poisoned herself with morphine. She left
a note: "I became a prostitute to infect the Poles."

But I am an art theoretician. I am a falling stone and, looking
down, I know what motivation is!

I don't believe the note.

And even if I believe it, what's it to me, pray tell, that the Polish
officers were infected?

They beat him for a long time. Then the Poles gave him back to
the Bolsheviks in exchange for a Polish priest.

Those of us in Petersburg had already given him up for dead.

He came back. He came to see me wearing a peaked cap with a
silent orderly in tow.

He had become stooped. He had a terrible look in his eyes. He
had ridden all across Russia, now under the New Economic Policy.

At night he slept at my place on the couch.

At night I often dream that a bomb is exploding in my hands.

That happened to me once.

Sometimes at night I dream that the ceiling is falling, that the
world is coming to an end. Then I run to the window and I see the
last fragment of the moon floating in an empty sky.

I say to my wife, "Lusya, keep calm and get dressed. The world
has come to an end."

The Communist slept very badly. He cried out and wept in his
sleep and had bad dreams.

I felt very sorry for him.

He was living in a small town near Petersburg and had little money, but you could get vodka for bread in that town and the high-school girls were taking up prostitution.

I think it would be terrible to sleep next to him at night.

Several days before my flight from Russia in 1922, I got a letter from the Communist. He was in prison.

The Special Section had quarreled with the local Cheka. The Communist had caught an agent of the Cheka following him and had beaten him up unmercifully.

He was arrested and found guilty on sixteen counts—among other things, for having willfully taken a shirt when he got out of the prison camp without any clothes.

And this is all about the Communist. He's already been released.

I was starving at that time, so I became an instructor at an automobile school on Semyonovskaya Street.

The school was in such a state that when we wanted something transported, we had to do it by hand. There wasn't a single car. The classrooms weren't heated. The life of the unit was concentrated on the commissary. A pound of bread was issued every day, as well as herring, several grams of rye and a piece of sugar.

When you got home, it was terrible to look at those puny portions. As if you were being mocked. Once beef was issued. What a fantastic taste it had! It was like the first time you slept with a woman. Something entirely new. Frozen potatoes were also issued and sometimes the Commissariat of Education gave out jam. Potatoes were issued by the bushel basket. They were so soft that you could squash them in your fingers. You had to wash the frozen potatoes in cold running water, preferably stirring them in the sink with a stick. That rubbed the peels off. Then you mashed them up with meat or herring, but you had to put in a lot of pepper. Horsemeat was also issued. Once they issued a lot—you could take as much as you wanted! It was almost runny. We took it.

Horsemeat was cooked in whale oil. At least, it was called whale oil. Actually, it was spermaceti(?), which works fine in face creams, but sets your teeth on edge.

We used rye flour and horsemeat to make beef stroganoff. Once we got hold of a lot of bread and invited guests. We fed them all on horsemeat and bread—as much as you wanted, with no ration cards and two caramels apiece for dessert.

The guests were soon in a good-natured mood and were only sorry that they hadn't brought their wives.

By that time, our book *Poetics* had come out. We had to use very thin paper, even thinner than toilet paper. That's all we could find.

The edition was turned over to the Commissariat of Education, but we all got royalties.

The bookstores hadn't been closed yet, but books were being distributed by the Commissariat of Education. This went on almost three years.

Books were being printed in enormous editions—generally no fewer than 10,000 copies and often as many as 200,000. The Commissariat of Education did almost all the printing. It picked up the books and sent them to the Central Printing Depot.

Central Printing, in turn, sent them to regional printing depots, and so on.

The result of all this was that there were no books in Russia. For example, 900 copies of astronomy charts would be sent to Gomel. What happened to them then? They just lay there.

Our book was distributed to the various Red Army reading rooms in Saratov. An enormous number of editions were lost in warehouses. Simply misplaced. Propaganda literature, especially toward the end, was used to roll cigarettes. There were some cities —Zhitomir, for instance—where no one saw a new book for three years.

Those books that were cranked out were chosen at random—except, of course, the propaganda.

It's fantastic how much more stupid a state is than an individual! A publisher will find a reader and a reader will find a book. And an individual manuscript will find a publisher. But if you add a State Publishing House and a State Printing Office, what you get is mountains of books—a Mont Blanc of books like Lemke's *250 Days at the Tsar's General Headquarters*. Literature was abandoned, sent away to foundling homes.

You heard such incredible stories! Milk's being collected. The order says to take all the milk to such-and-such a place by such-and-such a day. But there aren't any containers, so it's poured on the ground. This happened near Tver. The chairman of a commission for the collection of taxes in kind (a Communist) told me about it. Finally they found some containers—herring barrels. They poured in the milk, hauled it off, got it there and then had to pour it out. Even the smell made them sick. The same thing with eggs. Just think that Petersburg ate only frozen potatoes for two or three years.

All of life had to be reduced to a formula and regulated. A ready-made formula was imported. The result—we ate rotten potatoes.

In 1915, I was working in the Aviation School connected with the Polytechnical Institute. One time we received a certain paper.

It was a very important-looking paper and had been sent to all the schools and all the companies. On it was written: "Be absolutely certain that the aviation mechanics can distinguish the gasoline line from the oil line in the Gnome engine."

This is like sending a circular to all the villages telling them not to confuse cows with horses. It turned out, however, that they weren't joking.

Now a few words about the "Gnome" rotary engine.

The "Gnome" is an unusual, paradoxical engine. Its crankshaft stands still while the cylinders, with the propellers fastened to them, revolve.

I don't want to explain all the details of this machine to you right now. Let me just say that both the oil line and the gasoline line go through the crankshaft.

This engine takes castor oil (or, rather, used to—hardly any airplanes use this engine anymore). It takes a lot of oil. Centrifugal pressure even forces the oil through the valves into the cylinder heads.

If you walk up to this type of engine while it's running, you risk getting splashed with oil.

And the engine gives off the sweet, heady smell of burning castor oil.

In short, the cost of oil for this engine runs nearly as much as the cost of the gasoline. I don't remember the exact cost. Our mechanics, however, did get the oil and gas lines mixed up.

When that happened, the oil ran through the crankshaft into the bowels of the engine and from there through the piston valves into the compression chamber. The gasoline, when poured into the oil line, ran through the crankshaft into the connecting rods and from there through the piston cam into the walls of the cylinders. The funny thing is—the engines actually ran. They ran on the oil in the gasoline. They ran because they weren't accurately tuned up. There was no attempt at economy—"throw in some more" was the motto—and the gasoline would somehow go into the right place and explode. That system kept the engines running about five minutes.

Then the steel on the machines took on the color of stale water, the piston flooded and the machine stopped forever.

French mechanics were called in to look at them. I don't know whether they fainted or started to cry.

That's when the circular was sent around.

The Bolsheviks entered a Russia that was already sick, but they weren't neutral—no, they were a special kind of organizing bacillus, but of another world and dimension. It was like organizing a state of fish and fowl based on a double bookkeeping system.

But the mechanism which fell into the hands of the Bolsheviks, and into which they might have fallen, was so imperfect that it could run even when improperly serviced.

On oil instead of gasoline.

The Bolsheviks held out, are holding out and will hold out, thanks to the imperfections of the mechanism which they control.

However, I'm unjust toward them. Just as unjust as the deaf man who looks at people dancing and thinks they're insane. The Bolsheviks had their own music.

This whole digression is built on the device which in my "poetics" is called retardation.

Not long before his arrest, Professor Tikhvinsky was telling this story in my presence: "When we captured Grozny, we telegraphed right way that oil should be taken only from certain wells and not from others. Our telegram was ignored. They pumped oil with a high paraffin content into the tank cars and sent it to Petersburg. It's colder here. The oil congealed and wouldn't run out of the tank cars. The only places they'd used it before were on the Transcaspian roads. Now all our tank cars are tied up so we can't send them back for more and our supply's been stopped. About the only way to get the oil out of those tank cars is with your bare hands and then you wouldn't know what to do with it."

You had to listen to stories like this every day. If I could just relate the things that happened to automobiles alone!

People will ask, how did Russia ever permit such things to happen?

There's a migratory plot that the Boers in northern Africa tell about the Kaffirs and that the Jews in southern Russia tell about the Ukrainians.

A man buys some sacks of flour from a local farmer.

He says to him: "You don't know how to write, so I'll give you one new twenty-kopek piece for every sack of flour and then I'll pay you one ruble, twenty-five kopeks, for every twenty-kopek piece." The local farmer brought ten sacks and got ten twenty-kopek pieces, but he hated to give them back—they were brand-new —so he stole two and gave back only eight. This netted two rubles, ten kopeks, for the flour buyer.

Russia has stolen a lot of twenty-kopek pieces from herself. A few at a time, from every railroad car. She has ruined whole factories to make boots out of fan belts.

And meanwhile, it's not over yet. Russia keeps on stealing, a little at a time. Not a single railroad car could get from Revel to Petersburg in one piece—that's how people are living.

And as for me, I can't make any sense out of all the strange things I've seen in Russia.

Is it good to trouble my heart and tell about what happened?

And to judge without calling witnesses? I can speak only for myself, and then not everything.

I write, but the shore does not recede from me. I cannot lose myself like a wolf in a forest of thoughts, a forest of words created by me. The shores do not vanish. Life looms on every side, and not the verbal ocean, whose waters are nowhere in sight. The thought runs and runs along the ground and still, like a poorly built airplane, cannot take off.

And the blizzard of inspiration does not want to whirl my thoughts into the air, nor does the god of the shaman lift them from the ground. I lick my lips; they are without foam.

And all this because I cannot forget about the trial, about that trial which begins in Moscow tomorrow.

Life flows in staccato pieces belonging to different systems.

Only our clothing, not the body, joins together the disparate moments of life.

Consciousness illuminates a strip of segments held together only by light, as a projector illuminates a piece of cloud, the sea, a piece of shore, a forest, paying no heed to ethnographic boundaries.

But the madness is systematic: during sleep, everything is ordered.

And at this moment, with my life in fragments, I stand before the ordered consciousness of the Communists.

But my life is ordered, too, if only by its madness, whose name eludes me.

And you, friends of these last years, I grew up with you. In the reeking streets of Petersburg the simple and touching, we grew our works, needed, apparently, by no one.

I'll continue making a cross-section of my life.

By spring, I had come down with yellow jaundice, apparently caused by the bad food at the dining hall (not gratis) of the automobile company.

I got absolutely green and yellow, as bright as a canary. Even my eyes were yellow.

I didn't feel like moving, thinking or going out. Yet I had to get firewood and carry it myself.

It was cold. My sister gave me firewood and also some bread made out of rye flour with flax seed.

I was surprised by the darkness in her apartment. She wasn't on the reserved cable.[53]

Her children sat and waited quietly in the dark nursery, lit only by a "gasoline candle"—that's a metal cylinder with an asbestos fuse, something like a big cigarette lighter.

Two little girls: Galya and Marina.

A few days later, my sister died suddenly. I was shaken.

My sister Evgenia was the person closest to me. We were very much alike in the face and I could guess her thoughts.

What distinguished her from me was her indulgent, hopeless pessimism.

She died at the age of twenty-seven.

She had a good voice, had studied and wanted to sing.

There's no need to cry. The need is to love the living!

How hard it is to think that people have died and you haven't managed to say even a tender word to them.

And people died alone.

There's no need to cry.

The winter of 1919 changed me greatly.

At the end of the winter, we all got alarmed and decided to clear out of Petersburg.

When my sister was dying, she imagined in her delirium that I was leaving and taking the children of our slain brother with me.

It was terrifying. My aunt died of hunger.

My wife and her sister decided to go to the south. I was supposed to catch up with her in Kherson.

It was hard to get a travel permit. Kiev had just been occupied by the Reds.

My wife left. It was about the first of May.

I didn't see her for another year. Denikin began to advance and cut off the south. It was spring. There was dysentery in the city.

I was lying in an infirmary. Some syphilitic was dying in the corner.

It was a good infirmary and while I was there, I started to write the first book of my memoirs, *Revolution and the Front*.

It was spring. I walked along the quay. As I did every year.

During the summer, I continued to write. On Whitsunday I was writing in a dacha in Lakhta.

The glass was shaking from the heavy shell bursts. Kronstadt, hidden in smoke, was exchanging fire with Krasnaya Gorka.[54] My writing desk was shaking.

Mama was concocting piroshki. She was running wheat through a meat grinder. There was no flour. The children were overjoyed to be at the dacha because of the garden.

That isn't bad—it's life's momentum that enables you to keep living and the habit of repeating days heals wounds.

Back in the fall of 1918, a translators' studio had opened at Gorky's World Literature Publishing House on Nevsky Prospekt.

It had very quickly turned into a literary studio.

Here N. S. Gumilyov, L. Lozinsky, E. Zamyatin, Andrei Levinson, Kornei Chukovsky and Vladislav Shileiko gave lectures. Later B. M. Eikhenbaum and I were invited.

I had a very good young audience. We studied the theory of the novel. With the help of my students, I was writing my articles on *Don Quixote* and Sterne.[55] I never in my life worked the way I did that year. I argued with Aleksandra Veksler about the significance of the stock character in the novel.

It's so nice to go from work to work, from novel to novel, and to see what theory comes out of them.

Soon we moved from Nevsky Prospekt to the Muruzi residence on Liteiny Prospekt.

The Translators' Studio had already detached itself from World Literature.

It was a luxurious apartment in the Eastern style, with a marble stairway—all in all, very much like a bathhouse. The stove was kept going with Menshevik literature, left over from some sort of club.

During the fall of 1919, Yudenich attacked.

The defenders of Petersburg were shooting at Strelna from the Petropavlovskaya Fortress.

In the smoke, the fortress seemed like a ship.

Street barricades were being built out of wood and sandbags.

From inside the city it seemed that there wasn't enough manpower to resist; from outside the city, as I now read, it seemed that there wasn't enough manpower to attack.

Deserters were riding around town on streetcars.

And shell bursts—the shell bursts hung in the air like clouds in the sky.

It was civil war and two voids were attacking each other.

There were no Red and White Armies.

That's no joke. I saw the war.

The Whites stood like smoke all around the city. The city lay as if asleep.

The Semyonovsky Regiment finally concluded the treachery which it had been preparing for three years.[56]

And one of my soldier comrades came to me and said:

"Listen, Shklovsky, they say that even the Finns are going to attack us. No, I won't have the third Pargolovo conquering us. I'll join the machine gunners."

The besieged city had only cabbage to eat. Then the arrow of the manometer slowly moved past zero, the wind started to blow away from Petersburg and the Whites dispersed.

A new winter had come.

I kept alive by buying nails in Petersburg and taking them to the country to exchange for bread.

On one of these excursions, I met an artilleryman on the train. We had a conversation. He and his three-inch cannon had already been captured many times, first by the Reds, then by the Whites. He himself said, "I know just one thing—how to shoot."

That winter of 1919–1920, I worked in the Translators' Studio and on the newspaper *The Life of Art*, where I was invited by Maria Fyodorovna Andreeva. The salary was small, but sometimes women's stockings were issued. But how can I properly convey in memoirs all the activity that filled that winter?

I've decided to tell in this spot about Aleksei Maksimovich Peshkov—Maksim Gorky.

I first met Gorky in 1915, at the office of *Annals*. He was tall, with close-cropped hair—a little stooped, blue-eyed, very strong-looking.

Before I say anything else about Gorky, I must say that Aleksei Maksimovich saved my life several times. He interceded for me with Sverdlov and gave me money when I was about to die, and, toward the end, my life in St. Pete was spent among several enterprises that he created.

I'm writing all this not as a character sketch of the man, but as a fact of my own biography.

I was often at Gorky's place.

I'm a witty man and I love other people's jokes. At Gorky's place, we laughed a lot.

There was a special conversational tone—a special attitude toward life. An ironic nonrecognition of it.

Something on the order of the tone of a conversation with the stepmother in Tolstoy's *Boyhood*.

Gorky has an article in *The New Life* about a French officer who saw that his unit had been decimated and who cried out in the heat of battle, "Rise from the dead!"

He was French and consequently believed in fine words. And because many frightened soldiers had lain down during the battle and couldn't stand up because of the bullets, the dead did rise.

The French have sublime faith and no fear of heroics. But we Russians died spouting curses. Both we and the French have a fear of the ridiculous, but we Russians fear especially the grandiose and the dashing.

And so we die with a laugh.

Gorky has had a long life. Of all the Russian writers, perhaps he alone used characters with the dashing quality of Dumas's heroes. And in his first stories, the dead did rise.

Gorky's bolshevism is ironic, a bolshevism without faith in man. By bolshevism, I don't mean membership in the political party. Gorky never belonged to the party.

It's impossible to lead the dead into battle, but you can line them up, cover them with a little sand and use them for a roadbed.

I've gone off on a tangent, but everything that organizes an individual is external to him. He's only the point where lines of force intersect.

A nation, however, can be organized. The Bolsheviks believed that it's the design that matters, not the building material. They were willing to lose today, to lose biographies, in order to win the stake of history.

They wanted to organize everything so that the sun would rise on schedule and the weather would be made in their chancellery.

They couldn't understand the anarchy of life, its subconscious, the fact that a tree knows best how it should grow.

It's easy to see how the Bolsheviks made the mistake of mapping out a plan for the whole world on paper.

At first, they believed that their formula didn't conflict with life, that the mainspring of life was the "spontaneous activity of the masses," but regulated by their formula.

And now their words lie in Russia like so many defunct rhinoceroses and mammoths—so many of them!—"the spontaneous activity of the masses," "local power" and that ichthyosaurus "peace without annexations and reparations." Now children laugh at these dead, but not yet decayed, monsters.

Gorky was a sincere Bolshevik.

The World Literature Publishing House—a Russian writer mustn't write what he wants to: he must translate the classics, all the classics; everyone must translate and everyone must read. When everyone has read everything, he will know everything.

No need for hundreds of publishing houses: one will do—Grzhebin's—and this one publishing house will need a catalogue projected to one hundred years—a catalogue one hundred printer's signatures long, in the English, French, Indo-Chinese and Sanskrit languages.

And all the literati and all the writers, neatly classified and supervised by none other than S. Oldenburg and Alexandre Benois, will work from diagrams and then shelves of books will be born and everyone will read all these books and everyone will know everything.

There's no room in this scheme for either heroics or faith in people.

Why should the dead rise since everything will be organized for their benefit?

It wasn't chance that brought Gorky and Lenin together.

But Gorky was the Noah of the Russian intelligentsia.

During the flood, people were saved in the arks of World Literature, the Grzhebin Publishing House and the House of Arts.

They were saved, not to make a counterrevolution, but so that the literate people in Russia wouldn't die out.

The Bolsheviks accepted these concentration camps for the intelligentsia. They didn't break them up.

Without these centers, the intelligentsia would have degenerated and never done anything but hack work. Then the Bolsheviks would have gotten those who hadn't died—the dregs, but their property in every sense of the word.

Consequently, Gorky was ideologically incorrect, but he was practically useful.

He has a way of organizing energetic people—of singling out the leftists. The last group he organized before his departure in the fall of 1921 was the Serapion Brothers. He has an easy way with people.

Gorky has absolutely no faith in mankind.

Gorky doesn't like everyone—just those who write well or work well. . . .

No, I cannot write and I cannot sleep.

And the white night is visible from my window, and dawn over the fields.

And the tiny bells on the horses, let out into the forest for the night, ring—

To-lo-nen . . . to-lo-nen.

Tolonen is the name of the Finn next door.

No, I cannot write and I cannot sleep.

And the white night is visible from my window, and dawn over the fields.

And in Petersburg, that goddess of quotations stands watch in the sky—the needle-like spire of the Admiralty Building.

And from the window of the House of Arts, my wife sees green poplars and dawn behind the cupola of the Kazan Cathedral.

But here Tolonen. . . .

I cannot be happy.

I will not soon sit down at the stone table in my room to drink tea with sugar from glasses without saucers in a circle of friends and not soon will I see the rings left by the glasses on the table.

And Boris Eikhenbaum and Yury Tynyanov will not soon come to see me and talk about the nature of "rhythmo-syntactic figures."

The room floats by itself like "The Raft of the *Medusa*"[57] and we look for the *dominanta* of art and someone, strangely shaking his head, now moves his thought forward.

Lusya says then that he "champed at his cigarette holder." She says that because when a riding horse starts to move, he makes such a motion with his head and mouth.

Oh, the rings left by our glasses on the stone table!

And the smoke from our stovepipes! Our rooms were full of the smoke of the motherland.

Dear 1921! Lusya's year!

We slept under a blanket and a tiger skin. The tiger skin we bought in a Soviet store. It was a fugitive from some apartment. We cut off its head.

And Vsevolod Ivanov bought a white bear and made himself a fur coat lined in blue cloth—twenty-five pounds of it. To sew it, he practically needed the spire of the Admiralty building.

We slept under the tiger.

Lusya would get up and start the stove with documents from the Central Bank. Thin snakes of smoke rose from the chimney as from the nostrils of a smoker.

I would get up, put on my boots and scale a ladder to fill up the holes in the chimney.

Every day. I left the ladder right in the room.

And we couldn't get a stove man. He was the most necessary person in the city. The city was becoming winter-proof. Everyone had decided to live. We still couldn't run down a stove for Slonimsky.

He was cultivating a stove man, who called him Misha. The whole house called Slonimsky Misha. And he was admired because he (Slonimsky) could drink copiously without getting drunk.

But there was no stove to be had. And Akhmatova had a marble fireplace in her apartment.

I would get down on my knees in front of our stove and split logs with an ax.

It's good to live and sniff the road of life with your snout.

The last piece of sugar is sweet. Wrapped in its own little piece of paper.

Love is good.

And just on the other side of the wall looms the abyss, and automobiles, and the winter blizzards.

But we floated on our raft.

It was like the last spark in the ashes—no, not ashes—more like a dark coal flame.

But here is To-lo-nen. In a word—Finland.

All the land was being tilled and everything was almost all right.

Visas, peace, fences, borders, Russian dachas lying on their side and Bolsheviks—the Bolsheviks this, the Bolsheviks that. The newspapers were full of nothing but Bolsheviks.

They were squeezed into Finland from Russia.

So we see that Gorky is made of disbelief and piety, with irony for cement.

Irony in life is like eloquence in literature: it can tie everything together.

It makes a substitute for tragedy.

But in Gorky's books, things take on an inflated quality without being enlarged out of proportion.

It's like a card game played by some officers sitting in the basket of an observation balloon a mile up in the air.

Yet Gorky's a very important writer. All these foreigners—the Rollands and the Barbusses and Anatole France, with his book-dealer's irony—have no idea what a great contemporary they could have had.

Fundamentally, even at his dizzy height, Gorky is a very important writer known to almost everyone—with a background important for a writer.

The Kogans and the Mikhailovskys—that's a chapter heading.

A married man has thoughts which he thinks in his wife's presence and then rethinks without saying anything to her.

And then you're surprised when she doesn't know what matters to you.

And you never talk about the obvious.

I'm living now in Raivola (Finland).

People used to summer here. Now it's turned out that life has to be taken seriously. Nothing came out right.

I have nothing to read. I've been reading old journals that go back twenty years.

How strange to substitute the history of Russian liberalism for the history of Russian literature.

But Pypin related the history of literature to the history of ethnography.

They all lived—the Belinskys, the Dobrolyubovs, the Zaitsevs, the Mikhailovskys, the Skabichevskys, the Ovsyaniko-Kulikov-skys, the Nestor-Kotlyarevskys, the Kogans and the Friches.[58]

And they outlived Russian literature.

They're like the people who came to look at a flower and made themselves comfortable by sitting down on it.

Pushkin and Tolstoy got into Russian literature before these people knew what had happened. If they had known, they wouldn't have let them in.

It's no accident that A. F. Koni says Pushkin is dear to us because he foretold trial by jury.

There was no cult of craftsmanship in Russia, and Russia, like a fat, hefty wet-nurse, smothered Gorky in his sleep.

Only in his last things—especially in his book on Tolstoy—was Gorky able to write for someone other than Mikhailovsky.[59]

Tolstoy the craftsman, the man with his resentment against women. The Tolstoy who should absolutely not be considered a saint is described for the first time.

Damn Pavlenkov's biographical books anyway—all these little icons with their identical halos.

Everyone is good, everyone is virtuous.

Damn these mediocrities, these joint-stock companies for making people one-dimensional!

I think that we devoured a very important writer at the House of Scholars. That's Russian heroics—to lie in the ditch so that the heavy guns can be pulled across.

But Gorky's psychology isn't the psychology of a craftsman—a shoemaker or shoe repairman.

That's not how he lives: he doesn't live by what he knows how to do. He's perplexed.

And so are the people around him!

Let's go back to 1920.

It was winter and cold. My wife was far away. There were no wives. We lived in celibacy. It was cold. Cold filled the days. We made slippers out of pieces of cloth. We burned kerosene in bottles stuffed with rags. This instead of lamps. You get a kind of somber light.

We worked.

We were living on our last reserves. Our hardships kept piling on; we wore them like clothing. Life was such that we saw nothing in it, just as you can't see from a man's footprints what he's carrying.

Only the footprints—sometimes deep, sometimes shallow.

I was working in the Translators' Studio—giving lectures on
Don Quixote. There were five or six students. The girls wore black
gloves to hide their frostbitten hands.

I didn't have any lice: lice come from boredom.

Toward spring, I fought a duel.

Jews have rowdy, exhausting blood. The blood of Ilya Ehren-
burg-Imitator.

The Jews have lost their identity and are now searching for it.

For the time being, they make faces. However, the Jewish
bourgeoisie in the over-thirty age bracket is strong.

The bourgeoisie is generally strong.

I know one house where the inhabitants ate meat and wore silk
stockings all during the revolutionary period.

They had a terrible time of it. The father was taken away to
Vologda to dig trenches, was arrested, then forced to dig graves.
But he would run away and earn money somewhere.

It was warm by the stove in that house.

They had the usual kind of round stove: they put wood in it and
then it got warm.

But it wasn't just a stove. It was a relic of the bourgeois way of
life and therefore precious.

In St. Pete during the NEP period, a lot of signs were hung in
the store windows. Some apples would be lying there and over
them would be a sign "apples"; over the sugar, it said "sugar."

A lot, a whole lot of signs (it was 1921). But one sign was the
biggest of all:

ROLLS OF THE 1914 VARIETY

That stove was of the 1914 variety.

I used to go see that stove with an artist. He was doing my
portrait.[60] In it, I'm wearing a fur coat and a sweater.

A girl was sitting on the couch. The couch was big and covered
in green velvet. Like those on trains.

I forgot about the Jews.

Don't think I'm kidding.

A Jew was sitting there, too—young, once a rich man, also of
the 1914 variety and, what's more important, decked out to look
like an officer of the guards. He was the girl's fiancé.

The girl too was a bourgeois product and therefore lovely.

Such a culture can be created only with lots of silk stockings and
several talented people around.

And the girl was talented.

She understood everything and didn't want to do anything.

All this was a good deal more complicated.

It was so cold outside that it frosted your eyelashes; your nostrils frosted. The cold penetrated under your clothing like water.

There was no light anywhere. We sat long hours in the dark. It was impossible to live and we had already agreed to die. But we didn't have enough time. Spring was coming.

I hounded this man.

At first, I wanted to go to his apartment and kill him.

Because I hate the bourgeoisie. Perhaps I envy them, because I'm petty-bourgeois myself.

If I live to see another revolution, I'll break them into little pieces.

It's not right that we should have suffered in vain and that nothing has changed.

The rich and the poor remain, as before.

But I can't kill, so I challenged this man to a duel.

I too am half-Jewish and an imitator.

I challenged him. I had two seconds, one of them a Communist.

I went to see one of my driver comrades. I said, "Give me a car with a top. I don't have a requisition order." During the night he put a car together out of broken pieces. An ambulance, make—Jeffery.

The next morning at seven we drove to the other side of Sosnovka, a place full of tree stumps.

One of the girls in my class, wearing her muff, went with us. She was a doctor.

We shot at fifteen paces. I shot through the documents in his pocket (he was standing very much at an angle) and he missed me completely.

I went over and sat in the car. The driver said to me, "Viktor Borisovich, why did you want to go through with this? We could have run him down in the car."

I went home. I slept that afternoon; that night I lectured at the studio.

Spring had come. The Whites were pulling out of the Ukraine.

I went to look for my wife.

Why have I written about this?

I don't like the idea of wild animals in a pit.

This is from the folk tale about various wild animals that have fallen into a pit. The following animals were there: a bear, a fox, a wolf, maybe a ram. They didn't eat each other because they were in a pit.

When famine stood at the intersections instead of policemen, the intelligentsia declared a general peace.

Futurists and academicians, Kadets and Mensheviks, the talented and the untalented sat together in the studios at World Literature and stood in line at the House of Writers.

What a fall was this!

I always tried to live without changing the tempo of life. I didn't want to live in a pit. I made peace with no one. I loved and hated. Always without bread.

This state of affairs exposed me to the following possibility.

I could expect someone to kill me.

Therefore I sat in the kitchen, where it was warmest, and wrote. The table in Mama's kitchen was always spick and span. When you write at a kitchen table, though, you don't have any leg room.

During that time, I wrote a great deal; I wrote page after page, using a lot of paper.

By the time of the duel, I had finished my basic book, *Plot as a Stylistic Phenomenon.* It had to be published in parts. It had been written in snatches. But you won't find the seams.

I wrote and I ate rabbit.

That spring several trainloads of dressed rabbits were brought to Petersburg.

Rabbits were issued everywhere. People carried rabbits down the street; they cooked rabbits in their apartments.

Afterward, everyone wore rabbitskin caps.

Rabbits were issued at the House of Writers. Everyone stood in line and was given a rabbit and a half. We stood in line for rabbit. As one of the more reliable nonpaying customers, I often stood in line for days.

Lines of no mean proportions.

Aleksandr Blok stood in that line.

In all likelihood, I won't be able to indicate in these notes how much a rabbit weighs or what a bread ration is. It's as big as the biggest question.

In the meantime, a lull in the fighting.

I had to go to the Ukraine.

I sold all the rights to all my books to Grzhebin. I didn't hand over any manuscripts then. It came to about forty thousand rubles.

Then I started hunting up a travel permit.

The Soviet regime had trained everyone to be absolutely cynical about papers.

Anyone trying to live by the rules would have gotten nowhere.

We lived as we had to, but motivated by the Soviet regime.

We were plastered with papers. Entire trains ran on fake orders.

And this means everybody—workers, intelligentsia and professional Communists.

I got hold of a travel permit by pretending an interest in the "re-establishment of ties with the Ukraine." It wasn't easy to get. Everyone wanted to go. But once out of Moscow, no one ever asked for it.

Before leaving, I saw Semyonov. He had come to agitate for more of a shift to the left. We met as casual acquaintances. Our past friendship had ended. He proudly showed me a sack of rusk which the workers at the Aleksandrovsky plant had given him.

He said he was going to Germany so he wouldn't run into his old comrades at work.

And I left for the Ukraine.

Everything was fine as far as Moscow.

From Moscow to Kharkov it wasn't bad either.

In Kharkov some acquaintances helped me get hold of a paper giving me the right to travel in a car reserved for publishers.

I walked to the station. The train was somewhere down the track. It was muddy on the tracks.

With some difficulty I found my car. It contained several bundles of newspapers and two conductors, both high-school students.

One was the conductor and the other was his friend.

Nice kids. They were going mainly for flour.

The train was warming up. People kept knocking on the door of our compartment. They climbed in through every crack and then slipped the conductors some money.

They had credentials.

The train filled up with people and began to look like a red sausage. And suddenly, without whistling or pulling up to the station, the train jerked forward and started to leave.

And I had no ticket.

But that didn't really matter.

We rode a while, stopped, climbed out, rode some more.

During the first twenty-four hours, we covered six and a half miles. Most of that time we sat in the grass alongside the train.

There was some Jew with a big belly in the car.

At one particularly wearisome stop, he took me aside and suddenly asked me to put on his money belt.

It was all the same to me.

I go by my star and I don't know whether it's in the sky or not. It's a lantern in the field. But there's wind in the field.

I don't know whether one ought to take money belts from old Jews. But he was whispering and sweating with terror. The belt wound up on me. There were kerenkas in it. The belt was enormous, like a life jacket.

This was unexpected, but I adjusted. It became uncomfortable to lie on my side.

In the dark corner, a black-haired Ukrainian was making passes at a very blonde young lady.

They were talking Ukrainian with much conviction and gusto.

The train crept along.

It was impartial.

The high-school students were questioning everyone about how much things cost in various places.

It turned out that in Nikolaev and around Kherson, flour was a lot cheaper.

When they heard that, they suddenly started to sing.

"Glorious sea, sacred Baikal." I think it was that one.

Anyway, something quite unsuitable, but it was a rousing performance.

And the train crept along.

But the Ukraine was vast.

Some sailors were traveling with us. They had big baskets of "togs." In sailor language, that means "clothing." When an Anti-profiteering Brigade came along, the sailors took their plaited baskets and ran. The baskets, white and plaited, quickly receded into the darkness and disappeared into the bushes.

These sailors were a determined lot.

The train stood at one station in the steppe for three days. Maybe it was four.

The Poles were advancing from Kiev.

We crossed blown-up bridges. They had been repaired with

wood. They would be blown up again. There was talk of Makhno.

One time, three men came into our car.

One of them, wearing red pants and talking all sorts of nonsense, demanded our papers. He said he was the officer of the guard and a member of the local Cheka.

And he really was wearing the soft officer's service cap. The other two sat right down in the open door of the compartment and let their feet dangle. They had Mausers. The train was moving.

I was sitting in the door, too.

The wind was blowing in my face.

My neighbor quietly began to talk to me.

"Why did you show that windbag your papers? I'm in charge. He doesn't have the right to ask."

I said, "How was I to know? It's all the same to me."

"All of you are like that."

We talked.

The Ukraine quietly marched along the railroad ties beside us.

"In the next district," said my neighbor—and he named the district—"they caught a bandit. I was going there, since he was supposed to have hidden a lot of money, but those fools took him out and shot him. Now the money's lost."

I said, "But how would you have found out about the money?" That is, I was asking about torture. And my heart was aching.

"There are ways," my neighbor answered politely without ignoring the question.

We were silent for a while. Then he asked sadly, "Do you know Gorky?"

"Yes," I said.

"Tell me, why didn't he come over to our side right away?"

"Well," I said, "you use torture and the land is ruined. Can't you understand that it's hard to be on your side?"

This is a real conversation, not imagined.

I have a good memory.

If my memory were poorer, I would sleep better at night.

The man talking to me looked like a sergeant, probably a cavalryman, and he needed to feel that Gorky was on his side.

Before my departure from Petersburg, I had lectured in the House of Arts, before the mirror in the white hall, on the topic "Sterne's *Tristram Shandy* and the Theory of the Novel." The hall was full and excited by the formal approach.

The eyes of my friends were shining with joy. I felt surrounded by a resilient mass of understanding. I looked at myself in the mirror with satisfaction.

And now both the cavalryman and I were on this Ukrainian sea, where the train moved a step at a time, like a bull. We were both city people.

I decided to jump off the train and change to some other faster one.

The Jew and I installed ourselves on the tall heaps of our new train's coal supply. We were heading for Nikolaev.

Level with us, on top the locomotive or the tender, was a Colt machine gun. The train kept going.

It was night. By morning, we were as black as devils.

Our first train caught up with us, so we got back on it.

· Changing trains, and taking some typhus cases along, I finally got to Kherson. There were two men with typhus. They had gotten sick during the trip and had begged us not to put them off the train, to take them home.

Kherson had wide, quiet streets.

Wide because they were built that way, green because trees had been planted, and quiet because the port wasn't functioning.

The cranes were standing idle and the canvas of the sails was flapping. The wind had torn apart the threads of the cloth, then left.

The port buildings were abandoned.

This city, which had seen sixteen governments, was deserted.

I found my wife in Aleshki. Since my childhood, I had heard about Aleshki as the most godforsaken place in the world. I never expected to land there.

A small town on the other side of the Dnieper. Straw roofs.

There was still plenty of bread and bacon. Absolutely no sugar.

I spent the next month lying in a hammock. Apparently the sweetbrier had been blooming.

When I arrived on the first of May, everything had bloomed and already faded.

My wife was very sick.

She had had a hard time of it during this year we lived apart.

Under the Whites, there had been no work. She had lived without any warm clothing, by selling things. Now she was working at the Aleshki Theater for a scandalously low salary. She painted scenery on sacks that had been sewn together.

She said it had been miserable under the Whites in Kherson.

They hanged their victims on the lamp posts along the main streets.

They hanged them and left them hanging.

Children going home from school would gather around the lamp posts. They would just stand there.

This didn't happen just in Kherson. According to the stories, they did the same thing in Pskov.

I think I know the Whites. In Nikolaev the Whites shot the three Vonsky brothers for "bandit activity." One of them was a doctor; another was a lawyer—a Menshevik. The corpses lay in the middle of the street for three days. A fourth brother, Vladimir Vonsky, my aide in the Eighth Army, then went over to the insurgents. Now he's a Bolshevik.

The Whites hang men from the lamp posts and shoot them on the street out of romanticism.

They hanged a boy named Polyakov for organizing an armed rebellion. He was about sixteen or seventeen.

Before he died, the boy shouted, "Long live the Soviet regime!"

Since the Whites are romantics, they printed in the newspaper that he had died a hero.

But they hanged him.

Polyakov became a hero to the local young people; a local Communist Youth league was organized around his name.

When the Whites got ready to withdraw, they organized brigades of young boys from the area. They pulled out in the middle of winter. Their barges froze in the Dnieper. It was a ferocious winter, with temperatures down to 35 below zero. The wounded died. The boys ran away. Later on, their parents smuggled them back into the city disguised as women.

When the Whites left, everyone breathed easier. But after the Whites came, not the Reds, but some sort of outfit that didn't know what color it was.

They stayed a while and didn't do any looting, because the city was being run by the trade unions, with military backing.

Then the Reds arrived. The townspeople said they had wised up since the first time they took the town.

I lay in a hammock, slept the whole day and ate. I understood nothing.

My wife was sick.

Suddenly things got lively. Soldiers appeared in town. People started to pack their things. The steamboat stopped going to Kherson. A ramp for loading cattle was quickly attached to the pier.

The cattle were driven through town very quickly. You never drive cattle that way: it's hard on them. Obviously people were fleeing.

Things got lively in the infirmaries, too. I knew that an exodus was taking place. I went to Kherson to find out what was going on.

My friends in Kherson told me that Wrangel had broken through the front and was advancing. The Red units, which had been just sitting around Perekop for a long time, had fallen apart. Wrangel's men had broken through and they were fleeing.

I quickly caught a boat back to Aleshki. The pier was already seething with activity.

People were trying frantically to get at the boats. Heaps of things lay on the bank. Some commissar with a revolver was taking a boat away from another commissar.

My wife couldn't walk. With great difficulty I got her to the riverbank. I hunted for a boat all over the village, finally found one and, moving down the swampy Chaika River, or perhaps the Koika, we set out through the reeds and shrubs for Kherson.

That night, Aleshki was occupied by a mounted patrol of Circassians.

They promptly began to dance the lezginka. The Whites love to dance.

We pulled up to the shore at Kherson. Only they wouldn't let us land. They even shot at us. They said, "You'll start a panic." We pleaded with the sentry.

The Dnieper was running and it had two banks—a left and a right. On the right bank were the rightist elements; on the left bank, the leftist elements.

This arrangement varied with the current.

The left bank was wide open. There were no troops at all except for a Cheka battalion.

But the rightist group didn't advance, since it was advantageous for them to keep the Dnieper on their flank.

The mobilization of the trade unions began. No one would go. The mobilization of the Bolsheviks began. Apparently only a few went.

But the cannons were already firing. I love the thunder of

cannons in a town and the way shell fragments bounce off the pavement. It's great when there are cannons.

It seems as if you're going to meet the enemy later in the same day and fight it out to the finish.

My wife was in the hospital, terribly sick. I visited her frequently.

Now the mobilization of the Mensheviks and the Right-wing SR's got under way. The SR organization in Kherson was legal.

Not long before this, there had been elections for the Kherson Soviet. About half the representatives were either Mensheviks or SR's.

At the first meeting of the soviet, after listening to a greeting from the local Cheka battalion, the Communists announced that the soviet had decided to send greetings to Lenin, Trotsky and the Red Army. The Mensheviks announced that in general they didn't believe in greeting Lenin and Trotsky, but "taking into consideration. . . ."

It probably continued . . . "and insofar as. . . ."

In short, they agreed to sign the greeting.

But the Communists are a shrewd bunch. They moved that the soviet adopt the program of the Communist party. The Mensheviks wouldn't vote for that. Then they were expelled from the soviet.

The mobilization of the Mensheviks was carried out by their local committee without any enthusiasm. Only the local party leaders were in favor of it, among them my comrades from the first convocation of the Petrograd Soviet—Vsevolod Vengerov, who worked in the local trade unions, and Comrade Pechersky.

A total of about fifteen local students was about all that responded to the mobilization of the Mensheviks.

The SR's succeeded in mobilizing, in addition to their own committee, a few workers.

I couldn't resist, so I joined the Mensheviks—that's where my friends were.

At the meeting that was held, I vehemently supported the mobilization. We were all rounded up, put in big wagons and sent to the village of Teginka, on the right flank—about twenty-five miles from Kherson.

This was very hard for me. I had hoped to fight in the city or near the city so I could see my wife.

But this wasn't the first time I had gotten on a train without knowing where it was going. The man who mobilized the SR's was Comrade Mitkevich, a strong, narrow-minded man. During the war, he had been an officer with a demolition team. He was a very influential leader among the local SR's. This group was legal, but it supported the general SR platform.

We set out.

We rode through the empty fields, passing big wagons full of Jews running away from the Whites—from future pogroms.

The Jews were going to an agricultural colony called Lvovo, where they were piling up in such numbers that they weren't being beaten up anymore in that area.

I was never at that colony myself. They say that the farming isn't much good there. The houses stand all by themselves; there aren't any gardens. And they have special customs at Lvovo.

For instance, they travel in brigades when they go to do their trading and they ride in machine-gun carts, like Makhno.

And, like Makhno, they carry machine guns in the carts.

There's less anti-Semitism around Lvovo than in other places. Why, I don't know.

We rode into Teginka.

It was a large village with a church; the church had a bell tower; in the bell tower was an observer and below, a three-inch gun.

Wide streets. At night the company commander rode around in them and you could turn a troika without slowing down.

These streets were more like landing fields.

Various kinds of houses stood on both sides. Some had been built by the Old Believers. The people came from all over; they spoke more or less in Ukrainian, but, generally speaking, Novorossia is the dregs of Russia—without its own language, without its own songs or style—but its people imitate the Germans and put tile roofs on their houses.

They eat meat every day.

I was working on Thackeray. I had brought his novel with me.

We found life dreary. The whole company was Russian. This Petersburg company recalled Petersburg wistfully: "They say it's hungry there, but interesting."

At night, the command "Evening Prayer" was shouted and the men sang "This Is Our Last, Our Final Battle."

You think I wrote that line? I sang it.

I recently left Berlin for a few days. On my way back, I got caught in a strike. There were no streetcars or cabs. Since I don't know the language, I had to crisscross the whole country just to get back to my place on Kleiststrasse. Some people were walking toward me, a crowd of people, and some were riding bicycles. And that was all—just a lot of people—but my heart lifted. My beaten, disillusioned heart. My heart, which I constantly have to keep in check, leapt to see this crowd.

With such force!

The soldiers, apart from the "Internationale," were wont to sing "The Varangian" to the tune of "Lord, Save Thy People" and these soldiers, for the most part, were POW's.

A group not unfamiliar to me.

Not Communists or Bolsheviks—just plain Russian soldiers. They made us welcome.

The only thing that bothered them was being stuck in the Ukraine, where, obviously, they weren't wanted. All the men were griping.

They said, "If it wasn't for the coal in this Ukraine, the whole place could go to the devil. We've got all the grain we need in Siberia."

Then somebody else would disagree.

The Ukrainians—to be specific, those colonists who lived in Teginka—tolerated us.

They fed us on meat, sour cream and pork. But if they could have, they would have fed us to their pigs.

Broken mowing machines stood in their backyards. When we needed horses for our military operations, we helped ourselves. The populace didn't have enough clothing. There weren't even sacks for the grain or vehicles to haul it in.

The groundwork was already laid for famine.

One night, the Whites showed up. The peasants had brought them. The Whites attacked us that night. We took positions among the huts. There was the usual gunfire. And the Whites left for their right bank on the White side of the Dnieper.

In the darkness they had shot at their own men. My duties involved less commotion. I generally stood on guard at the bridge and checked everyone's papers.

I wore a linen cap with a brim—the peasants called it a bonnet

—a green suit made from some drapes and adorned with a sailor's collar, and a coat made from a good piece of thick carpet, with a buckle taken from somebody's knapsack.

No one in Petersburg was surprised, but the peasants were very upset.

Was I a man or a woman?

Once I went out with a scouting party.

First we went about ten miles along the bank to the left of our position.

It was quite a sparse front—about five men to every mile.

We were met by Caucasian cavalrymen in their black felt cloaks. Bending down theatrically from their horses, they spoke to us as they galloped down the bank. There was no one around the dark huts.

The Dnieper was calm and the boats weren't ready for us.

We got into some rotten hulks, with oars like toothpicks.

We pushed off and immediately started to sink. The boats were full of holes and we had a machine gun. We made it to a sandbank and got out.

We set out on foot through the short stubs of a recently cut cane field. Our wooden sandals kept slipping.

We ran across spotted, silken cows, pleasant to touch.

We reached a river and didn't know how to get across. No problem, just send out a reconnaissance party. The reconnaissance party didn't come back. We gathered in a small group, smoked and cursed our commander.

Our sergeant started a conversation with me about the general significance of communications. We smoked. The three-legged machine gun stood in the sand like a chair. No guards were posted. You got the impression that the men weren't taking the fighting seriously, that they had picked up the war and brusquely laid it aside.

The river had turned pink. We waded out into the warm water and pushed off our water-logged boat to take us back to the base.

We rowed back. The whole way we had to bail the water out with our caps.

Nothing was taken seriously.

I've traveled a lot in this world and seen various wars and I always had the impression of being in the hole of a doughnut.

And I never saw anything terrible. Life isn't so full.

War consists of massive mutual inability.

Perhaps this is true only of Russia. I was terribly bored. I wrote out a statement to the effect that I knew nothing about the infantry, but did know armored cars and, if worse came to worst, demolition work. Since demolition men were needed, I was sent to Kherson.

I've forgotten to say why I was absolutely superfluous in Teginka: I had no rifle. There weren't enough rifles to go around. I took off. I was put in a wagon, along with some prisoners. Two.

One big, heavy man, a commander of the local militia. The other was a small, quiet deserter.

I was armed only with a ramrod, but I wasn't alone. A small soldier, a former POW, went along as escort for the prisoners. He had a rifle, which was even loaded.

His legs hurt. He couldn't sit in the wagon or walk along beside it. He sort of squatted down on all fours in the back of the wagon.

One of the prisoners was very upset. He had been well worked over in Teginka, accused of speculation and practically of treason. He told us he was innocent.

He was tall and strong and we were in the middle of the steppe. And beyond the steppe lay the Dnieper and the Whites, and there were fewer Reds in the steppe than stone idols. Even if you tried, you couldn't find any.

And the steppe wasn't bare that time of year. A company, or even a division, could hide in the tall grass.

The small guard kept trying to convince the prisoner that he would be released in Kherson.

But he winked at me and looked significantly at his rifle; that meant the prisoner would be shot. And the steppe was all around us. It seemed to me that the prisoner should knock me and the POW guard on the head and escape, but he just kept saying he was innocent and sitting in the wagon as if he were bound hand and foot.

I didn't understand him, as I didn't understand Russia.

So we took him to Kherson.

And the other one was just a boy. If they didn't shoot him on the second day, they'd probably let him go on the third.

I got to Kherson.

In Kherson the cannons had been shooting so long that they had become a fact of everyday life.

Only the bazaar was nervous and fearful.

But, all the same, the trading went on. Cannons don't sour milk. People lived and traded in the city.

The lists of those who had been shot hung on the walls. Fifteen men a day. Very regular.

And the last five were always Jewish names—to show that there was no discrimination.

The cannons were right in the city. It was very cozy. But the women in the suburb wouldn't let them install a gun battery in their ravine.

They were right, of course. The Whites would come and go, and the Reds, and many others without any color; the guns would shoot; they would all come and go. Only the ravine would remain.

I started to organize a demolition squad. Mitkevich was due to arrive any day.

I sent requests to the regiments and took several boys from the Komsomol.

The squad began to take shape.

I found housing in an old fortress. I looked for demolition material in abandoned supply dumps. But it turned out that the dynamite had already been taken. I was too late. It was surprising that no one got the cannons, too.

There were a lot of cannons—long-range naval cannons. But no one knew how to shoot them. There was one special cannon for shooting at airplanes, but no one ever hit anything. Airplanes flew over every morning—white against the blue sky. They always arrived at the same time.

They circled. Then suddenly a good-sized explosion. Like someone striking a tambourine. Bombs. I got up. That meant it was seven o'clock and time to prepare the samovar. Time for the next act.

With a shrill whine, a red airplane would slowly rise from the city.

It would climb into the sky. The white airplanes would fly away.

Then the shooting started. The Whites shot at the former governor's mansion. Now it was the War Commissariat, with a gun battery next to it.

The Whites shot three-inch cannons. They generally hit the mark. The whole house was riddled, but people continued working there. And I went to work.

That was the right way to handle this war. There's no point in pretending that a civil war is anything like a real war and besides it's more convenient to fight from a city.

Mitkevich did a good solid job of organizing our brigade.

Like me, he had been part of a five-man outpost on the Dnieper, with hostile peasants on every side. These five Reds (in this case, SR's) had occupied a manor house and tried to give the impression that they were numerous. To that end, one man had been stationed at the door; he allowed no one inside.

Mitkevich was used to these four men and he brought them with him to Kherson.

He longed for this kind of job and he became fiercely attached to his brigade—just as Robinson Crusoe would have become attached to any white woman thrown up on his island.

In my lifetime I've seen so many men, especially Jews, who had been innocent of all responsibility under the old regime and who now became deeply attached to the job they were given to do.

Wait until the temperature in Russia drops to about 15 degrees; then take a man and a woman with anywhere from one to twenty years' difference in their ages, put them in the same apartment and they'll become man and wife. I don't know any sadder truth than this.

If the woman has no husband, she'll latch on to the man for dear life.

Man's nature requires substitutes. Mitkevich ate, drank and slept with the brigade. I did too.

I brought my Menshevik friends from Teginka into the brigade. They had been students. They arrived tired, gloomy and frightened. The day after my departure, they had attacked Kazachy Lager, an area on the other side of the river.

As this tiny band of men advanced, the peasants greeted them with the stern question:

"When will you have enough?"

Actually, the Russian revolution was already having to import interested outsiders.

Vengerov, who had a bad heart, often had to lie down; then he'd get up again. The men were cutting through a village, climbing over the fences. The Whites were slowly falling back. At the same time, our men were advancing on Aleshki. The plan was simplicity itself—a head-on assault. The men, mostly sailors, were rounded up, loaded on two boats and sent to Aleshki. There they fought and advanced. The Whites fell back and then struck from the flank. Our men started to run. They drowned trying to swim across the river. They discarded their boots and jackets. By nighttime, the remnants of the squads returned wet and almost naked. Our men had been repulsed from Kazachy Lager, too. But they didn't all return. Vengerov had taken a boat and pushed away from shore with several soldiers and a nurse. But he didn't reach the other shore. The body of the nurse was washed ashore.

We gave Vengerov up for dead. We searched for him and sent scouts to the other shore. Nothing.

The students reached my brigade in low spirits, completely worn down.

A day before they left, the battalion to which they belonged had been ordered to attack again.

The battalion had already dwindled to nothing. The men had somehow melted away.

They were ordered to attack. They were loaded on a flat-bottomed boat called the *Kharkov*. As a farewell gift, everyone was issued half a pound of sugar. It seemed just like a funeral. Sugar was scarce. It wasn't given away for nothing. The *Kharkov* traveled in silence. The men lay there. They were silent.

Fortunately, the boat got hung up on a sandbank, spent the prescribed amount of time there, then returned. The attack was called off. We arranged ourselves rather comfortably in the fortress. Bunks, floor mats. A telephone. Mitkevich gave the intellectuals a hard time and I felt sorry for them. However, I'm not guilty before anyone and therefore I don't want to take one person's part at the expense of someone else.

I took a trip to Nikolaev. No dynamite. I had to improvise. As a result, I brought back a carload of secrite, an explosive substance made in Norway—also some fuses and a smoke bomb.

And in the packages containing the combustible material for the smoke bomb, we found a safety fuse.

And so we launched our demolition industry à la Robinson Crusoe.

We learned how to throw bombs and make fuses.

The soldiers got smarter and more sure of themselves. Bombs and cars change a man's character.

During the evenings, I taught the soldiers fractions.

All over Russia, fronts were being opened. The Poles were advancing and my heart ached as it aches now.

And in the midst of all this misery, which I didn't understand, in the midst of the shells falling from the sky, as they fell one day along the Dnieper into a crowd of swimmers, it's very reassuring to say calmly:

"The larger the numerator, the larger the fraction, because that means there are more parts. The larger the denominator, the smaller the fraction, because that means it's more finely sliced."

That's a sure thing.

It's the only sure thing I know.

Sour green apples were lying on the table and tiny wild cherries. The gardens had been closed, nationalized.

No one knew how to pick fruit anyway, but the soldiers stole it. Troops always eat green fruit. If Adam had been a soldier, he would have taken the apple in paradise and eaten it green.

So I taught arithmetic. We had been given the job of blowing up the wooden bridge over a tributary of the Dnieper.

The bridge interfered with the navigation of our amphibious battery.

I don't know whether you can blow up wooden bridges.

The bridge had a central span of very elegant construction, made out of several layers of planks held together by oak pegs.

We removed the flooring of the bridge.

The soldiers worked wonderfully well.

One big, incredibly strong man had worked on bridges before. He was so big his muscles didn't show.

He hefted the bridge struts as if they were toothpicks.

The students worked hard, too.

The soldiers didn't like them because they were Jewish. Me they forgave for being Jewish.

To soldiers, I'm a strange man.

The men sitting on the wooden bridge were doing the same job and yet they kept riding each other.

One of the Jews in our outfit was from the Komsomol. His name was something like Brachmann.

He had enlisted. At this point, I should share a memory with you.

On a street in the city of Solozhbulak (in Kurdistan)—a city once famous for its leaves, its hides and its peacocks—I once saw a group of soldiers.

They had tied a kerosene can to the tail of a Persian cat and were having fun kicking it with their heavy boots.

The cat would play dead and lie there as if completely lifeless, then suddenly gather all its strength and make a frantic leap to get away, but the can held it fast; then the soldiers gave it another kick in the belly so that it seemed to be stretching as it sailed through the air.

The owner, either a Persian or a Kurd, stood to one side and wondered how to get his cat back from the soldiers.

In our demolition squad, Brachmann was like that cat.

He had entered the war with the idea of immediately going to officers' training school. But he was politely collared and told, "Stay in the ranks." And on the directive was written: "Keep him in the ranks."

And they were right.

You see, Brachmann was afraid of bombs.

He was forced to throw them. He got used to it. But this wasn't enough for the others. He was dirty, infested with lice, and he had festering wounds on his groin, to which he applied tobacco leaves.

He was a veritable walking advertisement for anti-Semitism.

But how the soldiers tormented him!

We were getting ready to blow up the bridge. We put dynamite on one of the abutments. We hung the dynamite sausages in the middle of the bridge. It blew up.

I remember the violent concussion. The bridge broke in half, but the debris hung in place on each side.

Then suddenly flame on one of the end beams. . . .

Within a minute, the entire bridge was in flames.

But we didn't want that. Only the center abutment was in our way.

This enormous bridge, over seventy feet high, had taken many years to build and it was burning like a tinderbox.

Poor Mitkevich!

The bridge was burning for all to see. And I had contributed to the destruction of Russia.

All Kherson gathered on the riverbank—jubilant. You see, in Russia people are sometimes jubilant about such things—"The

Bolsheviks don't have any firewood. Russia will freeze this winter." A nation as cunning as a cockroach! It has faith in its own life force and thinks, "The Bolsheviks will freeze, but we will somehow make it through the winter."

The nation knows how big it is. Meanwhile, the flame lifted the bridge—as if taking it to heaven.

All around the bridge, soldiers stood in the water with fire hoses. I don't know where they got them. They poured water on the bridge. They kept ducking under water. Their clothes were smouldering. The crowd on the bank—mostly women—was jubilant: "Go ahead! Take a good look! Burn up the whole country!"

But we had our own problems: the danger that the debris would obstruct the channel.

Mitkevich poled out to the bridge in a boat.

He tried to keep the falling debris from catching on the piles and blocking the passage. But luckily the bridge burned completely.

Crestfallen, we returned home. So much wood had burned!

And it was 1920, not 1917, which was the real year for fires.

We returned to Kherson.

I remember that the password in the city that night was "dreadnought."

We lived quietly in the moat of the old fortress.

We threw bombs, sometimes blowing up as much as seventy pounds of secrite at a time.

An explosion is a wonderful thing. You light the fuse and run back; then you get down and watch.

The earth swells up before your eyes.

In a split second the bubble grows, then detaches itself from the ground. A dark column rises up. Hard and solid. Big. Then it softens, fans out into the shape of a tree and falls to earth as black hail.

As beautiful as a horse's neigh.

Our explosives were bad.

But we had to train the men in a hurry.

All around Wrangel's army the earth was swelling into a giant bubble; the bubble was already detaching itself from the ground.

It might suddenly rise toward the sky!

In any case, we had to blow up bridges as we retreated. We were ordered to train the men within a week.

We worked night and day.

We had to learn to work under conditions which made the work impossible—for instance, to make explosions without a safety fuse.

In such cases, you can make an explosion by using the detonator (primer) from a hand grenade and fastening a cord to the linchpin of the primer.

When you pull out the pin, the primer ignites, and in three seconds there's an explosion.

Our hand grenades were on the German model. In this kind, the primer spring is held in place by an elastic disc, which is fastened to the grenade by the linchpin.

You pull the pin and then hold the disc in the palm of your hand so that it remains in place; then you throw it; the disc falls, the primer ignites. There's an explosion.

This is what we did one day. We inserted the primer into a tin can containing thirty pounds of secrite, tied a cord to the pin, hid behind a mound and pulled the cord.

We waited three seconds.

Silence.

We pulled again. That time we pulled the pin clear over to our mound.

Still no explosion. Perhaps the primer was no good.

According to regulations, you're not supposed to go up to the defective bomb in such cases. You're apparently supposed to wait half an hour. That makes sense.

But somehow the silence was total.

We got up and all of us started toward the bomb (defective).

Suddenly Mitkevich crouched down and shouted, "Shklovsky, smoke!"

And sure enough, the primer was emitting its quiet three-second smoke. It had just ignited.

That meant two seconds remained, maybe only one.

I ran up to the secrite, jerked out the primer and hurled it to one side. It blew up in the air.

Then I sat down on the ground. My legs had given out. The soldiers got up off the ground. But there hadn't been any point in getting down, because the crater would have been big enough for everybody. One of the men came up to me and said, "One of these days, you're going to blow yourself up for sure!"

By nighttime, that was the conviction of the whole squad.

What probably happened was this. We didn't have any wire to fasten the primer to the explosive in order to keep the primer from being pulled out by the cord along with the pin.

Instead, we set rocks up against the primer. Evidently one of them at first kept the disc from coming off and then somehow shifted. Then the primer ignited.

My wife asked every day, "Aren't you going to blow yourself up one of these days?"

I was still wearing that green suit made out of somebody's drapes.

Early every morning I walked through the park.

In the middle of the park was an oak; under the oak was a grave. Every new government removed the body that its predecessor had buried there and installed one of its own bodies.

If I had blown myself up, I think I would have been buried there.

The soldiers would have seen to it. They liked me a lot.

The sand is hot in Kherson and burns your feet when you don't have any boots. We were wearing wooden sandals with straps.

The footwear of the mendicant friars. When you wear sandals like these, every step feels as if someone is tugging on your feet.

But everyone was wearing them.

All over Kherson, you heard the clatter of sandals.

I was walking through Kherson. Lush foliage. I stopped at the bazaar.

In the bazaar, people traded or else they milled around in panic when the Whites bombarded the city.

Milk was sold in clay pitchers. It was thick from having been boiled. I lived on milk and apricots, at first using the forty thousand rubles that Grzhebin had given me, but they were hard to change. I had brought the whole sum in four bills and no one could change a ten-thousand-ruble note. Or else they would change them into the local currency—homemade thousand-ruble notes that no one would take. I paid two thousand rubles to get my ten thousand changed. I had to sell some things. I sold my coat. Then the good leather pants made from my suede couch. All the students at the Translators' Studio knew them. I had burned the wood in the couch.

I lived on apricots and milk. Then there was trouble in the bazaar. Why were the Jews buying bacon? According to their own law, they weren't supposed to buy pork. And besides, there wasn't enough for the Russians. If the Jews had that kind of rule, then why were they breaking their own rule?

I took my milk home. I walked through the park. The foliage, the cool of the shade, then lawn, and—the sun. I walked along and thought absent-mindedly about my past.

About Opoyaz. "Opoyaz" means "The Society for the Study of Poetic Language."

About something as clear to me as numerators and denominators. When you think, you get absent-minded. I blew myself up through absent-mindedness. This is how it happened.

We didn't have enough primers.

And primers are indispensable. We needed them in case of retreat and we needed them to destroy the bombs that the Whites were dropping on us. Those bombs didn't always explode.

I had brought from Nikolaev some little white cylinders of German origin that I thought were primers. Mitkevich tried to assure me they weren't. They actually did seem to have an aperture for a safety fuse, but it was too wide. You could stick your whole little finger in it and it was constructed in such a way that it was impossible to make the opening narrower.

I asked one of the men to make me a safety fuse out of a smoke bomb and I went to the edge of the ravine to try it out.

It was a nice day. The grass was green, the sky blue. In the distance there were some horses and a little boy. There were old trenches all around with dark holes at the bottom. What was inside those holes I don't know—probably just darkness.

I started to insert the fuse into the cylinder, which looked like a first-grader's round metal pencil case—about the circumference of a three-kopek piece and about six inches long. The fuse was too small: it wouldn't stay in the aperture.

I wound paper around it and measured it to go off in two seconds.

So I wouldn't get tired of waiting.

I lit a cigarette. A safety fuse is lit with a cigarette, not a match. Everything according to the rules. I puffed on the cigarette, picked up the cylinder and bent over it with the cigarette. What happened next I don't remember in detail.

Probably I accidentally lit the paper wrapped around the safety fuse.

My arms were flung back; I was lifted, seared and turned head over heels. The air filled with explosions. The cylinder had blown up in my hands. I hardly had time for a fleeting thought about my book *Plot as a Stylistic Phenomenon*. Who would write it now?

It seemed as if the explosion were still resounding, as if the rocks still hadn't fallen back to the ground. But I was on the ground. And I saw the horses galloping in the field, the little boy running. The grass all around was splashed with blood.

Blood is remarkably red against green.

My arms and clothes were all in shreds and holes. My shirt was black with blood and through the straps on my sandals I could see how twisted my feet were. The toes were out-of-joint and stood at various angles.

I lay on my belly, shrieking. The exploding bomb had already finished its shriek. I clawed the grass with my right hand.

I think the soldiers came running right away. They heard the explosion and said, "There it is. Shklovsky's blown himself up!"

They brought up a wagon. Fast. This was the wagon they used for potato expeditions. The men were badly fed, so they bought potatoes and cooked them at night.

The platoon leader and Matveev, the big fellow, came running and started to lift me into the wagon. I was already coming to.

The student named Pik came up, absolutely stunned.

They put me in the wagon and stuck my linen hat with the soft brim under my head for a cushion.

Mitkevich came up, as pale as when the bridge caught fire. He bent over me all out of breath.

There was still a ringing in my ears. My whole body quivered. But I know how to behave. It doesn't matter if I don't know the proper way to hold a spoon at the dinner table.

I said to him: "Take a report: the object given to me for purposes of experimentation proved to be too powerful for use as a primer. The explosion took place prematurely, probably because the outer covering of the safety fuse had been removed. Use regular primers!"

Everything was done according to the rules, as in the best of families.

There are rules about how a wounded man should behave. There are even rules about what a dying man should say.

I was taken to the hospital.

One of my soldier students sat at my feet and kept feeling them to see if I were getting cold.

We got to the infirmary. After some trouble with the orderlies, everything proceeded in customary fashion. I lay there and sadly began to recognize things. I was put on a table and soaped.

The flesh on my bones was quivering. Now that I hadn't seen before.

A fine tremor agitated my body. Not just the arms, not just the legs—no, the whole body.

A woman came up—the doctor.

I knew her from Petersburg. Hadn't seen her for eight years. We started to divert each other with conversation.

I was already being shaved, which is essential for the bandaging.

I talked to her about the great Russian poet Velimir Khlebnikov.

They bandaged me up to my waist and put me in bed.

My wife's sister came to see me the next day. I had told them not to disturb anybody until morning.

She looked at me, touched me with her finger and calmed down a little.

She went to tell Lusya that I still had my arms and legs.

Everyone already knew that I would blow myself up one day.

Actually, by living, maybe I'm helping fulfill some sort of unknown industrial quota.

I was severely wounded, with fragments of metal in my legs and chest.

My left hand had a hole clear through it, my fingers were mangled and there were fragments in my chest.

I was scratched all over, as if by claws. A chunk of flesh had been torn off my thigh.

And my toes were smashed.

It was impossible to remove all the fragments. To remove them, the doctor would have had to make incisions and the scars would have tightened up the leg.

The fragments came out by themselves.

I'd be walking along and something would sting. Something would scrape against my underwear. I'd stop and take a look and there'd be a small, white fragment sticking out.

I'd pull it out and the wound would heal right away.

But enough about wounds.

I was lying there and I didn't smell like fresh meat. It was hot.

The soldiers came to see me. They looked at me tenderly and diverted me with conversations.

Mitkevich came and said that he had written in his report to headquarters: ". . . and received numerous wounds all over his body, approximately eighteen in number."

I approved the report. That was the right number.

The soldiers brought me green apples and sour cherries.

It was hot lying there. My left hand was tied to a small aluminum grate. But I was well done all over.

Another wounded man was put on my right—an enormous man, but not intact. His right leg was missing all the way up to the pelvis.

He had a fine chest and fine, emaciated hands.

He was a local Communist named Gorban. His leg had been amputated long before and he had been wounded again in the following way.

He had been traveling with some agronomist on a matter of land management.

They had quarreled, and perhaps had a fight. The agronomist shot at him point-blank. The shot pierced his jaw and wounded him in the tongue.

Then the man threw Gorban out on the road and shot at him from the car.

He shot him in the scrotum, the chest, the arm, and then drove away.

Gorban lay on the ground under the sun. For a long time. He lay there bellowing in a pool of blood.

Peasants went by with their carts, but they left him there. He couldn't talk. The peasants went about their business.

The militia picked up Gorban that night.

He didn't at all want to die. He kept groaning, thrashing around, choking.

A gray-haired doctor stood over Gorban and injected him with camphor every half-hour. He was infused with a salt solution. Obviously everyone sincerely wanted him to pull through.

And he did pull through. The doctor would come to see him and look at him as lovingly as if he had given birth to this one-legged man himself.

Since our beds were next to each other, we soon became friends.

At first he couldn't talk. Others talked for him and he grunted affirmatively.

By profession, Gorban was a blacksmith. He had been sentenced to hard labor as an SR and beaten a lot.

He was released in 1917 and went to Kherson.

During the German occupation, he had kidnapped an *agent provocateur* who was out for a stroll on main street and taken him to his comrades. They killed the man.

But the Germans caught Gorban and took him away to be killed.

He unbuttoned his leather jacket and jumped out of it.

The jacket remained behind, but he jumped into the river in his boots and pants.

They wounded him in the water, but he got to shore.

He lived in the steppe. He never spent the night in a house; there was no finding him in the grass.

Then he fought against the Germans, against the Greeks (Kherson was occupied by Greeks for a while), then against the Whites.

He was wounded again in the leg. There was no one to bandage it.

That's how it was. When Makhno's men were forced to retreat, the typhus cases had to walk without any help.

Gorban's leg was apparently cut off with pocket knives.

When you cut off a leg, you have to cut through the muscles, pull back the flesh with forceps and saw through the bone.

Otherwise, the bone will eventually pierce through the stump.

If you don't like this description, don't make war. As for me, I'm ashamed to walk down the streets of Berlin and see the cripples.

Gorban wasn't properly operated on and when they got him to a real doctor, his leg had to be cut clear off.

Afterwards, when he went into battle, he had to be tied to his horse with ropes. A stick was fastened to one side of the saddle for him to hold on to.

He saw battle many more times.

He told us in Nikolaev how the men used to seize railroad

stations and declare them "up for grabs." That meant everybody
took as much as he could.

"Mostly all anybody got was maybe a lemon and a pair of
shorts, but it was fun."

He told how they had massacred trains full of refugees. One
train was massacred to the last man. They spared only one Jewish
woman who weighed about 350 pounds: she was a curiosity. Then
he took up land management.

Gorban's plan was to create a single economy for every ten
farms: the arable land and the produce remaining separate, but
machinery and repairs being a common responsibility.

You got the impression that he understood this whole business.

With a jubilant smile, he said of himself: "Now I'm a genuine
kulak. . . . You never saw so much grain. . . . Come and see me,
professor, and have yourself some apricots!"

A lot of people came to see Gorban. They sat and diverted him
with conversation. Students and soldiers came to see me from the
demolition squad. . . .

And here I've put together the pieces of an absolutely true story
—how Kherson was defended against the Germans. In general,
everything I write in this book is the truth. None of the names has
been changed.

Our soldiers had abandoned the front. They were traveling on
trains, in trains and under trains. Some of them remained on the
rails.

But with the help of the Russian god—a great and all-merciful
god—many returned home. With their rifles.

And still the people retained their faith in themselves. The
revolution was still going on.

The men came to Kherson. The port wasn't functioning. There
was nothing to do in Kherson. They went to the municipal duma.

Its members, being literate men, decided to set up some "national workshops."

Outside Kherson, and in, stood the ramparts of some old fortress. No one needed the soldiers and no one needed the ramparts.
Then why not let the soldiers tear down the ramparts?

The soldiers did a bad job of tearing down the ramparts. They
got into fights with the duma. The duma got together in secret and
decided to call in the Germans.

This is called "class consciousness."

The Germans arrived in small numbers and occupied the city.

The soldiers loved Russia, even though they had abandoned the front. They got together and drove out the Germans. Then they went to deal with the duma.

The members of the duma were terrified, but one of them got hold of himself, took a red velvet cushion from one of the chairs, laid on it the key to some safe and carried it out to those besieging the duma.

"We surrender. Take the key to the city."

The soldiers had often heard that phrase, "the key to the city."

They were completely confused. They took the key and let the members of the duma go home.

And then dictators appeared. The dictators were mainly escaped convicts, except for one who was a renegade Rumanian priest. A lot of Rumanians had been evacuated to Kherson. Even the king was supposed to be on his way.

The dictators, three in number, would walk their horses down the sidewalk.

Then troops started attacking the city. But Kherson didn't call a meeting or elect officers. The people decided to defend themselves "freely." The revolution was still going on.

Every time the Germans attacked, someone would dispatch cars all over the city to honk their horns; kids would run all over the city, knock on the doors and shout, "The Germans, the Germans!"

Then everyone picked up his gun and ran to the trenches to beat back the Germans.

First it was the Austrians who attacked. They surrendered when they got the chance.

I think it's generally hard to wage war against a leaderless city.

Then the Germans came, each regiment just like the other. They didn't understand that it's impossible to wage war against free men.

Before they arrived, the peasants came from the villages to fight against the Germans.

But the peasants lacked the necessary faith. They left, saying, "You're not well organized." They were landowners and feared for their homes—they had something to lose. Then, too, a peasant's heart doesn't take fire. The Germans were attacking.

The city's inhabitants fought outside the city, inside the city, on every street of the city. They locked themselves in the fortress. The Germans took the fortress. Order was restored.

The Germans didn't let anyone ride horses on the sidewalks.

They looked for guns everywhere, even in cesspools. If they found some, they burned the house.

This is when Gorban killed his *agent provocateur*. It was during the reign of Hetman Skoropadsky.

Then the Germans were driven out by the French. Skoropadsky was finished. The foulest period in Ukrainian history was finished.

But now, in addition to the Germans, there were the French to deal with.

They too have their "class consciousness." They decided to occupy the Ukraine.

Since the French didn't want to waste many Frenchmen on this affair, they made the Greeks responsible for the occupation of Kherson.

All told, I think the Ukraine saw as many as twenty governments.

But the inhabitants of Kherson spoke about the Greeks with the most rage.

"A trashy army!"

"Their cavalry rides asses!"

Then there were still the English and some others—Americans, too, but they apparently were human.

The Greeks occupied the city and then got scared. They were so scared that they cleared out entire sections of town and crammed the dispossessed people into grain elevators along the Dnieper.

Once the people were locked up, it wasn't so bad.

One time, the elevators caught fire and a lot of people burned to death.

There were various chunks of human meat lying in the ashes.

Meanwhile, Grigoriev had begun to attack. He pressed the city so hard that the front soon wound around the post office.

Grigoriev's men climbed over the back fences of Kherson and occupied the city.

The Greeks retreated, leaving their wounded in the same infirmary where I was then lying.

That morning, Grigoriev's men drove their wagons up to the infirmary and went to see the doctor.

The doctor was a gray-haired Ukrainian named Gorbenko.

An important doctor. A lot of people in Kherson had been cured by him and nearly all the men working in the infirmary were his former patients.

Grigoriev's men went up to the doctor and said that now they were going to kill all the wounded Greeks and that there would be no inconvenience because the wagons were all ready—they would haul off the bodies and dump them down a well in the fortress. There really was a well in the fortress—anywhere from three to six feet in width. When you lay on the edge and looked down, you could see that the walls converged in the distance like railroad tracks. Instead of a bottom, there was only darkness.

But Doctor Gorbenko wouldn't let Grigoriev's men throw the wounded Greeks down that well and they remained alive.

That man had strength of will—probably because he was a surgeon. I myself saw him save a man once. They had brought in a wounded enemy scout and put him in the bed next to mine. He had been mortally wounded by a hand grenade, thrown at him just as he was crossing into our sector of the front.

He was an enormous man with a red beard—a sailor, as it turned out, who had gone over to the Whites.

His death throes were already beginning. He kept plucking at his blanket and, choking all the while, he'd say, "Oh, Mama! My dear Mama! Christ protect me!"

The Cheka sent over a black-haired, décolleté sailor.

All the sailors had bared chests, but this one looked décolleté.

He put one foot on the chair and began the interrogation: "Well, speak up. How many of our buddies did you sell out?"

Apparently, these men had known each other before.

The red-haired sailor thrashed around and moaned. They injected him with camphor. He stared straight ahead and his fingers never stopped twitching.

The black-haired sailor left quickly.

But some soldiers were hanging around the door: "Give him to us!" They wanted to kill him.

The nurse looked at me in confusion and shrugged her shoulders: "You see?"

But Doctor Gorbenko scattered the soldiers like chickens: "I'm the doctor here. This is my business."

III

Toward evening, the red-haired sailor became quiet and died. He was carried into the chapel.

Those from our ward who weren't seriously wounded went to look at him.

They poked at the body.

The soldiers came back and told me that the "White" was fat and that he had an enormous . . . . That's what happened before Rasputin's body was burned in the furnace of the Polytechnical Institute. The men undressed the body, poked at it and took measurements with a brick.

A terrible country.

Terrible even before the Bolsheviks.

I felt very dejected.

The Whites were putting on the pressure.

You could already feel a cold draft blowing through Kherson. Uprisings were continually breaking out on our side of the river.

One night the order was given to haul all the wounded to Nikolaev.

Gorban didn't want to go.

A friend of his, the chairman of the local soviet, came to him and said, "You have to go while you can get through. All the peasants around here are up in arms."

We were taken out that night. The soldiers left very reluctantly. They believed that Gorbenko would cure them. We were put in wagons and hauled to the railroad station.

There we were transferred to railroad cars (the floors of).

Toward morning, they hooked a locomotive to the train and we pulled out.

That's how I left Kherson without seeing my wife.

The sun was baking hot. No one had accompanied us. The slightly wounded were looking after those who couldn't walk. There was no water.

We heard shooting in the distance—some village was revolting.

When a village revolts, the tocsin's sounded and people run every which way to defend themselves from the troops.

A field, in the field haystacks, behind the haystacks soldiers. They attack the village.

The next day, they take it. But behind that village lies another village and sometime it too will sound the tocsin.

The field is wide. The soldiers are always either attacking or resting up.

There's no hurry. The soldiers are spaced like teeth on a pitchfork.

And the Red train goes past. The wounded Red Army men lie on the floor of the train, Gorban delirious from the heat, and I look at my fate with indifference. I am a falling stone—professor of the Institute of Art History, founder of the Russian school of the formal method (or morphological). In this situation, I'm like a needle without any thread, passing through the cloth and leaving no trace.

There was shooting at the train. The telegraph wires hummed when the poles hadn't been cut down. There was shooting from the train.

But the track hadn't been dismantled and that night we arrived in Nikolaev. Trains carrying wounded men travel slowly.

I had seen my last gun-fighting. From now on, everything would be peaceful. That meant I could pause a while.

The Whites were advancing along the right bank of the Dnieper and trying to make landings around Rostov.

There were no Red troops between Nikolaev and Kherson. All the businesses in the area were packing up and pulling out.

We stayed for a short time in the hospital at Nikolaev. Then we were once again put aboard a train, which left for some unknown destination.

En route, the wounded sailors re-established justice by beating up the antiprofiteer brigades so that they could sell their "togs" and carry on to their hearts' content.

Next to me lay a Red artillery commander, who had been wounded in the legs by a bomb dropped from an airplane. By his bed stood a pair of yellow boots, made from saddle leather. They had been made to console him. Every time the train stopped, he put a boot on one leg, a slipper on the other.

And he went walking with the young ladies. He found them without any trouble.

All around lay wounded men, delirious, moaning from time to time.

The train kept going and going and finally stopped at Elizavetgrad.

We were taken off and put into a Jewish hospital.

The artillery commander wasn't walking anymore. Gangrene had set in and the yellow boots were set next to his bed.

I was walking on crutches.

And now I must explain my genealogy.

Viktor Shklovsky was born to Boris Shklovsky, a mathematics instructor who still teaches, and to Varvara Karlovna Shklovskaya, born Bundel, whose father, Karl Bundel, to the end of his days wouldn't set foot in the Russian church—even for the funerals of his children. A lot of his children died and, by law, they were Russian Orthodox.

My grandmother on Mother's side lived with her husband for forty years and never learned German. I don't speak German either, which is too bad, since I'm living in Berlin.

Karl Bundel spoke Russian badly. He knew Latin well, but what he loved most of all was hunting.

Now then, Varvara Karlovna Bundel was born in Petersburg to the son of the Wendish pastor—Karl Bundel, gardener of the Smolny Institute, who, without the permission of his parents, married at the age of seventeen the daughter of a deacon from Tsarskoe Selo, Anna Sevastianovna Kamennogradskaya. The name comes from an ancestor who cut precious stones. My mother's cousin Kamennogradsky was a deacon under Ioann of Kronstadt to the end of his days.

My father Boris Shklovsky, however, was a full-blooded Jew.

The Shklovskys come originally from Uman, a town in the Western Ukraine, but they were massacred in the Uman massacre.[61]

Those who were still alive went to Elizavetgrad, where the train had just brought me and the wounded Red Army men.

My great-grandfather, who was very rich, had lived in Elizavetgrad.

According to the legend, when he died, he left more than a hundred grandchildren and great-grandchildren.

My father had about fifteen brothers and sisters.

My grandfather was poor; he worked as a forester for his own brother.

As soon as the sons got to be fifteen or sixteen, they were sent out to seek their fortune.

When they found it, their brothers were sent to join them.

Mates for the daughters were taken from among the sixteen-year-old boys playing in the street, but they had to be of good Jewish stock. After the marriage, these fellows were taken in by the family, made pharmacists' apprentices and then pharmacists. It wasn't possible to do more than that.

These matches turned out well; they were happy, for the most part.

My grandmother didn't learn to speak Russian until she was sixty.

She liked to say that she had lived the first sixty years for her children and now she was living for herself.

It was said in the family that when my father, who had also married very young, at eighteen, arrived in Elizavetgrad with his first wife and his newborn son, my grandmother was breast-feeding her last baby.

When her grandson cried, my grandmother didn't want to wake up his young mother, so she nursed him along with her new daughter.

My grandmother had been abroad. She visited her son Isaak Shklovsky (Dioneo) in London and read him her book of memoirs.

Her memoirs begin with the stories of her nurse and her parents about Gonta; they end with Makhno.

The book is written in Yiddish. She translated some sections of it for me.

It's written calmly. Grandmother never stopped loving Russia.

There's one fine moment in it. Some officers and Cossacks had come to their house to loot. My grandmother was hiding her hand with the wedding ring on it. The officer said, "Don't worry. We don't take wedding rings."

"But we do," said the Cossack, pulling the ring off her finger.

Just a few days ago, I learned that my grandmother died of pneumonia in Elizavetgrad at the age of eighty-six. The letter from the Ukraine reached me in Finland via Denmark.

She had died in the ruins of the city.

Right now, the famine in Elizavetgrad is horrible.

I read the letter which Grandmother had written a few days before her death.

She wrote that the times were hard, but it didn't get her down. I believe she died without despair.

I saw her for the last time in 1920. I left the hospital and lived with her.

The apartment had been completely plundered. Dozens of bands of marauders had passed through the town; there had been an unusual number of pogroms. I'll note down one of their techniques: the quiet pogrom.

Organized marauders come to the bazaar and go up to the Jewish shops. They stand in line and announce: "All the merchan-

dise is going at prewar prices." Several of them stand there to take
in the money.

Within thirty minutes to an hour, the store is sold out; the
money taken in is handed over to the owner.

He can take this money to the next stall and buy a roll.

But usually they had the other kind of pogroms.

Sometimes the marauders examined passports and didn't bother
those who had been converted to Christianity. Sometimes they left
wedding rings.

They carried off furniture and pianos; they carried off the
maid's trunk.

As a general rule, they killed people after taking them as far as
the railroad station.

But the Jews hid and this, for some reason, was permitted.

One time, the workers at the Elvarti plant stopped a pogrom.

Several times, the whole city took a stand near the old fortress
and fought against some advancing band.

Grandmother told her grandsons to go and fight.

But the workers didn't take kindly to bourgeois Jews; they
didn't let the Jews fight at their side.

Now the town was quiet.

The shops were closed. People were trading in the bazaar, but
with trepidation.

I was in Elizavetgrad when the free sale of bread was forbidden,
even though the city distribution hadn't been set up. A bit strange,
that.

One night, two of my cousins showed up.

They were involved in some sort of speculation. They came at
night in a wagon.

They had come to Elizavetgrad and bought some bacon and
flour. Now they wanted me to go with them and take the whole
cargo to Kharkov.

They ran out at all the train stops and bought sacks of apples
and baskets of tomatoes. They spoke not in Yiddish, but in sailors'
jargon. "To grease the gills" meant to eat. Then followed other
interesting expressions. They were taking these provisions back
home to Kharkov to "grease their gills," not to sell. We changed
trains frequently and rode on top of the cars.

I was going to spend the night on the floor of a propaganda
bureau. But some soldier gave me his place on a table. I slept.

Lenin and Trotsky looked at me from the wall, not to mention choice aphorisms from Marx and the *Red Gazette*.

My chums slept on their things in the street.

I arrived in Kharkov.

They hauled me and the tomatoes to my uncle's house, out of which stepped my wife in a red calico dress and wooden sandals. When she had missed my train, she caught the next train out of Kherson. She looked for me in Nikolaev, then went to Kharkov. From there, she had planned to return to Elizavetgrad.

I sat for two days at the People's Food Commissariat trying to get permission to transport seventy-five pounds of food to Petersburg.

Within a week, we were in Petersburg.

The peat bogs around the city were burning.

The sun was hidden in smoke.

I quarreled with Lusya. She said that made it cloudy and I said sunny. I'm an optimist.

We arrived almost naked, with no underwear.

After the Ukraine, Petersburg impressed me as a city with everything.

I settled in a convalescent home on Kamenny Island. I gained ten pounds. I felt peaceful as never before.

Generally an active struggle against the Whites didn't figure prominently in the program of Russian intellectuals at that time, but no one was surprised when I returned from just such a mission wounded.

Whether out of affection for me or out of disaffection with the Whites, no one pestered me with questions.

The fragments were coming out of my wounds without any trouble. It was hot, but the windows of my room looked out on the Neva.

I was overjoyed to sleep on sheets and eat from plates.

The difference between Petersburg and the Soviet provinces is greater than that between Petersburg and Berlin.

Now begins an uneventful story—about the prosaic side of Soviet life.

I moved into the House of Arts.

There was no room for me. I just took my things, put them in a baby carriage and wheeled them to the House of Arts. My most important things were, of course, flour, groats and bottles of sun-flower-seed oil. I drove my baby carriage into the House of Arts without the permission of the administration.

I lived at the end of a long corridor. It was called "Pyast's Dead End" because it ended at the door of the poet Pyast.

Pyast went around in checked trousers—a fine, black-and-white check—in addition to which he wrung his hands and read poetry.

Sometimes he spoke very well, but then he would suddenly stop in the middle of his speech and be absolutely quiet for thirty seconds. During these minutes of silence, Pyast himself seemed somehow absent.

The other name for the corridor was the "Winter Monkey House."

It was like a monkey house: all those dark doors, all those stovepipes over your head—quite similar, all things considered— even an iron stairway leading upstairs.

Then—Eliseev's kitchen.

All done in blue and white tiles, with the stove in the middle.

The kitchen was clean, but there were lots of cockroaches.

A baby pig ran around on the tile floor, making its little grunts. It ate only cockroaches, but didn't put on any weight, so we sold it.

Next to me in the monkey house lived Mikhail Slonimsky.

He hadn't become a novelist yet. He was preparing something called *Literary Salons*. He had just finished a biography of Gorky.

When he had bread, he ate it greedily.

Farther down the corridor lived Aleksandr Grin, as gloomy and quiet as a convict in the middle of his sentence. Grin sat in his room and wrote the story called "Crimson Sails," a fine, naïve piece of work.

I was a bit cramped on my narrow bed. I was getting hungry, too. All I had to eat was buckwheat kasha—every day. Often followed by vomiting.

I had no writing desk and, in this matter, I'm an American. I demanded a desk. I absolutely terrorized the whole household.

Soon I was transferred to a room upstairs.

It had two windows overlooking the Moika Canal.

Nearby were the dome of the Kazan Cathedral and the green spires of poplar trees.

Everything in the room was massive.

There was a sink in the next room.

Now I started to live better.

I still had sugar left from the Ukraine. I ate it like bread. If you weren't in Russia from 1917 to 1921, you can't imagine how the body and the brain—the brain not as intellect, but as part of the body—can crave sugar.

The body craved sugar the way a man craves a woman; it kept insisting. How hard it was to get a few pieces of sugar home without eating them! It was hard, too, to be at someone's house where a sugar bowl with sugar in it sat casually on the table—hard not to cram all that sugar into your mouth and wolf it down.

Sugar and butter. Bread didn't have the same appeal, though I lived for years with the thought of bread in my mind.

They say that the brain needs sugar and fats.

Someday poems will be written about dried Soviet fish. To the starving, it was manna from heaven.

That fall of 1920, I was made a professor at the Institute of Art History. That was nice for me—I loved the institute. All my life, I've had to work in fits and starts. At the age of fifteen, I still couldn't tell time. Even now it's hard for me to remember the order of the months. They somehow never lodged in my head. But I worked, in my own way, a lot. I read a lot of novels and I know my business thoroughly.

I resurrected Laurence Sterne in Russia by knowing how to read him.

When my friend Eikhenbaum was leaving Petersburg for Saratov, he asked an English professor friend of his for *Tristram Shandy* to read on the train. His friend replied, "Forget it. It's a terrible bore." Now he considers Sterne an interesting writer. I revived Sterne by understanding his system. I demonstrated his connection with Byron.

The formal method is fundamentally very simple—a return to craftsmanship. Its most remarkable feature is that it doesn't deny the idea content of art, but treats the so-called content as one of the manifestations of form.

In a work of art, thought is juxtaposed to thought, just as word is to word and image to image.

Art is fundamentally ironic and destructive. It revitalizes the world. Its function is to create inequalities, which it does by means of contrasts.[62]

New forms in art are created by the canonization of peripheral forms.

Pushkin stems from the peripheral genre of the album, the novel from horror stories, Nekrasov from the vaudeville, Blok from the gypsy ballad, Mayakovsky from humorous poetry.

Everything—the fate of heroes, the epoch in which the action takes place—everything is the motivation of forms.

The motivation of forms changes faster than the form itself.

An example of motivation: at the beginning of the nineteenth century, the predominant literary fashion in novels and narrative poems was to violate the convention of the frame-novella.

Sterne left his *Tristram Shandy* unfinished. His *Sentimental Journey* ends in the middle of an erotic scene. Halfway through this same *Sentimental Journey*, he supplies the motivation for this ending by interrupting an inserted novella to tell about losing some pages of the manuscript. This same kind of motivation exists in Gogol's "Shponka and His Aunt," Byron's "Don Juan," Pushkin's "Evgeny Onegin," and Hoffmann's "Kater Murr." None of them was finished.

Another example: chronological displacement.

Chronological displacement is particularly characteristic of so-called romanticism (a nonexistent phenomenon).

The usual motivation is a story.

In other words, halfway through the novel, the action moves back in time by one of three devices: the reading of a "discovered manuscript," a dream or reminiscences of the hero (Chichikov in Gogol's *Dead Souls*, Lavretsky in Turgenev's *A Nest of Gentlefolk*).

The purpose of this device is retardation.

The motivation, as I've already said, is a story, a manuscript, reminiscence, a mistake by the bookbinder (Immermann), the forgetfulness of the author (Sterne, Pushkin) or a cat's coming along and mixing up the pages (Hoffmann).

There's no such thing as nonobjective art. There's only motivated art or unmotivated art. Art develops according to the technical possibilities of the time. The technique of the novel created the stock character. Hamlet was created by stage techniques.

I despise Iva ov-Razumnik, Gornfeld, Vasilevskys of all types —and the unfortunate Belinsky, the killer of Russian literature.[63]

I despise all newspaper trivia—all these "critics of modern times." If I had a horse, I would saddle up and trample them. Not having a horse, I will trample them with the legs of my writing desk.

I despise these men who break the blades of sharp swords. They destroy what the artist has created.

Just imagine—Koni asserts that Pushkin's significance lies in his defense of trial by jury!

Man absolutely requires butter. When my niece Marina was sick, she kept asking for butter—even just a little on her tongue.

And I wanted butter and sugar all the time.

If I were a poet, I would write a poem about butter and set it to music.

How much greed for fat runs through the Bible and Homer!

Now the writers and scholars of Petrograd understand that greed.

I was giving lectures at the Institute of Art History.

My students worked hard. It was cold. The institute apparently had wood, but not enough money to have it sawed. You froze. The curtains and stone walls of that luxurious house froze. The typists in the office were puffy from cold and hunger.

Steam hung over us.

We were analyzing some novels. I spoke carefully and they listened.

So did Grandfather Frost and the Arctic Circle. This great Russian civilization would not die or surrender.

Before me sat a student from a family of workers—a lithographer.

Each day he became more transparent. One day he gave a report on Fielding. His ears were translucent—white, rather than pink. After leaving the class, he fell in the street. He was picked up and taken to a hospital—hunger. I went to see Kristi.

He could give nothing.

His comrades, my students, got bread for him. They visited him.

He stayed in the hospital a while, then dragged himself out of there. He sold his books, paid his debts and returned to the institute.

Every day before coming to class, he pushed carts of coal around and got for his labors two pounds of bread a day, as well as five pounds of coal. He had dark circles under his eyes. So did almost all his comrades.

Don't think that art theoreticians are unnecessary.

Man lives not by what he eats, but by what he digests. Art is needed for ferment.

At home I stoked my stove with paper.

Try to imagine this strange city.

Firewood wasn't issued. Well, it was issued somewhere, but more than a thousand people stood in line for it—an endless line. All kinds of red tape were specially introduced so that people would give up and go away. There still wasn't enough.

And all you got was one bundle.

Tables, chairs, cornices, butterfly chests had all been burned up.

A friend of mine burned his library. That was horrible work. You have to tear all the pages out of the books and wad them up.

He nearly died that winter, but the doctor came to see him one day when the whole family was sick. He told them all to move into one tiny room.

They warmed it with their breath and survived. In that little room, Boris Eikhenbaum wrote his book *The Young Tolstoy*.

I floated on that frozen sea like a life preserver.

The absence of civilized life didn't bother me much, since I had lost the habit. It wasn't hard for me to become an Eskimo.

I visited my friends and buoyed up their spirits. I can think under any circumstances.

Let's go back to the stoking of stoves.

I was living in Eliseev's bedroom. In the corner stood a big stove, painted with pictures of wood grouse.

Part of this building had once been occupied by the Central Bank. I got hold of the key to the bank, walked in, and my head started swimming.

Rooms, rooms, and more rooms on the side facing Nevsky Prospekt, rooms facing Morskaya Street, still more rooms facing the Moika Canal. Opened safes, the whole floor littered with papers, receipt books, manilla folders. With the folders alone, I kept my stove going nearly a year.

It's true that the House of Arts did have firewood, but it was so wet that it never caught without a folder or two.

I wandered all through those empty rooms and rummaged through the papers.

For some reason, my head was swimming. For some reason, it made me sick at my stomach.

But that night I sat at Eliseev's small, round, inlaid table, with my back to the stove, and I sang.

I love to sing when I'm working. The poet Osip Mandelstam nicknamed me "the merry shoemaker."

A special way of life had already taken shape in that house.

When we presented our green cards, each of us was issued one bag and one wooden bowl; we all got hold of sledges.

In general, we adjusted to this life.

Most of us worked in several places and got food allotments at all of them. We were begrudged all these allotments. I myself never got two allotments at the same time, but, even so, it's not right to begrudge people their bread. People have children and they want to eat, too.

On the other hand, there were those who developed a psychological hunger and a cult about food.

One time I dropped in on a rather well-known writer. He wasn't home. I started talking with his white-haired, black-browed wife. She told me, "This month we've eaten twenty-five pounds of pork."

She was very proud of herself for having found that pork and eaten it. She looked down on those who weren't eating pork.

A lot of people were eaten along with the pork.

I was living comparatively well, since I got a firewood allotment from the House of Arts.

I didn't eat pork and didn't think about it.

Concerts were being given in the downstairs rooms of the house.

Akim Volynsky lived in a room with cupids on the ceiling.

He sat in his coat and hat and read the church fathers in Greek.

In the evenings, he drank tea in the kitchen.

I was kept busy installing new people in the house. Among the original inhabitants, there were two tendencies: the aristocrats, who tried to keep the number of inmates as small as possible, and I, who scurried all over the house finding apartments and installing people in them.

New people were making their appearance.

Vladislav Khodasevich, in a moth-eaten fur coat, with a scarf around his neck.

He has a Polish coat of arms like Mickiewicz's, the skin on his face is taut, and he has formic acid in his veins instead of blood.

He lived in Number 30. From his window, you could see the whole length of Nevsky Prospekt. The room was almost round, and Khodasevich muttered incantations:

> Illuminated from on high
> I sit within my chamber round
> And look up at the plaster sky
> My sixteen-candlepower sun.
>
> Around—illuminated, too—
> Some chairs, a table, and a bed.
> I sit, confused, irresolute,
> Not knowing where to put my head.
>
> In silence, palm trees, frozen, white,
> Upon the window panes are pressed.
> My watch, with a metallic sound,
> Fills the pocket in my vest.

When he writes, a dry, bitter sandstorm whirls him along. Microbes can't live in his blood: they curl up and die.

Osip Mandelstam wandered all over the house with his head tilted to one side. He writes his poems with people around and reads them line by line, day by day. His verses weigh a lot at birth. They come a line at a time. They're so burdened with proper names and archaic Slavonic words that they seem almost a joke. That's more or less how Kozma Prutkov wrote. Mandelstam's verses approach the ridiculous:

> Take, for pleasure, from my palms
> A little sun, a little honey,
> As the bees of Persephone decreed.
>
> One cannot loose an unmoored boat,
> One cannot hear a shadow shod in furs,
> One cannot quench the terror of clotted life.
>
> To us remain but kisses,
> Shaggy like the tiny bees,
> Which leave the comb and die.

Osip Mandelstam foraged in the house like a sheep and wandered through the rooms like Homer.

He's an extremely intelligent man in a conversation. The deceased Khlebnikov named him the "marble fly." Akhmatova said that he's one of our greatest poets.

Mandelstam loved sweets to distraction. Living in extremely difficult circumstances—without boots, without heat—he contrived to be treated like a spoiled child.

He was as disorganized as a woman and light-minded as a bird —and not entirely guileless in this. He had all the habits of the true artist. An artist will even lie to free himself for his all-important work. He's like the monkey, who, according to the Hindus, keeps quiet so that he won't be put to work.

On the first floor, walking without bending at the waist, was Nikolai Stepanovich Gumilyov. This man had strength of will—he hypnotized himself. Young people swarmed around him. I didn't like his school, but I know that, in his way, he knew how to train people. He forbade his students to write about spring, saying that there was no such season. You can imagine the pile of crap inherent in mass-produced verse. Gumilyov organized the versifiers. He took bad poets and made them not so bad. He had a passion for craftsmanship and the self-confidence of a craftsman. He had a good feeling for other people's poetry even when it was completely outside his orbit.

He was alien to me and it's hard for me to write about him. There was no need to kill him. No need at all. I remember his telling me about the proletarian poets in his studio: "I respect them. They write poetry, eat potatoes and cherish salt the way we do sugar."

Gumilyov died calmly.

A friend of mine was in jail, sentenced to death. We corresponded. That was about three or four years ago. One of the guards brought the letters out in his holster. My friend wrote: "I am suppressing in myself the will to live. I've forbidden myself to think about my family. Just one thing scares me"—it was evidently an obsession with him—"I'm afraid they'll tell me to take off my boots. I have high, laced boots that go clear up to the knees (drivers' boots) and I'm afraid of not being able to undo the laces."

Citizens!

Citizens, stop killing! Men are no longer afraid of death! There are already customs and techniques for telling a wife about the death of her husband.

It changes nothing. It just makes everything harder.

Blok died harder than Gumilyov: he died of despair.

Blok was not an esthete. At the base of his early craftsmanship lay the revival of the gypsy ballad. He used banal images in his writing.

Blok's strength lay in his use of the simplest forms of lyricism. It's no accident that he took the epigraphs for his poems from ballads.

He was not an imitator: he renewed a peripheral form.

He condemned the old world. He condemned humanism. Parliament. The clerk and the intellectual. He condemned Cicero, but took cognizance of Catullus. He accepted the revolution.

Shylock had been tricked. The senate of Venice offered to give him a pound of Antonio's flesh without spilling any blood. But it's impossible to cut into flesh or to make a revolution without spilling blood.

Blok accepted the revolution with its blood. That was hard for someone born on the premises of the University of Petersburg.

When I say he accepted the revolution, I'm not referring to his poem "The Twelve." "The Twelve" is ironical, like much of Blok's work.

By "irony," I mean not "mockery" but a certain device—either the simultaneous perception of two contradictory phenomena or the simultaneous relating of one and the same phenomenon to two semantic norms.

Neither the poetry of Vladimir Solovyov, nor his philosophy, nor the Moscow dawns of 1901–1902, about which Bely writes so well, account for Blok.

Blok, like Rozanov, is revolt. In Rozanov, it's the revolt of what we used to consider *petit bourgeois*—the backroom, the cowshed. Rozanov perceived as his holy of holies the revolt of "vapor" against the spirit. The common people sometimes say that animals have no soul, only vapor.

Blok is the revolt of pure lyricism. The banal and eternal theme of lyricism. In his images and word-combinations, Blok is a primitive poet. The gypsy ballad had long been sung in the streets; its theme had served as motivation for the great poets Pushkin, Apollon Grigoriev and Fet. Blok renewed the forms of this ballad.

Like Rozanov, who put his budget and his worry about the 35,000 rubles acquired from Suvorin into his books, so Blok dared to put the banal image into his poetry.

But Blok did not completely succeed in his attempt to elevate form to its rightful place. This rock, rejected by so many builders, did not serve as his cornerstone. He did perceive the gypsy theme as much-used building material, useful only as a point of departure; but at the same time, he perceived it and used it without significant alteration.

On this, he built his art.

In the same way, Leskov, an artist of genius who made the individual word palpable before Khlebnikov, could never present his word without motivation. He was able to use this new word only in his humorous *skaz*.[64] But what can you do in a country where Belinsky reproached Turgenev for using a provincialism in authorial speech, rather than in the conversation of his characters?

We Russians understand only representational art.

"The Twelve" is ironic. It's not even written like a chastushka.[65] It's done in argot, in the style of the hurdy-gurdy street couplet. The unexpected ending, with the appearance of Christ, gives the whole poem a new meaning. You come to understand the number "twelve." But the poem remains ambivalent and the effect is calculated.

Blok himself, however, accepted the revolution without ambivalence. The noise made by the fall of the old world bewitched him.

Time passed. It's hard to say what distinguished 1921 from 1918 and 1919. During the first years of the revolution, there was no normal life in any sense, unless you consider a storm normal. There wasn't a man alive who didn't experience periods of belief in the revolution. For whole minutes, you would believe in the Bolsheviks. Yes, indeed, Germany and England will collapse and the plow will plow under borders needed by no one! And the sky will unfurl like a parchment scroll!

But the weight of the world's habits was drawing to earth the rock of life thrown horizontally by the revolution.

The flight was turning into a fall.

Many of us had rejoiced to see that you could live without money in the New Russia. We rejoiced prematurely.

We believed in the studios set up for the Red Army soldiers. Some believed sooner, others later. As early as February 1918, a sculptor said to me, "I often go to the Winter Palace and the men there are always telephoning—'The Pskov Commune, connect me with the Pskov Commune, comrades!' It's great—right out of Mayne Reid!"

When Yudenich was advancing on Petersburg, my father said, "Viktor, you should go to the Whites and say to them, 'Gentlemen, why are you fighting us? We're men just like you, only we do our own work and you want to hire men to work.' "

For Blok, all this was more ominous. But the earth was drawing the rock down and the flight was turning into a fall. The blood spilled by the revolution had already turned into part of our daily life.

Blok said, "Killing can become the worst of professions."

Blok endured the collapse of the thing into which he had put his entire soul.

He had renounced the old prerevolutionary civilization; no new one came to take its place.

The new officers were already wearing jodhpurs and they carried riding crops, like their predecessors. Katka, the heroine of Blok's "Twelve," was sent to a concentration camp. Then everything became as before.

It hadn't worked out.

Blok died of despair.

He didn't know what to die of.

He came down with scurvy, though he lived no worse than anyone else; he came down with angina pectoris and then something else; but he died of exhaustion.

Since "The Twelve," he had written nothing.

He worked at World Literature and wrote for the "Historical Tableaux" department a very bad play called *Rameses*. The daily grind was already dragging him under. But he preferred to die of despair.

Before he died, he was delirious. He had been trying to get permission to go abroad. He had gotten it. I don't know whether going abroad would have helped. Perhaps Russia is better from a distance. In his delirium, he thought that his luggage was being carried out. He was going abroad.

Then he would sit down and figure out a special kind of bookcase to build for his library.

His library, however, had already been sold.

Blok died.

Friends carried his coffin to the Smolensk Cemetery in their arms.

There were few people. All who remained.

The nonbelievers buried him who believed.

I returned from the cemetery by streetcar. People asked me who had been buried. "Blok," I said, "Aleksandr."

"Genrikh Blok?" they asked again. And not just once, but many times during the day, I was asked that.

Genrikh Blok was a banker.

The death of Blok marked an epoch in the life of the Russian intelligentsia. The last faith was lost.

People were embittered. They eyed their masters like wolves and refused to take food from their hands.

And perhaps they began to care more for each other. To look after each other.

Whether our civilization is good or not, it's all we have!

Blok died. He was buried in the Smolensk Cemetery in the middle of a glade. No one spoke over the grave.

By the next winter, a stable way of life already existed. At the beginning of winter, I installed a stove. Pipes fifteen yards long. When we made a fire, we were warm. We weren't hauling paper from the bank anymore. You could buy firewood—even by the cart, but a cart was expensive. Usually we bought it by the bag. A bag contained about fifteen logs, I think. Sorry if I'm wrong. And the wood was usually dry. Don't ever buy birch for firewood if the bark is very white. That means it's just been sawed.

We bought wood every week. I hauled it home on my sledge.

On the night when they came to arrest me—it was March 4, 1922—I had arrived home late in the evening with wood in my sledge. I'd been detained downtown.

Just before that, I'd dreamed that the ceiling was falling on me.

From the Politseisky Bridge, I noticed that the lights were on in my room and in the room next door, a big room with four windows which had been Eliseev's dressing room (he had pedaled on his wheelless bicycle in that room).

I looked at the light in those windows at this unlikely time of night and decided not to go upstairs. Instead, I went slowly with my wood to the house of some friends. So since then I haven't seen either my room or my relatives.

That winter I'd been getting an "academic" food allotment as a writer, so I didn't have to go hungry. There was bread and, when not too many guests showed up, it sufficed. There was American bacon and even mustard. Provisions were being sent by the Finns and the Czechs. I couldn't contain myself! The whole city buzzed with the news. Sugar, ten pounds of sugar! People talked to each other about nothing else. When I had sugar, I ate it by the spoonful. The brain requires sugar and fats and you can't persuade it otherwise. Some chicken was issued, but mostly herring. During my entire Soviet existence, herring never left my side.

So it wasn't cold in my room, though it was often smoky, and there was something to eat. I could work, too. At that time, I took up publishing. Publishing is a favorite indoor sport in Russia. In my day you didn't need money to do it.

This is how I got started publishing things.

Vladimir Mayakovsky helped me publish *Poetics* with money obtained from the Commissariat of Education. There's a funny story behind my little booklet *Rozanov*.[66] I was working on the paper *The Life of Art*. I had already dropped out of the editorial board. As I remember, our board was simply dismissed. And for good reason. I was doing strange things with the paper. Of course, I wasn't printing counterrevolutionary articles in it (and I had no desire to write them or print them), but I was printing scholarly articles. The articles themselves were fine, but not in a theater newspaper. They belonged in a special journal, but there were no such journals. Certain issues of *The Life of Art* were extremely valuable. I remember a particularly good article by Boris Eikhenbaum "On the Tragic," articles by Roman Jakobson, articles by Yury Annenkov and a series of my own articles "On *Don Quixote*." This newspaper made it possible for me to work.

After the shakeup in the composition of the editorial board, *The Life of Art* became strictly a theater newspaper. Its heroic period had passed. I submitted to the paper a long article on Rozanov.

It was a report which I had just given at Opoyaz. It treated Rozanov as an artist instead of a philosopher. By chance, Stolpner, who had come from Kharkov, heard my report. Stolpner was one of the most intelligent men in Russia. He couldn't write, but he could talk. He had been made a professor at Kharkov University and given a fur coat with a beaver collar by way of a decoration. Wearing this fur coat, Stolpner had come to Petersburg for some books. He had made the rounds of his acquaintances, but no one was home. Night was coming on. Keeping calm and trying to decide what was the most sensible thing to do, Stolpner walked into a strange doorway, went upstairs and lay down in front of someone's door with his fur coat on. It was dark. Somewhat later the door opened, a man walked out, stepped on him and asked, "What's this?"

Stolpner answered truthfully even though he was sleepy: "A professor from Kharkov University." The man lit a cigarette lighter, checked the papers of the philosopher Stolpner, friend of Rozanov, and let him into his apartment, where he allowed him to sleep in an unheated room.

At that time, *The Life of Art* was just a leaflet.

"Rozanov" appeared a piece at a time. I asked the typesetters to save the galleys. The paper never printed the last part of "Rozanov," but I used those galleys to run off a little booklet. This book came out at a time when it was still impossible to publish. It was quickly sold out and I lived on the proceeds. I've told this to characterize Russian publishing houses.

I was no exception. A lot of people were publishing without any money. The typesetters treated them very well.

My regards to the typesetters! It was cold in the composing rooms and the metal type made your hands cold. It was smoky. The typesetters had scarves wrapped around their heads. It was so cold that the cylinder of the printing press kept stopping. Instead of running smoothly, it jerked continually as it rolled on the ink. Ink . . . no ink, of course. What we used was more like water. But the books didn't come out too badly. The men knew their business. Printers love books. When the man who makes up the page is good, he never lets a badly run-off book go through. Men who know their business are always good men.

If Semyonov hadn't been a half-baked intellectual, if he had had a trade, he wouldn't have become an informer. But there was a Torricellian vacuum in his soul, his hands were idle, he didn't know how to do anything, so he wanted to be able to say that he dabbled in politics.

No driver or metalworker would have done that.

I published quite a few books—mostly my own, naturally. Before my escape to Finland, I put out Eikhenbaum's *Verse Melodics* on fifteen printer's signatures. Ionov gave us the paper on credit. Part of the edition was sold for gold rubles to the Ukrainian State Publishing House, so we would have certainly paid for that paper. Unfortunately, however, Grigory Ivanovich Semyonov, a man

who knows nothing about work, kept Viktor Shklovsky, a man
who knows his business, from working.

Regards to the printers, too, and to all the workers in Russia!

I lived off books and not too badly. In the mornings, I made
cocoa on my little stove. I could even feed anyone who came to see
me. Of course, I lived worse than the poor people in Berlin, but
bacon was somehow more precious in Russia and the black bread
somehow whiter than a German roll.

Let me give a deposition. I declare the following: that I remained honest throughout the revolution. I drowned no one, I
stomped no one to death and I made peace with no one because of
hunger. I worked all the time. And if I had a cross to bear, I
always bore it under my arm. I stand guilty before the Russian
revolution of only one thing: I chopped wood in my room. That
made pieces of plaster fall off the ceiling below. I had enough
strength to chop wood for my friends, to install stoves and to help
young poets publish their books by telling the typesetters, "This
man is all right."

I got terribly tired. In the afternoons I slept on the couch under
the tiger skin. Sometimes it was hard because there wasn't enough
time to work. My books had to be dashed off. There wasn't time
for me to get seriously involved with myself. More was said than
written down.

I had a good writing desk in the House of Arts—with a marble
top and spiral legs.

I didn't work there, though, but in the corner by the stove.

Late in the fall of 1921, I ran into someone I had known in
Persia—an Aissor.

Remember those dark little men who sat on the street corners in
Russia with shoe brushes? They also led trained monkeys through
the streets. These men are as ancient as cobblestones. They're
Aissors—mountain Aissors.

One day I was walking down the street and decided to get my
shoes shined. I went up to a man sitting on the corner in a wicker
chair with the legs sawed off. Without looking at him, I put my
foot on his box.

It hadn't gotten cold yet, but I was wearing a white rabbitskin
cap and there were beads of sweat on my brow.

One boot had already been shined. I took off my cap.

"Shklovsky," said the man shining my boots.

"Shklovsky," he said, putting down his shoe brushes.

I recognized him. He was an Aissor named Lazar Zervandov, who had commanded a cavalry detachment of the Aissor army in northern Persia.

I looked around.

Everything was peaceful, except that the four black horses on the Anichkov Bridge were charging in different directions.

The Aissors lived in Mesopotamia, in the province of Van (eastern Turkey), and also in Russian Transcaucasia, around Dilman and Urmia. They're divided into the Maronites and Jacobites, who live in the area once dominated by ancient Nineveh, now the city of Mosul (hence the word "muslin"); into the mountain Aissors, incorrectly called "dzhelou" by the Persians (actually, that's the name for only one branch of the mountain Aissors); and into the Persian Aissors.

The mountain Aissors are Nestorians; that is, they don't recognize Jesus as God. The Maronites and Jacobites embraced Catholicism, but in Urmia, the ancient Christian, but heretical, souls of the Aissors were being pursued by missions of all denominations: English, American Baptists, French Catholics, German Protestants and a few others.

There were no missions in the Aissors' mountains. There the Aissors lived in villages governed by priests. Several villages form one branch—a clan governed by a malik, or chieftain—and all the maliks obeyed the patriarch, Mar Shimun.

The right to the title of patriarch belongs only to the branch descended from Simon, the brother of the Lord.

In January 1918, the Russian soldiers went home.

The Aissors' home was in Persia and even those who had come from Turkey stayed in Persia, because in Turkey they would have been massacred by the Kurds.

The Aissors formed their own army.

Even under the tsar the Russians had recruited two battalions of Aissors. Not all the Aissors went into these battalions; instead, they formed a guerrilla detachment under the command of Aga Petros, who was no one's fool.

This same Aga Petros I once took away from the soldiers of the Third Frontier Regiment when they were getting ready to bayonet him.

My friend Aga Petros! We will meet again sometime here in the East, for the East now begins in Pskov, but before it began in Verzhbolovo; now it goes uninterruptedly through India to Borneo, Sumatra and Java—as far as the duck-billed platypus in Australia!

But the English colonials have put the platypus in a jar of alcohol and made Australia part of the West.

No, never again will I see Aga Petros, since I will die on Nevsky Prospekt across from the Kazan Cathedral.

So I wrote in Petersburg. Now the place ordained for my death has changed: I will die in the flying coffin of the Berlin subway.

Aga Petros was a stocky man with an unusual chest, stuck out as if on purpose and decorated with the freshly polished gold of an Order of St. George, First Degree.

Aga Petros had shined shoes in New York and just possibly had led a trained monkey around the streets of Buenos Aires.

In any case, he had been sentenced to hard labor in Philadelphia.

Back home, he had lived in the mountains as a bandit. Then he was a vice-governor for the Turks and thoroughly pillaged the province. Then he became a big man in Persia. One time he got mad about something, arrested the governor of Urmia, put him in a cellar and let him go only when the shah gave him a medal.

He was the unofficial dragoman for our embassy and commander of the guerrilla detachment.

The Russian soldiers had gone home—vanished as completely as water into the ground. They left a lot of guns behind.

The Aissors were armed. The Armenians had organized into a national militia.

They started disarming the Persians.

Old scores were settled.

The first time the Russian troops had pulled out of Urmia (in 1914), the Persians massacred the Aissors who stayed behind because they had been fighting for the Russians.

The Aissors had taken sanctuary in the American mission, under the protection of Doctor Shedd. Bread was baked at the mission to feed the refugees. The Persians added ground glass and iron filings to the flour and the refugees died in droves. It was like throwing a bomb into a small pond full of fish.

The guerrilla detachment of Aga Petros intensified still more the enmity of the Persians toward the Aissors. Since most of them came from other regions, they had nothing of their own and we didn't feed them.

In short, they looted.

The guerrillas walked through the bazaar in their pants made from scraps of calico and their leather sandals; each of them had a bomb tucked into his sash. The Persian women pointed them out to their children and said, "There goes death."

As for me, if I had been in Persia then, I would have butted into this fight on the Aissors' side.

And I don't know why.

Is it possibly because in Petersburg I'm used to seeing the Turkish cannons that stand by the Monument to Glory on Izmailovsky Prospekt?

The Turks would have certainly massacred me—on purpose, not by mistake.

During the withdrawal of the Russians from Persia, there had been a skirmish. The Persians attacked the last Russian troops to withdraw and the Aissors attacked the Persians.

Aga Petros (I've just thought of his last name—Elov) put cannons on Jewish Mountain, which is just outside Urmia, and wrecked the town.

The Aissors generally understand the importance of occupying the commanding heights.

The Persian Cossacks had fought on the side of the Persians. They had been trained by Russian instructors as support for the counterrevolution in Persia.

In these battles, however, they fought not as representatives of the shah, but as representatives of the nation.

The Persian Cossacks were led by Colonel Stolder, a man with much influence at the Persian court. The Armenians and Aissors were led by Colonel Kondratiev and the Russian officers and sergeants who had stayed behind to help form the new national armies.

Many of them are in Mesopotamia now. They're splashed all over the world like drops of blood on the grass.

The Persians were beaten. Stolder and his daughter were captured and then killed.

The disarmament of the Persians began.

This was managed with artillery—forty to fifty shells lobbed into every village.

The villages in Persia are made of clay.

About thirty thousand rifles were confiscated.

Then the Kurd Sinko said, "Mar Shimun, come and see me. I too want to surrender my guns."

The Kurd Sinko occupied the Kuchin Pass—between Urmia and Dilman.

The Kurds have never had a state: they live as families and tribes.

The families form tribes, each governed by a khan.

Sinko wasn't a khan by birth.

He ascended to the Kuchin throne by means of intelligence and cunning. He duped the former Grand Duke Nikolai Nikolaevich, who had hoped to win a Kurdish unit over to the Russian side, and managed to get rifles and even machine guns from him and thereby rise even higher.

Sinko duped us constantly. Because of him we lost the hay stored in Diza. He had promised to give us camels and then didn't. He wasn't at all afraid of us. He said that forty Kurds could drive off a whole Russian regiment.

Aga Petros often recommended attacking Sinko's tribe in the winter, because when you drive these people from their homes in the winter, they perish.

Sinko wrote Mar Shimun: "Come and take our guns."

Mar Shimun took three hundred horsemen with him and they rode the fine horses just stolen from the Persians; he summoned his brother, got in his carriage and they all went to see Sinko.

The convoy rode into Sinko's courtyard. Mar Shimun and his brother went inside the house.

The Kurds started climbing onto the roofs and the Kurds had rifles in their hands.

The Aissors asked, "Why are you climbing onto the roofs?"

And they answered, "Because we're afraid of you."

"But why the rifles?"

The Kurds didn't explain the rifles.

Mar Shimun's brother walked out of the house.

He was cursing and he said, "There was no need to come and see this dog. No good will come of it. Let those who value their lives go home."

But they couldn't go home and desert the patriarch.

The Aissors stayed.

It's not I who tell all this, but Lazar, Petersburg bootblack, commander of a cavalry detachment and member of the army council—a Bolshevik by conviction.

Later he came to see me and drink tea.

He was calm. There was a meeting of Opoyaz at my place that day. Zervandov took off his heavy overcoat and sat down at the table. He drank tea. He refused butter because he was fasting just then. Then he turned to one of my comrades and said, "Look where I find Shklovsky!" To him, I seemed exotic here in Petersburg.

Lazar continued his story. . . .

Then Mar Shimun himself ran out of the house cursing.

The officer-instructor Vasiliev gave the command "To horse" and then from the Kurds on the roof came a volley of shots like a bell, then another volley; then machine guns opened up.

The horses reared, men shouted—complete pandemonium.

Those who could make it set off on the gallop, but most of them stayed where they fell.

Lazar lagged behind. He had a big horse, which took fright . . . so he was the last to gallop away.

He saw the patriarch running, running in mud up to his knees. Mar Shimun was running in the mud without a rifle.

On his chest near the shoulder a wound—blood.

A small wound—not fatal.

"Lazar," said the patriarch, taking hold of his stirrup, "Lazar, these fools have deserted me."

Lazar tried to get the patriarch on his horse. Just then blood covered his head and Mar Shimun fell back.

The Kurds kept shooting, shooting from the roofs.

Volley after volley, friendly as a bell.

Lazar urged on his horse. The remnants of the convoy made their way through Kurds armed with sabers. On the outskirts of the village, Lazar's horse was killed under him and he was wounded.

Another bootblack, the one who sits on Nevsky Prospekt across from the House of Arts and sells shoe polish, also got away—got away seriously wounded.

They rode to the next Aissor village and said, "The patriarch has been killed."

At first no one believed it. Then they saw the wounds.

They rode back to Urmia, collected an army of fifteen thousand men and set out. They hurried, but it's far from Urmia to the Kuchin Pass and the road goes through the mountains; it's far, too, from the pass to Sinko's village and all through the mountains.

They arrived at night.

They looked for the body.

They found the body of the patriarch.

Stripped, but not mutilated. The Kurds hadn't cut off his head, which meant they hadn't recognized him.

They were shooting, shooting from the roofs.

By morning, the Aissors had massacred everyone in the village.

But Sinko escaped.

He had scattered pieces of gold on the floor of his palace.

The soldiers rushed to pick up the gold and the khan escaped through a secret passage.

Mar Shimun was of less than average height; he wore a fez wrapped in a turban and a cassock; on his chest he wore an old Arabic crucifix, which he said dated from the fourth century.

He had red cheeks—a dark, rich red—the eyes of a child, white teeth and gray hair. He was twenty-six years old.

He always went into battle with a rifle in hand. His only complaint was that the three-shot French Lebel rifles which we supplied to the Aissors were breechloaders: these rifles burned their hands when they had to use the bayonets.

He had a simple heart.

When the Russians were pulling out of Persia, he had asked us for rifles and cannons (we gave him about forty rifles), as well as the rank of second lieutenant for all his maliks (chieftains) or else the right to confer the rank of second lieutenant; for himself, he asked an automobile.

Too bad we didn't comply.

Second lieutenant's epaulettes would have looked good on these men with their felt caps and their wide pants made from scraps of bright calico and tied with a rope below the knee; on this naïve and valiant army commanded by Mar Shimun, descendant of Simon the brother of Christ, those second lieutenants' epaulettes would have certainly looked good.

That's not Lazar speaking.

The Aissors were left without Mar Shimun.

The snow in the mountain passes is deep—up to a camel's nostrils.

But the snow had melted.

The Turks came through the passes and advanced on Urmia.

Colonel Kondratiev turned the Turks back with his Aissor and Armenian cavalry and took two battalions captive.

The situation seemed to have improved. Lazar complained to me about Aga Petros: "When you went to the home of a Persian, there you found already the men of Aga Petros. Aga Petros took much gold from Persia."

He complained further: "This Aga Petros was most interested in gold. He held a sector of the front and said that he had three thousand men; in fact, he had only three hundred men and the Turks broke through."

One Aissor cavalry unit was stationed in the mountains.

One morning the men went down to a stream to wash. On the other side of the stream they saw mules and packs.

And men also coming to wash.

Turks.

These men were startled to see each other at the stream.

If the Aissors had only seen the Turks come through the gorge below them in the night, they could have crushed them with rocks.

The Turks had broken through.

The Aissors had no shells for their cannons.

We had attempted to take all our ammunition back to Russia, but we simply abandoned it en route—we no longer had any use for it.

The small amount left behind had been squandered by the ecstatic Aissors when they bombarded the Persian villages.

They couldn't retreat to Russia: the route had been cut. In fact, the Turks were already heading for Tiflis.

The Aissors decided to head for the English in Baghdad.

They were joined by the Armenians, under the command of Stepanians—a Russian Armenian, Petersburg student, then a lieutenant and former chairman of the army committee.

In Persia he had quickly acquired the necessary savagery and turned out to be a born leader.

With him went his wife, a Russian med student. All told, 250,000 people set out from Urmia—men, women and children. A Russian detachment led the way; the Aissors who had previously served with the Russians brought up the rear; volunteers from among the Ashurite (mountain) Aissors guarded the flanks in the mountains.

Most of the people marched in the middle with the women and children.

There was no road. It was necessary to go along the Turkish front or, more exactly, through the Turkish and Kurdish mountains.

On all sides were Turks and Kurds and Persians—a hostile, choppy sea of Moslems—with shots from behind the rocks and battles beneath the crags in gorges where swift rivers flow through the rocks and rocks fall from the crags, and crags, always crags—the Persian crags like powerful waves, like the rock ripples of an entire sea of rock.

And beyond, the East—the East from Pskov to the duck-billed platypus, from Novaya Zemlya to old Africa—the eastern East, the southern East, the western East.

It was then that the Czechs were moving from the East toward the Volga.

And advancing to meet them were Russians, moving from West to East, and it was then that the Caucasian mountaineers descended from the mountains and crossed swords with the Terek and Kuban Cossacks.

And it was then that the Senegalese, after fighting the Germans, sailed back to Africa from France.

They no doubt sang.

They sailed and sang, they sang and thought, but what they thought I haven't any idea because I'm not a Negro. Just wait a bit and they'll tell you themselves.

Throughout the entire East, from the Irtysh River to the Euphrates, men hacked and killed.

The Aissors kept going because they're a great nation.

They left the gorges and proceeded through the mountains.

There was no water. They ate snow for twelve days.

The horses fell.

Then they took horses away from the old men and gave them to the young. It was no longer a question of saving individuals, but of saving the nation.

Then they abandoned the old women.

Then they began to abandon their children.

It took a month to reach English territory in Baghdad.

On the day of their arrival, they numbered 203,000 people.

The English said to them, "Stop here at our border, make camp, rest and wash for three days."

They stopped in the middle of a Persian village.

The day passed without event.

The following night, the Turks attacked and Persians began to shoot at the camp from their roofs.

The English detachment which had been sent to meet the Aissors saw for the first time how shots came from the right and from the left and from the rear and how the women and children cried out.

In the turmoil, the English soldiers jumped on their horses bareback and tried to gallop away.

But Colonel Kondratiev ordered the Aissors to set up their machine guns and to open fire on any who ran away.

The English stopped.

They were told, "If you came to help, then help us or we will kill you, because for four weeks we have followed a route known by all to be impassable. No caravan ever passed between Urmia and Hamadan, yet we have made this trip with women. Therefore if you refuse to help us, we will kill you with this machine gun, since we have eaten snow for twelve days."

The English got off their horses and joined the Aissors.

There was a battle.

The Persians were driven from the village. The Turks were captured and herded into a valley and the Aissors shot into this valley with machine guns; they shot into this valley with rifles.

Not one Turk emerged.

But the Turkish general was taken captive.

The Aissors asked him, "Why did you order your men to pick up our children and dash them to the ground?

"Why are we homeless now?

"Now we will shoot you."

The English said, "You can't kill a prisoner."

The Aissors answered, "He is our prisoner."

The general said nothing.

They killed him, but they did not cut off his ears and they did not cut off his head, because among the Aissors were men who had served with the Russians and because Lazar was a Bolshevik.

All the Aissors now broke camp, moved forward and crossed into English territory.

Here they learned that a detachment of Aissors from America was about to join them.

There are many Aissors in America; they even have two newspapers there.

When these Aissors heard about the battles from Oramar to Urmia, they had laid down their shoeshine brushes and closed their shops, left their businesses, used their gold to buy rifles from the Americans and returned to fight for their country.

If Aissors had been living along the Volga and starving, they would have left and gone all the way to India.

Because the Aissors are a great nation.

They waited for the detachment from America.

They decided to go with them to live among the English in Nineveh, in the land of ancient Assyria—near Mosul, the source of muslin.

It is said that in that land live serpents which can leap and plunge through the body of a man.

There monkeys and savage forest men live in forests always green and the heat is such that clothes are always drenched in sweat.

There in vaults beneath the houses, stone doors turn on stone pins; buried in vaults beneath the houses lie chests of precious stones.

There the English excavate.

Lazar didn't see these excavations.

The English came to his place and arrested him as a Bolshevik.

Before the withdrawal of the Russians from Persia, he had sat on the army committee as a Bolshevik.

Also arrested were several Russian officers and soldiers.

They sat in prison and wondered why they had eaten snow and gone to the English for help.

Lazar had been wearing a fine jacket with the wide—wider than usual—epaulettes of a sergeant major in the cavalry.

The English took him for a general.

They assigned him a separate room.

He wrote a note requesting spoons and dishes for all the prisoners.

He was given, in addition, twelve tomans.

The prisoners said nothing—they just laughed.

On the fifth day, a Russian officer with the English army came to take a look at this general, looked at him and said, "You're no general—you're just a sergeant major!"

Lazar replied, "Why should I not be a general if my captors call me one?"

At first, he was put in solitary confinement, then sent to Enzeli; in Enzeli he was released and ordered to go to Russia.

He went to Baku.

In Baku, however, were the Whites. They were recruiting a national militia and they ordered everyone to fight against the Bolsheviks.

They recruited an Aissor detachment, but the Aissors laid their rifles on the ground.

They wouldn't fight.

Then they were sent to Lenkoran Island.

Lenkoran Island is in the sea across from Baku.

The island itself is sandy, but the sea around is salty.

Before that, captured Turks had been held there.

Lazar had a wife.

I don't know whether I said that he was a naturalized Russian, even though his house in Urmia stood next to the French mission.

A fine house, with a long passageway leading between gray walls, an inner courtyard covered with grapevines and fretted stained-glass windows facing the courtyard.

With a peacock on the roof.

Peacocks have beautiful tails.

And the nights in Persia are beautiful.

And flamingos fly over Lake Urmia.

Lazar was a naturalized Russian. When the war began, he had chosen to serve in the artillery.

He was sent to Poland. When interpreters were being sought in all the armies, he was sent from Poland to the Caucasian front.

Lazar didn't see his family for four years.

He had left his wife pregnant.

He had no idea where his family was. He thought they were with a relative in Erevan. His home in Urmia had been abandoned and he was a prisoner on Lenkoran Island.

The sea around was salty.

Then the Bolsheviks arrived by sea from the Volga. Torpedo

boats arrived from St. Pete bearing none other than Fyodor Raskolnikov, student of S. A. Vengerov. With him was Larisa Reisner. Our life is well stirred. Also along was the poet Kolbasev, who now lives in the House of Arts. They took Lazar off the island.

He went to Erevan.

He went to see his relative and asked, "Where is my wife?"

His relative answered, "I quarreled with your wife and do not know where she is. I think that she left the city."

Lazar decided to go to America.

He went to the marketplace to buy some sausage for the road.

Sausage was inexpensive there.

A little boy was standing in the marketplace.

A nice boy and there was a family resemblance.

Lazar asked the boy, "Whose son are you?"

He replied, "Semyon's."

"Then you are not mine."

But Lazar's brother was named Semyon.

"And who is your mother?"

"Elena."

Lazar's wife was named Elena.

"Where is she?"

"She is there in the line to buy meat."

"Show me."

The boy led the way and showed him.

Lazar stood there.

It was not she.

Suddenly the woman began to cry, "Lazar, look, it is I!"

And she ran away.

Lazar stood in the middle of the marketplace and understood nothing.

Elena ran home.

Semyon was sleeping.

She grabbed him by the ear. "Get up, Semyon. Guess what good thing has happened? Lazar has come!"

Semyon gathered all the money that was in the house and gave it to Elena.

It came to 200,000 rubles.

Both of them ran to get Lazar.

But the third brother didn't run.

He had a carriage.

While Lazar was fighting the war, he had earned enough to buy a carriage.

Lazar stood there and understood nothing.

Then he saw running toward him Semyon, his wife and the boy.

And the boy was his son, only he had grown up with Semyon's children and was accustomed to think of himself as Semyon's son.

Because four years is a long time and Urmia, Poland and Baghdad are far away.

Running toward Lazar were his brother and his wife and behind them, driving his carriage, came the third brother, wearing a student's cap.

.   .   .   .

The Aissors are a nomadic nation.

The title of Mar Shimun was: "Patriarch of the East and India."

And the fact is that since at least the seventh century, the Aissors have been scattered over the entire world.

They were in Japan, in India on the Malabar coast and in Turkestan on the Chinese border.

Their alphabet served as the basis for all the Mongolian alphabets and for the Korean.

There are Aissor tombs in Tobolsk.

The Aissors have not lived in vain upon the earth.

Now they wander the entire world shining shoes.

There was nothing for Lazar to do in Erevan, so he moved his family to Armavir. There he fell in with a group of Aissors and traveled with them first to Moscow and then to Petersburg.

There are Aissors living in Petersburg.

There is Lazar, there is the translator for Mar Shimun, there is Hosha Alexander; there is even an Aissor in Petersburg from the family of Mar Shimun, only he doesn't shine shoes: he sits on his bed and reads books.

Lazar stands on the corner of Nevsky Prospekt.

It is cold in Petersburg.

The wind blows down Nevsky Prospekt.

And it blows down the other streets of the city.

The wind blows from the East, the wind blows from the West, and on its circuits the wind returns.

Here's the manuscript of Lazar Zervandov himself. All I did

was rearrange the punctuation and correct the cases a little. Consequently, it's come out sounding like me.

The Manuscript of Lazar Zervandov

After the departure of the Russians from Persia, the Aissor detachment was reorganized. At the head of this detachment were Russian and Aissor instructors under the command of Colonel Kondratiev.

The detachment was organized on January 29, 1918, in the city of Urmia.

A meeting was held in the presence of the patriarch, Mar Shimun, and the Persian governor, Etrattumai.

At the meeting, the Persians proposed that the Aissors surrender their weapons.

The Aissors refused.

On February 4, in the Urmian bazaar, sixteen mountain Aissors were killed and stripped.

This was followed by an attack on the post office. Lieutenant Ivanov was killed.

On February 8, 1918, all the Persians in Urmia rose up and surrounded the headquarters of Aga Petros. The battle lasted all night. Toward morning, Petros sent a dispatch to Mar Shimun.

Mar Shimun replied, "Do not fight the Persians."

At twelve o'clock noon, the Persians surrounded the corps headquarters where the commanding officer, Colonel Kuzmin, had his office.

Colonel Kuzmin sent a dispatch to Mar Shimun and asked for help in order to save the Russian instructors inside the building.

The Persians were pressing forward and shouting, "Ja Ali, Ja Ali." At that moment, Colonel Sokolov, commander of the artillery brigade, ordered four cannons stationed on Mount Charbat, which was a mile from Urmia, and two before the Degalin Gate.

They opened fire on the mob of Persians.

But, in spite of that, the Persians broke through the fence surrounding the headquarters building.

Comrade Lazar Zervandov and several of the Aissors ran to that place, took machine guns and hand grenades, and began to shoot at the Persians and Kurds.

The cannons continued to fire.

The Persians began running through the streets, but no matter where they ran, a platoon of Aissors was there. The Persians were killed to the last man. All night long there was looting in the city of Urmia. Doors were broken down and all the Persian rugs and property were dragged out. Patriarch Mar Shimun kept sending Aga Petros and Colonel Kuzmin dispatches saying that they should not fight, that it was better to surrender, because they were all on Persian territory and had come not to fight the Persians, but to escape the mountain Kurds.

There was a battle.

On February 12, at ten in the morning, the remaining Persians and Kurds frantically rushed to the American mission, where Doctor Shedd lived. He is the American consul.

The American consul and the Russian consul, Nikitin, and several Aissor priests began to make the rounds of the city and to pacify the Aissors.

At twelve o'clock noon, Lieutenant Vasiliev (an Aissor) and Second Lieutenant Stepanians (an Armenian) defeated the Persian Cossacks, who were commanded by Colonel Stolder.

He was taken captive.

The Aissors treated him not as a prisoner, but as a Russian officer. They sent him to the harbor at Gjulimkhan. En route, some Armenians intercepted the party and killed Stolder, his wife and his son.

On February 16, Patriarch Mar Shimun left Urmia for Dilman. Some instructors escorted him.

They reached Dilman on February 18. The distance from Urmia to Dilman is fifty miles.

The Dilman Persians already knew that the Urmian Persians and Kurds had been completely routed. The patriarch was summoned to a conference with Sinko in the town of Kenisher.

It had seemingly been decided that Sinko would conclude a peace with the Aissors.

This conference was attended by Mar Shimun, his brother Aga David and 250 Aissor delegates under the command of Colonel Kondratiev. During the conference, the Kurds occupied all the roofs and vantage points.

Aga David came out and said, "There is no use to talk to this dog!" He took two Aissors and left, but the rest all waited for Mar Shimun.

The patriarch came out twenty minutes later and Colonel Kondratiev gave the command: "To horse!"

They barely had time to mount. Suddenly from the roofs came a sound—a volley of shots like a bell.

There was confusion among the Aissors: some on their horses, some under their horses and some on the ground.

They frantically tried to flee.

Lieutenant Zaitsev was killed where he stood, as were the instructors Sagul Matveev and Skobin Tumazov.

The rest ran through the streets.

But the patriarch himself was running through the mud and blood flowed down his back.

He was surrounded by Ziga Levkoev, Nikodim Levkoev, Slivo Isaev, Lazar Zervandov, Ivan Dzhibaev, Yakov Abramov and Prince Lazarev. But they had no time to pick up the patriarch. A second bullet struck him in the forehead and he fell on the grass.

And the Kurds fired volley after volley at the running Aissors. At the edge of town, all that remained (and they without horses) were: Ziga Levkoev, wounded in the left leg; Lazar Zervandov, wounded in the head and the left arm; and Slivo Isaev, wounded in the left side. Our poor comrades had escaped beaten and wounded, but Patriarch Mar Shimun remained lying in the mud.

This happened at five o'clock in the afternoon.

The Kurds and Persians were all trying to find the body of the patriarch.

Because Sinko had received an official notice from the governor of Tabriz that if he sent the head of Mar Shimun, he would be granted twenty times its weight in gold.

The wounded reached the nearest Aissor village of Kostrobat and announced that everyone had perished—the patriarch and all the Aissors with him. No one believed them.

A few minutes later, Colonel Kondratiev arrived wounded and said that all had perished.

An army was gathered and sent to do battle against Sinko. At nine o'clock in the evening, the town of Kenisher was surrounded on all sides.

At midnight, the men hurled themselves into the attack and found the body of Mar Shimun.

But Sinko and his saber made their getaway to Chiri Kaleh.

Twenty days later, advance detachments of Turks made their appearance in the Salmas region—three battalions.

The Aissors went into battle and completely routed the Turks. March 25, 1918, the Turks made another attack. The battle lasted six days. The Aissors surrounded the Turks and captured two hundred and fifty soldiers and their two officers.

After this, Aga Petros went to Urmia with his detachment and announced to Colonel Kondratiev that he had assembled four thousand Aissors.

We launched a general offensive against the Turks in order to cut a road through to the Russian border; but, as it turned out, Aga Petros had only four hundred men, and those poorly armed. Therefore he was unable to carry out his assignment.

He was assigned to hold the left flank and maintain contact with the Armenians, who were advancing along the road to Khoi.

Colonel Kondratiev was holding the Aissors' right flank along the Bash Kaleh Road. The offensive was spearheaded by the Aissor Cavalry Brigade. At the head of this brigade were the following men: Lazar Zervandov, Ziga Levkoev, Nikodim Levkoev, Ivan Dzhibaev, Slivo Isaev, Ivan Zaev and Prince Lazarev.

We occupied the Kotul Gorge and continued to advance toward the Russian border.

Eight days later, Aga Petros and his detachment fell back to Urmia. The Turks had broken through at our rear.

At five o'clock in the morning, we went down to a stream to wash. There was a bivouac on the other side of the stream. We thought that Aga Petros had come to help us. The Turks thought that we were their army. . . .

At five o'clock that night, we received a message from the commander of the detachment that the Turks had broken through the sector held by Aga Petros and penetrated deep into the Salmas region.

We could not retreat because it was already night and rain was falling on us. At dawn, we began to retreat from the Kotul Gorge, but the heights on both sides of the road had been occupied by the Turks. Some said it was impossible to retreat, that we must surrender to captivity; others of my comrades said, "We have enough cartridges and our horses are all good—of Arabian stock. We can make a raid."

So, we fell upon one Turkish position and, indeed, they had no cartridges. They opened fire with a machine gun, but soon stopped. We rushed to the attack and sabered thirty-four Turks.

We captured one machine gun with no cartridges and then withdrew in haste.

We reached the city of Dilman, but saw no Aissors or Armenians. All the Kurds and Persians were looting the Aissor villages and driving away their sheep. We saw the bodies of those killed along the road and thought all the Aissors had perished.

We continued to withdraw without giving battle. For in the distance ahead of us, we saw a huge cloud of dust in the sky. We thought that a large Turkish detachment was advancing.

We reached Haitakhty, but did not find the Russian commander there—no one. We did see children crying along the road. It was impossible to take them, because there were many of them. It was sad to see them.

We ascended to the Kuchin Pass. The road had been cut off by Kurdish bandits. We went into battle against the Kurds and Sergeant Major Isaak Ivanov was killed. We had no time to take him; we left him there.

When we descended from the Kuchin Pass, we found the retreating Aissors heading toward Urmia and we asked, "Where is Aga Petros?"

"He has been in Urmia for three days."

We reached Urmia and spent fifteen days there. Then advance parties of Turks appeared around Urmia and skirmishes began with them.

On May 15, the city of Urmia was surrounded on all sides by the Turks.

It was evident that the Russians and Aissors were losing. A general meeting was held, with the Russian officers in attendance.

Aga Petros said that we had to surrender to the Turks because he had a letter from the commander of the Fourth Turkish Army, Halim Pasha.

But some of the Russians did not want to surrender. They said, "It's better to die," and they assembled a flotilla of rafts and tried to cross Lake Urmia to Sharafkhaneh.

All of them were killed by the Persians. Eight colonels and thirty-two officers and men perished. The Turks and Kurds began to attack. All the Aissors were fighting their last. There were no more weapons, no more shells.

On May 29, the Turks were three miles from Urmia.

The Aissors held a second meeting and decided the following: it was impossible to reach Russian territory because all Transcaucasia was occupied by the Turks; it was better to head east and attempt to reach the English.

The troops were instantly assembled—four thousand cavalry under the command of Colonel Kondratiev and six thousand infantry under the command of Colonel Kuzmin and an artillery brigade under the command of Colonel Sokolov.

Three miles from Urmia—in the vicinity of the village of Diza —twenty-four cannons were lined up.

Then the Turks thought that the Aissors would surrender that very day.

Colonel Sokolov ordered these twenty-four cannons to open fire. They directed a devastating barrage at the Turkish positions.

The Turks were on the mountain.

Four Turkish cannons were destroyed.

We began our general offensive.

All the priests and bishops held a church service in the open. It went well. The Turks were attacked and we broke through their lines.

But on the other side of Urmia, the Turks were already marching into the city.

All that remained in the city were the American and French missions and several thousand Aissors.

According to some Turkish deserters, all who remained were massacred by the Kurds and Turks.

We retreated along the road to Haidarabad.

In the lead were the cavalry and four cannons, in the rear the Aissors who were naturalized Russians, along the sides the Armenians and mountain Aissors.

The Turkish cavalry came in pursuit.

There were battles up ahead and battles in the rear. Everything was destroyed . . . houses . . . villages. . . .

It is thirty-six miles from Haidarabad to Solozhbulak.

The whole road was filled with bundles, sheep and people.

The road was narrow.

People dropped their bundles. They abandoned their children and hurried on. Day and night, we rode and rode without rest . . . nothing except shouts and noise, and the poor children cried.

There were no mothers and fathers. Some children were sleeping in the middle of the road; others were playing on the edge of the road, unafraid of the snakes, and there were many snakes.

We kept to the road as far as Ruwandiz.

About twelve miles from Ruwandiz, we learned that headquarters of a Turkish army was located there.

We turned left to Sain Kaleh.

On the fifteenth day after our flight from Urmia, we met the English. Some of us were overjoyed to be saved; others were crying—no children, no family.

The English ordered us to stay three days and rest.

After the third day, the Aissors began to move forward.

At four o'clock in the afternoon in Sain Kaleh, the Persians rose up and began to shoot from the roofs at the women and children.

The English discarded their machine guns and cartridges and jumped on their horses bareback. Things did not look good.

On the order of Colonel Kuzmin to turn the English back (to stop them), we aimed the machine guns at the English and turned them back.

Then we and the English attacked the town of Sain Kaleh. The Persians and Kurds were driven from the town, herded into a deep gorge and surrounded on all sides, then killed to the last man; the town was burned to the ground.

And we continued our retreat down that bottomless road—without bread or water—and finally came to Bijar in Kurdistan—270 miles.

One eighth of the nation had been lost along that road: some perished for lack of water, others fell in battle. We entered the Valley of Kermanshah. There is no dwelling in it, nothing.

Only dense fertile forests.

There wild beasts roam at will.

We saw large numbers of boa constrictors and vipers and monkeys.

We saw no bread there.

There was much water. We lived on sweet fruits and nuts.

We reached the town of Kermanshah.

There the people are different from those in Urmia. It was here that disagreements took place between the Aissors and the instructors.

The mountain and Urmian Aissors insisted on traveling from Kermanshah to Hamadan—a total of 130 miles—through the mountains.

But the Russian instructors followed the road and kept due east day and night.

The Russian Aissors from Karsk and some Russian officers headed toward the city of Baghdad and the brother of the patriarch went with them. There too it is a different world and different people.

We changed horses in the villages.

Here the people wash not in water but in sand, like chickens.

We stayed a total of eight days in the city of Baghdad, then turned again toward Hamadan and, after going 350 miles, reached Hamadan.

There the following men were arrested for being Russian Bolsheviks: Lieutenant Vasiliev, Second Lieutenant Stepanians and Instructor Lazar Zervandov.

By order of the English commander in chief, we were released. Our weapons were very good—they were all confiscated.

LAZAR ZERVANDOV

That's what Lazar wrote for me. I've already printed it in the booklet *Epilogue*. Mikhail Zoshchenko very successfully parodied that piece.[67]

Zoshchenko is a "Serapion."

The Serapion Brothers came into being in February 1921, on the ground floor of the House of Arts. They originated this way: Evgeny Zamyatin had been giving lectures to some students in the House of Arts. He spoke simply, but about craftsmanship; he was teaching them how to write prose.

He had quite a few students—among them, Nikolai Nikitin and Mikhail Zoshchenko. Nikitin is short and blond; we called him the "frustrated lawyer"—this with reference to his domestic affairs. He was under the influence of Zamyatin—perched on his right shoulder. But he doesn't imitate Zamyatin: his writing's more complex. Zoshchenko is dark and quiet—good-looking. He was gassed in the war and has a very bad heart. That's what makes him quiet. He has little self-confidence and never knows what to do about his writing. After joining the Serapions, he began to write well. His book *Stories of Nazar Ilich, Mister Bluebelly* is fine.

There are unexpected sentences in it that reverse the whole idea of the story. He's not so closely connected with Leskov as it seems. He can get along without Leskov, as, for example, in his story "The Female Fish." When his book went to press, the typesetters were told to set it up in standard-sized type; but they arbitrarily set it up in large type.

"A fine book," they said. "Make it so people can read it."

Right in the thick of the fraternity lies Mikhail Slonimsky. At first everyone respected him. He worked as a secretary for the Grzhebin Publishing House and wrote something called *Literary Salons*. Then he wrote a bad story called "Nevsky Prospekt,"[68] and then he started writing sketches and mastered the techniques of the absurd. He writes well. Now no one respects him because he's a good writer. He's rejuvenated and looks his twenty-three years. He lies in bed and sometimes works twelve hours a day—in the smoke. Before he got his "academic food allotment," like Nikitin and Zoshchenko, he suffered incredibly from hunger. His writing specialty is the complex plot with no psychological motivation. One floor down, in the monkey house, lives Lev Lunts. He's twenty years old. He just finished his studies in the Department of Romance and Germanic Languages. He's the Benjamin of the Serapions. However, they have three Benjamins: Lev Lunts, Volodya Pozner, who's now in Paris, and the true Benjamin— Veniamin Kaverin.

Lunts writes all the time. No two things are alike and a lot of them are good. He has a kind of wild, boyish zest for life.

When he finished his studies, the Serapions celebrated the occasion by tossing him up in the air. All of them. The then-gloomy Vsevolod Ivanov charged forward with the war whoop of the Kirghiz tribe and they dropped him on the floor and nearly killed him. That night Professor Grekov came to see him, ran his finger along Lunts' spine and said, "It's all right. We won't have to amputate the leg."

They had just about delegged him. Two weeks later, Lunts was dancing with a cane. He's done two dramas and a lot of comedies. He's bursting with ideas; he has something to say. Lunts, Slonimsky, Zilber and Elizaveta Polonskaya were my students. Only I didn't teach them how to write: I told them what literature is. Zilber (Kaverin) is a boy about twenty years old or less—with a broad chest and ruddy cheeks, though he and Tynyanov often sit at home without any bread. Then they chew their emergency supply of dried roots.

He's a sturdy sort.

I knew him when he was first starting to write. He's a very

individual writer, with a special interest in plot. He has a story called "Candles and Shields," in which some men are playing cards and the cards are carrying on their own intrigue. Kaverin is a mechanic—a plot constructor. Of all the Serapions, he alone isn't sentimental. About Zoshchenko, I can't say—he's too quiet.

Like A. Veksler, Elizaveta Polonskaya wore black gloves on her hands. It was the sign of their order.

Polonskaya writes poems. Out in the world, she's a doctor, a calm and strong person. Jewish, but not an imitator. Her blood is good and thick. She writes little. She has some good poems about present-day Russia. The typesetters liked them. Elizaveta Polonskaya is the only female Serapion Brother. The name of the society is accidental. The Serapions aren't crazy about Hoffmann—not even Kaverin is. They prefer Stevenson, Sterne and Conan Doyle.

Vsevolod Ivanov just kept wandering around Petersburg. He wandered by himself, in a worn-out fur jacket and shoes held together with string.

He had come from Siberia to see Gorky. Gorky wasn't in Petersburg then, so the proletarian writers took him in. They didn't have a thing themselves. They're not court poets. They gave Ivanov what they could—a room. He had nothing to eat. Next door was a depository for old page proofs, so Ivanov had plenty of paper to burn. He got the heat up to 50 degrees and then wasn't so hungry.

Gorky returned and settled Ivanov in the House of Scholars—not on a regular food allotment, however. Those allotments were not given to a man who had written no books. Gorky introduced Ivanov to me and I passed him along to the Serapions.

Vsevolod is a tall man with sideburns and chin whiskers, with slant eyes—like a Kirghiz, except for the pince-nez. He had formerly been a typesetter. The Serapions welcomed him very warmly. I remember the meeting in Slonimsky's room. We kept the stove going with the pieces of a table. Ivanov sat on the bed and began to read: "There are no palm trees in Siberia."

Everyone was overjoyed.

Now Ivanov writes a lot and it's uneven. I don't like his *Colored Winds*—and not because of its ideology, of course. What do I care about ideology! What I don't like is all this "Lacy Grass," as Zoshchenko put it.[69] Ivanov takes himself too seriously. His book's too mannered. In presenting things, a writer shouldn't emphasize himself too much. What's needed is not necessarily irony, but a light touch. His story "The Kid" is fine. It starts out like Bret Harte: some tough men find a baby and look after it.[70] But then the story takes an unexpected twist. The baby needs milk, so the men kidnap a Kirghiz woman with a baby. But in order to have enough milk for their baby, they kill the little yellow competitor.

Ivanov is married. His wife recently had a daughter.

The Serapion Brothers include the theoretician Ilya Gruzdyov, a student of Boris Eikhenbaum and Yury Tynyanov.

Toward the end of that winter, another poet arrived—Nikolai Tikhonov—of the Red Army cavalrymen.

He's twenty-five and his hair looks ash-gray, but he's actually a towhead. His eyes are frank, either gray or light blue. He writes good poems. He lives downstairs in the monkey house with Vsevolod Rozhdestvensky. Tikhonov used to tell good stories about horses—how, for example, the German horses taken captive indulged in sabotage and treachery.

Then there's Konstantin Fedin. He arrived fresh from a German prison camp. He missed the revolution because he was in prison. A good fellow, only just a mite traditional.

There, now I've let the Serapions into my book. I lived in the same house with them. I trust that the administration won't hold it against them that I drank tea with them. The Serapions grew with difficulty. If it hadn't been for Gorky, they would have perished. Aleksei Maksimovich immediately took them very seriously. They came to have more faith in themselves. Gorky almost always understands other people's manuscripts. He's successful with new writers.

Russia hasn't been entirely stomped and clobbered. People still grow in it like oats among the clods.

The great Russian literature, the great Russian science will live.

Meanwhile, the Serapions meet every Friday to eat bread, smoke cigarettes and play blind man's buff.[71] My god, how strong people are! And no one can tell what a man's burden is from his footprints—only whether it's heavy or light.

There weren't enough of the proletariat to go around; otherwise we'd have some metalworkers left.

In Russia, I saw a love for the machine, too—for the authentic material culture of today.

During the winter of 1922, I was walking down the street

where the transportation center was. It doesn't exist anymore; it's apparently been completely liquidated.

A young man came up to me in a driver's outfit: "Hello," he said, "Mister Instructor."

He gave his name—one of my students from the drivers' school.

"Mister Instructor," said the driver, walking beside me, "you're not in the party, are you? When you speak of the party in Russia, don't you usually mean a Bolshevik?"

"No," I said, "I'm in the Institute of Art History."

"Mister Instructor," said the driver, walking beside me—he knew me only from the school—"the machines are falling apart, the lathes are rusting, the castings already made are being discarded. I'm in the party and I can't bear that. Mister Instructor, why aren't you working with us?"

I didn't know how to answer him.

Men who stick to their lathes are always right. These men will grow tall in the field. They say that in Saratov Province, grain has come up from last year's sowing. That is how a new Russian civilization will grow.

We may expire, but Russia will continue.

No need to shout or rush things.

In 1913 the following incident took place in the Ciniselli Circus. One of the acrobats had invented an act in which he jumped from the trapeze with a noose around his neck. He had a strong neck. The knot on the noose was placed right at the top of his head; the noose itself evidently passed under his chin. Afterward, he would pull his head out of the noose, climb back up to his trapeze and wave at the crowd. The act was called "The Man with the Iron Neck." Once he made a mistake. The noose went around his throat; the man dangled there, hanged. A panic began. Ladders were brought. They didn't reach high enough. Someone climbed up to him, but forgot to take a knife. An acrobat got to him, but couldn't get him out of the noose. The crowd was howling, but the "Man with the Iron Neck" hung there and hung there.

Meanwhile, in an upper loge of the gallery, a man stood up—probably a merchant—a big man and, in all likelihood, a good man. He held up his arms and shouted to the hanging man:

"Climb down! My wife . . . is crying!"

That's a fact.

Spring came early to Petersburg in 1922. The last few years, the spring was always early, but with cold spells. That's because we took every thaw for spring.

It had been cold and we had little strength left. When a warm wind began to blow, it was like the land birds Columbus saw.

Spring, spring shouted the sailors from their ships.

Eikhenbaum said, "The main distinction between revolutionary life and ordinary life is that now everything is felt." Life became art. Spring is life. I think no hungry cow in her shed was more overjoyed to see spring than we were.

Spring, or anyway the thaw—actually it was only March—was coming.

David Vygodsky, who lived in apartment No. 56 at the House of Arts, had already opened his window to get warm.

The ink in the inkwell of his writing desk had actually thawed.

It was on just such a warm night that I walked away with my sledge from the lighted windows of my apartment.

I spent the night with friends, telling them nothing. The next morning I went to the State Publishing House to get a permit to publish my booklet *Epilogue*.

No one there knew anything yet, but a friend of mine happened to be there and he said, "The Cheka's waiting for you at home."

I lived in St. Pete another two weeks. I just changed my coat. I wasn't terribly afraid of being arrested. Why should anyone want to arrest me? My arrest was an accident. It was thought up by a man with no trade—Semyonov.

And because of him, I had to leave my wife and friends.

The thaw kept me from going across the ice.

Then it froze again. It was foggy on the ice. I came to a fishing shanty. Then I was conducted to a quarantine center.

I don't want to write about all that.

I remember one old woman—at least sixty or seventy—who had come to the quarantine center legally.

She was ecstatic about everything. She caught sight of some bread. "Ah, bread!" She idolized the butter and the stove.

But I spent all my time at the quarantine center sleeping.

At night I often cried out. It seemed to me that a bomb was exploding in my hand.

Then I went by boat to Stettin. The gulls were flying after us.

In my opinion, they were following us.

They have wings that bend like tin.

They have the voice of a motorcycle.

It's time to finish this book. That's a pity, even though it is heart-rending to finish it with that old woman warming herself at an alien fire. The ending of a two-part book should combine the motifs of both parts. That's why I'm going to write here about Doctor Shedd. Doctor Shedd was the American consul in Urmia.

Doctor Shedd drove around Urmia in a surrey. All four wheels of the surrey were just alike. A canopy with scalloped edges had been fastened over the surrey on four poles. The surrey was as simple and square as a matchbox.

The surrey was completely functional. Somewhere in America twenty years ago, such surreys were probably not unusual.

Doctor Shedd drove this surrey himself. He sat on the right side of the straight-backed front seat.

Behind, with her back to him, sat his gray-haired wife or his red-haired daughter.

His wife and daughter were not unusual.

Doctor Shedd had gray hair and wore a black frock coat.

Not an unusual one.

There was no machine gun or flag on Doctor Shedd's surrey.

Doctor Shedd lived near Urmia. The clay wall of the American mission extended for several miles.

No one was massacred behind that wall. That was America. The square surrey drove all over northern Persia and Kurdistan.

I saw Doctor Shedd for the first time at a meeting when we were demanding wheat from the Persians. That was December 1917.

The mullahs, wearing green turbans and stroking their red beards, studied their beautiful hands with painted fingernails and kindly said that they wouldn't give us any wheat.

General Karpov, the fat quartermaster for our army, studied his soft belly, with its numerous folds under the soft folds of his well-worn tunic, and kindly said that we would take their wheat. His nails weren't painted, but bitten.

The Russian consul, Nikitin (he was later killed during the withdrawal), fretted nervously.

Then Doctor Shedd suddenly appeared among us in his black frock coat.

He stood among us like a black pillar. His hair was washed and fluffy.

I was sitting in the corner. My field jacket was worn out and I had no coat—just a poncho with frayed edges.

I was ashamed and tried to hide the patches.

I had discarded my coat during the pogrom.

In that situation, I was like a jury mast. If a storm at sea fells the real mast, the sailors tie the jury mast to the remains of the old one.

I was a commissar in the army.

And my whole life consists of pieces linked only by my habits.

Doctor Shedd said, "Gentlemen! Yesterday in the bazaar, I found a dead six-year-old boy lying by the wall."

If Robinson Crusoe, wearing his shaggy pelts, had been transplanted from his uninhabited island to a London street, he would have seemed out of place there.

Doctor Shedd was just as out of place—counting corpses in the East, where corpses are not counted.

Once I met a caravan in the Kuchin Pass.

The camels were walking with their swaying gait.

Their backs, under those high packsaddles, looked like the backs of Russian wolfhounds.

Bells rang under the snouts of the camels. The horses were jogging along at a trot, their legs flashing in counterpoint to the long, easy stride of the camels.

I asked, "What are you hauling?"

They told me, "Silver for Doctor Shedd."

There were hardly any guards.

Silver continually arrived for Doctor Shedd and no one laid a hand on it because everything was changing; the people seeking refuge behind the clay wall of the American mission were changing, too, but Doctor Shedd fed them all.

Oh, bitter is alien bread and steep are alien stairs![72] Bitter were the lines at the House of Scholars!

And to fans of syncretic epithets, I'll say, "Bitter were the marble stairs at the House of Scholars."

And bitter were the nine pounds of Czech sugar. And bitter was the smoke from the cracked chimney of my stove. The smoke of disillusionment.

But steepest and most bitter of all are the wooden stairs of Berlin. Here I write on a card table.

I remember the way food allotments were distributed at the Degalin Gate in Urmia.

An immense mob of Kurds, almost naked in their rags, with striped rugs thrown over their shoulders (the familiar mode of dress in the East)—this mob was straining to get at that bread.

To one side of the distributor stood a man—or maybe two—with a thick whip. He was adroitly restraining the ardor of that mob with unhurried, uninterrupted, heavy blows of his whip.

When the Russians pulled out of Persia, they left the Armenians and the Aissors to the whims of fate. . . .

Actually, there's nothing whimsical about fate. If you don't feed a man, he has just one fate—to die.

The Russians pulled out of Persia.

The Aissors defended themselves with the heroism of a wolf that bites the headlights of an automobile.

When the Turks surrounded them, they broke through the encirclement and fled—the entire nation—to the English, to Baghdad.

They marched through the mountains and their horses fell; their packs fell and they had to abandon their children.

As everyone knows, abandoned children are no rarity in the East.

How does everyone know?

I don't know who collects news in the East.

But there's nothing whimsical about fate—abandoned children die.

It was then that Doctor Shedd got in his four-wheeled surrey and went after the fleeing Aissors.

Although what could one man do?

The Aissors were marching through the mountains.

There are no roads in these mountains and the ground is completely covered with rocks, as if rock rain has just fallen.

After sixty miles on such rocks, a horse wears out his shoes.

In the winter of 1918, a year marked by famine, people died in the midst of wallpaper covered with ice crystals and they were taken away and buried only with great difficulty.

We waited till spring to weep for our dead.

Spring did come, as always—with its lilacs and white nights.

We waited till spring to weep for our dead because in the winter it was too cold. The Aissors began weeping for their children only in Nineveh, only when the ground beneath their feet became soft and smooth. Bitter was the weeping that spring in Petersburg. Bitter will be the weeping when Russia thaws.

In Nineveh a quarrel broke out between the mountain Aissors and the Urmian Aissors.

There had been no animosity until then.

The same thing happened in 1918, a year marked by famine, in the midst of wallpaper glued to the walls by ice. People slept together because it was warmer that way. It was so cold that they didn't even hate each other.

Until spring.

The Urmian Aissors wanted to go back to take revenge for their devastated villages and to kill Sinko the assassin.

They had known, as they abandoned their children, that Sinko was following close behind. The mountain Aissors, however, had already spent their rage. They were too exhausted to cross the mountains for the third time.

At Nineveh they were almost home.

The Turks were no longer following.

The Aissors had only the Kurds to fight.

They passed through the Persians like a knife through butter.

The Urmian Aissors marched fast.

Sinko fled to Tabriz.

The Aissors besieged Tabriz.

Tabriz is a big city. There are many, many doors in the clay walls of its streets. Persian cities are judged not by the number of inhabitants, but by the number of doors. The doors are low, with wooden bolts, and what is behind them no one can tell. The Aissors wanted to find out, though they wouldn't have broken down the doors just out of curiosity.

It was then that Doctor Shedd got in the right side of the front seat of his surrey, his black surrey with the yellow wheels. Doctor Shedd, in his black frock coat, with his gray hair, drove through the Aissor troops to the city of Tabriz.

Doctor Shedd met these troops, with their worn-out legs and hearts—for the rocks in these mountains wear out not just iron horseshoes—and he had 3,500 children that he had picked up when he followed behind the fleeing Aissor people.

Doctor Shedd gave these children back to their fathers and he took Sinko by the hand, sat him down on the front seat of the square surrey and drove him to the English in Baghdad to be tried. No one blocked Doctor Shedd's way.

No, I shouldn't have written that. I warmed my heart. It . . . aches.

I pity Russia. Who will teach the Russians to load camels with their striped packs and to bind with woolen ropes the long snake-like caravans that will cross the deserted fields of the Volga basin?

Doctor Shedd, I am a man of the East because the East begins at Pskov, but before that at Verzhbolovo; the East begins, as before, at the Russian border and goes as far as the three oceans.

Doctor Shedd! Bitter are the stairs of exile. Doctor Shedd! Like a spotted rat, I made the journey from Ushnuiyeh to Petersburg with fleeing soldiers; I made the journey from Zhmerinka to Petersburg in a naked throng of prisoners of war coming from Germany.

Our train carried coffins and on the coffins was scrawled in tar: RETURN COFFINS.

Now I live among emigrants and am myself becoming a shadow among shadows.

Bitter is the wienerschnitzel in Berlin.

I lived in Petersburg from 1918 to 1922.

In your name, Doctor Shedd, and in the name of Doctor Gorbenko, who did not permit the killing of the wounded Greeks in Kherson, and in the name of the nameless driver who asked me to save his lathes, I finish this book.

TRANSLITERATION SYSTEM

NOTES

GLOSSARIES

INDEX

Transliteration System

For Russian words and for bibliographical material, this work follows the Library of Congress system of transliteration without diacritical marks. For proper names used in the text, with the exception of such names as Tolstoy, Ehrenburg, and Moscow, already familiar in another spelling, the following system has been used.

а	a	п	p
б	b	р	r
в	v	с	s
г	g	т	t
д	d	у	u
е	e	ф	f
ё	yo (o *after* sh, zh, *and* ch)	х	kh
ж	zh	ц	ts
з	z	ч	ch
и	i	ш	sh (s *before* t)
й	i	щ	shch
ый	y	ъ	(*omitted*)
ий	y	ы	y
к	k	ь	(*omitted except* i *before* e)
л	l	э	e
м	m	ю	yu (u *in the word Lusya*)
н	n	я	ya (a *after* i)
о	o		

Notes

1. A nickname for the two-kopek piece.

2. Because of the tsarina's German background, many people falsely attributed the disastrous policies of the tsar to pro-German sympathies on her part. In a famous speech to the Duma in November 1916, Pavel Milyukov charged that the incompetence of the regime bordered on treason.

3. Hero of a popular song describing how he debauched his master's wife. In addition to his baneful effect on the tsarina, Rasputin scandalized the court with his notorious debaucheries.

4. March 3 by the Gregorian calendar, which Russia adopted in February 1918. All the dates in this book are given according to the Julian calendar, which after 1900 was thirteen days behind the Gregorian calendar used in the West. Consequently, the February revolution (February 27) took place on March 12 by the Western calendar; the October revolution (October 25) took place on November 7.

5. When the local garrison proved too unreliable to control Moscow during the revolution of 1905, the Semyonovsky Regiment was dispatched from Petersburg to crush the uprising.

6. *Vechernee Vremia*, a right-wing newspaper founded by the well-known publisher A. S. Suvorin.

7. Probably Osip Brik.

8. *Letopis'*—a monthly journal sponsored by Maksim Gorky from December 1915 to December 1917.

9. According to rumors widely circulated in Petrograd, the minister of the interior, A. D. Protopopov, had ordered the police to set up machine-gun posts on the rooftops in order to shoot demonstrators. These rumors later proved to be unfounded, but they increased the bitterness of the populace toward the police.

10. After the collapse of the monarchy and the dissolution of the Duma, some conservative members of the Duma met and formed the "Temporary Executive Committee of the Duma" to maintain order and to urge the tsar to abdicate in favor of his son. At the same time, some of the Socialist members of the Duma and some Petrograd labor leaders met and formed the "Temporary Executive Committee of the Petrograd

Soviet of Workers' Deputies." The Soviet Committee immediately called upon the factories to elect deputies to a new soviet (one for every thousand workers) modeled on the St. Petersburg Soviet of 1905. That same evening, some two hundred deputies convened and declared the Soviet Committee a permanent body. The Petrograd Soviet immediately began to compete with the Duma Committee for popular support. While the Duma Committee was forming the Provisional Government, the Soviet Committee attempted to win the loyalty of the Petrograd garrison. Each company loyal to the revolution was invited to elect a deputy to form a "Soldiers' Section" of the Soviet. These soldiers met on March 1 to make known their demands, which were published the next day in the Soviet's new newspaper *Izvestia* as "Order No. 1." This "Order," among other things, created havoc in the army by providing for the election of committees to issue arms and to supervise the officers in each unit.

11. Abortive attempt of the Bolsheviks to seize power.

12. This was a provision of the "Declaration of Soldiers' Rights," passed May 9 (May 22). The commissars were expected to supervise the soldiers' committees established by Order No. 1.

13. Probably a reference to the German revolution of November 1918, which occurred under the pressure of decisive victories by the Allies. Kaiser Wilhelm II abdicated and a provisional government headed by Friederich Ebert was instituted. This new government had ruthlessly suppressed the activities of the newly created German Communist party by the summer of 1919, when Shklovsky wrote *Revolution and the Front*.

14. In general, the Kadets (Constitutional Democrats) favored continuation of the war. Zimmerwald is the town in Switzerland where an international Socialist conference voted in September 1915 to oppose continuation of the war.

15. A Finnic tribe centered mainly in the Volga region.

16. *Novaia zhizn'*—a daily newspaper sponsored by Maksim Gorky from April 1917 through July 1918. It served as a forum for the so-called "Internationalists."

17. Vserossiiskii Soiuz Revoliutsionnoi Sotsialisticheskoi Demokratii (All-Russian Union of the Revolutionary Socialist Democracy).

18. In a last desperate effort to strengthen his government against the growing power of the Bolsheviks, Kerensky called this conference on September 14 (September 27). He hoped to form a new cabinet based on a coalition between the moderate Socialists and the progressive parties, but the Socialists rejected any cooperation with the Kadets. When the conference reached an impasse, Kerensky simply proceeded to form a coalition cabinet that included Kadets—a step that further antagonized the Petrograd Soviet.

19. Abbreviated name of the All-Russian Regional Union for the

Assistance of Sick and Wounded Soldiers, voluntary organizations formed in July 1914 by individual provinces and towns to handle welfare, medical, and refugee problems created by the war. These organizations eventually played an important role in supplying the armed forces.

20. Turkey was claiming Persian territory up to Lake Urmia. In December 1914 the Turks crossed the mountains and drove the Russian troops out of Urmia. In June 1915 the Russians succeeded in retaking Urmia.

21. In 1907, Russia and Great Britain, fearful of Turkish expansion into Persia, signed a secret treaty which recognized northern and central Persia as Russian zones of influence, southern Persia as the British zone.

22. A revolution in 1906 had forced the shah, Mohammed Ali, to grant a constitution. To buttress his weakened position, he relied on the so-called Persian Cossacks, trained and led by Russian officers.

23. "Watch out!"

24. Nickname for the twenty- and forty-ruble notes issued by Kerensky's government.

25. "Khokhol" is a derogatory nickname for Ukrainians.

26. H. G. Wells, *The First Men in the Moon.*

27. A Russian military march.

28. Turkish, meaning "very, very good."

29. The English captured Baghdad from the Turks in March 1917.

30. By this treaty with the Turks, signed in December 1917, the Russians agreed to evacuate Persia. In order to concentrate his limited forces on the civil war, Lenin was forced in March 1918 to sign the Treaty of Brest-Litovsk, which deprived the Russians of 25 per cent of their territory.

31. Echo of a famous passage from Vasily Rozanov's book *The Apocalypse of Our Times* (1917–1919).

32. Shklovsky gives the next four towns in reverse order. After leaving Baku, he would have passed through Derbent, Petrovsk, Chirvonnaya, then Khasavyurt.

33. These receipts, obviously forged, were an attempt to stamp the Bolshevik leaders as German agents—an accusation frequently made by Lenin's enemies and vigorously denied by him. However, the German archives captured by the Allies during World War II prove that Lenin did receive money from German agents prior to 1917.

34. This lyrical leitmotif echoes a passage from one of Spinoza's letters. See Letter LXII (LVIII) in *The Chief Works of Benedict Spinoza* (New York, 1951), 2: 390.

35. Probably the Commission of Workers' and Peasants' Inspectors and the Commissariat of Education for the Collection and Evaluation of Antiques and Art Objects.

36. Primary city of the maritime province of Siberia. In June 1918, Socialist Revolutionaries expelled the soviet and proclaimed eastern Siberia an autonomous republic. In August, small contingents of Japanese, British, French, and American troops landed to assist in the overthrow of the Bolshevik regime. This White government remained in power until October 1922, when the Japanese finally renounced their claims to this territory.

37. During World War I, a brigade of Czechs, composed of deserters and escaped prisoners from the Austro-Hungarian Army, served with the Russian forces. After the Treaty of Brest-Litovsk, the Allies requested that this brigade (approximately forty thousand men) be allowed to leave Russia via Vladivostok in order to continue fighting on the western front. The Russians agreed, but in May 1918, Trotsky ordered Soviet officials to disarm these troops. The Czechs refused to surrender their arms and rose against the Bolshevik regime. Throughout the summer of 1918, they moved west along the Siberian railroad, provoking in their wake a general anti-Bolshevik uprising in eastern Russia.

38. Early in July 1918, under the leadership of Boris Savinkov, the Left-wing Socialist Revolutionaries instigated anti-Bolshevik uprisings in several cities. The insurgents gained complete control of Yaroslavl on July 6 and held the city until July 23, at which time the uprising was cruelly suppressed by the Bolsheviks.

39. Shklovsky eventually finished this article and published it in the anthology *Sborniki po teorii poeticheskogo iazyka*, [Studies on the Theory of Poetic Language], vol. 3: *Poetika* (Petrograd, 1919). It was republished in his *Theory of Prose* (1925).

40. Several Socialist Revolutionaries were indicted at this time in an investigation of the party's role in all the assassinations and attempted assassinations that took place in the summer of 1918. These leaders mostly denied that their acts had the official sanction of the party, but Semyonov turned state's evidence and attempted to incriminate the party leadership. He also gave false evidence against Shklovsky, who had to flee from Russia in March 1922 to escape arrest on these charges.

41. As the Red Army began recovering territory in the east during the winter of 1919–1920, Kolchak retreated with his White army to Irkutsk. There an uprising took place, apparently staged by the Bolsheviks, and Kolchak was executed in February 1920 by the new rulers of the city.

42. Shklovsky never published a book by this title. Most of this material was eventually included in his *Theory of Prose* (1925).

43. The Socialist Revolutionary Dora Kaplan seriously wounded Lenin on August 30, 1918—the same day that Uritsky was assassinated—but there was apparently no connection between the two acts.

44. A reference to "How the Whale Got His Throat," from the *Just So Stories* by Rudyard Kipling. In that story, a resourceful sailor swallowed by a whale uses his suspenders to effect his escape. Shklovsky probably means that he was able to survive his adversities by never forgetting his writing desk.

45. A reference to the Russian proverb: to sell oneself for a mess of pottage. The proverb comes from Genesis 25:29–34, where Esau sells his birthright to Jacob for a pottage of lentils.

46. An echo of Ecclesiastes 1:6.

47. Probably a reference to Turgenev's story "A Quiet Spot," whose Ukrainian heroine is depicted in a rather patronizing manner.

48. In the wake of the Czech advance, two rival White governments came into being in the east. The one in Samara was composed of SR's who had participated in the Constituent Assembly and who hoped to see it re-established; the one in Omsk was more inclined toward restoration of some kind of monarchy. In September 1918 these two governments called a conference in Ufa to settle their differences and to consolidate their opposition to the Bolsheviks. The delegates compromised on a directory of five men, who were to sit in Omsk. In November, Kolchak overthrew the Directory and became dictator, to the despair of the SR's. In December he arrested the SR's who had headed the Samara government, which had moved to Ufa after the capture of Samara by the Red Army in October. The Red Army captured Ufa on December 31, 1918, and completed the rout of those SR's hoping to restore the Constituent Assembly.

49. Volsky had been a leader in the Samara government. After Kolchak's forcible assumption of leadership, he and his faction, embittered, made their peace with the Bolsheviks, in return for which the SR party was temporarily legalized in Soviet territory.

50. The article in question is Boris Eikhenbaum's famous study "How Gogol's 'Overcoat' Is Made."

51. The Bolshevik government had granted Finland its independence in December 1917. Civil war broke out early in 1918, and with the help of the Germans, the Finns had driven out the remaining Bolshevik units by May 1918. There were signs, in the fall of 1919, that Finnish troops might support Yudenich in his attack on Petrograd.

52. Early in 1920 the Poles began a general offensive against Russia, which culminated in the capture of Kiev in May. The Red Army successfully resisted and pursued the Poles as far as Warsaw before being routed. The war with Poland ended in March 1921.

53. Although most residents of Petrograd had electricity only a few hours each night, the apartments of Cheka members and Party officials were connected to a special cable that provided a constant supply.

54. In May 1919, General Yudenich advanced on Petrograd. On June 12 he occupied Krasnaya Gorka, whose Red garrison mutinied

and joined the Whites. Heavy firing from Kronstadt, however, forced the Whites to retreat four days later, when help expected from the British fleet was not forthcoming.

55. These articles appeared in *The Life of Art* (1920), as separate booklets (1921) and in Shklovsky's *Theory of Prose* (1925).

56. During the siege by the forces of General Yudenich, the Semyonovsky Regiment deserted to the Whites.

57. Painting by Gericault.

58. Critics whose approach to literature was extrinsic.

59. Gorky's famous reminiscences of Tolstoy, first published in 1919.

60. Probably the portrait done by Yury Annenkov in 1919, reproduced as the frontispiece to this book. See Yury Annenkov, *Dnevnik moikh vstrech* (New York, 1966), 1: 35.

61. Ukrainian city where a notorious massacre took place in 1768, when a band of Cossacks under the leadership of Ivan Gonta revolted against their Polish overlords, seized control of the city, and slaughtered thousands of Poles and Jews.

62. Shklovsky means those instances where an author opposes ideas or characters, such as Don Quixote and Sancho Panza or Anna Karenina-Vronsky and Kitty-Levin, in order to make the reader think carefully about their similarities and their differences.

63. Critics whose approach to literature was extrinsic.

64. Scholars have never agreed on a precise definition of this term, but it is basically a prose narrative designed to exploit the peculiar speech and point of view of an unusual character.

65. Short songs, usually two or four lines in length, often humorous and epigrammatic, often about love.

66. This work appeared first in *The Life of Art* in 1921, then as a separate booklet during the same year. It was included in Shklovsky's book *Theory of Prose* (1925).

67. Shklovsky refers to *Stories of Nazar Ilich, Mister Bluebelly* (1922), the book which catapulted Zoshchenko to fame.

68. Slonimsky never wrote a story by this title. The reference is probably to "Srednii Prospekt." See Hongor Oulanoff, *The Serapion Brothers* (The Hague, Paris, 1966), p. 10.

69. Zoshchenko wrote a parody of Ivanov's style by this title. See Oulanoff, p. 12.

70. The reference is to Bret Harte's story "The Luck of Roaring Camp."

71. According to the overwhelming testimony, the Serapions met on Saturdays.

72. An echo of Dante's *Divine Comedy*, "Paradiso," 17: 58–60.

Glossary of Persons

Persons rather extensively discussed in the text are, for the most part, not included in this appendix. Those included are described in terms of the special significance which they have for the period covered by the book or for Shklovsky himself.

AKHMATOVA, ANNA ANDREEVNA (1889–1966). Acmeist poet who published several volumes of superb lyric verse between 1912 and 1923, and who was a dominant figure in the intellectual life of Petrograd during those years.

ANDREEVA, MARIA FYODOROVNA (1872–1953). Gorky's common-law wife, a well-known actress.

ANNENKOV, YURY PAVLOVICH (born 1889). Artist, director, and writer.

BENOIS, ALEXANDRE (1870–1960). Painter, theatrical designer, producer, art critic, and art historian. He was the intellectual force behind Sergei Diaghilev's journal *Mir Iskusstva* [The World of Art] (1898–1904), which was oriented toward the symbolist movement. Benois was known as an implacable foe of the futurist movement.

BONDI, SERGEI MIKHAILOVICH (born 1891). Expert on verse theory, textology, and Pushkin.

BRIK, OSIP MAKSIMOVICH (1888–1945). Leading exponent of futurism, formalism, and LEF.

CHERNOV, VIKTOR MIKHAILOVICH (1873–1952). Chief theoretician of the SR party, minister of agriculture in the Provisional Government, and chairman of the Constituent Assembly.

CHKHEIDZE, NIKOLAI SEMYONOVICH (1864–1926). Leading Menshevik, first president of the Petrograd Soviet.

CHUKOVSKY, KORNEI IVANOVICH (1882–1969). Prominent critic,

287

translator, and children's author, known especially for his monograph on Nekrasov and his translations of Walt Whitman.

CUNCTATOR, QUINTUS FABIUS MAXIMUS (d. 203 B.C.). Roman general who foiled Hannibal during the Second Punic War by avoiding decisive contests, while constantly harassing him with marches, countermarches, and the like. His name is used as a synonym for being cautious and dilatory.

DENIKIN, ANTON IVANOVICH (1872–1947). Tsarist general, chief of staff, and then commander in chief of the south and southwest fronts under the Provisional Government. He was arrested for his support of the Kornilov insurrection, then escaped to the Don region after the October revolution and helped organize a volunteer army as aide to General Kornilov. He took command of this army after Kornilov's death in April 1918. In March 1920 he retreated to the Crimea, where he placed his troops under the command of General Wrangel and fled to Constantinople on a British battleship.

"DIONEO" (Isaak Vladimirovich Shklovsky, 1865–1935). Shklovsky's uncle, who went to London in 1896 as English news correspondent for the Moscow daily *Russkie vedomosti* [Russian Gazette] and the monthly review *Russkoe bogatstvo* [Russian Wealth]. He was the author of several books.

EHRENBURG, ILYA GRIGOREVICH (1891–1967). Prominent novelist, poet, critic, and translator.

EIKHENBAUM, BORIS MIKHAILOVICH (1886–1959). Leading Russian formalist, who made major contributions in the areas of *skaz* "How Gogol's 'Overcoat' Is Made," 1919), verse theory (*Verse Melodics*, 1922), and literary history. He concentrated especially on the work of Tolstoy (*The Young Tolstoy*, 1922, and a long, unfinished monograph, 1928–1960).

ELISEEV, GRIGORY GRIGOREVICH. Former occupant of the rooms used by the Serapion Brothers in the House of Arts. He was a wealthy merchant who fled the country after the October revolution.

FILONENKO, MAKSIMILIAN. Ambitious captain whom Kerensky appointed as commissar to the Russian army. When General Kornilov was made commander in chief of the Russian armies in July 1917, Filonenko was appointed chief commissar attached to general headquarters, where he was to serve as liaison between Kornilov and Kerensky.

GONTA, IVAN (?–1768). Leader of a Cossack uprising against the Poles in 1768. When the Cossacks under his command were dispatched to suppress a serf rebellion in 1768, he and his men joined forces with the rebels and seized the town of Uman, which they held until defeated by Russian troops. Gonta was drawn and quartered. He became a hero in Ukrainian folklore.

GRIGORIEV, —— (?–1919). A Ukrainian peasant leader who initially served Petlyura, then turned against him and served the Bolsheviks. His followers occupied Kherson in March 1919. When the Bolsheviks ordered him to march on Rumania in May, he refused and led a revolt against them. His raids seriously hampered their efforts to defeat General Denikin. He was shot by one of Makhno's men in 1919; most of his followers then joined Makhno.

GUMILYOV, NIKOLAI STEPANOVICH (1886–1921). Leader of the acmeist movement in poetry; first husband of Anna Akhmatova. He was shot in August 1921, despite Gorky's efforts to save him, for alleged involvement in a plot to overthrow the Bolshevik regime.

IONOV, ILYA. Director of the State Publishing House in Petrograd.

JAKOBSON, ROMAN OSIPOVICH (1896–1982). Charter member of the Moscow Linguistic Circle and prominent formalist critic.

KALEDIN, ALEKSEI MAKSIMOVICH (1861–1918). Cossack general elected ataman of the Don Cossack army in July 1917. Kaledin supported the Kornilov insurrection in August. After the October revolution, he made the Don territory a refuge for anti-Bolshevik elements and in January 1918 proclaimed the territory's independence. The German invasion of the Ukraine, however, stimulated among the Cossacks a certain resurgence of loyalty toward the Bolshevik regime. Feeling that he no longer had the complete support of his men, Kaledin committed suicide in February.

KERENSKY, ALEKSANDR FYODOROVICH (1881–1970). Socialist Revolutionary who became minister of justice after the February revolution, then minister of war and navy in the new cabinet formed after Milyukov's resignation in May. He became prime minister in July and remained head of the Provisional Government until the October revolution, at which time he fled abroad.

KHLEBNIKOV, VIKTOR (Velimir) VLADIMIROVICH (1885–1922). Prominent futurist poet, known for his efforts to create a new verse language.

KOLCHAK, ALEKSANDR VASILEVICH (1873–1920). Admiral who, after the October revolution, established an anti-Bolshevik government in Omsk, Siberia, and asserted his authority over rival White governments elsewhere in Siberia, notably in Samara and Ufa. After an unsuccessful offensive into eastern Russia in the fall of 1919, he fled to Irkutsk, where he was captured by the Bolsheviks and shot in February 1920.

KONI, ANATOLY FYODOROVICH (1844–1927). Outstanding lawyer

and writer who became a professor at the University of Petrograd after the October revolution.

KORDI, VASILISA GEORGIEVNA. Shklovsky's first wife—the Lusya to whom *A Sentimental Journey* is dedicated. He is now married to Serafima Gustavovna Suok.

KORNILOV, LAVR GEORGIEVICH (1870–1918). Commander of the Petrograd garrison, then commander of the Eighth Army on the southwestern front, then commander in chief of the southwestern front, and finally supreme commander in July 1917. Dissatisfied with Kerensky's vacillation, General Kornilov headed an abortive coup against the Provisional Government in August. He was arrested but, after the October revolution, fled to the Don region, where he organized and commanded a White army. He was killed in battle in April 1918, at which time Denikin assumed command of the army.

KRASNOV, PYOTR NIKOLAEVICH (1869–1947). Cossack general who supported the Kornilov insurrection. He was elected ataman of the Don Cossacks in May 1918, after Kaledin, the former ataman, committed suicide in February. He and his Cossacks cooperated with General Denikin and his Volunteer Army to drive the Bolsheviks from the Don and Kuban regions by the summer of 1918.

KRYLENKO, NIKOLAI VASILEVICH (1885–1938). Commissar of military and naval affairs after the October revolution, then commander in chief of the armies in November 1917. In 1918 he organized the revolutionary tribunals and in 1922 was appointed deputy commissar of justice of the RSFSR and chief public prosecutor of the supreme court.

LIEBER, MIKHAIL ISAAKOVICH (1880–1937). Member of the right-wing Mensheviks and the Bund, as well as an important leader on the Executive Committee of the Soviets.

LINDE, FYODOR (?–1917). Mathematician and philosopher who instigated the demonstration of the Finland Regiment in May 1917 to demand the resignation of Milyukov.

LOZINSKY, MIKHAIL LEONIDOVICH (1886–1955). Scholar and poet especially known for his translations of Dante.

LUNACHARSKY, ANATOLY VASILEVICH (1875–1933). Old-time Bolshevik, commissar of education after the October revolution.

MAKHNO, NESTOR IVANOVICH (1889–1934). Anarchist peasant leader who fought against the Germans, Petlyura, the Reds, and the Whites. During the fall of 1919, he gained control of large sections of the Ukraine and harassed Denikin's White Army. Throughout 1920, his band made raids on the Bolshevik forces and on the White

Army, now commanded by General Wrangel. After the defeat of Wrangel's army, the Red Army liquidated Makhno's followers, but he escaped abroad.

MEREZHKOVSKY, DMITRY SERGEEVICH (1865–1941). Symbolist writer who emigrated to France after the October revolution.

MILYUKOV, PAVEL NIKOLAEVICH (1859–1943). Leader of the Kadet party and first foreign minister in the Provisional Government. A note sent to the Allies in his name assured them of Russia's intention to remain in the war. The demonstrations which this note provoked among the soldiers and workers led to his resignation in May.

MURAVYOV, MIKHAIL ARTEMEVICH (1880–1918). Lieutenant colonel who sided initially with the Bolsheviks, then joined the uprising of the Left-wing Socialist Revolutionaries in Moscow in July 1918.

NADSON, SEMYON YAKOVLEVICH (1862–1887). Minor Russian poet immensely popular during the late nineteenth century, but later regarded as the epitome of bad taste.

OTTO. An Estonian who served as interrogator for the Cheka.

PAVLENKOV, FLORENTY FYODOROVICH (1839–1900). Well-known publisher who produced for popular consumption a series of biographies of the major Russian authors. The biography of Tolstoy was written by E. Solovyov.

PETLYURA, SIMON VASILEVICH (1877–1926). Leader of the Ukrainian nationalist movement during the civil war. He and his army took control of the Ukraine after the withdrawal of the German troops and their puppet, Hetman Skoropadsky, in November 1918. When ousted by the Bolsheviks in February 1919, he signed an agreement with Poland and took part in the Polish campaign against the Bolsheviks in 1920. After the Polish-Russian Treaty of Riga, which left the Ukraine under Russian domination, he emigrated to France.

PRUTKOV, KOZMA. Pen name under which A. K. Tolstoy and the Zhemchuzhnikov brothers wrote humorous poetry during the second half of the nineteenth century.

RASKOLNIKOV, FYODOR FYODOROVICH (1892–1939). Husband of Larisa Reisner and commander of the Soviet Volga Flotilla during the civil war.

RASPUTIN, GRIGORY EFIMOVICH (1872–1916). Licentious Siberian monk who gained great influence over the tsar and tsarina through his ability to control the hemophilia from which the heir apparent Alexis suffered. His unscrupulous use of his power created scandalous situations and provoked members of the court to assassinate him in December 1916.

REID, MAYNE (1818–1883). Irish novelist.

REISNER, LARISA MIKHAILOVNA (1895–1926). Bolshevik commissar in the campaign against the Czechoslovak Legion. She was widely known for her beauty, courage, and journalist talent.

RODZYANKO, MIKHAIL VLADIMIROVICH (1859–1924). President of the Third and Fourth Dumas (1911–1917) and a loyal monarchist. After the February revolution, he headed the provisional executive committee of the Duma, which approved the Provisional Government. After the October revolution, he fled south and joined the Volunteer Army; after its defeat, he emigrated to Yugoslavia.

ROMANOV, NIKOLAI NIKOLAEVICH (1850–1929). Uncle of the tsar, he became commander in chief of the Russian army after the outbreak of World War I. In August 1915 he was relieved of his command to become viceroy of the Caucasus and commander in chief of the Caucasian front.

ROZANOV, VASILY VASILEVICH (1856–1919). Russian philosopher, critic, and prose stylist of surpassing originality. His apotheosis of sex led him to criticize Christianity for its ascetic tendencies even though he remained deeply attached to it. His marriage to Dostoevsky's mistress, Polina Suslova, contributed insights to his critical studies on Dostoevsky, which are still considered fundamental. His general hatred of dogma included the printed page, whose rigidity he combatted by inventing a new genre, composed of short, paradoxical statements arranged in disjointed fashion and imbued with a strong oral intonation (especially *Solitaria almost in Manuscript Form*, 1912, and *Fallen Leaves*, 1913 and 1915). He achieved financial security in 1899, when he began writing for Suvorin's conservative newspaper *The New Time*, but he aroused great indignation when it was discovered that he was simultaneously contributing, under a pseudonym, to the radical journal *The Russian Word*. His *Solitaria* and *Fallen Leaves* strongly influenced the direction in which Shklovsky's style developed. Shklovsky's booklet on Rozanov in 1921 was a major contribution in that it ignored Rozanov's controversial philosophy to focus exclusively on the originality of his style.

SAVINKOV, BORIS VIKTOROVICH (1879–1925). Leader of the terrorist organization associated with the SR's during the early years of the party (1902–1906). He became deputy minister of war under Kerensky and then governor-general of Petrograd, but was dismissed by Kerensky for his support of the Kornilov insurrection. After the October revolution, Savinkov fought against the Bolsheviks. In July 1918 he organized the revolt of the Left-wing SR's in Moscow, which triggered revolts all over central Russia.

SEMYONOV, GRIGORY IVANOVICH (1891–1937). Star government witness at the Moscow trial of prominent SR's in June 1922. He testified that he had committed terrorist acts against the Soviet regime at the behest of the Central Committee of the SR party and attempted to incriminate the party leadership of authorizing the assassination of Volodarsky and the attempt on Lenin's life. He evidently also gave false evidence against Shklovsky at this trial.

SHEDD, WILLIAM A. (1865–1918). American missionary in Persia. The son of missionaries in Persia, Shedd returned there to work after receiving his medical education in the United States. He was highly respected by all the nationalities pitted against each other in the Urmia area and worked incessantly to maintain the precarious order and save lives. In December 1917 the United States government appointed him honorary vice-consul, in the hope that this title would enable him to deal more effectively with the explosive situation created in Urmia by the evacuation of the Russian troops. When fighting began between the Persians and the Aissors, Shedd succeeded in establishing an uneasy truce; after the assassination of Mar Shimun in March, he managed to prevent the Aissors from massacring the Kurdish refugees in Urmia. When the Turks surrounded Urmia in June, Shedd tried to persuade the Aissors and Armenians not to flee the city and leave the Christian converts at the mercy of the Turks, but he could not stop the exodus, which began on July 31. Shedd and his wife left with the fugitives, but he never reached Baghdad. He died of cholera shortly after the battle at Sain Kaleh on August 9, 1918, and was therefore, unbeknownst to Shklovsky, already dead when *Revolution and the Front* was written. See Mary L. Shedd, *The Measure of a Man* (New York, 1922).

SHILEIKO, VLADISLAV KAZIMIROVICH (1891–1930). Poet and Assyriologist, translator of the *Gilgamesh Epic*, and second husband of Anna Akhmatova.

SKOROPADSKY, PAVEL PETROVICH (1873–1945). Head of the puppet government installed by the Germans during their occupation of the Ukraine between April and December 1918.

STIRNER, MAX (pseudonym of Kaspar Schmidt, 1806–1856). Minor German philosopher who espoused a program of individualism bordering on anarchism.

SUKHANOV, NIKOLAI NIKOLAEVICH (1882–1940). Menshevik journalist, known for his memoirs about the revolution; editor of Gorky's journals *The New Life* and *Annals;* member of the Executive Committee of the Petrograd Soviet; economist until his arrest in 1931.

SUVORIN, ALEKSEI SERGEEVICH (1834–1912). Conservative newspaper owner and publisher, known especially for his newspaper *Novoe vremia* [The New Time].

SVERDLOV, YAKOV MIKHAILOVICH (1885–1919). Chairman of the Central Executive Committee of the Congress of Soviets and secretary of the Central Committee of the Bolshevik Party.

TERESHCHENKO, MIKHAIL IVANOVICH (1884–1956). Minister of finance in the Provisional Government, then foreign minister after the resignation of Milyukov in May. He emigrated after the October revolution.

TYNYANOV, YURY NIKOLAEVICH (1894–1943). Leading Russian formalist, known especially for his brilliant comparative study "Gogol and Dostoevsky," 1921, and his remarkable book on verse theory *The Problem of Verse Language*, 1924.

URITSKY, MOISEI SOLOMONOVICH (1873–1918). Chief of the Petrograd Cheka. He was assassinated by Socialist Revolutionaries in August 1918.

VOLODARSKY, MOISEI MARKOVICH (1890–1918). Prominent Bolshevik assassinated by a member of the Socialist Revolutionary party in June 1918.

VOLYNSKY, AKIM LVOVICH (1863–1930). Well-known symbolist critic, to whom the first edition of Shklovsky's *Epilogue* is dedicated.

WIED, PRINCE WILHELM OF (1876–1945). Erstwhile king of Albania. Albania took advantage of the First Balkan War to declare her independence of the Turkish Empire. By the Treaty of London ending that war in 1913, the great powers appointed a commission to determine the boundaries of Albania and, in 1914, designated Wilhelm, prince of Wied, as ruler of Albania. He was forced to abdicate during the same year, with resultant chaos.

WRANGEL, PYOTR NIKOLAEVICH (1878–1928). Russian general who fought with Kaledin and Denikin against the Bolsheviks. In April 1920 he succeeded Denikin as commander of the White Army in the south. Taking advantage of the Polish invasion of the Ukraine in May, he launched an anti-Bolshevik offensive from the Crimea in June 1920. When the Bolsheviks resisted and forced him back into the Crimea in October, he and his troops were evacuated by Allied ships to Constantinople.

YUDENICH, NIKOLAI NIKOLAEVICH (1862–1933). White general in command of a Russian volunteer army based in Estonia. In May 1919 he launched an offensive against Petrograd in which he advanced as far as Krasnaya Gorka but was forced to withdraw when shelled by gun positions at Kronstadt. In October 1919 he launched a second offensive against Petrograd and reached the very gates of the city before the Reds succeeded in repulsing the attack.

ZAMYATIN, EVGENY IVANOVICH (1884–1937). Consummate prose

stylist whose writings and lectures strongly influenced the Serapion Brothers and other young writers of the twenties.

ZINOVIEV, GRIGORY EVSEEVICH (1883–1936). Important Bolshevik leader closely associated with Lenin. He was party secretary of Petrograd.

Glossary of Places

ALEKSANDROPOL. Now Leninakan.

CHERVONNAYA. Probably Chiryurt.

CHORNAYA RECHKA. A sparsely populated, heavily wooded section in the northern part of Petrograd.

CZERNOWITZ. Now Chernovtsy.

DILMAN. Now Shahpur.

DZELAMEROK. Now Colemerik.

ELISAVETPOL. Now Kirovabad.

ELIZAVETGRAD. Now Kirovograd.

FIELD OF MARS. A parade ground located across the Neva from the Petropavlovskaya Fortress. Only victims of the October revolution were honored by burial there.

HELSINGFORS. Now Helsinki.

KOLPINO. An industrial suburb south of Petrograd.

KRESHCHATIK. The main street of Kiev.

LAKHTA. A small village six miles northwest of Petrograd on the Gulf of Finland. Now Lakhtinsky.

ORANIENBAUM. Now Lomonosov.

PARGOLOVO. Three villages called Pargolovo lay along the old border between Russia and Finland and were used as summer resorts both by the inhabitants of Petrograd and by the Finns.

PETERSBURG SIDE. Oldest quarter of the city, comprising the islands circumscribed by the Neva, the Great Nevka, the little Nevka, and the Little Neva.

PETROVSK. Now Makhachkala.

REVEL. Now Tallinn, capital of Estonia.

SAMARA. Now Kuibyshev.

SOLOZHBULAK. Now Mehabad.

St. Pete. In Russian, *Piter*, an affectionate nickname for St. Petersburg. To eliminate the Germanic sound, the name of the city was changed to Petrograd in August 1914, but many people continued to use the old name.

Tiflis. Now Tbilisi.

Tsaritsyn. First changed to Stalingrad, now Volgograd.

Urmia. Now Rezaiyeh.

Verzhbolovo. A village on the old frontier between Russia and Germany. It was an important switching center for trains going between Germany and Russia.

Yamburg. Now Kingisep.

Glossary of Parties and Groups

"ACADEMICIANS." Members of a right-wing student organization that advocated that students not participate in the political affairs of the country.

ANARCHIST COMMUNISTS. A left-wing group that hoped to establish cooperative communism by abolishing the political state.

BLACK HUNDREDS. A reactionary society opposed to Jews and revolutionaries.

BOLSHEVIKS. The left wing of the Socialist Democratic party. They repudiated any cooperation with the liberal bourgeoisie and sought an alliance of peasant and proletarian interests as a means to the development of industrial capitalism and the almost immediate overthrow of the middle class and the establishment of a Socialist state.

THE BUND. A Jewish labor and Socialist party that combatted persecution of the Jews and advocated a Russian federation in which the Jews would have national-cultural autonomy.

CONSTITUTIONAL DEMOCRATS (Kadets). The large moderate-liberal party that advocated the establishment of a constitutional monarchy in Russia. In general, they favored continuation of the war. When the party was outlawed by the Bolsheviks on November 28 (December 11), 1917, many Kadets joined the anti-Bolshevik forces gathering in the Don region.

DUKHOBORS. A peasant religious sect that rejected all external political and religious authority, including that of the Bible.

INTERNATIONALISTS. Those left-wing Socialists, including the Bolsheviks, who opposed continuation of the war; in particular, the faction of the Socialist Democratic party that advocated Russia's withdrawal from the war at the Zimmerwald Conference. They were closely associated with Maksim Gorky's daily newspaper *Novaia zhizn'* [The New Life].

KADETS. Popular name for the Constitutional Democrats, *q.v.*

MOLOKANS. A sect opposed to the taking of oaths and to civil authority.

MENSHEVIKS. The right wing of the Socialist Democratic party. They believed that the Marxists must ally themselves with liberal bourgeois elements in order to achieve the bourgeois revolution, after which the proletarian revolution would be possible.

SOCIALIST DEMOCRATS. The orthodox Marxist party, which sought, through first a "bourgeois" revolution and then a "proletarian" revolution, to establish a Socialist state in Russia. They demanded an immediate end to the war. In 1903 the party split into two factions, the Bolsheviks and the Mensheviks, qq.v.

SOCIALIST REVOLUTIONARIES (SR). The party that dominated the Provisional Government during Kerensky's term as prime minister. Its members viewed the peasantry as the main hope of the revolutionary movement and were especially concerned about land reform. The Right-wing Socialist Revolutionaries (RSR) were the faction of the party that believed in continuing the war until conditions for a just peace could be achieved. The left wing of the party favored Russia's immediate withdrawal and a peace "without annexations and reparations," in the belief that Socialists of all the countries involved would also insist on such a peace. The Left-wing SR's collaborated with the Bolsheviks from December 1917 until March 1918, when they ceased to cooperate because of opposition to the Peace of Brest-Litovsk. After their pivotal role in the abortive Moscow revolt of July 1918, they were outlawed by the Bolsheviks.

TOLSTOYANS. Those who follow the teachings of Lev Tolstoy, hence people strongly opposed to violence, all forms of governmental compulsion, and the institution of private property. They frequently abstain from the flesh of animals, intoxicants, and drugs.

UNION FOR THE REBIRTH OF RUSSIA (Soiuz Vozrozhdeniia Rossii). A coalition of anti-Bolshevik elements formed in April 1918 and dominated by Right-wing SR's. This organization was especially interested in gaining control of the lower reaches of the Volga, thus blocking the Bolsheviks' access to the Caspian Sea. Headquarters of these underground activities were in Saratov, from which the group allegedly encouraged the Czechoslovak Legion to rise against the Bolsheviks. According to the deposition of one Dashevsky: "Shklovsky was transferred to Saratov a month before I was [i.e., in early July]; he was assigned the task of organizing demolition work along the Ural front. He made Atkarsk the center of his work, got hold of some pyroxylin from a demolition squad, and proposed to blow up all trains heading for the front, a proposal not accepted by the majority. He had to leave Atkarsk because he was being followed." This evidence was given at the trial of the Right-wing SR's, held in Moscow during June 1922—

the trial that Shklovsky fled from Russia to escape and that he mentions in the text. See " 'Rabota' eserov v 1918 godu" [The "Work" of the SR's in 1918], *Krasnyi Arkhiv* [Red Archive], 20 (1927): 153–174, especially p. 155.

The Union included not only rightist socialists but also leftist liberals, drawn together primarily by their dismay at the Bolsheviks' dissolution of the Constituent Assembly in January 1918. The members of the Union hoped to salvage the Constituent Assembly and, in general, to press for the revival of democracy in Russia. Toward this end, the Union exerted influence over the Ufa Directory (see n. 48). Its program included continuation of the struggle against the Bolsheviks and the Germans; funds for those purposes were provided by the Allies.

The Union's underground outposts in Saratov and Atkarsk, where Shklovsky was working in July 1918, were directed from Samara, which was the center of opposition for those Right-wing SR's determined to restore the Constituent Assembly. After the Saratov group was arrested, Shklovsky fled in disguise to Moscow and then immediately to Kiev, where he resumed his ties with the Union. Kiev, occupied by the Germans at this time, was ruled by their puppet Hetman Skoropadsky, whose armored cars Shklovsky sabotaged. The life of the city during this surrealistic period is depicted in Mikhail Bulgakov's superb novel *The White Guard,* where Shklovsky appears as the character Mikhail Shpolyansky.

By the fall of 1918, the Socialist Revolutionary Party had become increasingly unhappy about its ties with the Union, so in October, while Shklovsky was still in Kiev, the Central Committee of the SR's forbade its members to join the Union, on the ground that it had become too independent. In November, Shklovsky was stunned to hear that Kolchak had dismissed the Directory to set himself up as dictator. This meant the end of hopes for the reinstatement of the Constituent Assembly and also the end of the Union as a viable force. The SR opposition government in Samara now felt obliged to make peace with the Bolsheviks, in return for which the SR Party was (temporarily) legalized in Soviet territory (see n. 49).

In February 1919, the Bolsheviks proclaimed an amnesty for those SR's who had previously engaged in illegal activities—that amnesty whose retraction Shklovsky indignantly mentions. Two years later, when the Bolsheviks decided to move against the SR's, the indictment indicated that the amnesty covered neither the members of the Central Committee nor those who had engaged in terrorist activities before the amnesty. The government's case relied heavily on the testimony of Grigory Semyonov and, to a lesser extent, on the testimony of Lidia Konoplyova, both former SR's who had been persuaded by the Bolsheviks to betray their comrades. Both Semyonov and Konoplyova died in the Purges. See Marc Jansen, *A Show Trial under Lenin* (Boston, 1982).

Index of Names

Adam, 211
Agnivtsev, Nikolai, 157
Akhmatova, Anna, 191, 237, 287, 289, 293
Anardovich, 13, 21–22, 25, 31, 35–36, 38, 40, 42, 51, 64, 67–68, 70
Andreeva, Maria, 187, 287
Annenkov, Yury, 176, 243, 286 n. 60, 287

Baburishvili, 97, 104
Barbusse, Henri, 59, 192
Bek, Halil, 58
Belinsky, Vissarion, 192, 233, 240
Bely, Andrei, 239
Benjamin, 267
Benois, Alexandre, 189, 287
Blok, Aleksandr, 196, 233, 238–242
Blok, Genrikh, 242
Bogdanov, Fyodor, 14–15
Bondi, Sergei, 177, 287
Borovikovsky, Vladimir, 135
Brachmann, 211–212
Brik, Osip, 177, 281 n. 7, 287
Bundel, Karl, 227
Byron, Lord, 232–233

Catherine I, 119
Catullus, 239
Chekhov, Anton, 74
Cheremisov, General, 32, 57, 64, 68–69
Chernov, Viktor, 72–73, 289
Chichikov, 233
Chinarov, Captain, 34–35
Chkheidze, Nikolai, 18, 23–24, 72, 287
Chukovsky, Kornei, 186, 287
Cicero, 239
Crusoe, Robinson, 169, 209–210, 273
Cunctator, Quintus Fabius, 22, 288

Dante Alighieri, 286 n. 72
Dashevsky, 299
Davidova, 159
Denikin, Anton, 147, 186, 288
Dioneo, see Shklovsky, Isaak
Dobrolyubov, Nikolai, 192
Dolgopolov, 55
Dostoevsky, Fyodor, 80
Doyle, Arthur Conan, 268
Duclos, Armand, 159–160
Dumas, Alexandre, 188

Ehrenburg, Ilya, 194, 268, 288
Eikhenbaum, Boris, 176–177, 186, 190, 232, 235, 243–244, 269, 271, 285 n. 50, 288
Eliseev, 231, 235–236, 242, 288
Elov, Aga Petros, 83, 85–86, 108–109, 124, 246–249, 252, 259–260, 262–263
Ern, Colonel, 105, 117
Erofeev, 64, 71

Fedin, Konstantin, 269
Fet, Afanasy, 239
Fielding, Henry, 234
Filonenko, Maksimilian, 20–23, 25, 28, 31, 35, 39–40, 42, 44, 56, 62–64, 67, 69, 137, 140–141, 288
France, Anatole, 192
Friche, Vladimir, 192

Geobbekian, 80
Géricault, 286 n. 57
Gogol, Nikolai, 89, 233
Gonta, Ivan, 228, 286 n. 61, 288–289
Gorban, 219–221, 223, 225
Gorbenko, Doctor, 223–225, 276
Gorky, Maksim, see Peshkov, Aleksei

301

Viktor Shklovsky in 1919. The portrait is by Yury Annenkov and is reproduced from Annenkov's *Portrety* (Petrograd, 1922).

A leading figure in the Russian Formalist movement of the 1910s and 1920s VIKTOR SHKLOVSKY (1893–1984) had a profound effect on twentieth century Russian literature and on literary criticism throughout the world Many of his books, including *Zoo, or Letters Not About Love*, *Third Factory Theory of Prose*, *Bowstring*, *Literature and Cinematography*, and *Energy o Delusion*, have been translated into English and are available from Dalke Archive Press.

Petros Abatzoglou, *What Does Mrs. Freeman Want?*
Michal Ajvaz, *The Golden Age.*
The Other City.
Pierre Albert-Birot, *Grabinoulor.*
Yuz Aleshkovsky, *Kangaroo.*
Felipe Alfau, *Chromos.*
Locos.
João Almino, *The Book of Emotions.*
Ivan Ângelo, *The Celebration.*
The Tower of Glass.
David Antin, *Talking.*
António Lobo Antunes, *Knowledge of Hell.*
The Splendor of Portugal.
Alain Arias-Misson, *Theatre of Incest.*
Iftikhar Arif and Waqas Khwaja, eds., *Modern Poetry of Pakistan.*
John Ashbery and James Schuyler, *A Nest of Ninnies.*
Robert Ashley, *Perfect Lives.*
Gabriela Avigur-Rotem, *Heatwave and Crazy Birds.*
Heimrad Bäcker, *transcript.*
Djuna Barnes, *Ladies Almanack.*
Ryder.
John Barth, *LETTERS.*
Sabbatical.
Donald Barthelme, *The King.*
Paradise.
Svetislav Basara, *Chinese Letter.*
Miquel Bauçà, *The Siege in the Room.*
René Belletto, *Dying.*
Marek Bieńczyk, *Transparency.*
Mark Binelli, *Sacco and Vanzetti Must Die!*
Andrei Bitov, *Pushkin House.*
Andrej Blatnik, *You Do Understand.*
Louis Paul Boon, *Chapel Road.*
My Little War.
Summer in Termuren.
Roger Boylan, *Killoyle.*
Ignácio de Loyola Brandão, *Anonymous Celebrity.*
The Good-Bye Angel.
Teeth under the Sun.
Zero.
Bonnie Bremser, *Troia: Mexican Memoirs.*
Christine Brooke-Rose, *Amalgamemnon.*
Brigid Brophy, *In Transit.*
Meredith Brosnan, *Mr. Dynamite.*
Gerald L. Bruns, *Modern Poetry and the Idea of Language.*
Evgeny Bunimovich and J. Kates, eds., *Contemporary Russian Poetry: An Anthology.*
Gabrielle Burton, *Heartbreak Hotel.*
Michel Butor, *Degrees.*
Mobile.
Portrait of the Artist as a Young Ape.
G. Cabrera Infante, *Infante's Inferno.*
Three Trapped Tigers.
Julieta Campos, *The Fear of Losing Eurydice.*
Anne Carson, *Eros the Bittersweet.*
Orly Castel-Bloom, *Dolly City.*
Camilo José Cela, *Christ versus Arizona.*
The Family of Pascual Duarte.
The Hive.
Louis-Ferdinand Céline, *Castle to Castle.*
Conversations with Professor Y.
London Bridge.

Normance.
North.
Rigadoon.
Marie Chaix, *The Laurels of Lake Constance.*
Hugo Charteris, *The Tide Is Right.*
Jerome Charyn, *The Tar Baby.*
Eric Chevillard, *Demolishing Nisard.*
Luis Chitarroni, *The No Variations.*
Marc Cholodenko, *Mordechai Schamz.*
Joshua Cohen, *Witz.*
Emily Holmes Coleman, *The Shutter of Snow.*
Robert Coover, *A Night at the Movies.*
Stanley Crawford, *Log of the S.S. The Mrs Unguentine.*
Some Instructions to My Wife.
Robert Creeley, *Collected Prose.*
René Crevel, *Putting My Foot in It.*
Ralph Cusack, *Cadenza.*
Susan Daitch, *L.C.*
Storytown.
Nicholas Delbanco, *The Count of Concord.*
Sherbrookes.
Nigel Dennis, *Cards of Identity.*
Peter Dimock, *A Short Rhetoric for Leaving the Family.*
Ariel Dorfman, *Konfidenz.*
Coleman Dowell, *The Houses of Children.*
Island People.
Too Much Flesh and Jabez.
Arkadii Dragomoshchenko, *Dust.*
Rikki Ducornet, *The Complete Butcher's Tales.*
The Fountains of Neptune.
The Jade Cabinet.
The One Marvelous Thing.
Phosphor in Dreamland.
The Stain.
The Word "Desire."
William Eastlake, *The Bamboo Bed.*
Castle Keep.
Lyric of the Circle Heart.
Jean Echenoz, *Chopin's Move.*
Stanley Elkin, *A Bad Man.*
Boswell: A Modern Comedy.
Criers and Kibitzers, Kibitzers and Criers.
The Dick Gibson Show.
The Franchiser.
George Mills.
The Living End.
The MacGuffin.
The Magic Kingdom.
Mrs. Ted Bliss.
The Rabbi of Lud.
Van Gogh's Room at Arles.
François Emmanuel, *Invitation to a Voyage.*
Annie Ernaux, *Cleaned Out.*
Salvador Espriu, *Ariadne in the Grotesque Labyrinth.*
Lauren Fairbanks, *Muzzle Thyself.*
Sister Carrie.
Leslie A. Fiedler, *Love and Death in the American Novel.*
Juan Filloy, *Faction.*
Op Oloop.
Andy Fitch, *Pop Poetics.*
Gustave Flaubert, *Bouvard and Pécuchet.*
Kass Fleisher, *Talking out of School.*

WALLACE MARKFIELD,
Teitlebaum's Window.
To an Early Grave.
DAVID MARKSON, Reader's Block.
Springer's Progress.
Wittgenstein's Mistress.
CAROLE MASO, AVA.
LADISLAV MATEJKA AND KRYSTYNA
POMORSKA, EDS.,
Readings in Russian Poetics:
Formalist and Structuralist Views.
HARRY MATHEWS,
The Case of the Persevering Maltese:
Collected Essays.
Cigarettes.
The Conversions.
The Human Country: New and
Collected Stories.
The Journalist.
My Life in CIA.
Singular Pleasures.
The Sinking of the Odradek
Stadium.
Tlooth.
20 Lines a Day.
JOSEPH MCELROY,
Night Soul and Other Stories.
THOMAS MCGONIGLE,
Going to Patchogue.
ROBERT L. MCLAUGHLIN, ED., Innovations:
An Anthology of Modern &
Contemporary Fiction.
ABDELWAHAB MEDDEB, Talismano.
GERHARD MEIER, Isle of the Dead.
HERMAN MELVILLE, The Confidence-Man.
AMANDA MICHALOPOULOU, I'd Like.
STEVEN MILLHAUSER, The Barnum Museum.
In the Penny Arcade.
RALPH J. MILLS, JR., Essays on Poetry.
MOMUS, The Book of Jokes.
CHRISTINE MONTALBETTI, The Origin of Man.
Western.
OLIVE MOORE, Spleen.
NICHOLAS MOSLEY, Accident.
Assassins.
Catastrophe Practice.
Children of Darkness and Light.
Experience and Religion.
A Garden of Trees.
God's Hazard.
The Hesperides Tree.
Hopeful Monsters.
Imago Bird.
Impossible Object.
Inventing God.
Judith.
Look at the Dark.
Natalie Natalia.
Paradoxes of Peace.
Serpent.
Time at War.
The Uses of Slime Mould:
Essays of Four Decades.
WARREN MOTTE,
Fables of the Novel: French Fiction
since 1990.
Fiction Now: The French Novel in
the 21st Century.
Oulipo: A Primer of Potential
Literature.
GERALD MURNANE, Barley Patch.
Inland.

YVES NAVARRE, Our Share of Time.
Sweet Tooth.
DOROTHY NELSON, In Night's City.
Tar and Feathers.
ESHKOL NEVO, Homesick.
WILFRIDO D. NOLLEDO, But for the Lovers.
FLANN O'BRIEN, At Swim-Two-Birds.
At War.
The Best of Myles.
The Dalkey Archive.
Further Cuttings.
The Hard Life.
The Poor Mouth.
The Third Policeman.
CLAUDE OLLIER, The Mise-en-Scène.
Wert and the Life Without End.
GIOVANNI ORELLI, Walaschek's Dream.
PATRIK OUŘEDNÍK, Europeana.
The Opportune Moment, 1855.
BORIS PAHOR, Necropolis.
FERNANDO DEL PASO, News from the Empire.
Palinuro of Mexico.
ROBERT PINGET, The Inquisitory.
Mahu or The Material.
Trio.
A. G. PORTA, The No World Concerto.
MANUEL PUIG, Betrayed by Rita Hayworth.
The Buenos Aires Affair.
Heartbreak Tango.
RAYMOND QUENEAU, The Last Days.
Odile.
Pierrot Mon Ami.
Saint Glinglin.
ANN QUIN, Berg.
Passages.
Three.
Tripticks.
ISHMAEL REED, The Free-Lance Pallbearers.
The Last Days of Louisiana Red.
Ishmael Reed: The Plays.
Juice!
Reckless Eyeballing.
The Terrible Threes.
The Terrible Twos.
Yellow Back Radio Broke-Down.
JASIA REICHARDT, 15 Journeys Warsaw
to London.
NOËLLE REVAZ, With the Animals.
JOÃO UBALDO RIBEIRO, House of the
Fortunate Buddhas.
JEAN RICARDOU, Place Names.
RAINER MARIA RILKE, The Notebooks of
Malte Laurids Brigge.
JULIÁN RÍOS, The House of Ulysses.
Larva: A Midsummer Night's Babel.
Poundemonium.
Procession of Shadows.
AUGUSTO ROA BASTOS, I the Supreme.
DANIËL ROBBERECHTS, Arriving in Avignon.
JEAN ROLIN, The Explosion of the
Radiator Hose.
OLIVIER ROLIN, Hotel Crystal.
ALIX CLEO ROUBAUD, Alix's Journal.
JACQUES ROUBAUD, The Form of a
City Changes Faster, Alas, Than
the Human Heart.
The Great Fire of London.
Hortense in Exile.
Hortense Is Abducted.
The Loop.
Mathematics:
The Plurality of Worlds of Lewis.

SELECTED DALKEY ARCHIVE TITLES

WALLACE MARKFIELD,
  Teitlebaum's Window.
  To an Early Grave.
DAVID MARKSON, *Reader's Block.*
  Springer's Progress.
  Wittgenstein's Mistress.
CAROLE MASO, *AVA.*
LADISLAV MATEJKA AND KRYSTYNA
  POMORSKA, EDS.,
  Readings in Russian Poetics:
  Formalist and Structuralist Views.
HARRY MATHEWS,
  The Case of the Persevering Maltese:
  Collected Essays.
  Cigarettes.
  The Conversions.
  The Human Country: New and
  Collected Stories.
  The Journalist.
  My Life in CIA.
  Singular Pleasures.
  The Sinking of the Odradek
  Stadium.
  Tlooth.
  20 Lines a Day.
JOSEPH MCELROY,
  Night Soul and Other Stories.
THOMAS MCGONIGLE,
  Going to Patchogue.
ROBERT L. MCLAUGHLIN, ED., *Innovations:*
  An Anthology of Modern &
  Contemporary Fiction.
ABDELWAHAB MEDDEB, *Talismano.*
GERHARD MEIER, *Isle of the Dead.*
HERMAN MELVILLE, *The Confidence-Man.*
AMANDA MICHALOPOULOU, *I'd Like.*
STEVEN MILLHAUSER, *The Barnum Museum.*
  In the Penny Arcade.
RALPH J. MILLS, JR., *Essays on Poetry.*
MOMUS, *The Book of Jokes.*
CHRISTINE MONTALBETTI, *The Origin of Man.*
  Western.
OLIVE MOORE, *Spleen.*
NICHOLAS MOSLEY, *Accident.*
  Assassins.
  Catastrophe Practice.
  Children of Darkness and Light.
  Experience and Religion.
  A Garden of Trees.
  God's Hazard.
  The Hesperides Tree.
  Hopeful Monsters.
  Imago Bird.
  Impossible Object.
  Inventing God.
  Judith.
  Look at the Dark.
  Natalie Natalia.
  Paradoxes of Peace.
  Serpent.
  Time at War.
  The Uses of Slime Mould:
  Essays of Four Decades.
WARREN MOTTE,
  Fables of the Novel: French Fiction
  since 1990.
  Fiction Now: The French Novel in
  the 21st Century.
  Oulipo: A Primer of Potential
  Literature.
GERALD MURNANE, *Barley Patch.*
  Inland.

YVES NAVARRE, *Our Share of Time.*
  Sweet Tooth.
DOROTHY NELSON, *In Night's City.*
  Tar and Feathers.
ESHKOL NEVO, *Homesick.*
WILFRIDO D. NOLLEDO, *But for the Lovers.*
FLANN O'BRIEN, *At Swim-Two-Birds.*
  At War.
  The Best of Myles.
  The Dalkey Archive.
  Further Cuttings.
  The Hard Life.
  The Poor Mouth.
  The Third Policeman.
CLAUDE OLLIER, *The Mise-en-Scène.*
  Wert and the Life Without End.
GIOVANNI ORELLI, *Walaschek's Dream.*
PATRIK OUŘEDNÍK, *Europeana.*
  The Opportune Moment, 1855.
BORIS PAHOR, *Necropolis.*
FERNANDO DEL PASO, *News from the Empire.*
  Palinuro of Mexico.
ROBERT PINGET, *The Inquisitory.*
  Mahu or The Material.
  Trio.
A. G. PORTA, *The No World Concerto.*
MANUEL PUIG, *Betrayed by Rita Hayworth.*
  The Buenos Aires Affair.
  Heartbreak Tango.
RAYMOND QUENEAU, *The Last Days.*
  Odile.
  Pierrot Mon Ami.
  Saint Glinglin.
ANN QUIN, *Berg.*
  Passages.
  Three.
  Tripticks.
ISHMAEL REED, *The Free-Lance Pallbearers.*
  The Last Days of Louisiana Red.
  Ishmael Reed: The Plays.
  Juice!
  Reckless Eyeballing.
  The Terrible Threes.
  The Terrible Twos.
  Yellow Back Radio Broke-Down.
JASIA REICHARDT, *15 Journeys Warsaw*
  to London.
NOËLLE REVAZ, *With the Animals.*
JOÃO UBALDO RIBEIRO, *House of the*
  Fortunate Buddhas.
JEAN RICARDOU, *Place Names.*
RAINER MARIA RILKE, *The Notebooks of*
  Malte Laurids Brigge.
JULIÁN RÍOS, *The House of Ulysses.*
  Larva: A Midsummer Night's Babel.
  Poundemonium.
  Procession of Shadows.
AUGUSTO ROA BASTOS, *I the Supreme.*
DANIËL ROBBERECHTS, *Arriving in Avignon.*
JEAN ROLIN, *The Explosion of the*
  Radiator Hose.
OLIVIER ROLIN, *Hotel Crystal.*
ALIX CLEO ROUBAUD, *Alix's Journal.*
JACQUES ROUBAUD, *The Form of a*
  City Changes Faster, Alas, Than
  the Human Heart.
  The Great Fire of London.
  Hortense in Exile.
  Hortense Is Abducted.
  The Loop.
  Mathematics:
  The Plurality of Worlds of Lewis.

SELECTED DALKEY ARCHIVE TITLES

FOR A FULL LIST OF PUBLICATIONS, VISIT:
www.dalkeyarchive.com